MEANWHILE, ELSEWHERE

SCIENCE FICTION *and* FANTASY *from* TRANSGENDER WRITERS

Edited by Cat Fitzpatrick and Casey Plett

Library of Congress Cataloging-in-Publication Data is available.
ISBN 978-1-62729-018-0 (paperback)

10 9 8 7 6 5 4 3 2 1

Table of Contents

For Rachel Pollack, who's been doing this for over forty years

MEANWHILE, ELSEWHERE

Control

RACHEL K. ZALL

Marble, glass, steel. Cameras above the doorways. He looked directly up at the old building, one of few left from the early days of the city, and a gargoyle spread its jaws back at him, its granite claws digging into a cornice. Inside its mouth one glass eye stared passively back, a bright red LED drawing in the attentions of anyone who looked up, just to let them know they were watched, to let them know they were safe, to let them know that if they looked up from a crowd of people, someone somewhere was going to look back.

Somewhere, a computer ran the picture of his face through the databases and confirmed that he lived nearby and that his score was acceptable: no outstanding warrants, no criminal records, no radical activities or associations with extremist religions, solid credit, good job. Owner of a luxury condo in the district. That he'd had a name change raised a red flag, but an officially approved doctor's letter on file confirming he was transsexual lowered it. His score was a 96, the computer decided: a good citizen who could be reassured that the cameras were only there to keep him safe.

The woman to his left, on the other hand, was difficult for the eye to interpret. Her hair made scribbles across her face that baffled the software, puffed out like a black and white spray of frizzy spikes and hid her from view. The computer calculated her height as above average and she seemed to be walking with the 96, so it could guess what sex she was assigned at birth from that, but without a clear picture it couldn't determine if she had filed the correct paperwork to even be considered a "she." Her picture was passed along to a human operator, who took one look at her and knew perfectly well that she didn't live anywhere nearby.

The operator sent a signal out, and a nearby police officer set down his coffee and drove slowly past them. The camera on his car was a next-generation model capable of thwarting the standard ways of avoiding facial recognition software. It had her in seconds. Bad credit, questionable associations, an arrest for soliciting but no conviction, officially male. No outstanding warrants. Claimed legal residence in one of the northern districts, but no lease or utility bill registered in her name to prove she actually lived there.

The officer took into account her companion was a 96 and decided not to stop and frisk her, though he drove slowly past several times as they walked so she would know she'd been noticed. As though she'd had any doubt.

But then they walked north and crossed the line out of his district, into the place where she probably belonged. The officer wondered what a 96 would be doing walking over that line with her – there was no record of drugs or even public intoxication for him, but why else would someone from the district be walking so far north? The officer pulled into a "no parking" zone right near the line and decided to sip his coffee and wait. He notified Central that cameras should keep an eye out for where the 96 re-entered and do a full analysis on his behavior.

Old brick, broken. Weeds like trees waving over their heads from the toothgaps where row houses once stood. Wood panels nailed over windows. He'd never been up this far, but he'd swept through panoramic views online and he knew what the neighborhood looked like. That's why last week he'd demanded she visit his place first.

"Shit," she'd sighed, slumping into his leather sofa, eyeing the artisan cheeses he'd set out before she arrived, "next time you come visit me, alright? I showed you the way now, you're a grown ass man and you can come up yourself for a Craigslist hookup. I fucking hate going down to the district."

"Why?" He looked at her. "The district is safe, and it's clean. I like the district."

She snorted, "Yeah, that's cause they score you good when they see you. When I go down there I gotta get in and get out. You saw that cop circling us, didn't you?"

"They don't score people! That's a conspiracy theory," the 96 laughed. "Most of those cameras probably don't even do anything."

Thinking back to that now, she sighed and shook her head. Was she really taking this idiot to her place? She considered sneaking in the back of an abandoned building and slipping away to let the rats scare him back home where he belonged. But then she remembered last week, the hard muscles in his back tensing as he came inside her, her legs wrapped around his tight ass, and he was so damn beautiful with a split lip. She didn't cum – she was so used to faking it that she didn't know if she could come from a guy fucking her ass anymore – but she wanted to. At the very least he owed her a blowjob.

So whatever, it wasn't like she was fucking him for his brains.

She stopped in front of a house with boarded windows and a mushy-looking roof. Vines poured out where some boards had been pried off the upstairs windows. She stepped onto the concrete steps and they crumbled a little under her boots.

"You live here?" He asked, leaning away from the house slightly.

"Fuck you talking about? No one lives here," she snorted, knocking three times on the door. It fell open and musty air carried a gush of mold into his face. He cringed. "I thought we were going to your apartment," he said.

"I didn't say that. My roommate wouldn't even put up with your ass. I said I'd take you to my *place*—this is it."

She stepped in, and trying to keep his breath shallow, he followed. Inside was a living room with rotted floorboards and an old couch bulging with moldy wet stuffing. There were cigarette butts and shards of broken glass everywhere. There was a bare wooden staircase with no railing that went up to a closed door with flecks of white paint still lingering on its surface. It was missing two steps. "This was my mom's place. I got it when she died." She walked up the stairs and looked back to see if he would follow.

He stepped gingerly onto the first step and it held. At the top of the stairs, by the closed door, she crossed her arms and sighed. He hopped over the missing steps and was pleasantly surprised that the stairs didn't break and kill him. As he came close to her on the staircase, she turned the old brass knob and opened the door. On the other side was nothing but darkness.

She stepped in.

He called her name, but she didn't respond. He went right up to the threshold but still couldn't see inside. How could it be so dark upstairs with the roof half gone? He felt around with one foot, and grit on the floor crunched under his foot, but the floor seemed firm. He took a step inside. Behind him the door crashed shut and he swiveled in terror. Then he looked up.

"Wait what?" He looked back at the door, then up at the stars overhead; he'd never seen so many. He didn't even know there were so many. The moon was enormous and blue, directly overhead as if it was midnight. The floor was still wood but where the walls should have been it just faded out into a plain of dust that stretched in all directions around them. They had to have been on the second floor, but the space seemed to have no edges. The door still stood behind him, hanging in the air as if it had been pasted in.

"This is my place," she said. "I told you I was taking you to my place, right?" He took a deep breath. The air was pure and cool, like the air by a stream in the woods. In the corner on the floor, just where the dust met the floorboards, was a queen-sized bed with brass rails and a bare, blue-striped mattress. It was so quiet her words didn't even echo. There were red mountains he'd never seen before ringing the horizon. He looked around, expecting to see the lights of the district or even just streetlights, but there was nothing.

"Holy crap," he murmured. "So, um." He looked all around him, as though maybe he'd just missed the city lights on his first pass. Nothing. "What is this? Where are we? I mean... do I get the tour?"

"The tour!" she spat. " I didn't bring you here to be a god damn tour guide. Get over here. Take off your fancy clothes," she said, unbuttoning his dress shirt. "You don't want them to get all covered in dust, do you?"

"I should have brought a broom," he smiled weakly. She didn't smile back, just focused on working each button through its hole. She slid the shirt down his arms, exposing his flat breasts and big shoulders.

"Mmm, those shoulders!" She murmured to herself. "Yeah, now that's what I brought you here for." She gripped the pale muscles of his arms, pulled him in and kissed him violently, and he put his arms around her and squeezed. He tried to ignore the pained, terrifying groan of something somewhere beyond the mountains.

She pulled back and shoved him, and he tumbled into the dust, an explosion of it puffing out from beneath him. Specks sparkled in the moonlight; they could have been tiny diamonds or miniature polished skulls. She fell through the glittering cloud and landed on top of him, grabbing his hair and smashing her lips into his. His little cock was hard between his thighs; her clit was tenting her skirt.

"Where are we?" he asked, his mouth dry with dust.

"Nowhere. Bitch, you don't shut up I'm gonna shut you up," she said, slapping him. He breathed in, tiny diamond skulls sucking into his sinuses, and he coughed. "You want me to shut you up?" She asked, lightly placing her hands around his throat.

"Please, yes, please——" He whispered. She tightened, and he hoped this time it wouldn't bruise anywhere visible. His lungs spasmed frantically for air and his mind started to blur. Better than drugs. The cloud parted over his head and in his juddering vision he could see the blue moon and the stars and her, black and white spines of hair falling into her face. She was looking straight into his eyes. The danger of accidentally killing him flashed through her mind, but she was pretty sure the cameras hadn't identified her, and she figured a body would probably just fade into the dust here. She could do it. She could kill him if she wanted to. In this place she could do anything: for once she had full control.

She looked down at his rolled-back eyes, the rivulet of spit running down his chin. His body started to go limp in her hands and abruptly she opened them and let him slump into the dust.

He coughed and sputtered and when he could he gurgled the word "again."

"No," she said. "You got work to do. Look at me." She grabbed his hair and turned him to look at her face. A trickle of drool hung from his lip. He wanted her to strangle him until he passed out, he half wanted her to strangle him until he disappeared, here in this noplace where he'd never be found or heard from again. But she slid off her skirt, her erection bouncing in her white lace underpants. She slipped off her shirt and her bra, then finally her panties and stood naked above him, silhouetted by the moon. "We ain't here for you. Not this time."

"Yes ma'am," he croaked, smiling up, eyes half-lidded.

"You wanna suck my clit?" She asked. "That's what you're good for. That's why I brought you here. Get up."

He raised himself on his arms and slid his ankles beneath his ass. He leaned forward with his dry mouth toward her. She put one finger on his forehead. "I asked you a question," she said. "I ask you a question you answer. I could leave you here, take the door with me. Never come back. You better answer and you better obey."

"I want to suck your clit," he said, reminding his hands to not creep to his own pants. He stole a glance at the featureless dust all around them before his attention snapped back to her. His cock was a little wet, and it ached in its sheath. "May I jack off while I do?"

"No you can't jack off, you're here for me. You jack off when you get home."

He whimpered, and wondered if he could make it all the way home without cumming. "Yes. I'm sorry. May I suck you? Please?"

She smiled, looking down at his desperate face, his little red mouth that he forgot to close, his hair all mussed and glittery with dust, his cheeks still burning as oxygen returned to his blood. She could kill him and leave him here and he'd beg her for it. But knowing that was enough. She just wanted him to suck her clit.

"Yeah," she said, shoving her fingers into the tuft of blond hair on his head, that expensive haircut, and yanking his face in to her. He opened his mouth obediently and slid his lips along the shaft, wiggled his tongue up the length. Yeah, that's why she brought him here. That's why he was worth putting up with.

With her free hand she squeezed her tit as she thrust her hips into his face. Her clit pressed far enough into his throat to trigger his gag reflex, and he choked back bile and need. He thought about grabbing her ass, but he didn't have permission and didn't want to push his luck. She balled his hair tighter in her fists and he squirmed, hungry to be treated the way she wanted to treat him. It was such a relief to let someone else be in charge, to surrender himself completely to some trashy girl from the northern districts. (Just for a night, of course. Just once in a while.)

His mouth felt so good and his tongue was so eager to please. She shoved her clit as deep as she could, burying his face in her pubic hair, trying to make him disappear from sight completely, to have him be nothing but a talented tongue and a need to please. She dreamed of him only ever being what he was here, in her private space where the power was all hers. He slipped his tongue around her rigid clit and she closed her eyes, grimaced, breathed deep.

A warm light trickled all over her body; above her the stars seemed to glow brighter as he sucked. He saw nothing, he saw her, he only knew her clit growing stiffer in his mouth, knew that he'd done well. She looked straight up and the stars above seemed to go nova, the light inside her burst and she howled and pulled his head all the way down onto her. Her cum was a warm stream splashing on his uvula and he tried to keep his own orgasm quiet and secret, but he wanted to buck his hips and scream on her clit. She clutched his hair so hard it hurt and he began to quake from restraining himself as his orgasm stabbed to its peak and dropped off.

Above him she was out of breath. She let go of his hair and tried not to stumble as she stepped back, a thin stream of semen bridging the space between his lip and her clit. "Clean me off," she gasped. He shuffled forward and leaned eagerly in to suck her softening clit, kiss the stickiness away and lick off the cum. She pulled away and he stayed kneeling there, exhausted and breathing the clean air in deeply. She slumped down on the floor and put her forehead in her hand.

"Kay," she said. "You were good. We're done, though, you can go."

"No cuddling?" He asked. She shook her head. She looked up at the distant moon, her hair toppling back, face tinted by the blue light.

"I just want some quiet."

He hesitated, trying to think of something to say, then murmured "OK" and put his shirt back on. He walked to the door, tentatively opened it and took a step forward.

He was back on the crumbling staircase, in the light of the broken roof, the wall covered in unreadable pseudonyms. Behind him the door was closed.

He thought about going back, just to prove to himself that what he'd seen was real. But he didn't know what he'd say to her if he stepped back into that place. He wasn't even sure what he'd see if he opened the door.

A week later, and not a word from her. He expected that, though. She'd call him when she wanted him. He could wait.

But he wanted to go back to that house, that house was worth leaving the district for. The cameras saw him walking back in the same direction, one he'd never walked before last week, and alone this time. They added a small possibility of participation in the drug trade to his record. But he was still a 91. There was a cop car waiting at the edge of the district as he passed. He was sure it was a coincidence.

He walked back to the house, feeling awkward walking through this neighborhood alone, keeping his eyes out for muggers or drive-bys or whatever they did up here. But all the while he was thinking about the possibilities of that house. A lunar desert right in the heart of the city; absolute quiet and privacy. No cameras and no danger, which was all everyone really wanted anyway, right? The taxes hadn't been paid in years; he could get the building for a song at sheriff's sale.

The borders of the district would have to shift, but the borders of the district were always shifting. Buy a few properties, install a few cameras. The district was a living thing, after all, and living things grow into available space.

He could spearhead an economic revitalization in a dead neighborhood and boost the tourism industry for the city, and everyone would know it was a transgender person who'd done it. It would be a windfall of good PR for the transgender community.

He knocked twice on the door and then it just fell open. He stepped into the spotty light from the damaged wall and walked up the broken stairs to the door. He put his hand on the knob and turned, but the knob just slipped off.

The door drifted open. Beyond it there was nothing.

Delicate Bodies

BRIDGET LIANG

The first thing she noticed was the familiar scratchiness of cheap carpet. What was she doing on the floor instead of in bed?

Little bits of memory trickled back into place.

She recalled staggering into her apartment clutching her side, delirious with pain earlier this—

Morning?

Why the hell was she back at home?

She should be at Ontario Works dealing with her shitty caseworker. The woman would only refer to her by the name on her ID and not as... Wait, what was she again? Oh yeah. Her name was Beryl. Her favourite colour was green. And she had just survived a strange attack.

She had been just walking to the OW office when sharp nails came out of nowhere dragging against her shoulders and cutting through her Value Village blouse. She turned around and saw a pale, sickly woman mumbling and growling something unintelligible. The woman was covered in blood and dirt and her filmy blue eyes were blown out. She stared straight at Beryl. Was she maybe on that drug, bath salts?

Before Beryl could react, Bath Salts attacked her like a wild animal, nails digging into her hips. Beryl recognized the sensation from the man who groped her during her introduction to clubbing as a girl last week. But unlike a man, Bath Salts didn't squeal in pain and fall to the ground when Beryl slammed her palm into her nose. Instead she bit Beryl's shoulder. Beryl kicked the woman in the face and ran, heart thumping and limbs jittery.

As she ran, she fished around her bra for her phone. Her fingers trembling, she called 911. She didn't get through to the dispatcher, it was busy somehow. As she stumbled back into her apartment, she thought to herself that she had lost her jacket. At least that was the only thing she lost. That was the last thing she remembered.

Now, here she was, she was covered in scratches, almost like she had been attacked by a herd of cats, and her shoulder still throbbed. She also felt... different? She wasn't quite sure how to describe it. She decided to stop doing an impression of a beached whale, and try dialing 911 once more. It kept ringing.

She booted up her laptop and checked Facebook. Amidst the usual Buzzfeed articles and cat videos were some posts that were a little... strange? One of her trans girl friends, Chloe, was freaking out about an apocalypse. A genderqueer friend named Alyxx who was studying to become an Anglican Priest was quoting Revelations and asking their God to protect everyone. What the hell was going on? She scrolled faster, until she saw it.

The man's skin was ashy instead of the warm brown it was supposed to be and blood covered his hands and face. His eyes were vacant and the way he held his body was unhinged.

Like Bath Salts.

More posts. A white gay boy named Dan she used to work with was planning on creating a zombie killing team. She wondered why she hadn't unfollowed him before. He was just as cisscummy as any other white cis dude.

Finally, her 911 call went through. It was a voice recording. A calm, clearly enunciated female voice: "Parts of Toronto are under attack from an unknown enemy. At present, it is being contained to the Jane and Finch community. We are asking all residents in Toronto and the GTA to lock their doors, obstruct their windows, and not leave their homes under any circumstances. We are working to resolve this issue swiftly. I repeat—" Beryl hung up and frowned. Of course the attack/zombie apocalypse was being contained to her neighbourhood. One of the poorer and black/immigrant neighbourhoods of Toronto. But if not zombies, maybe people were actually taking white terrorists seriously now.

Back on Facebook, there were more posts about attacks in her neighbourhood. But as quickly as she read them, they were disappearing right before her eyes. There was a media blackout going on! Holyfuck this was such a Big Brother moment. There were fucking zombies and no one would come in and save them!

Beryl noticed that her hand resting on the mouse looked different. The first couple joints of her fingers looked ashen and sort of waxy. She pulled off her mismatched socks and saw that it had also reached her toes.

Trembling, she took a picture of her discoloured hands and posted it up on Facebook. Within moments, she had worried comments asking if she had been bitten, Dan started yelling in caps lock that he was going to kill her if she became a zombie. Other 'friends' started posting "RIP Beryl" gifs. The responses reminded her a bit too much of coming out as Beryl.

She'd come so far over the past year. She'd lost some friends, and some (mostly queer ones) had stuck with her But the shitty memories stuck with her too. Especially of people "mourning" the loss of the boy she never was. And now she was becoming a zombie and Facebook was making her feel shitty all over again!

Beryl pushed away from her desk in shock. If these lemmings she called friends were right, she was going to die soon... Or would it be un-death? Would she become some kind of monster on the other side? Would she be a Romero zombie or would she be like a zombie from the remake of *Dawn of the Dead*? Or maybe from *In the Flesh* or *iZombie*...

She switched to Tumblr. But the rumours of a zombie apocalypse were there too. Apparently, the first recorded zombie attack was in the parking lot of Yorkgate Mall, outside Vince's No Frills. It had spread from there and the city had quarantined from the 400 to Keele and Steeles to Sheppard. And of course, Beryl lived a ten-minute walk from Jane and Finch. Shit. There was no escape for her. Of course the city would quarantine instead of rescuing people living in the area. It's not as if black lives mattered or something. Or the lives of other poor people like her.

She checked on her hands again and the gray, waxy skin had progressed to her wrists. And her tummy growled. Not just your usual tummy growling, it fucking hurt.

She got up and went to rummage through her fridge and cabinets. She had some fried dumplings from the local Chinese grocery store, enough cucumber and garlic to make a quick salad... the thought of it turned her stomach. She made a sandwich and took a bite, then spat it out. She had a sinking feeling the only thing she wanted now was brains...

But that was revolting! Her belly growled at the thought of eating human brains? Or just human flesh in general? Suddenly all she could think of was the salty warmth of blood pumping from a fluttering heart. Every fiber of her body was crying out for her to feed. Tear. Rip flesh. Bathe in the blood. Rinse. Repeat.

This was worse than testosterone! She was a vegetarian. Her family was Buddhist. She could barely stand the thought of eating meat, let alone her own kind!

Although, she thought to herself, were they really her own kind? People like her certainly weren't seen as fully human. Not many professional queers were willing to hire a weird Chinese trans girl dropout who'd barely started her medical transition. They'd just smile and hire another white trans guy. And straight people? They'd keep on using her dead name, call her nasty things, and try to get her fired for the smallest mistake.

Granted, they were assholes. That didn't mean you could eat them!

Maybe she could get away with just eating meat from a supermarket? Ironically, Vince's No Frills. It was only a couple blocks from her apartment complex. She'd be like the Twinklight vampires who call themselves vegetarian! Well, vegetarian by undead standards. If she was a zombie, the other zombies wouldn't attack her, right? Well, it was now or never. She changed out of her ripped blouse, showered the crusty blood off, put on a fresh top, and braved the world.

And the world was on fire! How long had she been out for? Beryl made her way down Finch. She spotted a group of rotting zombies crowding around what was likely a human body. She shuddered and was glad she couldn't see it, hoping that the person's death was fast. As she reached the supermarket, she saw two dark-skinned black women exit the building with a shopping cart full of groceries. They looked like a mother and grandmother duo working together. Mom used the shopping cart as a battering ram, hitting zombies coming at them while Grandma wielded two cast iron pans smacking any zombies left over.

Beryl walked right through the jammed sliding door to the No Frills. The place was a mess. Cans smashed into walls, displays wrecked, produce scattered all over the floor, bodies, and blood. She tried to avert her eyes from the worst of the gore and made her way down to the deli. She saw the bloody remains of what was likely the butcher and felt the pull towards the picked over carcass, but refused. Not with other animal carcasses nearby.

Beryl got behind the counter and reached for a slab of beef, gripping it with her thumb and forefinger. As daintily as she could, she dangled it in front of her mouth and took a small bite, scrunching her nose in disgust. The cow flesh felt cold and chewy as her teeth cut through it. She swallowed mechanically, then took a moment to be mindful of her body, like her old therapist taught her. She was able to stomach it, but her hunger had not abated. Her arms were still grey. It looked like she'd have to go back home and find a way to survive her zombification. She really didn't want to hurt anyone. Even if they were terrible people.

As she reached the entrance of the supermarket, she bumped into someone. A very human someone. Tall, blond, blue eyes, tanned white skin, muscles and very definitely male—

Suddenly it hit her who it was. The human's name was Sean. She hadn't heard from him in months. Want tugged at her heart, her belly, and coiled right above her abdomen, and she wasn't sure which kind of want it was.

It was perhaps a year ago when they first met. Beryl received a message on Grindr from this guy who was charming and intelligent (not to mention Chris Hemsworth hot). She thought he was a figment of her imagination. She had just started playing with gender and was still more of a femmey gay boy. Guys didn't message her much. She quickly realized being a femmey mixed Asian gay boy wasn't sexy to these guys. The guys who were into Asians only talked about smooth, elfin Asian ass (which she wasn't skinny enough to be...) And here was a guy who was interested in her and was treating her like a human being. He was studying to become a diplomat to China and talked with her about Chinese culture respectfully. Not like a fucking rice queen.

"What are you doing here?" Beryl said, incredulously overcome from meeting someone she knew. Sean's boyish expression changed to one of surprise. He looked over her and it slowly dawned on him who it was. Beryl repressed a wince. She forgot that she was still probably male to him.

"I could ask you the same question," he responded guardedly. On second glance, Sean looked ruffled and less put together. His normally sky-high faux hawk was mussed, as if someone had run fingers through it and tugged on it—in a stress way, not a sexy way. Ugh, she needed to stop thinking about sex at a moment like this.

"Um, gathering supplies. I was going to-"

Sean suddenly exclaimed, "And why are you wearing girl's clothes? Why is your hair so long?" He tapped his thumb against his lip contemplating something, then his face lit up. "Oh! You're trans! Right? Did I get it right?"

Beryl responded, "Yes, I'm a girl now. No, it's not a phase. I go by Beryl now."

"Cool. I knew you were a girl from the start," he said matter-of-factly.

Beryl felt like Sean's comment stabbed her in the chest. Well, the world was ending and she was probably going to die soon anyways. So she asked, "Really? Then why message me, go out on a date with me, but then hook up with someone else right after?"

"I mean, I thought we were just going out as friends... You didn't assume we were dating right? I didn't mean to lead you on or anything... I've only ever been into twinks. We all have our preferences." Sean responded, brushing off her main question. He pulled out a pipe from behind his back and swung it at her and added, "Oh, and I'd never fuck a zombie."

Beryl jumped back in surprise as the pipe whooshed past her face.

Everything changed. The hunger rose to the surface; and with it a lot of anger. He said it had been a date. Said she was cute. Why the fuck did he lie and say that it had never been a date? Fucking gaslighting white boys. She shared all the Mandarin she knew and helped him pass his contemporary Chinese culture class. And then after their actual date, he showed her the grindr profile of a skinny white twink he was going to hook up with later. Fuck white boys, they really were garbage. But she also wished that he would have been that someone who'd finally see her as sexy and worth dating.

And now, he just tried to kill her.

She charged at Sean even though he was covered in perfectly toned muscles. He swung at her again, catching her square in the chest, but it didn't hurt her. There might be some advantages of being a zombie after all. Her nails made contact with his arms, drawing blood. Sean yelped and flinched, which gave her enough to close in.

Beryl could smell it. She could smell his warm, supple flesh, the blood under the surface of his skin pumping life through his body. Using her bulk, she knocked him to the floor of the supermarket. His pipe went flying. Without thinking, her mouth closed over one of Sean's toned biceps and bit into it, tearing into the flesh. Sean screamed. He tried to buck Beryl off, but she was quite firmly latched onto his body and her weight made it impossible for him to dislodge her. She didn't mind if he tried to beat her with his free arm, it didn't hurt. She had him pinned and there was no escape.

Sean tasted hot and metallic with blood and the inner growling changed to a purr. She felt good. Warmth flooded her body, making her feel hot and aroused in ways she never thought she could be. Lifting her head, she looked into Sean's terrified baby blue eyes and smiled revealing her bloody teeth.

"You know, I thought you were really hot when we first met. You were one of the few guys who's ever treated me right. Or so I thought. I thought you were smarter than that."

Beryl ran a blood-caked fingernail down Sean's tight, bloodied muscle shirt and down to his jeans. "Pity someone so hot has such an ugly heart."

Sean tried to squirm away the closer her finger got to his crotch. When her finger reached his belt buckle he squealed, "Y-you're a woman! Y-y-y-you're b-b-beautiful! You're strong and powerful and sexy! You're s-s-s-s-s-s-sexy!!!!"

Beryl glared at Sean. She sat up pinning his legs down and intentionally ripped his shirt exposing waxed, toned abs. She was seething mad at him. Everything that he stood for, everything that he took advantage of, everything he said.

Beryl slid her hand down between Sean's legs and undid the buckle to his jeans, pulling the front wide open. The lump within a pair of designer boxers twitched in interest. The shaft of Sean's cock was pushed to the side. She ripped into the fabric, exposing the whole thing to the air. So this was the cock that had been inside of so many boys... No, it wasn't worth calling a cock. She would call it a growth, like a disease. She saw that once in a shitty fan fic. There really weren't derogatory words to describe a penis really. But many to describe a vagina.

Sean furtively raised his hips trying to buck her off his legs, but she was expecting it and fell back on top of Sean hard, knocking the wind out of him. She grasped Sean's growth, stroking it slowly, curling her wrist around the head and it grew within her bloody palm. So it was as big as he claimed it was. Her mouth twitched into a wicked smirk. She placed a hand in the middle of his chest to hold him in place. Fuck yeah superhuman strength. She moved down and took the growth between her small, cupid lips. It tasted warm and Beryl just wanted to bite it off. She never felt so powerful before. She took the whole thing down her throat sucking on it.

Sean let out a low moan. Beryl found it amusing how she was able to make him feel good. He must not have had anyone deep throat him like this before. This must be such a huge surprise for him that he could enjoy sex with someone who was not a twinky white boy.

Beryl bobbed on his shaft teasingly, taking enjoyment in the act of bringing pleasure to someone who could have been in an Aberzombie and Kitsch catalogue. Her girl friends said how hot she looked. How funny and awesome she was. They got her and if only she was able to date them. But the guys that passed by her life barely saw her. She was just too trans. Too Asian. Too fat. Too crazy. Too poor. And if they were cool with one or two of those things, they weren't cool with the rest of them. It was like she was a monster. Well, now she was a monster for real.

She pulled off, licking the head as she looked over at Sean's face. He was panting now, the still oozing wound forgotten. He was hooked. Beryl smiled to herself as she took his whole growth back down her throat, sucking and bobbing on it vigorously. She wanted his cum. She wanted his blood. His flesh. His soul. She caressed his hard, warm body, so different from her own. Like how he was alive and she was...dying.

Sean convulsed and she felt him throb as he pumped his cum down her throat. She unsheathed her teeth from behind her lips and bit down hard. Sean's moan quickly turned into a howl of pain. Swallowing his growth, she imagined it was a veggie dog. She decided to end it. She attacked his chest, clawing and ripping into his pecs with her teeth. Bodies were such delicate things. In his chest cavity she found what she was looking for: the beating, pulsing muscle. She chewed and swallowed and as she felt Sean's life force leave his body, covered in his blood and viscera, Beryl growled in pleasure. His heart satisfied her hunger in a way that made her shiver. His heart was now a part of her.

She continued feasting on his body until only a bloody mess was left. It felt like her body had stopped rotting, but part of her torso and the whole area below her belly button had turned that sickly grey. Beryl got to her feet, looking around.

Home seemed like a good place to go and try to curl up into a ball and cry. She wanted to throw up over what she had done, but the hunger was still pressing on her.

Her gait had become uneven, like a real zombie. Her limbs just wouldn't move the way she wanted them to. It was like part of her brain couldn't control her body anymore...

As she made her way back home, she saw other zombies wandering the streets. Most were covered in blood; a couple were missing limbs or were badly injured. She watched them shamble and wondered if there was still a person inside the rotting body. Would she become the same sort of empty husk? She saw a brown male zombie stumble and fall and a second zombie, a brown woman, lean down to help the man back up. She garbled something that sounded like concern towards him. Huh.

Beryl reached her apartment and saw the door open. She made her way in cautiously to find a shabby figure rifling through her stuff and bagging anything that looked valuable. Like the jade bracelet that had belonged to her nainai! How thankful she was that her nainai hadn't lived to see this horrible day come. Beryl howled and jumped on the burglar, instinctively about to go for the jugular, then she stopped.

Curly fawn-brown hair and matching eyes that once commanded adoration, and still decked out in a plaid shirt and skinny jeans—Josh! What the hell?!?! What was another guy from her past doing here? What was this? Some kind of fucked up rom com?

Josh screamed, his eyes wide in horror as he saw Beryl's bloody face. "I thought this apartment was abandoned! I heard that whoever lived here was dead!"

Beryl had had a major crush on Josh when she was 16. He was the hot leading man in every school play (she always got the bumbling fools, meant to be humorously pitied). Josh was sweet, funny, and his brown eyes were so warm and kind that she just couldn't help but fall for him. And the best part was, he was openly bisexual.

Her mouth opened in a bloody, toothy smile as she responded, "I live here and I'm dead. And I'm not dead too. I'm a zombie."

Josh shrieked. He looked so much like a young deer about to get eaten. In the years since high school, Josh had kept his skinny, boyish figure, so it wasn't too hard for Beryl to hold him in place. She leaned forward slowly as he squirmed in her arms. She didn't really hate Josh—but he got everything handed to him on a silver spoon. He had acting, dancing, and singing lessons and always got lead roles. He was one of the hottest people she had ever met and genuinely sweet. He had tons of people (including herself) who wanted to date him. And she was the exact opposite.

She pressed her lips to his, forcing him to taste Sean's blood. Josh tried his best not to give in to the kiss, gagging, repulsed. Beryl kissed him more forcefully, cradling the back of his head with one of her hands fisted into his curls, pushing her tongue into his mouth, sucking on his tongue. Her hunger pulsed incessantly, like an insatiable living thing begging to be fed. Beryl pulled away, a thread of clotted blood connecting their lips.

"Is there something still wrong with me?" she whispered.

She released Josh and cupped her modest breasts, which the rot had just begun to touch. She was a day away from getting her hormone prescription. Still, being fat had its advantages, she came with some breast tissue already.

Josh tried to make a run for it. Beryl gave chase down the hall howling for reals and managed to catch him before he reached the stairwell. Josh shrieked hysterically, hitting her weakly. So this was what became of the boy she had so admired. Even though he was bisexual, he wasn't into people whose genders were complicated. She had hoped that he might like her better than the gay boys, who all called her, "a lesbian" or "too flamboyant". But he dated only masculine cis boys and feminine cis girls throughout high school.

Despite all the unearned privileges he had been given just for being cute and white and everything, Josh had grown up to be a petty thief, a pretty boy with no real substance to him after all. Why had she developed feelings for such a shit guy? She was better than that. She was now the one at the top of the food chain. Quite literally.

She decided to play with this shadow of her high school crush just a little longer. She wanted to mark and claim him in the worst way. Hunger overrode any feelings of revulsion and horror over what she was doing. Her fingers dug hard into his hips, leaving bruises. Tears welled up in his eyes as she left a trail of bloody kisses along his neck. She licked up his tears and chuckled to herself. White Male Tears. She finally got to drink some. And yet she felt hardness pressing against her thigh. Part of her purred happily, and another weakly tried to protest this was wrong, as she left heated, bloody kisses along Josh's neck.

"Bet this is like what you did with all the girls and boys you fucked." Beryl slipped a hand into Josh's tight skinny jeans. Fuck, his crotch felt warm against her clammy, rotting hand. She wrapped her hand around his half hard dick and stroked it. There really wasn't much room in Josh's restrictive jeans. He fit nicely in her hand, the head of his dick reaching a little above her fist. She freed it from its cage giving her more space to stroke him. Her teeth gently grazed Josh's throat and his adam's apple bobbed reflexively. With just one bite... She bypassed his throat to place another kiss on Josh's lips. This time, he was more willing to reciprocate.

Josh bucked into her hand and she could taste his pulse quickening. He looked gorgeous like this, desperate for an orgasm and terrified of what she would do to him. When he came, rutting and grinding against her palm and screaming into her mouth, she broke the kiss. Even though it was everything her sixteen year old self would have wanted, it wasn't enough. With the force of a fierce predator, her mouth closed around Josh's windpipe, cutting off his air. Her teeth ripped and tore into his throat as her hands held down his arms so she could feed. Blood spurted everywhere as life left the gorgeous faun eyes that had formerly enthralled her. His bloody, ripped out throat looked gorgeous oozing blood and she thought, "he looks like mine." She had left her mark. Her claim. And now he would become a part of her.

Pausing, she kissed his slack lips once more before tearing them off with her teeth. It was a rush. Better than any drug. Much better than sex (although she hadn't had that many opportunities and none had been great). The feeling of tearing into flesh, feeling hot blood against her skin, taking life, and then consuming it made her feel powerful. Like she could do anything. It scared her how good it felt.

Once Josh was little more than tattered jeans and flannel, she tossed the bloody mess down the stairwell. This would likely be the last time she returned here. Beryl felt a bit of remorse for her neighbours. There were bloody handprints smeared going down the hallway and one large blood splatter she made just outside their doors. She knew they could hear Josh's cry and the sounds of her feeding on him. They were good people for the most part and was sad that what she had become may have harmed them.

She'd miss Liang nainai, the old Chinese widow who was like the nain-ai she had never met because of her deadbeat dad. She taught Beryl how to cook dandan mian and make the most ma la sauces from scratch. She taught her Mandarin and exposed her to a few of the most famous Chinese tales like Sun Wukong and Bai Suzhen. Beryl's mom was never home and was working three jobs and didn't have the time to teach much of their shared culture.

Beryl returned to her room and signed back onto her computer. She needed something to distract herself from the horrors that she just commit-ted. Her dash had an article from Buzzfeed- helicopters were being sent to York University to rescue the students and faculty trapped there. No rescue plans for anyone else. she noted. There was a post from Dan (why hadn't she deleted him?) where a photo was taken of him beside some police offi-cers which he captioned as, "OUR FRIENDS THE POLICE HAVE COME RISKING THEIR LIVES TO SAVE US FROM THE ZOMBIE PLAGUE! I THINK THIS OFFICER WAS FLIRTING WITH ME GRRROWL! BLUE LIVES MATTER! THEY'RE FIGHTING TO SAVE US!!! HE SAID HE WANTS TO BE ON MY ZOMBIE KILLING TEAM!!!!"

Even though Beryl's hands were covered in gore, she facepalmed. Ugh, how was it that someone like Dan was working at the Centre for Hu-man Rights as a queer advocate even though he's still doing his undergrad? Oh yeah. White male privilege. That was why he was being saved whilst all of Jane and Finch was being left to become zombies.

Beryl had to stop reading this shit. It was making her upset and it wasn't helping to keep away the things she didn't want to even think about or process. Where was brain bleach when you needed it? She vigorously un-friended Dan, then watched a few cat videos to calm down enough to finish saying her goodbyes to everyone. Including herself. She looked through her selfies, smiling sadly. Even though guys treated her like shit, she had a solid core of amazing friends, especially other trans girls. But now she was prob-ably about to become a mindless zombie. She hadn't gotten to actually ex-perience love and had barely had any time as a girl. Maybe in another life...

Maybe in another life she wouldn't be a murderer and a... she couldn't even think it to herself. These people she lived around, they were her com-munity. They didn't deserve being fucked over by a country that was de-signed to keep them down. They didn't deserve being trapped with monsters that wanted eat them. If anyone deserved to be eaten, it was be the politicians, the businessmen, and all the shitty people in positions of power making things this way.

She took a selfie of her bloody, undead state and wrote a final post to her friends. Her real friends.

Friends. I love you. All of you. I never said that enough. I'm a zombie now, but being a zombie isn't anything like we see in movies... I'm not a good zombie, but I'm not a mindless monster. I'm still me, but different. I'm not human anymore. I need to feed on humans to survive and I hate it. I don't expect any of you to understand what I'm going through.

I don't know what caused the zombie outbreak, but how it's being handled is fishy. I mean, why save everyone at York University but leave the rest of us to become zombies or die? Who the fuck does shit like this? There are so many kids here. Isn't the government all for saving kids? Or just white kids? I'm beyond saving. I expect I'll be killed by some douchebro joyriding with his brodude friends pretending this is all a game. But save the humans still living here. They didn't do anything and even though I'm no longer human, I want them to live. I'd rather kill and eat scummy white dudes if I can help it. Or anyone terrible really.

Anyways, this'll probably be the last time I ever sign into Facebook. I'll miss all of you, but live. Live for me. Become amazing, powerful trans women. Become defiant fatties. Let your disabled freak flag fly and don't care that some people see you as broken or useless. Find love, laugh, and party. Have good lives even though this government clearly wants people like us to die

Later, after Beryl was gone, her friend Alyxx would reply to this post. They'd say Beryl was right that it was fishy. That they'd seen a post with photographic proof that some famous psychiatrist at the university, who had military funding to develop neuroviral weapons, had been testing them on homeless people around Jane and Finch. On what he called disposable people. And that there were plans to clear out all the zombies once he was done studying the effects of the virus. Then the land could be used to build more condos. But Beryl would never see this comment.

Beryl slipped on nainai's jade bracelet before closing and locking her door. She felt soooo tired... Without really thinking, Beryl shuffled her way out of the building for the last time, not sure what to do or where to go anymore. There were crowds of zombies clawing at windows and doors of the malls and apartment buildings in her area. Most of the zombies were non-white, and probably just as poor as her. She shambled off among them, and soon lost track of just what street she was on.

She passed by a pack of freed dogs gnawing on a decomposing zombie. It was still moving, snapping their teeth weakly at the dogs. Beryl didn't blink as she witnessed this. The dogs had to eat too. At least it was for survival and not for sport. Humans were so strange. They killed for sport. They were needlessly cruel. But so was she, and she had been human until very recently. She was beyond caring about the harm she had caused by now.

She caught the sight of a human running by with a few zombies in hot pursuit. Was she supposed to cheer on the human now or the zombies trying to catch them?

Beryl glanced at herself in an apartment building window, ignoring the children hiding inside. Her shoulder-length black hair was matted with blood and looked brittle as straw. She looked gaunt and starved. She missed her moon-shaped face, her dimples and naturally pink cheeks, She had never appreciated them. Blood stained her face and gore caked her hands. She was now just as ugly and monstrous as she had been made to feel by so many people. Beryl absently ran a hand down her body; everything felt brittle and dead. A fingernail came off. It gave her a terrible idea.

She undid the front of her pants and pulled her junk out. With a hard shove, she created a hole of sorts. She ripped off the poison factories and surveyed her shoddy work. It took zombification for her to get sexual reassignment surgery (of sorts), even if it was a DIY job.

She was sure the rot had taken over her entire body. Her limbs dragged sluggishly and the hunger constantly throbbed. She thought of hot, warm, blood (especially directly from the heart) gushing into her mouth. Was this why none of the zombies were speaking? Were they too traumatized by what they did? Did they carry the same guilt for killing and eating people they might have known or loved? What had she become? Was there any redemption for her?

Beryl meandered her way mindlessly onto a field with power lines which she recognized as directly south of York. A gust of wind brought the scent of a live human on it. Her hunger stirred and without even thinking, her rotting body was loping towards the tantalizing scent of living human flesh. She couldn't think of anything else except ripping into flesh. The scent led her to a tall, broad-shouldered man scrambling through a field and heading right towards her. She thought she recognized him—but it didn't matter. Standing quite still, Beryl waited. And the man ran close to her. With a speed she would have loved to have had as a kid playing Octopus on the playground, she sunk her claw-like hands into his side, moaning hungrily. Beryl's nails tore into his t-shirt and her face contorted into a visage of mindless hunger for the beating heart within. But the man had a height advantage and seemed to have some martial arts training. He batted her clawed hands away and gave her a solid kick to the stomach. She was knocked over to the ground, which gave him a moment's reprieve. Instead of running away or killing her, he looked directly at her. His eyes widened in disbelief and he exclaimed,

"Julian? Is that you? I haven't seen you in years!"

That was the wrong move. Beryl launched herself at this man who recognized her, and this time, she struck true, her mouth coming into contact with his chest. Her teeth raked across his skin as he fought to push her off. Her nails tore at his shirt, leaving it in ribbons and were soon tearing at flesh. Soon, there'd be more lovely scars than the twin lines she found underneath each pectoral. This human had a good layer of warm fat that she tore through. Her blood lust peaked as she hit blood, coppery and warm. She left his chest deciding to come back to it later as she made her way further up. When she came face to face with the man's fluttering eyes, she froze.

Eyes almost like hers in shape, skin a shade darker, and black hair that he often neglected to cut.

It was Aaron. Her only crush she didn't have any resentment towards. Just guilt. (Why did she end up bumping into and eating so many of her past crushes? Seriously!) He was a fellow outcast and one of her best friends. She was the only Chinese kid and he, the adopted, ambiguously brown trans kid. (She was still figuring things out at the time). He was taken from his family as an infant by CAS and adopted by some well-meaning white couple. He was also born with a barely visible physical disability called microtia that he had been bullied for his entire life. He always hid the undeveloped ear by growing his hair long on the sides. They met at a presentation on queer youth homelessness that was put on by the GSA. She fell for him almost unconsciously. Like it was breathing. Then they became friends, good friends. Like Connie and Steven from Steven Universe. And she found out that he had a skinny, white lesbian-identified girlfriend, but that didn't stop her feelings towards him. Still, what did she have that this white lesbian didn't? Why would Aaron even look at her at all? Ugh, she was always a disaster over whoever she fell for.

One day right after graduation, they were hanging out in Chinatown and standing so close together. Their eyes had met; Beryl had leaned closer and she thought Aaron was leaning closer, and she freaked. He had a girlfriend, which meant kissing him was wrong, so she ran off. Then she moved across the city, out of his life like a ghost. And now somehow, here he was in front of her, dying by her hand.

Beryl managed to push away her hunger and get away from Aaron's body. She crawled away from him; a toe came off in her shoe. She collapsed in a pile, curling into fetal position in the grass. She broke. The last spark of what made her human broke. She hurt someone that she cared for even after all these years. She had become the monster she was always afraid of becoming. Her last message on Facebook? It was pure posturing trying to find a way to justify her actions. She took lives, forced sexual acts upon her victims, and ate human-animal flesh. Her mind flashed back to each of the people she had consumed in just a few hours. She could never go back to being human once again. She was a freak in life just for being born different and was treated as a freak. Now she was an undead freak. She clamped her will down on the hunger. She wanted to just stay here until she rotted away or was eaten by dogs. Like much of society would have cared even if she were alive. She was wretched.

Beryl stewed over her own existence for an hour or so, and didn't hear the sounds of someone squirming about and shouts of pain as Aaron's body was wracked by the zombie virus. Then: His eyes opened and he sat up. Aaron got to his feet and his eyes fell on Beryl huddled in a pile on the ground. He knelt down near her (but far enough to be out of lunging distance). "Hey. Are you okay?"

Beryl turned over faster than one would expect a rotting corpse to do. Warm suffused where her heart was. She looked up at Aaron in surprise. "You're alive! Err, I mean a zombie. Like me! This is all my fault."

Aaron lent a hand to Beryl helping her up. "Thanks for killing me." He rolled his eyes. "I ran from a bunch of zombies only to be attacked and zombified by someone who I thought was one of my closest friends until she blocked me from all social media and disappeared. The universe must really hate me or have an ironic sense of humour."

Beryl bit her lip (slicing it open of course). "I'm sorry..." She hunched her shoulders forward trying to look small. Fuck, this is exactly what she was always afraid of. She hurt... and how would she pay for her actions? Maybe she should just die now and get it over with already.

"Sorry? That's all you can say? Where the fuck did you go?" He lightly pushed her shoulder angrily. "I thought that I fucked up when you left and disappeared!" Aaron's bushy eyebrows knit in concern. "I never had a chance to speak to you... To explain."

"I get it. You don't need to tell me. I mean, why would you want a freaky gender weird fat Asian over a skinny white cis girl?" Beryl half mumbled to herself unable to meet his eyes.

"You're not listening. Fuck! And now you're... Still sentient. Huh." Aaron frowned and looked at the ground introspectively.

"Yeah... Being a zombie isn't all bad? I'm sorry I attacked you. I'm—I mean we—aren't exactly human anymore. And we do eat human flesh, it's really hard to resist." Beryl tried to explain and was about to wring her hands but remembered that they'd probably break off if she did.

"Alright. It could be worse I guess..." He sounded less angry than before and almost sounded like the Aaron she used to know.

"You could be dead. I could have eaten you completely," Beryl said lightly dimpling into a small smile.

"Argh, why does it feel like the universe doesn't want me alive? But maybe being a sentient zombie is better than being dead..." Aaron looked visibly calmer, but Beryl didn't feel the need to respond. She was the one who attacked him after all...

"By the way, what are your name and pronouns now?" Aaron looked her over for the first time and Beryl felt like she was being inspected. This was awkward, although probably nothing in comparison to giving someone a virus that'll probably kill them sometime soon.

"Yeah, I go by Beryl. As in the evil queen from Sailor Moon." Beryl felt something in her melt just a tiny bit. For the first time since she became a zombie, she felt a touch of warmth. There was something special about being recognized by another trans person. It was silly, but Aaron felt like

her compliment. Both as a human being and now as a zombie. She smiled brightly as best as her brittle flesh would allow.

Aaron, whom hadn't started rotting yet, laughed and rolled his eyes. "Figures you'd name yourself after an anime character."

"What? She was really awesome and I really felt for her. She was in love with a guy who never noticed her. I think she was misunderstood! And she was killed by Sailor Moon instead of being saved. All for loving someone! She deserved better than that," Beryl retorted.

"Well, I see you Beryl." Aaron said formally responding with the proper name affirmation response.

Beryl didn't know what to say. She was still a monster and now had made another... She was literally Bath Salts. "Wait, you said that you wanted to explain something back then? Before I disappeared?"

"It doesn't matter now. It was years ago. You really hurt me when you disappeared. I really cared about you." Aaron said softly.

Beryl looked up at her former crush and paused, revealing a flash of her teenage insecurities as she replied, "Why would you care?"

"Because of this," Aaron replied, before pulling Beryl into his arms, wrapping her up safe and secure and pressing their lips together. It was a soft kiss, but it was more significant than any other kiss she'd ever had.

The hunger flared hotly once more inside Beryl. She wanted to tear into his flesh and devour him, but at the same time, she wanted him to devour her. It wasn't the same hunger she had experienced since her undeath. It wasn't like she actually wanted to just tear into his flesh, or she would have done it already. What happened between two zombies? Would they magically become human again like in *Warm Bodies*? Would the power of love (friendship is magic!) bring them back to life?

Aaron pulled away from the surprisingly sloppy (bloody?) kiss and said thickly, "I loved you... I guess I still love you. We're different people now, but I can't help but feel something for you still. I'm such a Scorpio."

Beryl whined. "You had a girlfriend... I know this is a little anachronistic, but I'd hate to be the Crazy, Jealous Homewrecker Trans Woman."

"Sorry. I didn't realize that I was poly until I met you. I was kinda a mess."

"It's okay I guess. I'd say we need to do a lot of processing, but we don't have much time."

"Yeah I get it... I'm still angry at you, but you're right, we don't have much time. So what do you want then?" Aaron asked softly.

"I need more. I may never get the chance again. Please?"

Quickly as her rotting body would allow her to, she shimmied out of her jeans and tossed her blouse off. Screw modesty and any body image problems. He'd like her anyways because he was Aaron. That and zombies. This was really under-negotiated, but she just wanted... now. Whatever happened would happen.

Without needing any prompting, Aaron did the same but much faster. He just tore off the dangling strips left of his shirt and hastily undid the buckle to his pants and pulled them off. Even though Aaron was freshly (un)dead, it had already impacted his body. Rigor mortis had taken an interesting hold on a part of him. Aaron's cock stood straight out from his body without the need to pump it, pointing towards the now naked Beryl. Wait, Aaron had a cis cock? Oh wait, she noticed the skin graft on the arm and realized that he had phalloplasty. Cool! How and when did that happen? And she needed it in her yesterday. Zombie-ism was totally the perfect cure for trans related genital dysphorias. She shuffled towards Aaron, reaching for his engorged flesh and pulled it to the hole she had created between her legs.

"It may not be perfect," Beryl said, "but I wanted you to fuck this hole I made. You'll be my first and only," She pressed the head against the gaping gash. Without needing much encouragement, he pushed his length through the hole until he had the whole thing inside. It was a tight and somewhat awkward fit and felt okay. It didn't really hurt which was a plus. Zombies apparently didn't feel pleasure the same way humans did. It was more like the memory of pleasure that she had dreamed about as he slowly pulled his cock out and thrust back in.

Zombies didn't really feel pain either. Beryl clutched Aaron's body, marveling in the act of actually getting to have sex face to face standing up. Well, she was pressed against a tree and he had to kneel down to get the right angle.

"F-f-fuck. Can't believe I get to do this. With you. So smart. Who else would think of doing SRS because they're a zombie?" Aaron uttered between clenched teeth.

She moved against his thrusts and ran her nails lightly down Aaron's cooling body. She motioned for Aaron to bend down as their lips connected again and their inner hungers rose as if to meet each other. They growled as they managed to restrain the bulk of their want; their mouths collided frantically as they nipped and bit into the other's lips. Clawed hands raked along each other's bodies as their hips slammed together.

As Aaron thrust hard into her, he leaned forward, taking a bite out of her neck. Blunt teeth scraped across her shoulder eliciting a shiver of imagined memory and he shared his mouthful with her in a kiss. Beryl accepted the proffered piece of her own flesh and they passed it back and forth between their mouths. Kinda like they were snowballing. It was strangely hot and intimate and made her smile.

Beryl felt as if Aaron's death-engorged cock was smashing things apart deep inside her. Even though it wasn't pleasurable, she still found fucking like this really hot. And it felt right in her skin. It felt right to be in his arms and the way they were fucking. She growled her response and bit Aaron's chest right along one of his top surgery scars. Fucking beautiful scars that she wanted to worship and create more of.

"Wonder if zombies can cum. Harder, fuck my brains out." Beryl said hoarsely.

"Going to wreck you then, love," Aaron gripped her hips and drove his cock harder. It jarred her with each thrust, but what really got to her was the fact that he had called her love.

Beryl cried out as Aaron's cock battered her hole. Her nails dragged along Aaron's back as she pulled their bodies as close as they could go. With a high pitched keen, she surprisingly came, what was left of her toes curling as waves of white hot pleasure pulsed through her body. Aaron pulled her right against his body and she knew he was cumming too.

After a couple moments, he pulled out and collapsed to the ground. Beryl joined him, snuggling up against him affectionately. One arm came loose and was now useless, hanging on by a bit of muscle. Fuck Hollywood and their story about redeeming zombies with love. Being human is over-rated.

She didn't really remember much of what happened after that. Her memory was seriously beginning to slip. What she did remember was that she felt warm, complete, protected, and desired. She felt... sexy.

Beryl's last thoughts were that she didn't regret a thing. Yes, she was wretched and people would wish her dead but how was that different from before? They were the wretched, the unwanted. Perhaps this zombification was a blessing in disguise. It gave her a way to fight back. She was the wretched through and through. She was among her kind.

What Cheer

RJ EDWARDS

Apparently the record store on Hope Street is a hookah bar now. Every storefront on the east side of Providence goes through a hookah bar stage: larva, pupa, hookah bar. Then, if we're lucky, it emerges as a decent pizza or burrito place, or if we're unlucky, another kitschy gift shop selling over-priced anchor-motif jewelry and funny cat postcards. I don't have time to wait for the next phase, so I stick my hands in my pockets and start walking home.

It's two days until Christmas and I'm still trying to find a stupid present for my brother-in-law Jared, about whom I know very little despite going to school with him since we were five years old. No one warned me, back when we were sipping peach schnapps at Martin Otelli's parents' beach house after junior prom, that he'd end up working with my sister and falling in love and I'd have to buy presents for him every year for the rest of our lives. I would have paid more attention. I would have drank less schnapps. But I'm sure he's not thrilled to have annual holiday quizzes on me, either.

I get to Blackstone Boulevard and veer left. I rub my hands together and pull my scarf up over my mouth and nose. It's cold as balls but I didn't bring a hat because I don't like my hair to get messed up. If it stays like this, maybe we'll get snow on Christmas. There's even a patch of it on the ground in front of the cemetery.

I pause. It's the first snow I've seen this year. I can't remember it snowing.

Maybe it happened last night? There wasn't snow on the ground at my place. Maybe someone piled it up there when they were clearing the walkways. But it's a bizarre spot – I walk towards it. It's a perfect white mound in the browning grass, smooth and untouched except for a pine-cone half-buried in the pile. Did someone put this at the mouth of a grave-yard as some kind of obtuse art project? Or like – a way of paying respects? I crouch down to inspect it.

The pinecone is not a pinecone, but some other kind of coniferous plant that I don't recognize – a sphere with brown spikes in every direction. Too big to be a chestnut, and not quite the right shape. I've lived around here my whole life and never seen it before. I take out my phone and try to snap a picture to send to Nancy, but the light's no good.

If someone did leave it here on purpose, I probably shouldn't touch it. This is what I tell myself as I reach out and immediately prick myself on one of the spikes. I curse out loud, and then look over my shoulder because: oh yeah, squatting in front a cemetery after dark is creepy behavior. I decide to just dig the thing out of the pile.

The snow isn't cold – it feels more like ash. When I pick up the sphere and carefully turn it over in my hand, its weight shifts, as if there's liquid inside. It's definitely not any plant I've ever seen, but doesn't feel plasticy or fake. Something about it nauseates me – like it's slightly out of focus even when I'm looking right at it. A chill tells me I should leave it where I found it – but instead, I dump it in my pocket and walk home as fast as I can.

"Addie. Do you know what fucking time it is?" Nancy is leaning to-ward her camera, wearing nothing but a black bra and a gold necklace.

"It's ten-thirty," I reply. "You don't go to bed until like two."

"It's quarter of eleven, actually. And it's still late for get-online-now text messages from you. Unless... are you attempting the lamest, most needlessly elaborate booty call?"

I roll my eyes. "Yeah, no. I wanted to show you something."

I fish the sphere out of my pocket and try to hold it near the laptop camera without messing up the focus. It feels heavier than it did when I picked it up and the spikes have curled a bit at the ends – maybe I killed it.

"Ew, gross! What is that?" Nancy leans closer.

"I don't know. It's like, a weird plant or something."

"And you just picked it up and brought it into your house?"

"Yeah, I guess." The bizarre unfocused feeling has faded, and looking at it in the light, it is gross – kind of veiny. "I found it in front of Swan's Cemetery, in like, a pile of fake snow."

"Oh my God, Addison, you're so fucking weird. Throw it out!"

"But what is it?"

"Who. Cares. Throw it out."

"Someone probably put it there. Is it like an art thing?"

"What the fuck is this, CSI? Addie."

"Yeah, yeah, ok," I say, but I just put it down on my desk where she can't see it for now. "I thought it was interesting."

"What were you doing at the cemetery anyway?"

"I was on my way home from Hope Street – out looking for a Christmas present for my brother-in-law."

"What did you get him?"

"Nothing, yet. The record store I tried to go to isn't there anymore," I lean back in my chair and sigh. "I don't know what the hell he likes."

"So don't get him anything," she shrugs.

"That's not really how it works in my family. I have to be twice as generous and whatever as everyone else or I'm, like, *being difficult*."

"Cause you're the trans kid?"

"It started before that. It's like, an adoption thing. But yeah, no, that didn't help."

"Well, fuck them. You should do what I did after I came out and move two thousand miles away. Does wonders for the mental health."

I chuckle. "Then we couldn't hang out."

"Sure, but you could still chat me in the middle of the night to show me some nerd shit you found on an unmarked grave." She smiles and rests her head on one hand. Behind her, I can see the shelves and shelves of her candle collection, half of which she never uses. Nancy cultivates this witchy image. She's never given me the impression that she actually believes in any of it, but I think it suits her – willowy, dark, and witchy. In my corner of the screen, I can tell my hair is still perfect. "Or you could just spend Christmas with me."

"What are your Christmas plans, then?"

"I'll be here. My family sends cards. I'll probably order Chinese food and get drunk."

"That sounds ok."

"Yeah, well. Maybe I'll watch *It's a Wonderful Life* while I get drunk, too."

We stay online and complain for a while about work and whatever. We finally say goodnight and sign off around midnight, after lots of chatting and teasing and half-flirting. Nancy has become a lifeline since we met in a spring semester class, interrupting my work-school-thesis-sleep-repeat routine. I sort of gave up on social life after the people I grew up with all moved away or stopped making any sense to me – but Nancy and I clicked. I find myself hoping that she's not drinking alone on Christmas, that she gets to do something nice, but if I told her that she'd make fun of me for being a sap.

I dope around on Facebook for a bit before shutting down my computer for the night – then I look around the room with the feeling I forgot something. I stare at the desk until I realize the plant thing: it's not where I left it.

I check my pockets, move stuff around on my desk, and reluctantly kneel down to look for it on the floor. I'm not sure, at first, what I'm looking at under the desk. There's an unfamiliar brown something, but it's way too big to be what I'm looking for. No – a sick dread seizes me, making it difficult to move. It's there.

The plant has grown larger than a watermelon. It's pressed up against the wall, about two feet from my face. As I watch it, pinned to the spot, I realize that it's pulsing.

After a long moment of the blessed thoughtlessness of shock, I decide I need to deal. So I break it down into options:

Reach out and touch the thing.

Get a broom and touch the thing.

Call Nancy.

Call animal control.

Call the plant equivalent of animal control – maybe poison control?

Ignore it and go to bed.

Panic and call the cops.

Ok. Ok. I slowly stand up and look for the broom.

I'm able to pull the thing out so I can see it. It has grown even more in the last several minutes, and it's definitely moving. It gently expands and shrinks, as if breathing. I crouch next to it and use the broom to spin it. No mouth that I can see. No eyeballs or claws. It still looks mostly plant-like. I tap the surface with the broom's handle. Not hollow.

And suddenly, it cracks.

"Shit shit shit!" I shout as I scramble backwards, all my senses springing alive with adrenaline. Did I kill it? Is it attacking? I hold out the broom defensively.

The seam across the pod's surface turns a milky white, and as it spreads I realize it's something inside leaking out. It drips and pools on the floor. The shell of the thing splits apart like a melon being halved, or an egg perfectly cracked. From inside spills the huddled form of an animal, covered in the thick white liquid and folded in on itself. It doesn't move for a long, tense moment. Maybe I *did* kill it.

I hear it before I see it – a hiss. But it's not the creature. Bubbles are spreading across the surface of the white goo. It's boiling there on the floor. I cover my mouth with my sleeve to filter the strong acidy smell, but before I can decide whether to throw water on it or a blanket over it or what, it's evaporated.

I can see the hatched animal clearly now. It starts to stir and blink. It's human.

It's me.

They stretch their legs which are my legs and they roll onto their back, which has all the same moles and zits and hair as my back. They squint their eyes, which are the same shade of brown as my eyes, and with an eerie kind of grace they rise and spin, taking in the room. It also gives me a view of them – of me – from every angle. There's a pod person in my bedroom wearing my skin and my hair and my bones and my tits and my junk and my face. They're looking at with me with my own face. I shift the broom in my hands.

"Hi!" They say brightly. In my voice.

A new option suddenly occurs to me:

Run into the bathroom and lock the door.

In my hurry to execute the new plan, I neglected to grab my phone. So I can escape through the window, stay here hugging myself and pacing until I die, or eventually, go out and face them. I think I could probably take me in a fight. If I can stop shaking first.

"Hello?" I can hear them hovering outside the door. "Excuse me. Politeness. Excuse me! I did not mean to be rude. Or scare. Scare you. I am learning very rapidly. But I will not harm you. Usual, usually, there is a, uh, a bonding that we perform now. But your biology's bonding process is slow, I think?"

"What do you want from me?" I attempt to sound less terrified than I am.

"I came to walk with you."

"Ok. So," I hug myself tighter and lean against the door. "You're an alien, yeah?"

"Correct! I came on a, uh. I think there is no equivalent word. Spore?"

"The spiky thing."

"Yes, yes!" They're so loud. Is that what I sound like? I cringe.

"Listen," I say. "I want to talk more. I have a lot of questions, obviously. But before I come out, can you – be someone else?"

"I don't understand."

"You look like me. Look like someone else."

"But I connected with you," they say plainly. "The walk is begun."

"What are you talking about, walk?"

"My kind have this ability. We connect with a host and replicate their shape so that we may walk with them. It allows us to..." They struggle for the correct word. "To know."

"So, that's how you know English and stuff? You've got my brain, too?"

"Yes, we must draw on this to use our new shapes."

A chill runs through me. "You have my memories."

"Yes. Maybe," they say. "Memory is a strange word. Images of past experiences. I have my own. But I have other parts. Very interesting. Language in one place, feelings in another. But memories all over between everything. I can only remember with as much speed as you can."

This is not very clarifying, or comforting. "So, you've got my body and my brain and you're here to... what? Lay eggs? Blend in and get a job?"

"To know."

"Intelligence? Recon? What for?" I refuse to simplify out of spite.

"We know to know. We arrive, we walk, we know, we leave. We do not come back."

I consider this. An alien anthropologist walking around in my body. "So... maybe you should connect with someone else."

"The walk has begun. I cannot change shape again until I go back."

I exhale, and it feels like the first time I've done so in hours. I stare at my reflection in the bathroom mirror and try deep breaths. "You're stuck here. Looking like me."

"This is correct."

"For how long?"

"One full waking-resting cycle."

"...and how long is that?"

"Twenty-nine hours," they say.

"Wow, ok, Jesus. I'm going to open the door."

They don't answer. I turn the knob and open it a crack. They're there, real, my face, all of it. They're giving me a big, earnest grin – *how cheerful*, I think. A phrase bubbles up from a high school history class memory of a Narragansett man's first words upon meeting the settler Roger Williams: *what cheer, friend?*

"Can you, uh, put on some clothes?"

"Oh!" They're immediately mortified. Jesus. I taught shame to an alien species. Am I the colonized or the colonizer in this scenario? Their posture becomes shrinking – more like mine.

"Hey, whatever. It's ok," I tell them. "There are some clothes on the floor in the room where you... hatched."

They nod and go to put them on. "Nudity is taboo."

"Yeah, uh," I step out of the bathroom.

I go to the bedroom closet to grab some pillows and a blanket. Out of the corner of my eye, I watch them put on a t-shirt and a pair of my underpants. "Do you have a to-do list to hit, or...?"

"I don't understand. I have no mission but to walk with you."

"And when you leave, you go back to your own planet?" I try to imagine them as another person. But it's me, me in 3D with surround-sound.

"It's not quite a planet. But yes."

"So... what's it like there? Some utopia where everyone's graceful and cheerful?"

"Utopia." They taste the word. "No. We don't have a thing like that. There are many of us who go out, and we all come back with different knowing. So, it's very complicated."

"Sounds like Earth," I say. "Ok, well, right now it's super late. I'm not walking anywhere. We need to sleep. *I* have to sleep, I don't know about you."

They start to interrupt with some fun fact about how our physiology is completely identical and I hold up a hand to stop them.

"So we're going to sleep. We'll get up early and... I don't know, fuck. I'll figure something out."

I get them set up on the floor and apologize for not having somewhere better. I turn off the lights and tentatively get into bed.

"Don't kill me in my sleep, ok?"

"No, of course not," they say softly. "Utopia – that's very interesting, but I don't think it's real."

"...Ok, so, goodnight."

My guest doesn't try to chat any longer. I lie awake for another hour or so, watching them, waiting for some more sinister creature to emerge. But it's just me – drifting to sleep. It feels dangerous to watch myself in such a vulnerable state – I want to wake them up, say: hey, there's an alien in the room! I focus on the shadows of their face until, like a magic eye puzzle, my vision shifts and their features look new and unfamiliar enough for me to close my eyes and relax.

I dream that my mother and my sister are tearing up my apartment, looking for something embarrassing. My face is burning and I know they're going to find it. The two of them tower over me, mirror images of high cheekbones and long blonde hair, and they lecture me about keeping secrets from the people who care about you. My mother starts throwing out everything in my refrigerator. My sister turns and I see it's actually Nancy – she's grown my sister's brilliant hair and she looks incredible. She's angry with me and rushes out the front door. I try to follow her, but the door only leads back inside.

"Hey. Hey, uh, Addie Junior. Wake up."

They're asleep on their back, with their hands folded across their stomach. I've been tiptoeing around them as I got showered and dressed this morning, and for a moment it feels kind of normal that they're here. Then their eyes pop open and a big smile spreads across their face.

"I had visions in the night."

Moment of normalcy over. It is the creepiest and the funniest thing to see those words come out of my own mouth. "Good ones?"

"Yes, I think so. I did not feel distress."

"Dreams can be cool," I say.

They scrunch their face a bit and wipe drool from the corner of their mouth. "I can't remember them now."

"Yeah, that's normal," I say.

"Did you dream?" they ask.

The image of Nancy with bright blonde hair reappears in my mind. "I don't remember. Hey, how many more hours until you go?"

They pause. "Approximately twenty-one and one-quarter hours."

"Ok. Ok. If you want to, uh, wash up or anything and get ready – I'm working on a plan."

They sit up and stick their arms out straight, stretching their muscles in a way that looks uncomfortable to me. "Yes, I think I will enjoy washing up."

I can hear them in the bathroom experimenting with faucets before they start drawing a bath. I try calling and skyping Nancy while the clone is busy, but she doesn't pick up. A moment later, she texts: *Hey whats up?*

I need your help with something

I start picking out an outfit for Addie Jr.

More CSI shit?? Nancy shoots back.

More like X-Files I type, but erase it. I send: *Something went really wrong last night, need your advice, in person preferable*

She would never believe me if I told her without showing her. She's the only person who might believe me at all. It's a shit plan, but who else do I go to? The police? My *parents*?

I lay a pink t-shirt, a sports bra, dark blue jeans, and a puffy coat that I haven't worn in years on the bed. I scrounge in a drawer and find some long-neglected eye makeup.

I'm having brunch with Chad atm

I'm not sure how to respond. I know Chad – guy that she's seen on and off since this summer. Is she on a date?

Can you meet me after?

I listen to the water sloshing in the other room during the long wait for a response.

Sure babe, is it ok if Chad joins us?

I let myself be furious with her for a moment. Then excuses come: how would she know how serious this is? As far as she knows, I talked to her from home last night and then fell asleep. Maybe Chad is trustworthy enough. Maybe more witnesses will be a good thing.

yeah of course, but he can't tell anyone what I tell you

I hit send even though it sounds a bit paranoid. I think: I deserve to be paranoid. Addie Jr. pokes their head out of the bathroom and I look away while they get dressed.

Before we head out, I apply thick black liner around their eyes and give them a hat with ear flaps. On the bus, I see our reflection in the windows and try to slouch more than usual. We don't look identical from afar, but I'm still hoping we don't run into anyone I know. Maybe I can pass them off as a relative. A look-alike cousin or something. From that birth family I never knew. Totally.

An older guy keeps glancing at the two of us. I wonder what he sees: a heterosexual couple, a pair of ugly lesbians, a brother and sister? How novel, a sibling who looks like me. I wonder how much of a difference looking alike would have made with my sister and me – but I don't let myself chase that train of thought too far.

My pod person is practically bouncing in their seat for the whole ride, occasionally flashing me a manic smile. I told them we were going to meet some friends of mine. The eye liner job looks terrible – the whole disguise reminds me of myself around twenty, closeted and transparently false. But Addie Jr. has none of the grim self-consciousness or anxious mannerisms that I did.

The ear-flap hat is cuter on me than I would have thought.

I step into the café and spot Nancy and Chad in the corner. She waves, then looks quizzically at my counterpart. I grab Addie Jr's arm and hurry past the signs advertising eggnog lattes, past the counter, towards the booth.

"Hey, uh, let me talk them through this ok?" I say to Addie Jr.

"Yes, I imagine your explanation would include finer social nuances than – "

"Hey Addie," Chad says warmly as we take a seat. He removes his hand from Nancy's – definitely a date – and extends it towards my pod person. "Sorry, I don't think we've met?"

I jump in: "This is... AJ. I met them last night."

After staring at his palm for a moment too long, AJ gives Chad a firm handshake.

"Look, I had – we had a, uh, really weird night, and I'd like to keep it between us."

"Oh yeah, sure," Chad says.

"Is everything ok?" Nancy asks. She looks at my guest, trying to piece something together.

I take a deep breath and swallow. "You remember the plant thing that I showed you?"

"Um," Nancy gives me an are-you-high face, but answers, "Yes."

"Well... I didn't throw it out." I'm not sure where to go from here. "It was a pod. Like, a person-pod. Like, a pod person."

Chad and Nancy just stare at me. I put my elbows on the table, bury my face in my hands, and I lose it.

"This is crazy, but it's not. Ok? Ok. Aliens are real, and they visited me – one visited me. And I don't know what the fuck to do. I don't know what the fuck to do. Like, how the fuck do I explain this? AJ is an alien. They're me. They're a pod person version of me."

Nancy slowly raises her chin, then turns it into a nod. "Ok. Ok. Addie, we believe you."

"Really?" I say, meeting her eye. *I* wouldn't believe me.

"We believe that this is what you experienced, ok? And we can, uh, figure out what happened," Nancy says. This is a very supportive way of not believing me.

"Holy *shit*," Chad says. Nancy and I both look at him. He's looking at AJ. "This is you. Like, this is *you*."

AJ smiles politely. Chad reaches over and removes the ear-flap hat.

Don't touch them, I want to say. *Don't.*

Something shifts on Nancy's face. "Holy shit. Holy fuck."

"This is amazing!" Chad whispers. He leans over the table, looking at AJ from every angle. My stomach churns. This was a mistake.

Stop staring at them. Stop staring at them. Stop it.

I nod. "Oh my god, Addie. What are

say. "So – I don't know. I guess tell-
d."

d this time I do say it: "Don't touch

bles an apology.
people touch you. Ok?"
walk?"

Nancy says.
r... I don't know! This is incredible!"

s. You shouldn't have even brought

expression makes me feel like I've

Oh my god. Are we the only people
people? It doesn't even know what
I don't know, record an interview or

sus stop stop stop looking at them.
s.

n AJ. I feel suddenly like lead has
breathe again.

to Addie if anyone found out about
uld get hurt?" She shakes her head
again. "This is a fucking disaster. A trans alien? It's a fucking joke. I don't even know... it would be bad. Fuck."

AJ looks to me with concern. I don't know if they understand, but I find their hand under the table and give it a squeeze anyway.

"Well, we don't have to tell *everyone*..." he continues.

"That's not how this fucking works, Chad. You know it's not." Nancy looks at me. "Addison, I can't believe..."

"I don't know what to do," I say quietly. "I thought... you always know what to do."

"Well, I don't. I don't know what you've gotten yourself into."

"They're not evil or anything," I say. "I don't think."

"You're not curious?" Chad asks Nancy. He puts his arm around her and gently brushes his thumb over her shoulder. "You don't want to know... where they're from, what they think of us?"

She looks down into her Bloody Mary. "Stories like this don't end well. Especially for people like us."

"It's very nice to meet you," AJ says suddenly, startling all three of us. None of us know how to respond, so we don't.

Before we go, they both swear they won't tell anyone. Chad asks AJ some questions about space and they give him their polite, vague non-answers. I know Nancy is mad at me but I don't really know why. Maybe I do, but it feels unfair. I'm the one this is happening to.

"I think I am hungry," AJ says to me as we step out of the café. We never bothered ordering anything in there. I check my phone. It's a little past one, and my stomach is growling, too.

"Ok," I press my hands against my eyes and take a deep breath. "Ok, let's get you some food. I have some errands I need to run before tomorrow, anyway."

I can remember when the Providence Place Mall was built – adults around me grumbling that the one-million-square-foot shopping centre being erected right on top of the Providence River was "changing the character" of the city. But of course, once it was finished, they all shopped there. Other developments soon followed: condos down the river, a gaudy glass office tower right across the street. Across the street from the mall is also Waterplace Park, a patch of green by the river where homeless people sleep and bored teens sometimes hang out and where Gay Pride festivities were once held. After the office tower, Pride moved to the east side, with the hookah bars. The homeless folks drifted deeper downtown. The teens went into the mall, I guess. There sure are a lot of them there on Christmas Eve.

The food court is packed with teens hunched over tables in groups of four or five, or else coupled off and making out. A few lean against the floor-to-ceiling windows facing the shiny tower and the empty park. AJ is watching one of these couples closely as they gyrate against the glass. The humping teens don't notice.

"Hey, your Sbarro's getting cold," I say.

"Oh," AJ says, and manages to tear their eyes away. They rip off the point of their cheese pizza with their hands and eat it, looking meditative as they chew.

"I like Sbarro," they declare, then touch their face. "It feels warm, to like something."

Leaving the food court, we pass the line to see Santa Claus. Despite the fact that today is a pseudo-holiday, or maybe because it is, the line twists and turns and stretches at least one hundred stressed-out parents and screaming babies deep. Their impatience is palpable. The whole scene is scored by shrill-voiced chipmunks begging for toys.

"Christmas is very important." AJ is solemn, like Christmas has just died and they are saying a few words.

"Yeah, it's kind of a weird time to be here," is all I can think to add.

After they touch and smell *every single fucking thing* in Lush and I buy a bath bomb to pair with a gift card for my mom, we head down the escalator. I can see AJ's breath catch and their neck crane as they take in the elaborate Christmas decorations hanging overhead. In Newbury's, I plant them by the shelf of floppies where they flip through one after another, entranced. I pick out Sufjan Steven's stupid Christmas box set for Jared and hope he doesn't already have it. As we're leaving, AJ holds up an issue of Thor: God of Thunder.

"Can we bring this with us?"

"Yeah, whatever," I say. As I pay for it, I'm already thinking about how long I should wait after they leave to throw it away. Maybe they'll take it with them – maybe this will be all that aliens will know about our religions and concepts of outer space. Norse Mythology and Jack Kirby might be too much for me to explain to them in one day. I guess it's half a day now.

My phone goes off while we're waiting for the bus, and I fumble to answer it. "Hello?"

I expect Nancy's voice – she figured something out, or told the FBI, or just wants to smooth the day over.

"Hey," my sister says. My stomach drops as if she can see me standing with this suspicious body double at Kennedy Plaza. Why didn't I check the stupid number?

"Oh, hey," I say. I gesture wildly to AJ: motioning YOU, palm-up STAY, pointing HERE. They watch me and don't respond. I try the give-me-one-minute finger and step away. "Sorry, I'm outside, it's a little loud. Everything ok?"

"You're coming tomorrow, to my place, yeah?"

"Yeah, of course. I thought I told you."

"No, you didn't."

"Well, I told mom."

"Anyway, I wanted to tell you Nan and Poppy are going to be there too."

"Ok? Great?" I look over my shoulder to make sure AJ hasn't followed me or wandered off. My sister starts talking at me about the logistics of the dinner prep, not saying what she called to say which is: *don't ruin Christmas.* But I don't hear her.

Someone is with AJ.

He's tall, but youngish, and he's leaning in and AJ is just smiling the same way that they smile at me and the world drops out from under my feet watching a person wearing my body being cornered as this guy puts his arm up on the bus stop plexiglass.

"Will you?" My sister says on the phone.

"Yeah," I say. "Yeah, of course."

"Ok. Don't burn them this year. And wear something, like, kinda nice? You know how mom is."

"Uh-huh, I know. Sorry my bus is here see you tomorrow."

I hang up and bee-line to AJ.

"We gotta go, sis," I say, too loud and too high.

"Bus isn't here yet," the dude says.

I don't bother with fake excuses. I grab their arm and pull them away from him – the earflaps hat collides with his arm, but stays on, and we slip away.

He follows.

"Hey," he says. "Your friend and I were just talking."

I push past the other passengers and towards the crosswalk.

"Hey! What the fuck's your problem?" He shouts after us.

We're almost across the street. The light's going to change, please change.

"Fucking bitch!" He says, then changes his mind. "Fucking faggot!"

The light changes and cars pass between us and him. I can't hear him anymore but I don't turn around.

"We're gonna walk home," I say, as much to myself as AJ. "It's uphill, but it's not too far."

I let go of AJ's arm when we get across Memorial Boulevard and we walk side by side up the forty-five degree slopes of College Hill. We pause to catch our breath at the Brown University gates; I support myself with one hand on the wrought iron. They finally ask: "Did that person mean to harm us?"

"Jesus," is all I can say.

"Are they an enemy?"

"No, it's..." I'm still shaking, panicked and mad, mad at them for not understanding. "Fuck, how do you have my brain and not get this stuff? How do you just stand there and – "

They're looking at me, waiting. Scared. In my oversized coat, they look like a teenager. I remember that they're younger than that. What the fuck am I doing? Why did I bring them to the fucking mall?

"It's complicated. But we're ok now. Ok? We're ok. Let's just go home."

We get to my place and I crank up the heat. AJ is still dazed, so I leave them to read their Thor comic while I wrap the presents and make some tea.

"Here you go, AJ," I place a mug next to where they're perched on the floor. "Careful, it's still pretty hot."

"What does AJ mean?"

"Oh," I sit at the desk and wrap my hands around my cup. "I was just, uh, giving you a nickname. Cause I was calling you Addie Junior. AJ for short."
"Oh." They return to the comic book. I'm struck with guilt, which is possibly misplaced, but still. I never even asked.

"But, uh, maybe you should name yourself."

This sparks their attention.

"I would like that," they push the comic away and pause, deep in thought. "Could I be... Nancy?"

Absolutely fucking not is my first thought, but I can't say that. I feel my face going red. "Why do you want to be Nancy?"

"I don't know. I feel affection for this name."

"Oh. That's like, residual me, I guess. Nancy is my friend you met today, remember?"

"Yes. She was very nice to me," they say.

I don't know if she was.

"Your friend," they say the word slowly and glow with happiness, then tilt their head. "You love her."

"Uh," I feel the nauseous, panicky urge to deny it, followed by the blissful anxiety of realizing it might be true. I consider explaining the difference between *friend-love* and *love-love*, but *holy shit* why do I care? I have to stay, like, cool and invulnerable, even though I'm never going to see this person again? This person who is literally me? "Yeah. I think I love her."

They run a hand over their stomach, then squeeze it into a fist above their chest. For the first time, their expression is inscrutable to me. "Does she love... you?"

I think about it. Nancy flirts, for sure. But I have a hard feeling in the pit of my stomach about the answer. "No."

"Does it hurt you?" they whisper.

"No," I say slowly. Then I push down the hard feeling; go back to being cool, invulnerable Addie. The Addie that Nancy likes. "Well, it might."

I can see them thinking of more questions, so I get up and pull my pipe off the dresser.

"Hey, you wanna try smoking?" I say.

After some explaining about what the stuff in the pipe is and what it does, we both get stoned and I order Chinese food for delivery. I don't know what they'll like, so I just order a ton of shit. When it all arrives, it comes with four sets of chopsticks. It turns out they like crab rangoons. They say it reminds them of pizza. I guess that makes sense?

"You feel ok?" I ask.

"Oh yes," they say. I can't note any change in their demeanor, so I wonder if maybe their born-yesterday brain and body can't process the weed. But they did eat a whole carton of fried rice, and they're reaching for another, so.

I look at the clock. It's seven-thirty, so they have like ten hours? Ten-ish? Fuck, I'm bad at math when I'm not high. I think about, I don't know, trying to give them the cliffnotes version of human history, or maybe I could explain dinosaurs, but that doesn't feel right. I don't want to get us all stressed out again. What do I actually want to share with them? What I would want to do if I had one night on Earth?

I take another hit, then turn on my computer and queue up *Spirited Away*.

I figure they'll like *Ponyo* best, but it turns out they're a *Kiki's Delivery Service* fan. Between each movie I ask them if they want to do anything else, but they're content to keep watching anime in our underpants and munch on leftover food.

"Can my name be Kiki?" They ask me without taking their eyes off the screen.

"Sure, whatever."

I'm still stoned, and so is Kiki. I take out my phone. It's one in the morning, the same time they arrived the night before. Five hours left. I find myself wishing that they could stay one day longer and go out to breakfast with me the next morning – I want them to know about eggs and home fries. Then I remember what day it is. I pause the movie.

"Hey, come here," I say and hold out my arm. They scoot over, erasing the foot or so that had been between us on the bed. I drape one arm over them and hold up my phone with the other hand to record a video. "Christmas morning, 2013, I'm here with Kiki. They're totally real. You're not crazy, Addie. Say hi, Kiki, I'm recording a video."

"Hi," Kiki says. Their eyes are a bit red. I put down the phone and look at them. Their face, which is my face, is so close to mine, and they're smiling again. They smile so much more than I do. They don't fucking get it. It breaks my heart.

"I think I'm going to miss you," I say, and my mouth hangs open after the last word. Their lips part, too, and I can feel their breath brushing with mine. They put a hand to my face and it feels so warm; their whole body is warm and pressing against mine. My nose collides with Kiki's and I kiss them.

They kiss me back, confident but gentle, and I feel dizzy with lust. The impossibility of the situation, their impending departure – it feels so important and so liberatingly meaningless at once. The words *they don't care* loop in my head as the tonguing grows more intense, *they don't care* – don't know, haven't learned to be self-conscious about the way my fat stretches my clothing in the wrong places, to be uncomfortable with the hair coating my stomach and breasts and outlining my nipples. When they press against me they're not caught up with acting out a faulty impression of one thing or the other; their hands aren't asking me for anything but touch. What do they see when they look at my body? *Don't care.*

I run my fingertips up their leg and they runs theirs up mine; they're feeling what I'm feeling just how I'm feeling it. I scratch my fingernails over the thick brown hairs on their thigh, on my thigh, and they do the same to mine, to theirs, sending heat through both of us like a circuit. My body is touching my body and it's the only body that it knows, the only body that it's ever wanted. It's all so fucking hot and I push myself up, so I'm kneeling over them. We're still making out while I fumble to take off my top.

When we finally break the kiss, I see them looking up at me – their glassy-eyed expression – and the crazy lust stops dead. This is fucked up. Not like, the having sex with myself part, but having sex with someone who's functionally twenty-four hours old and high.

"Uh, sorry," I say. I readjust my shirt.

"What's wrong?" They ask.

"Nothing," I say. "I mean, sorry if that was weird. I got, uh, carried away. I think we should watch the movie."

"Ok," they say. If they're hurt, they don't show it.

I lean down and kiss them again, a peck this time, a punctuation mark. We sit closer together for the rest of the film, but nothing else happens.

I wake up with that sickening jumping feeling and see that *Princess Mononoke* is over. My phone is ringing. Kiki is gone.

I check the clock – it's four. It's not time, it's not fucking time!

I can't breathe as I push myself up and stagger across the room. I grab my phone to see who the fuck could be calling me at –

It's Nancy.

I press it against my ear.

"Hello?" I choke out.

"Addie?" Nancy says, almost too quiet to hear.

The bedroom door is open – it wasn't before, right? Kiki's not in the bathroom. I notice the front door is ajar, too. Jesus, Kiki.

"What's wrong?" I ask Nancy while I look for my shoes.

"It's so stupid. It's so stupid. We got in a fight," she sounds like she's been crying. She's definitely drunk.

"A fight?"

"Me and Chad."

"Did he hurt you?"

"No, it wasn't like that."

"Is he still there?"

"No," she says with a gulping post-sobbing sound.

"Shit. I'm sorry, Nancy. Do you want me to come over later? I can come in the morning, you can tell me about it." Keys, keys, where are my keys. When did I fall asleep? How far could Kiki possibly get? Fuck, why did I get us so high?

"Can you come over now?" She asks in a tiny voice.

I freeze. "Right now?"

"I'm sorry, fuck, I'm sorry Addie, I'm so dumb."

"No, you're not. It's ok. It's ok. Are you ok? Are you going to be ok alone?"

"I just really want to see you," Nancy repeats. When I don't answer for a moment, she asks: "What are you doing?"

"Fuck. I'm sorry, Nancy. Kiki's gone. I woke up and they were gone."

"Who's Kiki?"

I find my keys under the earflap hat.

"Oh my god. Are you talking about that fucking alien?"

"I'm sorry, I'm really sorry Nancy."

"Oh, fuck you."

"Nancy, I'm sorry. They're alone. They might get hurt."

"No, no, no, fuck, Addison, they're not even real. I'm real, I'm a real person and I'm asking you please, Jesus, please Addie, forget them and just come over, please, Addie?"

I hesitate. "I can't..."

She hangs up on me.

Fuck.

I grab my keys, pull on my shoes and book it down the staircase, out into the yard.

Relief floods me when I see their silhouette – barefoot, no pants, no coat, but still on this planet. Just standing in the yard. Goddammit, Kiki.

"Kiki," I say in a frustrated stage-whisper.

They turn around and there are tears streaming down their face. I rush to their side.

"Are you ok?"

They point across the street. I don't see anything.

"Isn't it beautiful?" They say in a shaky voice.

I look – it's snowing. I can see it clearly because every single house on the block has left their Christmas decorations illuminated overnight. Windows are outlined in twinkles of red, green, and blue. LED icicles give the appearance of white light dripping from rooftops. Fir trees that seem to bear glowing fruits greet us from inside almost every living room. Fluffy snowflakes dance towards the ground and everything – everything – is coated in delicate frost. I wonder if Kiki knows what it all means, but maybe it's better not to explain.

"Yeah, it's beautiful," I whisper back. I touch their arm and they're shivering, so I lead them back inside.

For the last hour or so they sit in my living room, wrapped in a blanket. I try to call Nancy back, but I'm not surprised when she doesn't pick up. I ask Kiki if there's anything else they want to know.

"No," they say, "Knowing isn't about asking questions. It's about the walk."

"It's not a very long walk," I say, and they just nod. "I guess maybe it's different, in different places?"

"I suppose so," they say. They look peaceful as they say, "I think I will miss you too."

The sun is starting to come up, so we get dressed and go outside to watch it.

The street is empty – no pedestrians, no cars on the road, no footprints in the new snow but ours. Everyone is inside with their families, opening their first presents, or else begging their children for five minutes more sleep, or else just lying awake in bed with an unmatched kind of feverish anticipation. In a few hours, I realize, I'll have to go to my sister's place and pretend everything is normal.

"It's time," Kiki says suddenly, their eyes still focused on the horizon. The sky bleeds orange and pink.

"Wait," I blurt out. My heart is pounding. "Can I come with you? Is it possible?"

I don't know if I mean it, but I don't know what else to do. This can't be it. They can't just leave. They can't – Kiki turns to me, and for a moment I think they're considering it. But they shake their head. They take my hand and squeeze it.

"You belong to this world, Addison." They drop my hand and start to back away.

"Wait," I don't have anything else, so I repeat it. "Wait."

"Thank you," they say. The clothes that I lent them start to drop away as if they're made of air.

"Wait, please wait."

Their skin and hair turn white, and then something past white, something too bright to look at directly. I blink a few times. My eyes won't adjust.

"Kiki, wait!"

But they have no ears to hear me, and no mouth to reply – they have dissolved, become something else than human again. When I can finally look directly at them, they're floating away, up: a pile of ash caught in the wind, or snow returning to the sky.

I stand in the yard and watch the spot in the sky for long after they're gone. I hear a car door open and close somewhere and take the cue to duck inside.

I shower, put on a maroon sweater and black pants. Do my hair. I pick up the Thor comic and put it on the desk for now. I put all the presents in plastic bags.

I feel my phone vibrate and take it out of my pocket. It's from Nancy.
Did you find them

I decide to make some coffee before I leave the apartment. I lean back on the kitchen counter; wait for it to brew. I take out my phone again, read the text again. I watch the video I took the night before.

"You're not crazy, Addie. Say hi, Kiki, I'm recording a video."

It ends, and I watch it again.

I hover over the delete icon long enough for the screen to go black. I wake up the phone and hastily delete the video.

I consider staying home, but my family would use it against me just as much as showing up. I send a reply to Nancy: *yes. they're gone now. sorry about last night. hope your Christmas doesn't suck too much. call if you want.* I add *love you.* I delete it. I rewrite it. I hit send. I pour myself a cup of coffee. I decide I am going to keep their stupid comic book.

I don't know what they learned while they were here. I don't think they really learned anything.

Satan, Are You There? It's Me, Laura

AISLING FAE

It was Friday night and Laura was summoning the devil. Because she was manic tonight and she thought, why not? Laura wasn't very given to the occult arts, but she had googled around and found really all it took was to draw a circle and a pentagram, and say an incantation.

However, because she was in this manic mood she went several extra miles. She drew a goat's head inside the pentagram. She turned the circle into a trans symbol. Around it she wrote: *"In Nomine Diabulus et Belial Satan Lucifer Astaroth et Yahve"* (which sounded like a badass incantation but was really just song lyrics).

Laura liked to draw, sometimes she thought she should drop out and pursue it full time, but she didn't feel like being a trans girl starving artist would be a good life path for her. Instead she carried on going to engineering school, working her shitty part time job at the library, and occasionally skyping her girlfriend who was doing a semester abroad. She was quickly getting bored of the mundanity. Therefore, Satan.

Once she'd finished drawing the circle, she started on the incantation. Slowly, in a loud, thundering voice, she said the words she'd written around the circle. She spoke in Latin, and ominously, because she had always believed Latin should only be spoken ominously.

And then, nothing happened.

Of course nothing happened. Laura felt silly—she felt really silly. It wasn't like she was actually expecting anything to happen, she told herself. Defeated, she got into bed—and of course, she couldn't sleep. She lay awake on her bed, staring at her ceiling. She probably should have spent all her extra energy finishing her homework, she'd just have to rush it before class. She turned around to look at the clock on her bedside table.

"Ok, 2:04, that's 2 times 2 times times 3 times 17. 2:05, that's 5 times 41."

She factored the time into prime factors until she finally fell asleep.

And then, something did happen.

A strong draft of hot air suddenly hit her body. She sat up—the wall with the mural was smoking, absolutely smoking. Out of the smoke a figure emerged, a big man, seven or eight feet tall. Skin red as blood, hair black as the void, furry cloven hooves. He looked around first, muttering to himself, then noticed Laura, staring at him, mouth agape. In a loud booming voice, he said: "You! You dare to summon the deceiver, the lord of flies? You call upon Lucifer, the Morningstar?"

"Holy hell!" Laura screamed.

The Demon laughed.

"What do we have here? A little girl summons Satan. For what? Perhaps she has a wish she thinks I could grant. Is that the case?"

"Uh. Uh. Uh. Wait, yes, kind of." Laura needed a few more seconds to process what was going on, but after that, she got it. "I mean. I kind of just—wanted to meet you."

"Meet me?" The demon seemed taken aback for a moment. Then he regained himself. "Is this some sort of joke? You called on Satan to meet Satan? Oh little girl, you're going to meet him all right!"

"Ok, then, hey, like, how do you do?" Laura extended a hand to the demon.

"What? No, I'm not going to shake your hand! How dare you? You sinful sinner, I should condemn you to hellfire for all eternity for wasting my time!"

Laura took this in her stride. Then she had a thought. "Since when do you condemn people to hellfire?"

"Well since always." The devil's face turned worried. "That's my thing, I run hell."

"Isn't that more God's thing? Like he sends them down, you burn them up. Satan would WANT me to sin."

"That's blasphemous!" the devil screeched.

Laura scratched her face. "Wait. *WAIT.*" And then it dawned on her. "God, is that you? Holy shit are you trying to punk me or something?"

Satan uttered a nervous laugh.

"Why," he said. "What could possibly lead you to say that? God? God wouldn't bother with, I mean he..."

"Nope, that's it, I'm sure. You're God."

"No! I am myself! Satan! The most beautiful Ang- "

"Cut the *crap*, God, I know it's you."

A sigh.

"All right, it's me."

The satanic figure shrunk down a bit, both literally and figuratively. The swirling smoke and fire began to clear. Furry cloven feet became sharply pressed pant legs ending in shiny black shoes. The red bare chest transformed into the white fabric of a three-piece suit. The goatee grew into a full, but neatly trimmed, white beard. Where previously an imposing demon had stood, now stood a man. He looked Middle Eastern and, despite herself, Laura found him very attractive.

"I'm usually not into guys, but dayumm."

"Thank you!" God said, in a voice that was much higher than you'd expect. "You like the suit? It's an original Armani design. I used to wear Dolce and Gabanna, but I'm boycotting."

Laura sat on her bed in quiet contemplation.

"It doesn't feel like a dream," she said. "I've had lucid dreams before, but not like this."

"That's 'cause it's not a dream, toots," God reassured her.

"Then what's going on?" She gestured towards him. "Why is God in my bedroom right now?"

"Well, what did you want? You were summoning Satan; I gave you Satan."

"But," Laura said, feeling strangely sad. "Why didn't Satan come himself?"

"Oh. Well shhh..."

"You're shushing me now?"

"No, I meant, um, he... Satan and I are not together anymore."

"Together, you say?" She grinned.

"As in, we don't work together anymore." God sounded snippy.

"You used to work together?"

"Well, sure. We collaborated a lot. We had an amazing thing going with the whole good and evil duality. We got the idea from Ahura Mazda. Gave us Hegemony. A two deity system, no more gods needed. Satan tempts, I condemn, Satan tortures. It was really elegant. But then, we stopped."

"Well there's my Catholic indoctrination blown out the window."

"Oh my God, yes! Indoctrination is super important. That's how you keep people faithful, which keeps us strong. It doesn't matter if they believe we're good or bad, so long as they believe. And it worked. We're still up there, still the biggest names in religion, after all these years!"

"So, why did you stop?"

"Oh, you don't want to know," God muttered.

"No, I do," Laura said softly. "I'm actually really curious."

"Well, I don't think I should share this with you."

"Come on. You obviously want to talk about it, otherwise you wouldn't still be here." She tapped a space on the edge of her bed. "Sit."

The God of David sat down on her bed. Ran his fingers through his hair. He looked distraught.

"It all happened because of Jesus. Not that I blamed him. He's a good kid. Just... 'For so he loved the world, that he gave it his only son.' Which was great, but I always had to be the tough love dad. 'Let him spend 40 days in the desert, it'll build character and he wants to do it anyway.' And his mom would say 'But he'll get cold and hungry. He's our baby, let's at least give him some snacks for the road'."

"His mom? You mean Mary?"

"Oh no, she was just the surrogate. He was *our* baby. And we thought it would help, we really did. Work was going good, but we'd fallen in a rut ever since her... stuff... happened. And she'd always wanted children, but it just made everything worse. Ok, it wasn't all bad. It was nice seeing her so happy for once. Not once in our relationship had I seen her so happy as with that kid. But she was too soft on him, and let him go on spouting all those horrid ideas. Hanging out with prostitutes and thieves, my own son? I was mortified."

"Huh?"

"And we all know how that turned out! Death on the cross. And then he was like, 'let me go back!' But she didn't want him to. And they argued for three straight days until finally he said something so awful. He said,

'You're not my real mom, you can't be anybody's mom.' She was devastated. So she let him go."

"Wait I'm confused..."

"She hasn't talked to me since. She made up with Jesus, but *he* won't talk to her on my behalf. All he does is lounge around on the Internet, reading Tumblr and talking about videogames or something. 'Dad, they say it's about ethics in Journalism, but it's just an excuse to be awful and misogy-'"

"OK stop! Who's Jesus' mother? Who left whom? What are you talking about?"

"Well, isn't it obvious? You asked me about her... Oh! That's right!" God smacked himself in the head dramatically. "Your Bible still uses her old name and pronouns. I'm talking about Satan, Lucifer. Well, she goes by Lucy now."

Laura's face brightened. "She's trans!"

"Yeah."

"That's so cool! Oh, sorry for misgendering her earlier, by the way."

"Oh, it's fine, you didn't know."

Laura rolled her eyes. "Yes, obviously, but I should still apologize— Wait, if I didn't know, it's because you didn't tell me. Why didn't you tell me?"

"You didn't ask?"

"True, true, but you did come in disguised—like, the idea we have of her. Is she—is she ok with that?"

God deflated. "She doesn't know I've been doing this," he said.

"You've done this before?"

"Only a couple times."

"That's really fucked up!"

God went on the defensive. "I'm just keeping her memory alive in the hearts of the people, because everything would fall apart if I didn't. People would sin, or stop sinning. Or, God forbid, start blaming *me* for their shit, She can be so selfish, she never once stopped to think about how this affected me!"

"But you're showing her old self. You're keeping that person. Demon. Angel?"

"They're all kind of correct."

"Anyways, you're keeping him alive instead of her. No one even knows about her."

"What do you think people would think, if they knew their terrible Devil was some tranny and their God a fag?"

"I don't know what they'd think, but I know you can't just go on misgendering a trans woman and doing... whatever the hell you call what you're doing."

"What do you want me to do? I don't know what she wants, and I can't ask her what she wants because she won't speak to me!" God was getting worked up. "And anyways, I don't see how you have any room to talk, you had a whole thing with her old name written in big bloody letters on your wall didn't you?"

"I know and I'm sorry and I would fix it now but you just happened to destroy the wall with your grand entrance! Fuck! I guess I'm not getting my deposit back!"

"Ugh, whatever. Why do you care so much about this anyway?"

"Because I'm trans, you jerk! "

"Oh wow! I had no idea."

"You didn't? Whatever happened to omniscience?"

"Oh, that's an exaggeration. I'm not omnipotent either."

"Well, yeah, I'm trans. That's why I had a mural with a huge trans symbol AND the head of Baphomet."

"Don't even talk to me about that asshole. He's the one who put all these gender ideas in her head. At least Lucy has an actual gender, unlike him."

"Holy shit, are you shitty?"

"Well, what do you want me to do—uh. Your name?"

"Laura."

"What do you want me to do, Laura? I told you, she won't talk to me! She hasn't talked to me in two thousand years!! And I, I... I... I miss—I miss—Her..."

God started to cry. At arm's length, Laura patted his back. "Uh. There, there."

This night was not turning out as she expected. She didn't have the slightest interest in meeting God but she REALLY wanted to meet Lucy now.

And then Laura got a dangerous idea. An idea that might have been as dangerous as flooding the earth for forty days.

"Hey, how about I talk to her?" Laura said.

"What?"

"What if I talked to her? I bet she'd talk to me."

God brightened up.

"She would! She really would! She loves talking to your. Your. People."

Laura rolled her eyes once again.

"Ok, let's do it. How do we call her? My circle didn't work, obvi."

"Circles only work sometimes. She doesn't check her notifications that much."

"How come you saw it?"

"Just because you tagged her doesn't mean it's a private channel. And my name was on there too."

"Ok, sure," Laura relented.

"But there's a better, guaranteed way to get her attention."

"Awesome, what do I need to—" but before she could finish, he grabbed her by the hand and spirited them away.

They arrived at a place outside. Where a dirt road met another.

"To summon a demon, we come to the crossroads."

"Dude! Why would you bring me here? I'm cold."

"Oh, come on. We're down south, it's so warm."

"Well..." she gestured down.

"Oh, I see. Nice panties."

"Thanks. Now can you get me something to cover up?"

"Sure, I can summon you some pants."

"I don't really wear pants."

"Well here, have this."

Laura inspected her newly appeared attire. Long, hooded, woollen robes. "Really? I look like the Virgin Mary!"

"What were you expecting? A Versace dress?"

"No, but now that you mention it, yes, why not?"

"Ugh, ok fine."

Now Laura was wearing a beautiful, long sleeved, blue dress, with golden buttons down the front.

"Nice, I like this," Laura said.

"It's from the Winter 2014 collection, so it's a couple years late, but I just loved that line so much, better than anything this year."

"Well, thanks, it's cute and it's warm."

God gave her a smile of dubious sincerity and started walking to the centre of the crossroads, before Laura, looking dazzling in her new evening wear, stopped him.

"Wait a second, though. Let's talk about this."

"Talk? What's there to talk about?" God said.

"I just. I'm having second thoughts. I... do you think she'll like me?"

"Who cares if she likes you? We're here to talk about me."

"If you're going to be like that, we should just call this off."

"No. No. Please?" God's voice got really high. "It would mean creation to me if you did this, and I know she'll listen to you. Of course she'll like you, she likes all of you people."

Laura frowned at him. She was excited to meet Satan, but also really nervous. God didn't seem to know shit, and not all trans girls like each other, Laura had learned.

"Fine, but only because I really want to meet her," she finally answered.

"Phew. Ok. Can I take a bit of your blood?" God continued.

"Sure," she offered her arm.

God instead touched her chest and somehow pulled out a small vial of red liquid.

"Ok, case in point—good advice in how to treat trans women, or any woman really: don't touch her without permission. Specially not in the chest."

"But you told me I could take your blood!"

"Yeah, out of my arm!"

"Whatever, this was quicker."

"Just keep your hands away from my boobies, only my girlfriend touches those. Well and me. Well and some other girls sometimes. Well..."

"I got it."

God marched to the centre of the crossroads and pulled a small wooden box out of his suit pockets. He put Laura's blood in the box and then buried it. The ground shook. Laura could feel it from where she was standing. Smoke began to rise where the box had been buried. The smoke blocked her view and rose in a large column that soon dissipated, leaving behind a smartphone. It was ringing.

God picked up the phone.

"Hello."

...

"It's not for me. It's for this lovely lady that I brought with me."

...

"Ok, fine," he turned to Laura.

"It's her secretary."

"P.A..." she heard faintly from the phone.

Laura grabbed it. "Hello?"

"Hello, I understand you wish to speak with Lucy."

"Yes please."

"Ok, can I get your name, and age—oh should I just put her on? Oh, ok."

"Hello, darling. How are you?" The voice was at once sweet and terrible, like a fire consuming a building you set ablaze because you needed the warmth.

"H... Hi," Laura stammered.

"Do tell me, what can I do for you?"

"Um, well God wanted me to talk to you. About you maybe possibly getting back together with him," Laura walked a bit to make sure God was out of earshot. She looked back and he gave her a big grin and a thumbs up. "OK, listen, God brought me here, but I don't actually care if you get back together with him. Actually I'm against it. I wanted to talk to you because I wanted to talk to you!"

"What do you mean?"

"I'm such a big fan of you like holy shit!! The fact that I'm even speaking on the phone with you is blowing my mind!"

"Well, I'm flattered, but darling," said Satan, "I'm really busy. Unless you need help or would like to make a deal, I should really get going."

"Sorry sorry, I just got carried away—because again, such a big fan, and I never even knew you were trans, and-"

"Hold on just one second, hon. You didn't know?"

"No, nobody knows," Laura said. "The Bible kind of paints you as male."

"Nobody knows? NOBODY?!!..." The phone suddenly got hotter and hotter, Laura almost had to drop it. Until she heard, "One second," and then there was a click.

And then there was a bang, and a tremble, and then from a plume of black smoke and red fire burst forth the most beautiful woman Laura had ever seen. She had bright red skin, like the flames that embraced her, and her long dark hair was tipped with fire—not red hair, actual fire. From her forehead sprouted two magnificent curly horns. Laura, her mouth agape turned her gaze downward. The woman wore a beautiful red and silver dress, backless, showing her wide shoulders, with a long skirt from which protruded an elegant pair of cloven hooves.

She turned to Laura and gave her the warmest hug she'd ever received. And yet Laura did not burn.

"Oh, it's ever so nice to meet you, darling. If you would, give me just one second." She let go and turned to God.

"YOU!!!"

God swallowed his own spit, hard.

"Did you, or did you not, release my updated biography?" She started walking towards him. God retreated.

"I, I tried, but you know how the Pope is, he said it was heresy!"

"The Pope works for you, dammit!!" The flames that tipped her hair grew hotter and brighter.

"Not anymore, you know that!" God whined. "You know he says whatever he pleases now. And he's not even the top authority on these matters anymore."

He continued to retreat as Lucy bellowed. "Well then, DO TELL: WHO THE FUCK IS?"

"No one! There's all the different Protestant churches, and the Mormons, and the Muslims, and the Jews, and they all think different things."

"Do ANY of them know me for who I am? Do they know my name?"

God hesitated.

"DO THEY?" Lucy asked as the sky erupted in flames. Laura wondered if anyone else could see that.

"Look, honey, angel," God said weakly. "I'm sorry, I tried. I really did."

She turned to Laura. "Tell me, Laura, is this true? Did he try?" Laura could feel the electrifying heat of her stare, but she was aware that it was not aimed at her.

"Last I heard, the Pope thinks I'm a nuclear bomb, so, whatever he did doesn't seem to be working very well."

"What? Nuclear bomb?" The demoness seemed genuinely confused, and for a moment, the fires and explosions receded.

"It's this silly thing," Laura replied, "It's like, saying we're dangerous and unnatural."

"Unnatural," she scoffed. "Why, I am a primal force of nature! As are, I suppose, the interactions which produce nuclear armaments and energy. But that's besides the point! And I am as much a woman as you are, or that fucking precious Virgin Mary of his."

"Fucking Virgin Mary, sounds like an awesome porno."

"Oh I wouldn't say so. Sounds nasty if you ask me."

"I guess it might attract the wrong crowd."

"Goodness," Lucy groaned. "He has a point, I suppose. He can't control what people do or think, but he could at least have GIVEN. THEM. MY. CORRECT. NAME." She punctuated the last five words with slaps on God's shoulder.

"Sweetie, boo, I'm sorry," God wheedled. "I'll make it up to you. I'll go right now and fix it, on every bible, Talmud, Qur'an, anything that mentions you, I'll go right now."

"Yeah, you better."

God exploded into a cloud of white doves, which scattered in every direction.

"So dramatic, him. He's always been." Lucy looked at the desert around her. She sighed, like an avalanche in the distance. She looked forlornly at the horizon.

"Lucy?" Laura said.

Slowly, Lucy turned around to face her.

"Oh sorry darling, I was just thinking. I haven't even so much as looked at earth for two thousand years. To be honest, I couldn't stand to think of it. After the people here killed my son, and what's even worse, absolutely wrecked my relationship to him, I wanted nothing to do with this place. I just threw myself into my work back home."

"I can understand that. I just." Laura was silent.

"What is it, darling? You can tell me."

"I don't know. It's a mixed feeling finding out you're trans. Like, that's really cool. Trans girls get demonized so often that, hell, even before today, I always identified with you. You know, there's this dude at work, and every time he says something about how the world is going to hell in a hand basket, he always glances at me. Like, people think because I'm trans that I'm some devil worshiper who wants to kill God. So I embrace it. I mean, now that I've met God, I don't know that I want to kill him, but I definitely want to punch him. Anyway, I convinced myself I was a demon, and that that was a good thing. But you, you live that, you literally are the demonic trans girl we all aspire to be. I just... I wish we'd known. I wish we'd had you around."

Lucy turned away and was silent for a moment.

"I'm so sorry. I should have known things wouldn't be good for you. I suppose I told myself I was just too busy to pay attention. Taking leadership of Hell, establishing full communism there... Oh, I just holed myself up in my office and I mean, I did read the emails and take the calls from trans women, but I never dealt with them directly. I always delegated, I just couldn't bear it."

She turned around and Laura could see she had tears in her eyes.

"I really have no excuse. I knew something was wrong, how couldn't I? So many of you were writing to me. Asking, pleading for help. And I just, I just." Lucy was trembling, the tears flowing freely from her eyes. The fire in her hair dimmed, almost going out.

Laura hugged her.

"It's ok, you don't have to save everybody. You have to take care of yourself or you can't take care of anyone."

At this, Lucy gave the warmest smile Laura had ever seen. Everything about her was warm, she noted, when it wasn't flaming hot fury. The tears on her eyes evaporated into little steam clouds.

"Thank you for this. For dragging me out of hell and giving me a good talking to. I needed that."

"It's really my honour, Lucy."

"I must tell you, though, there's something that has me utterly perplexed. I only took emails from trans women, and they always gendered me correctly. If no one told them, how did they know?"

Laura smiled. "We can usually tell our own."

Lucy chuckled

"But seriously," Laura continued "It's one of those things that even if you hadn't thought about it before, it makes sense. We are drawn to you."

" A lot of them called me Lilith. I suppose they couldn't tell the two of us apart. I didn't mind, Lilith is such a sweet girl, I really should find the time to catch up with her... Oh, here I go rambling, I almost forgot. Since you were calling for me I have to assume you were looking to make a deal."

Laura thought.

"I mean, yes and no. I can think of a lot of things I would ask for you. But like, getting to meet you, that's better than any wish."

"Darling, stop, you're going to make me cry again!"

They shared a nice laugh and a smile, then Lucy spoke again.

"But, really, do ask for anything, it's the least I could do. Although, I must let you know that I won't make you cis."

"Oh, no, HA! no no no no no, that's not what I want."

"Well, good. You'd be surprised how many girls ask for that. A soul is not worth that, and a trans soul is worth so much more than that."

Laura hummed a few bars of Against Me under her breath. Lucy spoke again.

"There are a few other caveats. For one thing, we have to make a deal or I can't do anything for you. Consent is very important in these matters. Although, you don't always have to give a soul in return. With girls like you, like us, I sometimes make sure they get their wish for free. Only if it's something small, of course. For instance, a lot of girls ask for a, well let's say, bigger bosom. I can do that for free."

"Well, that's not what I want either."

"So tell me."

Laura leaned in and whispered in her ear.

"Well that's a first."

"If it's too weird, you don't have to do it." Laura said hastily.

Lucy chuckled. "Darling, you certainly are strange, but I like strange. I'll see what I can do." She surveyed the landscape one more time. She looked towards the mountains on the edge of the desert. The sun was rising on the horizon.

"Oh, honey, I'll try to take a look around here when I can. I'll try to be here for my sisters from now on."

"Sisters, yeah. Though, I don't know, I'd almost say you're more my mother than you are my sister."

This struck a chord with Lucy.

"I've been a mother. Not a very good one, I'm afraid. And yet, it seems that despite myself, my children have become wonderful people. Yes, you are my daughters, and I'll make sure you are protected." Now Lucy was standing tall, in all her magnificent fiery glory. As the sun rose behind her, the light she gave was even brighter. She gave Laura one last hug before saying: "Wherever you go, don't forget, always, somewhere, someone is fighting for you."

Then she let go. "All right, I'll put you back where he snatched you from."

"Do I get to keep the dress?"

"There's a reason they say 'the lord giveth, the lord taketh away'. What I give, I never take, but he's always been a bit more fickle. He'll probably want that back."

"But, it's a Versace! Oh all right. I guess I shouldn't get too greedy."

"Exactly. Greed is a capital sin after all."

"Aren't you all about sin, though?"

"Don't get me wrong, I love sin, but I hate capital. Now come on, let us away."

Laura awoke with a start. She looked around her room. Everything was where she left it. There were no signs of the destruction God had caused.

"Oh, it was just a dream, it was just a dream. Whew. What a weird dream."

The mid-dawn sun was streaming in through the window casting a soft light on her surroundings. She turned around to inspect the sigil on her wall and gave a start.

"*In Nomine Diabulus et, Belial, Satan, Lucy, Astaroth, et Yaveh.*" So it had been real after all.

"I wonder if she remembered, I wonder if she did it."

She tugged at the band of her panties and peered into them.

"Oh, yes! I'm going to have so much fun with these! Two dicks! Fuck yeah!!"

It Can Grow!!!

TRISH SALAH

Tuesday July 19th, 2016 10 am

Lily Roy has a problem. Several in fact. But they are not what you would think. Knowing about her fatal illness, or the fact that she just lost her job, and is struggling to know whether or not she should make peace with her family, or her girlfriend, before she dies, you might think that these things are what occupies her mind. You wouldn't be entirely wrong. The girl can think of more than one thing at a time. But they are not the problem. As in THE PROBLEM.

In her head, she tried to formulate the problem in epistolary form:

Dear Dan Savage,

Let me get straight to the point. The problem is getting off, pardon my French. My "pal" can't get off and it is pissing her the fuck off.

She spent a long time getting off (or more often, not getting off) in ways that fucked with her shit, and then a stupid numbers of years in therapy, more or less asexual—asexual without a name for it, asexual with a name for it but in denial about it, asexual by choice, asexual and proud, asexual and resigned, asexual and proud, asexual and bored—and then she was a hooker for, like, five minutes and that was oddly alright even though she wasn't into the dudes she saw particularly.

And then she could afford her surgery. (Not because of the five minutes of hooking, but because the province reinstated public funding for SRS. Thank you, Ontario Human Rights Commission, and countless trans activists she's mostly never heard of who, you know, fought for that.) And then she got her doctors' letters, and then she got her surgery, and then the doctors—don't get her started on the doctors, how useless if well meaning, but ever so blissfully wrapped up in their own beautiful self importance, etc.—they said it might take a few months before she could get off, and then it was six months, and now going on two years later it has really been trying her patience, especially since she fell head over heels for this total genius of a diesel femme power top.

Anyhow the problem was getting off, but then she got sick.

My friend's thing about being sick is that she's always had a crap immune system so she's kinda sick all the time, but she's also got metric tonnes of willpower so mostly she just powers through it. Plus with GID in the DSM isn't she just categorically sick all the time anyway? Which is to say as far as she is concerned society makes her sick and furthermore, the social construct of illness and wellness are such able-ist bullshit, anyways, but ... then she got sick.

Which is to say, she got the amoeba. In her brain. IN.HER.BRAIN.

Which sounds dumb, right, an amoeba in the brain? Like amoeba are single celled organisms, so what is that, even? Like, at that level of scale, is it even her brain her amoeba is in? Couldn't it just pass through a cell wall and like, be in her hair or her hat? She also can't believe she is mentally referring to it as her amoeba. Like it was her car or her boob or her girlfriend. Her ex-girlfriend.....

Sooooo..... have there been any instances where people were cured of a brain sucking Amoeba through orgasms? Asking for a friend!

Thanks, umm, L.

Ps For real! My friend would write you herself but she hates your column because of your transphobia and homonormative entitlement! Plus she is a total know it all...

Lily is the kind who fancies herself the nerd in the couple even when they're both nerds in the couple. "Firefly, sure, but let's talk Farscape!" You likely know the type. Scrawny, tall, oversized hipster glasses. Dark brown hair when it isn't pink or white or violet. Vintage with combat boots when she was a student living at home with her parents but not actually that good at Sally Ann style, even after seven years on her own. Lazy punk with painted, nibbled nails. White as the day is long.

Lily kind of hates that she reads Dan Savage often enough to compose a letter to him in her head. But she does need to get off. And she hasn't, since, well, maybe since before her bottom surgery? Yes, she thinks so... At least since before the neo-vagina, the neo-clit, the new junk, as her favourite trans writer Imogen Binnie would say. That's right, right?

Lily is a bit ambivalent about having a favourite trans writer, in the same way she is ambivalent about those words: neo-vagina, neo-clit. Binnie is a writer and Lily has a clit, if newishly made. But this is exposition and polemic, and Lily also hates both of those things, unless – and this is important, so pay attention—unless, they transpire in the muted and sepia tones of a novel of an idyllic and bygone era: say, *Pride and Prejudice*, or *White Teeth*, or *Childlike Life of the Black Tarantula by the Black Tarantula*. It's true. once upon a time Lily was an English major, the kind who if life hadn't intervened, might have ended up in grad school.

At first she thought the Amoeba meant she was losing her mind. Which it literally did, or would, but not in that moment or that quickly. The Amoeba is a brain eater but it is also very small. Being single celled and all. But Lily hasn't lost it yet. She can tell because she can still keep it together around Serena. Or at least she could until—

She lost her job because she was stealing. It was clear cut and she knows that and so did her bosses. She was underpaid, and it was a designer cookie store, so on one level so what if she was—they were fucking COOK-IES, right? And, anyways, Marcie and Bryna, the owners, were fucking ass-holes who got off on pretending to be their employees' friends, just because they're lesbians, right, while paying them, like, barely fifty cents more than minimum wage, and asking them to double shift on no notice, and really, why should she give a rat's ass! Except now she didn't have a job, or a refer-ence. And part of her thinks that if she could afford really good drugs she probably could get off and that would be very very helpful.

She lost her girlfriend because she picked up this hot trans guy at the bar last night, when she was trying to drink her other problems away. They have an open relationship, so this wouldn't have been such an issue if Serena hadn't been the one tending bar and tending to her right up until she left with said guy.

So Lily also feels sad and sucky and guilty, but she is trying not to be-cause THAT IS NOT THE PROBLEM.

The problem is getting off and its relationship to the end of the world. Again, implausibly, there is this Brain Sucking Amoeba. It is going to end the world. Not the way you think—it is not just that by eating Lily's brain, it is going to end Lily and by extension, the world for all intents and purposes as far as Lily as a particular subject is concerned. That would be bad enough.

The problem however is much—pardon me, but MUCH—larger than *that*. And so, as it happens, is the Amoeba. Lily isn't sure how she knows, and again there is the impulse to say she fucking doesn't know shit, that it is some sort of hallucination or delusion, some such shit, that she is in fact losing her mind—but that would be copping out. Lily knows what she knows. And what she knows is this. The Amoeba is the tip of the iceberg. The Thing It Will Be, is the Iceberg. And eating Lily's Brain will bring the whole schlemiel into view.

It may be a single celled organism, but it can grow.

Monday July 18, 2016, 1:41 am

Lily is in bed with a hot trans guy. A hot guy, rather, who is trans and was at a dyke bar and she generally isn't into guys and she is into this guy and she tells herself it isn't just because he is trans because as Lily knows that would be fucked up!

He is hot. She has forgotten his name. Maybe it is DUKE???

If only he knew how to eat pussy properly. Whoever heard of a trans guy who couldn't eat pussy? Lily can't even—

Earlier that Spring

Of course she researched it. Or she tried to. It shouldn't be so hard, what with the google and all that. She had even seen it in the news—the first time was that little girl from Arkansas who actually got better, which nobody does. Heartwarming story. Lily has a notebook chock full of notes:

Naegleria fowleri, commonly known as "brain-eating amoeba," are typically found in warm freshwater bodies, such as lakes, rivers, hot springs and particularly, man-made bodies of water. Though naturally occurring, proximity to industrial sources of heat seem to correlate to higher than usual concentrations. The amoeba typically enters the body through the nasal passage as people are swimming or diving. Once within the body it travels to the brain, causing primary amebic meningoencephalitis.

Initial symptoms usually start within one to seven days and include headache, fever, nausea and vomiting. The disease progresses quickly, with other symptoms manifesting such as stiff neck, confusion, vertigo, seizures, hallucinations. The infection is normally fatal within two weeks from the manifestation of first symptoms.

But Lily also has notes on that that little girl who survived, seemingly thanks to early detection and experimental treatment with a breast cancer drug.

That is not what Lily has, not exactly. Then there is the other one, *Acanthamoeba*, that is apparently present in dormant form in a statistically significant percentage of the population who live in tropical zones, but normally suppressed by healthy immune systems. In those cases a combination of their host immunes response and amoebal proteases cause massive brain swelling leading to in death in 95% of those whose Amoebas wake up.

Lily laughs to see that she wrote that, "wakes up." They certainly didn't put it that way in the news story or on Wikipedia. It was—a premonition maybe? Lily thinks hers might be more like *Acanthamoeba* than *Naegleria fowleri*, because the former expands – it just grows bigger – whereas the second reproduces by mitosis, splitting itself up. *Acanthamoeba* can grow to a length of sixteen millimetres.

More like, but not the same as. Because in all the reports of Brain Eating Amoebas that Lily has read, she's found no reports—none, zero, zilch—that report that the hosts could hear their Amoeba's dreams.

Monday, July 18, 2016, 5:59 am

DUKE's name isn't even Duke. So he's wondering why he told Lily that it is. Except of course he knows, he needed to get her away from the bar, away from that bitch of a girlfriend, who would be bad news even if she were not standing in the way of the next messiah, but who is very deliberately if possibly unconsciously doing that particular harm to the world—he needed to get her alone. Because Lily is Chosen. No, not a Vampire Slayer, or The Slayer or—

(There was that one time when Lily and Serena were first getting together when they had that conversation. The one that let Lily know that even though she was used to being 'the nerd in the relationship,' as she was in all her relationships, all bets were off now.

"Wait! did you like that show?"

"I liked that show!"

"Me too! I loved that show!"

"I have a whole thing about that show!"

"Ya, you and every transsexual girl ever."

"Every white transsexual girl ever?"

"Maybe."

"And, also, other people... do have a thing... about that show too."

Which is just what Duke thought while dreaming their relationship the night before walking into the bar where he would meet Lily. She didn't look the least like Buffy, not that he expected her to.)

No, no—not chosen, not like that. Lily has been chosen to be the mother of his children. His? No—It is a weird thought. Whose thought was that? Duke has no children, not yet, not here, not in this *now/here* or whatever. So when? who? But he, *no, not he*—It has children to be born, and not of Duke's own body, of Lily's. They are like legion, and they—and all it would take is for her to cum, even just once—*and they/it will grow.*

So after he stole her away, he fucked her while she was asleep. Before she was asleep too, and that was hot—she is surprisingly good in bed, for someone who can't stop drunkenly complaining about how she can't get off—but he couldn't give her his children then. For that, he needed the Amoeba. And for that, she needed to be asleep.

Earlier that Spring

Duke got used to repeating this part in therapy. That he used to dream about the Amoeba when he was a kid. It was a grey scale dream, and at first everything was ocean, winter stormy and in grey it was hard to tell water from sky. Everything was heavier. The air swirled wet and slow, not so dense as the sea churning below and through it, thick as heavy cream, but clear and burning cold as deep ocean floors. He thought they were jellyfish at first, the thicker undulations of motion dull speckled like salt. Abrasive as sandpaper or scales, that brittle on his skin.

Was he he then? His therapist kept coming back to that when Duke retold the dream in session; Duke only looked through her uncomprehending, his eyes full of salt scale seas, and the massive form barely emergent from the nightmare skyscape—seascape—it filled.

The dream repeated itself, and sometimes colours crept in, the dream's monochrome stained at the margins, one night ochre, another blue velvet.

"If a girl appears to you in your dream," he asked his therapist, "and she has your old face, but she is old, really old, who is she?"

Monday, July 18, 2016, 5:59 am

Serena is asleep. In her dream she is punching Lily in her pretty pretty face, and crying. She is surprisingly sad. In the dream she has lost her. In real life too, but in the dream she thinks it is just a dream and punching Lily in the face is just a metaphor and probably it is herself she is hitting, now that she thinks it, remembering that bit from *The Interpretation of Dreams*, she can even see that Lily with her face bloody and broken looks a bit like her own used to. God. She is so sad and she is crying. Her face is all these rivulets of salt water (or blood?) but mostly salt water and she wishes she had never traded her voice for legs and left her sisters deep below.

What?!?! Who said that?

Before she wakes up, a couple hours from now – this now – she remembers that she did it to save the world, but she also did it to save Lily whom she was in love with long before she walked on land.

Then when she wakes up she is not/no longer Ariel from the Littlest Mermaid crossed with some savior sea princess averting the apocalypse.

She is just Serena, who had a fight with her girlfriend Lily last night and who feels like something much bigger than her relationship is going to shit.

Earlier that Spring

Acanthamoeba can grow to a length of sixteen millimetres. But it kills you in less than two weeks. The Amoeba in Lily's brain has been there for almost six months and as far as Lily's been able to work it out, it's dreams are filled with oceans, deserts, mountains, stars. Or more precisely, it dreams of being filled with oceans, deserts, mountains, stars.

And as far as Lily's been able to work it out, the only thing that can kill it is an orgasm.(How in the world is that something she could have "worked out?" That is a very good question. Don't worry, Lily is working on that one too.)

As if not being able to cum hadn't been incentive enough, now she really needed to figure that shit out. *Paging Dr. Kinsey. Paging Eugen Steinach. Good luck!*

And so it was once more into the breach. Lily became a collector. Serena would go to work and Lily would reach across the futon for the Rabbit, the Bullet, the We Vibe, the Rumbler, the Bunny Bullet and God and the maxed out credit card only knew how many AA, AAA, N and C cell batteries. To say nothing of all of the squash, cucumbers and other would be natural aides de camp. At the end of the night though it wasn't enough. Even the superpowered combo of Serena's tongue and Mr. Pointy couldn't do the trick.

Suddenly, last summer

Long before Lily and Serena got together they were circling one another like predators. Like scaredy-cat, shy as fuck but still hopeful of an ethical, if non-vegan, meal non-predatory predators. At least that is what Lily tells Duke that night in the bar—*was that last night or was it the night before?* The truth is Serena followed her around and Lily pretended not to notice and at first wondered if she was making it up and then felt embarrassed about how much she liked it. Whatever, they didn't know one another, but they knew about one another and since Serena didn't yet work at the coolest queer bar in town and Lily had really just started going by that name and it was easier than talking and...

Anyways they lived on the same street in the same rapidly gentrifying bit of west Toronto. West of Queen West, just before it was Queer West. Oh yeah, Parkdale.

Mostly it was just alternately sketchy and speculative eyes made across the bar at the Rhino, where Serena used to work before she started at the Henhouse, but also in the produce section at the No Frills, and at the Tennessee, this old timey diner where Lilly used to hang out when she was on E.I., high and trying to write poetry, before her highly lucrative and fulfilling gig at the designer cookie store.

One would notice the other and there would be that stiffening of the air between them, say over bins of onions, and the other's eyes would roll up from the shopping cart or pint of lager one of them was holding, along the unlikely toughness of the other's prettiness and... bammm. A small inaudible explosion would send them scurrying in separate directions, clammy, stupid, and wanting.

How it changed was like this. Serena would be walking home from the Rhino, and Lily would be sitting on her porch getting high, and Serena would walk by, looking really fine in combat boots, and cut offs and some kind of faded band t-shirt that had been cut into a tank top so her shoulders were on display and the cut of her biceps, and Lily would want to whistle, but would know or worry that was creepy, and maybe even looking at Serena up and down, taking in her long black hair and muscular legs, and—maybe that was creepy, maybe that was like what a man would do.

So she just pretended not to do those things and let a lazy smile creep across her face. And then she'd catch Serena looking at her, with a look that said, *I want you pretty girl,* and she would look away and keep smoking and Serena would keep going and they did that for two weeks of muggy August 4 ams, before she asked if Serena wanted a toke, and Serena said "Sure." And looked her in the eyes, and this time she didn't look away.

Instead, felt—what?

Crude.

Stupid.

Wet.

Flushed, but also pulled very far away from anything like having her body.

Obliterated, almost. It wasn't great but it was something... But then Serena was speaking again.

"Do you want to go down to the Lake?"

Half an hour later they were neck deep in the water, making out. Did she cum that night? Lily couldn't say—though she'd like to think so. The truth is that night was a grey black blur of clouds like mountains, the wet air churning slow and heavy like a dream of much deeper oceans. It was quite a while before she'd worked out the math.

The following night Serena didn't look at her when she walked by. Or the night after that. Lily was hurt, then furious, then determined. So on the third night, instead of watching stunned as the tall girl strode past her, or cursing Serena out under her breath, she offered to make her pancakes. "Hey dipshit!" she growled.

Serena turned, looking way too tired to get into it, but also really annoyed.

Lily put on her peppiest impression of pep. "Do you like pancakes? I like pancakes. Maybe we should go for pancakes?"

The other girl's face scrunched then opened and scrunched and reopened in a weird gif of fight and confusion, relief and giddy and sauce. She realized she didn't know what she was waiting for. Maybe this. "Sure. Why the fuck not?"

The next night it was burgers.

Serena was surprised about how sweaty Lily got. Her skin was silky, that was the first surprise, but the sweat, the saltiness of her. She wondered if that was hormonal or what. Still she loved to touch her; to caress her while she was asleep was best. Serena would make up names for her, pretend witch names, and whisper them in the sleeping girls' ear while stroking her hair, nuzzling her neck, cupping the sleeping girl's bony ass.

Lily would pretend to be asleep while Serena would touch her there, and between her legs, all over really, and felt so strange that Serena really didn't seem to know she was awake. But then Lily would wonder if she even really was. If she was pretending to be asleep or dreaming that she was awake. After all, all those times she never said a word, or moaned or even moved, it was almost like she was frozen in one of those dreams of waking, but not quite awake, aware of what was going on around her, but stuck still just on the other side of sleep. Or was it just that she didn't want to spoil it, Serena touching her, reverent and tender, like that, so crazy different from when they fucked?

Monday July 18, 2016, 5:59 am
"I feel like I'm made of jelly." Lily said not even sure what she meant or what she was asking for. Her jaw hurt. She thought she was speaking to Serena, but Serena wasn't there. Was she dreaming? Waking up?

The Amoeba opened a mouth like a shark's and smiled with all its teeth. The night fell in, a hole in the moon, and Lily knew then that she was dreaming, maybe Serena's dream, maybe Duke's; she didn't know. But something. It was like in Lovecraft, or Caitlín Kiernan, when you got close to knowing the thing, and then your capacity to know twisted into some other violently violet thing, incalculable and impossible. The world or your mind at the limit of its math. Old gods type of thing. A fossilized remnant encrypted with some prehistoric incursion from the sublime. A magical special hermaphrodite to make all the genders implode like rotten teeth.

"Do you want a smoke?" Lily had asked Duke after he'd finished trying to mystically impregnate her while sleeping.

"You're awake?" Duke was confused. How could he have not known? She lay so still, but not stiff, bending with his movements, giving soft sighs. He thought he was giving her a magical sleep experience.

"You kinda raped me." Lily said as if it was a minor complaint. "And when you went down on me I could barely feel it. I mean, really. Barely at all."

"Could I, ah—could I bum a cigarette?" Duke asked.

"I don't smoke," Lily replied.

Earlier that Spring

In therapy Duke sometimes felt like his therapist wanted him to explain things to her. Not about him, but about the community, you know, gender politics. Her eyes got scrunched up and bright whenever he got gossipy or mean, like he was suddenly interesting. What kind of counseling degrees did they give at that university anyway? He'd thought it was a teachers' college but she'd set him straight. "Let me set you straight on that," she'd said.

He wondered if he would end up in a paper somewhere, a case study. Or if she thought about him sexually. He knew therapists weren't supposed to think of their patients that way but she was young, not much older than him, and pretty, with hazel eyes, and glossy black Betty Page bangs.

From the Amoeba's point of view it was just slow moving shit, trying to be born. It cried a lot in pain, and of course no one heard. It was very small. To the Amoeba it seemed even insects were indifferent, but on one level who doesn't feel like that? You think Amoebas don't have history, dreams? Layers? The Amoeba had once aspired to play bass guitar in a not half bad *Thompson Twins* cover band, *The Believing*.

When light falls on you in a way that can be utterly annihilating your first impulse may well be to call the doctor, but who knows, the universe could have bigger things in store for you.

Tuesday July 18, 9:15 pm

It was too hot out to be inside, and no matter how much she wanted to, Lily couldn't make herself go to her girlfriend's—her ex—to Serena's, who had AC. Not yet. They hadn't talked and wouldn't for a while. After she left Duke's Lily walked to the library in a daze and sat there until it closed. Then she walked around the neighborhood like a mouse in a maze, trying to find a way out. You see, she had this problem...

When the sky broke open and the rain came down like a lake, Lily could swear it turned to steam when it hit the pavement and only made the air even hotter. She did like the feeling of her wet clothes clinging along the length of her body though they felt heavy and then she felt heavy and sleepy. And then she felt, or thought she felt, the Amoeba waking up a little bit more.

She thought: *I don't have a lot of time.*

When she got home she sat on the front porch and pulled her damp wallet out of her damper backpack. At least the porch was roofed. She pulled Serena's photo of the wallet and it was only a little bit wet.

She loved her girlfriend and that was a fact. But less than twenty four hours ago she'd walked out on her screaming in the bar, with some guy she didn't know at all, and now that he'd fucked her in something near sleep, she thought he was less sexy, and of course she hadn't cum and she didn't know why she thought it would be different with him but she did, more fool her. Maybe the Amoeba was affecting her. Was Duke a hallucination? Or maybe the Amoeba's dreams were bleeding over into her own?

If only if she could cum then she just knew everything would be alright with her and Serena and the world. Her and Serena and the world— she liked the sound of that. Alright.

The Amoeba sure hoped so. Lily's brain was like being incased in soft cabbage, and even though there was food literally everywhere, it was not very exciting fare at all. If only the girl would get off then the Amoeba could take a bigger, tastier bite. It could grow.

Lily thought she heard something, just then. A wave or a murmur, and suddenly she felt like it could happen. Shivers went through her, and the whisper of arousal.

When Serena found her, hours later, Lily Roy was still sitting there studying the girl in the photograph, wondering who she was.

Rent, Don't Sell

CALVIN GIMPELEVICH

Mara was supposed to drive her to work, but she slept late and wouldn't leave her room without putting a face on. Nok shouted at her, thought about taking the bus, realized she didn't have time. Mara swore she could get dressed in a minute. Their mother woke and shouted at Mara to shut up, get up, and find a real job.

"I have a job!" Mara yelled, still doing her makeup.

Mara's job entailed little skirts and high heels with brand name bikinis. She walked up and down the beach with her big lips and her just-tousled hair, not-quite-glancing at men until the good ones, the rich ones, offered to buy her nice things.

"There." She opened her door and blew a kiss at her sister.

"I'm going to be late," Nok said.

"Not in the Scion."

She revved and swerved around traffic, racing up the back lanes. Nok gripped the dash as Mara cut off a biker. "I met an agent," she said. "On the beach. He wants to sign me."

Nok snorted. "Everyone you meet is an agent—or a producer, or a director, or a multi-fucking-billion dollar trustee." She leaned back. "I'm waiting for an astronaut or the president or, I don't know, something totally crazy and out there—maybe a dentist."

"I think he's for real. He took my picture—"

"I hope you charged him."

" —And showed me his card." The streetlight ahead turned yellow. Mara gunned the engine, missed it, and sped through the red. "He has a whole business."

"Will you watch the road?"

"I am! Anyways, he said there's lots of work and it pays well and, I don't know, it's pretty glamorous, right? Like being a movie star."

"Like being a hooker."

"Escort," she said. They pulled up to the gym. "See?" Mara pointed to the clock. "You're on time."

Nok grunted. She twisted left for her seatbelt, right for the door.

"Hey," Mara said. "Shoelace."

Reflex took over and Nok reached for the laces. Her right hand met nothing. The stump burned. Her left arm stopped at the elbow.

Her sister touched her leg. "You okay?"

"Peachy."

Mara dealt with the shoe. "I can't pick you up."

"I'll take the bus. You're gonna meet with that agent?" She nodded. "Don't fuck him 'til he signs you a contract."

SciFit was the new mega-gym chain, all about high-tech and science. Doors opened and shut by themselves, sinks came on with a sensor. Every machine listed calories burned, from the cable pulleys to the treadmills. Dumbbells changed weight depending on strength, ease, and program. Their swim caps measured strokes-per-hour, their lockers remembered your touch.

Nok flashed her ID, grabbed a clipboard, and shouldered her way to the staff room. She checked her load for the day and tucked the board under her stump. Four clients. She made hourly plus a commission.

Her first job was already prepped, client unconscious in the swapper. She was a regular. Carol, middle aged and caucasian, nine months into the program. With Nok, she had lost thirty pounds. They were starting to build her some muscle.

Carol's body lay in the machine. Her mind received an electrical pulse that mimicked an anesthesia. Like drugs, it knocked the mind out, but it didn't effect the body. She wore electric blue elastic capris with matching headband and sneakers. Her tank top was smart. It cooled as her temperature rose, and warmed her as it cooled down.

Nok stepped into the adjoining chair. She pulled the metal cap down and onto her head. Little pricks form the sensors. Acupuncture from robots. The lab tech checked her cap, checked Carol's, gave a thumbs up and went back to the desk. Nok closed her eyes.

It felt like somersaulting off a cliff, like napping in zero G. Vertigo. She remembered parachuting out of a jet and into the wind, and blowing blowing blowing—

She opened her eyes. She clapped her hands. The palms stung from contact. Nok/Carol stood up. She was plump, her knees ached, she was taller. Nok laced the fingers of her two hands together and pushed out, feeling the stretch in her wrists, the rotation and cracks of her shoulders.

She knew this body. She rolled her head. Carol's neck always hurt, a stiffness in that and her shoulders. As Nok took over, that tightness released for the latticework of her own tension.

Her other body, the Nok-skin, lay slack. Carol's mind was sedated inside. The techs would watch the body. She removed the staff badge from the limp form and clipped it to her blue pocket.

Cardio first, ten minutes, a warm-up, followed by yogic stretching. She did core on the mat before heading out to the weight room. Resistance training combated the client's demographic risk for osteoporosis. Free weights helped stabilize joints, another target. Today was triceps and chest, meaning bench press, some dips, a range of push motions. Carol came three times a week. Her body remembered the forms.

When her arms were spent, Nok hit the treadmill. Her pulse knocked up, her lungs protested, sweat piled under her breasts. In her first month of boot camp, when recruits ran five, ten miles under humid sun and were half-crazy from weeks of four-hour sleep, Nok repeated the slogans. *Pain is weakness leaving the body. The Few. The Proud. The Marines.* She said them until the words cut. She felt the scars as she hammered out Carol's weakness.

Forty-five minutes. She sprinted the whole last mile. Carol's time slot ran out and Nok headed off to swap out. The whole body was shaky, pumped up with endorphins. She chugged a bottle of water.

The towel girl blocked her way to the staff room. "I'm sorry," she said. "That's restricted." She held a white folded half-towel. Nok grabbed it and wiped the sweat from her face. "Trainer," she panted. "Swapper."

The girl looked down to her badge. It read: *Nok Montri. GCTG Private Trainer.* There was no picture. "Shit." She blushed. "I'm so sorry." She was pale and the flush took over her features. "I keep forgetting—it's still my first month."

"Don't worry."

"Nok."

"You've seen me." Nok had seen her. She was clumsy, always dropping the towels, catching her hips on the desk. "Asian. Five-two. Short hair."

"Oh! With, um—"

"One arm?"

The blush spread. "I was going to say tattoos on your neck."

"Natasha," Nok read off her tag. "Funny name for a ginger." She glanced at the clock. Time to switch out her clients. "See you around."

The lab had a dozen swappers, each with space for two bodies. You could not have a body without a mind, and you could not have two minds in one body. She wasn't sure if those restrictions were legal or technical, but that's what they said in the training.

Her twelve-o-clock lay blank in his chair. She switched Carol into herself, rubbed the end of her stump, sat, called the tech, and went into the new body.

The man was new. She held his chart with blunt fingers. Thin bright veins spidered over his hands. He was obese, bald, and arthritic. She felt alcoholic sludge in his pores. Liver stats confirmed the theory. He smoked, he drank, he had prepaid six months of training. Gordon. Occupation: Landlord. He wanted to lose fifty pounds.

She trudged back to the main center, endorphins replaced with new toxins. She felt heavy in ways beyond weight. The first three workouts were hardest.

"Hey again," she said to the towel girl.

Natasha frowned and checked her badge. "Nok?"

"You're learning." She reached for a towel. Natasha handed it over, careful their hands didn't touch.

She wondered, during opening stretches, if she had said something wrong, or if Natasha didn't like touching fat bodies. A lot of people didn't— especially here. They acted like it was contagious. Or maybe she didn't like men.

His sex moved under the shorts. It moved without her permission. Because of this, because she found it so awkward, Nok preferred to train women. Her mind had trouble acknowledging the extra flesh. She didn't like when it shifted.

Natasha seemed like a student. They got a new batch every fall. She was pretty, and there was something in the way that she moved, a certain awkwardness of motion. Nok watched her push a cart of laundry past, her weight positioned all wrong. Short people—Natasha was, at most, an inch taller than her—were usually better at putting their weight behind them. She bent over, like the cart was too low, and pushed with only her arms. She wore a cheap flattering dress beneath the SciFit monogrammed shirt.

Nok hadn't meant to think about what was under the dress, but it happened, and the thing in her shorts popped a boner. She jerked forward and crossed her legs, pretending to do a back stretch. "Fuck," she whispered. "Shit fuck damn."

She checked to see if anyone noticed. Dan, her immediate boss, had just entered. A group of people trailed behind in street clothes. "This is a great room for Pilates, core work, warm-ups. The mats are self-cleaning, you can see a stack over there" The group nodded, stared. "And here—you're in luck—is one of our G-C Trainers. Nok, you wanna wave hi?"

She grimaced. Her legs pressed as tight as they could. The tour group nodded and stared.

Dan laughed. "See, that's a typical trainer—too busy getting *you* fit to have small talk. We're actually the only sports facility in the county with a licensed G-C Transmorphic Generator. Expensive, but worth it. All gain, no pain—we save *that* for the trainers." He slapped her (Gordon's) thigh. The flesh rippled. "On your left is a more traditional approach, you'll see a personal trainer working out *with* a client, building the foundations for them to do more on their own." They walked on.

Nok uncrossed her legs and was relieved to find herself flaccid. She hit the elliptical for low-impact cardio—better on joints for his weight—breathing hard. Two minutes in and the body thought it was dying. The stomach turned, she gasped for breath, she was dizzy. It didn't matter how many times she had done this before, the body perceived it as torture. Every heart beat pulsed in her head, driven in with a hammer. She gave up. She was done. She kept running.

It could be worse, Nok thought. She could be Mara, getting scammed by some wannabe agent. She could be Joe. She could have an erection.

She met Joe on third tour around the Golan Heights. He was discharged early and made good money swapping. He had hooked her up in the trade.

He was also crazy, doing total immersion packets. He would eat, sleep, and shit in someone else's body for six weeks while they detoxed. She tried once, but never again. It was awful. Three grand for someone else's withdrawal. They kept her in a locked room while the body shook and expelled toxic smells—shits like you wouldn't believe. Every bone felt like it was being crushed in a vice. Not worth it. She remembered panic attacks, thinking LA and Golan had mixed, that there were bombs getting dropped overhead, the streets ripped apart under fire.

Joe eventually lost it. They caught him nodding off on his breakfast, track marks fresh up one leg. Big lawsuit. He was lucky they didn't arrest him. He got hired as a janitor somewhere else, far away from loose skins.

She couldn't blame him. In the hospital, after losing her arm, she would have killed if it got her more morphine. She remembered visiting Dawson, who got hit in the same raid. He lost both legs, his nose, and a good chunk of midsection. They had him hooked up to so many painkillers he didn't care. Probably got quite a habit.

Of course, in the long run, it didn't matter. Dawson was in bad enough shape to get wait-listed for a new body. He got a con straight off death row—6'8", built like a gorilla, with these soft hazel eyes. He looked like a model. She'd seen him on talk shows a couple of times: *The Man Who Lived Twice.* One of them got lucky during that raid. Nok just wasn't sure who.

After the arm, she tried to get a new body. She had protected and served—she sacrificed for her country. Everywhere, she had to see civilians who had never sacrificed anything, never cared for more than themselves, but they got to keep both their hands. Rich people with birth defects, or who had accidents, they paid for new skins. If anyone deserved that, it was her. She had done it for them.

The VA said it wasn't going to happen. They signed her up for a million trials instead, rubbing burning oils onto the stump, willing herself to be one of the half percent of people who experienced growth, begging, praying, for the bone to regrow. Measuring the tissue every day. Trying to convince herself not to give up, that the bump was getting bigger.

She left the hospital and moved in with her girlfriend. She had trouble eating, sleeping. Trouble getting up out of bed. Nok didn't have a good temper. Everything Grace did provoked her. The way she spoke and chewed and shed hair. She—Nok—couldn't help it. Grace wouldn't look at the arm. She would have been more patient if it wasn't for the lost arm. It ended with Grace screaming at her to do something. Get up, make friends, get a job.

For a while, she only left her mom's house to go to the gym. Physical therapy three times a week. She added cardio and then weights. Then serious body building. She went to the gym every day. Got obsessive. Counted calories, protein. Forty-three grams of protein in a cup of chicken, six grams per egg. She stopped drinking—too many empty carbs. If she couldn't have her arm back, she would sculpt the rest of her body. Nok trained harder than a normal person—harder than she ever would have, on par with the weight lifting addicts who needed that pump to feel real. For a while, she could pick any muscle on her body, traps, delts, whatever, and decide if she wanted it a millimeter bigger, or if she wanted to bring the size down.

She wouldn't stay out late because it messed with her workouts. Wouldn't eat sugar. Invested in a variety of supplements, powders. Drank eight glasses of water a day. Before, if someone asked her why she worked out, she would have said for the girls. Then later, to help do her job. Marines were the first responders (more slogans: *First to go. Last to know.*) It helped to get built like a tank. If someone asked, after, about the hours of gym, she couldn't have answered.

"You're pushing too hard," her mother said.

"You need a life," from Mara.

She got some gym buddies, spotters. Dan helped her balance the one-arm bench press and they started to talk between sets. Eventually, he found out she was a veteran, that she'd swapped in the detox program, and offered the G-C training job.

It suited her. There were only so many hours she could push her own body—whose gains had already plateaued. Other people, when they needed it as much as she did, stopped gaining and started steroids. She got to start on new flesh. The—what the VA called post-traumatic depression, was fading, taken over with rage.

She hated the clients. She hated herself. They took what they had for granted. She worked those bodies until they were ready to collapse and pass out between sets. She pushed Gordon's body to a violent nausea, to a point he was gasping for breath. She had to pause the machine, bend over, and wait for her heart to calm down. The sickness got worse. She ran to the bathrooms. They had women's and men's. She picked the latter.

In a stall, on her knees, the sickness came forward. Hot, acidic, disgusting. She hated this man. She hated everyone looking at her—judging her, avoiding the arm, when she lost it protecting them. They didn't know what it was like to see your friend with his stomach ripped out, or to spend so many hours shooting dummies that the shots became automatic—and stayed that way when the dummies turned into real people. And they certainly didn't have to wake up every day with a physical reminder of how much they had lost. The best parts of herself were gone—and she didn't mean her left hand. If Nok had known, she never would have enlisted.

Her mouth tasted like astringent and rotten wine. She was hungover. Someone knocked and asked if she was okay. She pushed the door open and shrugged the other man off. "I'm fine." She splashed water on her face and tried to rinse out the mouth.

Later, after she had clocked off and done her own workout, Nok looked for Natasha. She had seen her once more, while working out, and watched her duck under a doorway. Nok realized that the little woman walked like someone uncomfortably tall.

Natasha had her polo off and was smoking outside the building. The dress was cut high and wide, a tunic or long peasant blouse. It flowed like water through a creek bed, some gentle billowing fabric. Had Natasha been graceful or posed in front of a soft-lit tree in a grove, she would have looked ethereal.

Instead, she was perched on the curb, the square mega-gym behind her. Natasha flicked the butt down, and again, Nok had the thought: she moved like a stranger to her own skin.

"Do you want to get dinner?" Nok asked.

"What? Right now?"

"My treat."

Natasha blinked. "It's nice to see you out of your work clothes." She smiled.

"You too." Nok crouched so they were at eye level. "You look nice. Food?"

"I can't."

"Come on. I promise I won't tell your boyfriend."

Her cheeks burnt worse than red. "I'm single—just busy." She paused. "I could do it tomorrow."

"Okay," Nok said. "Yeah, I'm free. Let's do it." She crossed the stump over her chest and rubbed it with her right hand. "I guess I'll see you tomorrow."

"Where should we meet?"

"Give me your number. I'll call."

Nice, that she could still get a date. It took about five minutes for the glow to fade and for her to wonder why Natasha said yes. Thrill seeker? Fetishist? Someone who thinks a date with a one-armed veteran made them oh so worldly and cool.

The bus stopped, let her on, and jerked back to its lane as she was paying her fare. It threw her off balance. She reached for the rail, but the fare was in her right hand, so she reached with the left—and crashed her shoulder into the bar. Quick, blinding pain. Coins rolled under the seats. Everyone, the old women up front, the high school kids, the guys in gym wear, stopped talking.

She crouched and grabbed at the coins. One of the teenagers ran up and started helping. "I can do it!" she barked. The boy backed away. She dumped what she had in the toll—not her whole fare, but the driver didn't argue—and stalked to the back. Bus chatter resumed. The arm—the missing arm—felt like it had been stabbed. She held the stump, breathing hard, trying to calm herself down as the arm split apart, trying not to look strange.

She would give anything to make the pain end. To make herself whole. Her body, her family, her memories, her self. Anything. The creams weren't working. The stump didn't grow. The doctors were worthless.

She wanted another body.

Anything—*anything* whole. Race, sex, she didn't care. If they gave her a body, she'd finish her tour. Go back to combat. She told them that, but it didn't matter. They wouldn't even waitlist a body. She wore other people's meat sacks all day, but had to give them back at the end of their session. If she could keep one—run away – . She wouldn't, but she liked to imagine. Get a new body, get a new life. Go somewhere else and start over. She thought about that while her arm throbbed, while she walked the last blocks to her house.

Mara was there, when she got in, balled up and painting her toenails. Nok collapsed on the couch. "Cheer me up," she said. "I'm having bad thoughts. I had a bad day."

"Ooh," Mara said. "See, that's really too bad, because *I* had a great one."

Nok pushed her.

"Hey! Don't mess with the nails. I have to look good for my contract."

"Contract?"

"He signed me."

"Wait—what? That agent? No way."

"He was for real. But shh." She nodded at the kitchen, where their mother was turned to the stove. "Don't tell her," she whispered. "I want it to be a surprise."

"Come on, Mara. You're twenty-five. Get a real job."

"*You* do it," she hissed. "And besides," she glanced back at their mom, at the compression stockings she had to wear because she had varicose veins and her legs swelled from forty-odd years of standing behind a register. "No thank you."

Nok shook her head. "You saw the contract?"

"He took me to his office. It's a whole company." She put the final strokes on her nails. "I'm really excited."

"Okay." Nok looked at the ceiling. "Tell me about it. What's the score?"

"Well, first they took a whole bunch of pictures. Professional photographer, makeup artist, the works. Then they put me in their database and set up a few holos so the customers can see how I look in 3D. After that I wait and if someone likes what they see, I come in, and they rent me." She exhaled. "He thinks I have a good chance. He said that I'm really pretty."

"You knew that."

"They have one of them, the, ah—"

"Galviston-Chang Transmorphic Generators."

"Exactly. I've never done it before. He said I walk in and the next thing I know it's over. A few hours have passed and they pay me. It's, like, literally the easiest job in the world."

"What're they going to do in your body?"

"That's confidential. Besides—I don't want to know. They're not allowed to hurt me."

Nok thought back to her first clients. To the private things that she did. She peed out of them. She pooped. She took the first man straight into the handicap stall to get that out of the way, to see how guys felt getting off. "They might do some weird things."

"Does it matter? I mean, I'm not there. It's a shell. It's not like your body remembers."

Nok shrugged.

"I'm not stupid. I know they want to have sex. It's what I do now, just easy—and legal." She leaned back. "I won't have to worry about not getting paid or assholes or cops or whatever. They've got a whole system."

Mom finished and brought the food out. When they tried helping her in the kitchen, she shooed them out. When they didn't help, she scolded. Nok and Mara gave up a long time ago. "I don't understand," she said, continuing an old argument, "why you don't marry one of those men."

Mara gave a look. Said, "I rent, I don't sell."

She picked a Greek place for dinner, sandwiched between a taqueria and the Halal butcher. Nok showed up early, accepted the menus, and played with her ghost hand. She wrapped it around her water and felt the ice cubes, the cold. She made a fist. With her eyes closed, the hand was still there.

Her therapist at the VA had set her up with a mirror to manage the pain. She would sit in a chair and have the mirror reflect her right hand. From the right angle it looked like two hands. The reflection served as her left. Her therapist massaged her right hand and Nok watched her left. It helped. Her missing limb tended to cramp. The mirror tricked her into thinking it was still there, that she wasn't helpless.

When it started to hurt and her eyes perceived nothing, that absence escalated her pain. It hurt, but it wasn't there. It wasn't there, but it hurt. She went round and round with the paradox, until she was crazy, burning, and mad. The first time she punched a doctor. The orderlies came and knuckled her down. After that she just yelled.

Everyone in the hospital came in from Golan. People hit, people screamed. People gave up and stared at the ceiling until a nurse took them to the bathroom or brought food. In the real world that wasn't an option. Temper tantrums meant jail, with no special treatment for being a veteran. She learned to catch it. To close her eyes and feel the hand.

She tried lifting the salt. It felt real—more real, maybe, than her physical body. The phantom limb drained her other sensations, putting all her feeling on the one absent point. She seldom noticed new cuts or new burns. She sprained her ankle last month and it took a week to realize that anything hurt.

With a new body, those issues would all go away. She needed the chance to start over.

Natasha came in with a little black dress and a gold Star of David hung over her chest. She looked breathless, like she had jogged the last blocks. "I'm sorry I'm late—my bus was off schedule. I had to catch the next line."

"Don't worry. Sit down." Nok pushed her a menu. "You want water? Appetizers? Anything, just tell me. It's done." What else did she have to spend on? The military gave her a stipend. She didn't have friends. She didn't pay rent.

"Thank you."

The waiter came by and they ordered. They made small talk. Natasha knocked over her glass. Nok watched her sop up the water, trying to figure out the best way to phrase what she wanted to ask. Nothing polite came to mind. She gave up and leaned forward. "Can I ask you a personal question?"

Natasha shrugged. "Go ahead."

"How did you do it? How did you swap?"

Natasha pulled back.

"You're not a veteran. Did you get into an accident? Are you in witness protection? I've never met a civilian—"

"Is that why you asked me out?"

Nok didn't answer.

"Okay," Natasha said. She looked at the table. Nok hadn't felt guilty in a long time—but the woman's expression—she hadn't thought the other woman actually wanted a date. She figured Natasha was being polite. Natasha stood. "I should go."

Nok chased her down. "Hey—stop. Please stop. I'm sorry. That was rude. Forget I asked." Natasha waited. "Really, I thought you were cute. Are cute. I've been watching you since you got hired—and that sounded creepy." She exhaled. "Look, I haven't been on a date in a long time and I'm fucking this up, but I would really like to buy you dinner. Can I do that? We don't have to talk about swapping."

"Good." Natasha pushed the hair out of her face. "Because I haven't had a date in a long time either."

They returned to the table. Food came. They shared a platter.

"It's good," Natasha said. "I like it."

"I'm glad."

There was a pause as she pushed the tzatziki around. "I'm transgender."

"Really?"

"That's how I swapped. I didn't feel like a man and the normal transition—the surgery and hormones—I wasn't sure that it'd work." She looked down. "I mean, it would have worked if I'd done it. I watched other people do it, but it didn't seem like enough." She picked up a round of pita bread and shredded it with her hands. "I thought that I was too tall, that I wouldn't pass." She ran out of pita. "It seems silly now."

"So you switched bodies?"

"I met someone in a chat room. A trans man. He wanted a dick. The surgical ones don't work very well. He was local. We met a few times. I thought he was pretty." She looked down at the mess. "I'm not in the closet. I don't mind people knowing."

"Do you like it?"

Natasha shook her head. "I'm suing right now to swap back."

"Wait—what? You want to live as a man?"

"Oh, God, no," she rushed. "The estrogen's great. Dream come true. That part—it's like there was a fist in my back just pushing my whole life and now, all of a sudden, it's gone. I can't even describe it—." She paused. "I feel like myself, but when I look in the mirror, it's someone else's reflection.

"I want to start over, do it old fashioned: estrogen pills twice a day." She looked up. "That's the whole story."

Nok told hers. The sanitized version. They were in a hot zone, a bomb went off, the truck flipped, she passed out. Woke to her arm caught under the metal. The left hand was crushed. She didn't remember being in pain. The medic had a needle in her chest, was telling her to count breaths. She didn't come to until after the surgery.

"I'm sorry."

"Don't be. I'm not sorry for you." Nok didn't mention wanting a permanent swap, or the military's rejection. Natasha regretted hers, but Nok wasn't Natasha. "Think you'll win the lawsuit?"

Natasha shrugged. "Do you know what the worst part is? I see him around town. There's someone else in my body and I have to watch."

"Does he come to the gym?"

"No. I have an old picture. Do you want to see?" She pulled a photograph out of her purse. Nok saw a man. Bearded, slavic, brunet. Tall, but not a giant. She examined the eyes, the expression, trying to find an obvious thread, some proof of connection or gender. "I wouldn't have showed you before—but now I don't care. I don't even care if I pass. It used to hang over my head—the most important part of transition, you know? Be a woman, look like a woman. That's why I swapped."

"You have an accent," Nok said. "I didn't notice before."

"I moved here when I was eight."

"It's not the words so much as the cadence. There's a lilting aspect." It sounded nice. A nice voice. Was it different in her old body? She tried to remember what she sounded like at work, inside other skins. She couldn't remember. She wanted to touch Natasha's lips. The ghost hand reached. The stump moved. The empty part ached and made her self-conscious. She hadn't pinned it under long sleeves, but had left it exposed. She wore a tank top. The pain flared and she grimaced. Rubbed the end of her arm.

"It hurts?" Natasha asked.

"Let's go somewhere else."

They walked to the park. They sat on a bench. Natasha was on her left side. "Can I?" she asked, meaning the stump. Nok nodded. Natasha cupped the rounded end. She stroked it. Nok shivered. "I go to school for massage."

"It feels good." Relaxing. Natasha's delicate intelligent hands. She remembered the client before, the erection. Stupid irrational jealousy flared. That body wanted Natasha. Nok wanted Natasha. Not for the client's skin to want her—for Nok to be the only one with that desire. She leaned forward. They kissed. Nok ran her hand up the dress. She felt the curves that were not always Natasha's and wondered what it would feel like to touch her the other way, the Natasha of before. On the bench were three people, two forms.

Natasha thought the same thing. She pulled back. "I'm sorry."

"We can go slow."

"It's not that. It's—this isn't mine. It doesn't feel right. I'm sorry."

"It's fine."

"Can we talk? Just sit here and talk?"

"Yeah. Sure." Nok sighed. "Start talking."

Natasha sat silent. "You're disappointed."

"No! Yes—some. I like you. You know? That's not normal for me." Not since the discharge. Not her girlfriend, and not the rebound after. "I want to get to know you. Really. You. Not that body. So, talk. Let me know who you are." She stopped. "You're blushing. Did you do that before?"

"Not often."

"So that's a new thing. I'll put it in the new thing category. 'Not Natasha.'"

She laughed. "It isn't that simple."

"Why not? I'll only like the things that are you. That way, it won't throw me off when you get your real body."

"That doesn't make any sense."

"Sure it does. You just have to promise not to like me at work. Okay? I don't want you liking me while I'm someone else." Nok grinned. "Not unless it's a permanent change."

"I like your body."

"You would have liked it better before."

Natasha started to answer, thought better and stopped. She changed the subject. "Do you know what bothers me now? For the surgery—when I get the vaginoplasty done—they'll knock me out, but it isn't actually a knock out. Your brain is awake. The anesthesia just keeps the different parts from talking to each other. You don't remember, but maybe the body does. It has to, right? Maybe a part of you is horrified. Or maybe the memory lives in you, but it doesn't matter. Maybe things are only bad if you're interpreting them as a horror."

"I don't remember anything from my surgery. And I don't remember anything from the work swaps. The techs could do anything with my body—I wouldn't know. I don't even think that I'd care."

"No," Natasha said. "It makes a difference. You would."

Mara worked all the time.

She had a popular body. The first month, they said it was normal. Clients wanted to try the new girls. She spent more time out of her body than in, counting paychecks and sleeping—they didn't pay the body to sleep. That she did on her own.

Renting started with celebrities on their way down, the has-beens, who couldn't get parts, but wanted to spend like before. Not the elite, but people were still willing to pay a fortune to spend a few hours as the lead of a telenovela, or shoot hoops as an NBA star. The fad trickled down. Aspiring actors and models found it easier to get rented than parts. Their agents already had rosters of good looking people; they started connecting talent to renters. Actresses used to wait tables. Not anymore.

The second month, work didn't slow. If anything, it seemed higher. Mara had a good look. Exotic. People loved her. Three months and a backlog of clients. Nok didn't even see her at home.

The money could have been better. Mara's agent, the company, and the estheticians all took a big cut. She came home exhausted, having done nothing more than wake up. Her eyes started to line in ways that didn't reflect her. Nok caught other traits in her face, evidence of other habits, a sharpness, experience, different knits to her brow.

She had nightmares. Dreams of being in her body, but riding back-seat—rigor mortis, while others were at the controls. She woke up, after one session, to hands that were painfully stiff. Both wrists had a bruise. The company gave her a bonus. She didn't complain. Her eyes bagged. She started to age.

Nok told her to quit.

"Are you kidding? I almost have enough for a down payment."

"All you do is come home and sleep. You don't need your own place."

Mara rolled her eyes.

Nok blamed the agent. She hadn't liked his look. They swung by his house once, her and Mara, to get paperwork. He had a mini-mansion in the Hollywood Hills. His deck looked over the lake. He was terribly handsome—and young. "He swapped," she told Mara. "He found some desperate immigrant kid and bought out his body. That's the only way."

"You think *everyone* swapped."

"It's the new trend."

She complained to Natasha at work. They spent so much time together that, when she was talking to Mara, Nok heard Natasha's ideas coming out of her mouth. That whatever the clients did, it would stay in Mara's body, carry over—effect her. "I work out in my clients," she said. "They keep the gains. What are you keeping from yours?"

Even the old fantasy—running off with a stolen body—seemed less appealing. She used to think about it when she felt trapped. When the pain didn't end, when the stump threw her off, when she couldn't tie her own shoe and the thought of her whole life like that got too overwhelming, she imagined how she would do it. Made plans. She had some money and a blank passport. She wasn't going to use it, but it helped, sometimes, to know she had an escape.

"I'd like to kill that fucker," she said, meaning the agent.

Natasha bit her thumbnail. Brushed the hair from her eyes. Nok loved those little gestures. She was deeply in love—or deeply infatuated. "Have you?" Natasha asked.

"Her agent? Not yet."

"Killed someone?"

Nok shrugged.

"I suppose it's a silly question." She chewed the thumbnail again. "Do you ever feel guilty?"

"Only about not feeling guilty."

"What a strange transition." Natasha was perched on the curb, smoking. Nok sat next to her with a coffee. "In one place, the killing earns you a medal—and then they send you back home. If you did the same here, they'd give you the lethal injection."

"The swapper, more likely—if you're young." Nok sipped her coffee. "It's like a fairy tale: my sister's youth sold to a crone." Someone entering the gym whipped back to stare at Nok's arm. She flipped her middle finger. "Best part of my job," she told Natasha, "is nobody knows that I work here. I can do what I want."

Her memory flashed to Mara, but much much younger, with her round eyes and dark hair in pigtails, with her round sweet little girl's face. She remembered the three of them getting ice cream, Mara, as a toddler, running up and down past the case full of flavors, wearing pink shoes, with the ice cream scoopers and all the other customers watching, smiling at their mother like, Oh, you have such a wonderful girl, and she thought, now, about walking with Mara, about how people still smiled, but like, Oh, give me a piece of that ass. She thought about the little girl holding her ice cream, feeling such a blend of pride and nostalgia and anger and sadness, she wasn't sure how anyone could hold so many things and survive. She crunched the empty coffee, telling herself to stop it, because she had plenty of better memories to haunt her, and if she let one in, the rest would sneak by. She focused on the future, on Natasha. She said, "Your court date's next week."

Natasha nodded. "It is."

"Maybe I'll meet your old body soon."

She crushed the cigarette butt. "I don't even know what I'll do if they say no. This skin is driving me crazy. It makes me feel things that aren't mine—I swear, his memories live in this body. I feel it in his stomach. The body wants to turn me into him. To make us into a fusion.

"Is that bad? I don't know. People change, but I want to change as myself. I want there to be a barrier."

"Once," Nok said, "They switched me into this guy, and he was a detoxing alcoholic. It didn't show up in the screening. But, I woke up in him, and I hadn't had a beer or anything in six months—which wasn't too hard, I didn't have any cravings—but then I was in this guy and all of a sudden." She paused. "It was insane. Like, if my mother was there, and she had a drink, I would've punched her in the face to get it. No second thoughts. I would have punched her and chugged."

"What happened?"

"We swapped back. They referred him to a detoxification center."

"It's real." Her voice caught. "I can't keep living this way."

Nok put her arm over Natasha's shoulder. "They'll give it to you. They have to. If not—don't even think about that. I'm gonna wear my dress blues to court. Show them who they're messing with." She hugged the woman closer. "I won't let them screw you."

The judge ruled against her. Property contracts were binding—bodies belonged to the mind.

Nok finished her day with a round of pull-ups. She had worked her way up to one-arm pushups in her own body, but the pulls were too hard. It was a work pleasure. She felt the man's lats lift and squeeze and contract until they could do it no more.

She hit the lab and swapped into herself. Her left arm had atrophied from lack of use. Her right bulged from excess. Every single time she entered herself, the loss hit anew.

Dan stopped her before she could leave. "Can I talk to you for a minute?"

"Depends." She eyed him. "Am I fired?"

Her boss laughed. "That humor! Come in. I've got something for you."

He had a little office over the lab. There was enough room for a desk and computer, a chair and many many charts. Nok found her name and read over her schedule while Dan opened a drawer. He handed her an envelope. "Go ahead," he said. "Open it."

It was square and unsealed. She pinched the bottom under stump and pulled out a card. It said 'Thank You' over a printed bouquet. Inside that was a check and a message.

Dear Nok,

We've never met, but I wrangled your name from the gym. But, of course, that's wrong. You've met me. Over the last year, you have spent quite a lot of time in my body. I'm diabetic. My doctor recommended aggressive weight loss and the gym assigned me to you. Well, it's been a year and I've just come back from a check-up. I lost more than fifty pounds and was told that I no longer need insulin to manage the diabetes. I wanted to tell you how grateful I am. I hope you consider the check a bonus. I couldn't have done it without you.

-Janet Martinez

"I talked to her for a little while," Dan said. "She was *very* impressed with your service, and as your supervisor I can say the same thing. We value all our employees, but the trainers are special. This isn't the kind of work you age out of. It's a career." He shook her hand.

Mara picked her up. They were supposed to catch a movie, but the agent called and insisted they reroute to his place. "It'll only be a minute," Mara promised. "We can still catch a film." She had a new car. The veins stood out on her hands.

"You can say no when he calls."

Mara shook her head. "Clock's ticking down. They won't want me forever."

"Great," Nok said. "They'll use all that youthful energy up, and throw you back when you aren't wanted. That's a great use of your twenties."

"Can you not?"

"You should have told them you're busy."

"I'm not going to fuck myself over."

"You don't have to. They're doing it for you."

"Look!" she slammed her hand down. "I want to *be* something, okay? I didn't ask to look like this, but I do, and I put up with shit for it every fucking day. When I was goddamned twelve years old and got a good grade, people asked if I was blowing the teacher. When I walk down the street, people holler. It doesn't matter *what* I do—people are going to think it was my body, so fuck them. I'm going to use it for what I can get."

"Mara—"

"You don't know what it's like! Not everyone can be a marine, alright? I'm sorry I'm not a macho."

"Fine." Nok slid down in her seat. "Whatever."

She followed Mara into the building where a new client wanted a live inspection. Nok hung back while the woman prodded. She pinched her triceps, examined her breasts. Mara held still. "I'll take it," said the client.

"She's open tomorrow," the agent told her. "We can arrange something."

"Oh no. I need it now." An old woman. Liver spotted, turkey necked, flesh layered in makeup. "It's an emergency."

"I had plans," Mara said.

The woman pulled out her wallet. "I can pay extra. I need it right now."

Mara glanced back at Nok, who was trying to imagine the old woman in Mara's body. Mara in hers, unconscious. They were the same. The thought was unwelcome. She and the crone were the same. She rented bodies. She used them to remember life with two hands.

The agent paid a car to take her home.

Her mom wasn't in. She tried watching TV, but the shows went over her head. The apartment was too quiet, but the music she played sounded wrong. She called Natasha. "You were right," she said. "About everything. It's too fucked up. I can't do it."

"Nok – "

"I'm not going to let them do this to you. Or me. I'm done."

"What happened?"

"I'm coming over."

They talked in the car. Nok had Mara's old one, she steered with a knee when she had to shift. "You know what the military taught me? If you can take it, it's yours. It's what countries do, what rich people do, what politicians and muggers and bastards all do—it's yours."

They got his address from the court order. They stalled the car out front, Nok wishing they had a driver, a third.

Marines were riflemen. That was out, but she could still shoot a pistol. She had one in the glove. That was her right, from the service, to carry concealed. She loaded and cocked the thing with one hand. She squeezed Natasha. "Let's be the bad guys."

Natasha walked to the front of his house while Nok padded in through the back door—which was open, fan on. She could be so quiet, a cat. This was nothing. She once ambushed an enemy compound in broad day.

He was flipping through a magazine on the couch. The man from the picture. If he turned around he would see her. Nok would have to shoot or run. She waited.

The bell rang and he went to the door. "Hello?" Behind his silhouette was the woman. Her hands were empty. She watched her watch him, and the woman's face broke.

"Natasha," he said. His back tensed. "I'm sorry. I don't want to see you again."

Nok crept forward. As he spoke to Natasha, she pounced.

He didn't have time. She had the gun pressed into his neck, the front, so the muzzle pushed up at his jaw. "Don't move." His mouth opened. "Don't talk."

In a way, she was touching Natasha for the first time.

She waved her stump at the woman. "Now." Her voice was relaxed. She hadn't been so calm since Golan. The adrenaline brought her into the moment, slowed everything down. Natasha was shaking, a new recruit panicked in the face of her first firefight, her first charge. Nok had been a corporal, she'd walked privates through it before. "Take a deep breath and do it. I need you to do it right now." To the body: "You move, I shoot. Okay?"

She tried making a face, to Natasha, like she wouldn't actually shoot him, like, you're not getting involved with a psychopath because I'm just bluffing here. She told herself to smile. Her face was so stiff that it came out like a maniac grin. Fuck it, she thought to Natasha. I *will* shoot. There's only one rule in a battle, and it doesn't have anything to do with higher morals or powers. The rule is to do what I say. If you break it—it's your own fault, whatever happens, because I am in charge, and you do not disobey.

The skin knew. Her seriousness kept him from moving. To Natasha, she thought: This is me. I'm fucked up. You should know this. But also: Baby, I promise I'll never hurt you. I'll kill this body if I have to, but after you're in it, I'll never hurt you again. She thought: You have to believe that, Natasha. Believe so much that you make it true.

Natasha pulled the rag from her pocket. It stunk of chemicals, chloroform. She pushed it over his mouth and he panicked. He started to thrash. Nok pressed the gun harder. She pinned him as well as she could with her armpit, but lost him as he jerked back. Natasha tried to follow. She lost her balance. Nok hit him in the back of his head. She used the gun butt. It popped like a coconut when you rapped it. Not a nice sound, but not the horrible one of a skull actually cracking. Natasha got the rag back on him and pressed it until he collapsed. "Sorry," Nok mouthed. That bump would hurt the next day. They zipped him up in a blanket and dragged him back to the car, trying not to rough it up any more.

She – Natasha – did not cry.

Nok scanned her thumbprint into SciFit's back door. The scans were recorded into their system. Between that and the cameras, they'd know it was her. She made a face and flipped off the first cam.

She had to shoot the lock off the swap room. It was loud. She had to work fast.

They dragged the limp body into a chair and Nok placed the right bands. She put the cap on his head and checked on the sensors. Her right hand shook. The phantom was calm.

"You know how to do this?" Natasha asked. "You won't make a mistake?"

Nok shrugged. "I've watched a million times."

"Will it kill him?"

"Only if it goes wrong."

Natasha didn't answer. She pressed her lips to a line. Was she worried about the body? Nok wondered. The soul?

She looked over the control pad. It was easy. Fool-proof. Operators didn't even need a degree. She took a deep breath. She told it to prep him for transfer.

For a moment the machine did nothing and her heart was too loud. Then it whirred up into the noises she had heard so many times. He jerked once and was still. The electrical pulse had him out. He was ready.

Natasha sat in the next seat. Nok took the controls and this time double and triple checked everything before pressing the button and—

Later, when they were bodysnatchers, bogeymen getting by with LA Spanish, when they were lovers and Natasha was on hormones, and the money ran out, and they found more, and Nok's arm stopped hurting, she dreamt of that place and the body abandoned. When the Irish skin crumpled and the stranger filled with her girl.

No Comment

AYŞE DEVRIM

Mary Walker considered herself to be a blessed woman. Newly twenty-four years old, she was a year away from the nursing degree she had been dreaming of since she was barely tall enough to see over the marsh grasses behind her grandmother's North Carolina home. Her parents, Phil and Helen, supported her in everything she did, from the cheerleading squad to nursing school to her impending marriage to Joe Carpenter (only THE hottest guy in their high school). The childhood they gave her was safe, quiet, and full of wholesome Christian values. Hopefully, she thought, Joe would give her her greatest blessing soon enough: motherhood. The chance to feel a heart beating in time with her own, to see eyes look into hers with the most intimate and unconditional of loves – other than God's love, of course – was almost too much for her young heart to hold.

One morning in early 2030, Mary woke up with a complete feeling of warmth and purpose. "Feeling truly blessed 2day. God is great :-*" she texted Joe as she left her apartment for work. Little did Mary know the true miracle she was experiencing.

Today was a good day, a holy day. Mary, the virgin, was pregnant, although she had no way of knowing it yet.

After texting her fiancé, she walked down the street to her car. The air felt purer, the sun shone brighter, and the songbirds seemed to be singing just for her. She thanked God and told her car to take the usual path to school. Down Main Street, right on Hancock, left on Elm. A half-mile from her destination, Mary's car was jolted as an SUV slammed into it.

The SUV's driver was Marcus Hansen, a 38 year old attorney spe-cializing in family law. Only moments earlier the biggest problem in his life had been an ex-wife who was still litigating for increased child support payments even though the courts had long ago issued their judgments. His friends and family had begged him not to conduct his own divorce, but he did it anyway and it had been a true work of art, goddammit. Why the hell couldn't that bitch see it?

Now, though, he had a bigger problem on his hands. A car accident? Who the fuck gets into car accidents these days? Oh shit, she's not moving. Fuck, if Terry's lawyers find out...

He looked around and saw no other cars, pedestrians, or cameras. Like a good, red-blooded American man, Marcus saw his chance and he took it. He peeled off down the open road and refused to look back for even a moment, as if doing so would turn him to salt.

"God, why the fuck did you do this to me today of all fucking days??" he said as he sped away.

God had no comment.

Within an hour of the accident, Mary's useful organs were parceled out for transplants. One kidney made it to an ailing 58 year old man living in Connecticut. His recovery was so astonishing that before the end of the year he was able to personally oversee a corporate merger that would lead to $35 million in executive bonuses, 5,478 personal bankruptcies, and the foreclosure of a rape crisis center that would eventually be converted into a nightclub notorious for the high volume of date rape drugs trafficked there. He and his family regularly thanked God for years after the transplant, but He could not be reached for comment.

Mary's other kidney was reserved for 17 year old Estefania Gonzalez from the South Bronx, but the kidney mysteriously disappeared an hour before the surgery. For the next two months leading up to her death, her mother urged her to hang on and not give up hope, pointing to the news that the head of a famous megachurch in Virginia had been healed of his own kidney ailments through a miracle from God. God could not be reached for comment, but the EMT who was paid $20,000 by the pastor's lawyer for the kidney eventually would be.

Mary's uterus and ovaries went to a 28 year old nurse, Maryam Jalaali, in one of the first such attempts on a transgender woman in nearly a century. Unlike Lili Elbe's, Maryam's doctors had some inkling of what they were doing, at least medically speaking. Transplants in cisgender women had been achieving reliable fertility since 2020. The research was spearheaded by FUQR – Foundations United for Queer Rights, a massive coalition of LGBT rights groups fearing their own obsolescence – in tandem with an all-star team of obstetric surgeons from Columbia University. Together, they managed to secure $15 million in NIH funding. The queer community was largely overjoyed, except for roughly 150 people in South Philadelphia who were too busy fretting over their HIV clinic being shut down due to its grant being revoked. God was not consulted, but the HRC was there to refuse to comment in His place.

Out of the hundreds of volunteers from around the world who had passed the initial round of exams, Maryam seemed like an utterly terrible choice. She was nearly 29 and her career had led her to spend the vast majority of time with runaways and sex workers suffering from the epidemic of antibiotic-resistant syphilis. Moreover, most people just didn't find her pleasant to be around. Her best friend Lena, the only person who unequivocally tolerated her, had written a personal motto for her – "single, surly, and sauced" – which Maryam had tattooed in translated Arabic circling her waist like a belt. She slept around with impunity and only formed "relationships" on the rare occasion it suited her purposes – like when she was running low on credit, needed to prove a point to her family, or was applying for a uterus. She dumped Evan, the unremarkable cisgender white man she'd been dating when she applied to the program, as soon as she knew things had progressed too far for the doctors to back out.

The first round of testing included 25 trans people at seven sites "around the world," which was still somehow the New York Times' way of referring to North America and Europe. What ultimately made Maryam one of them was some peculiar physiology (thanks to an intersex condition diagnosed during her transition) and the best damn connections a middling career in queer health care activism could provide.

Sitting in her underwear and smoking a joint, finally finding a use for her degree in biological engineering, Maryam marveled at the elegance of the concept. All we needed to tear the human sex binary a new one were advanced 3D tissue printers, six months of scans, and an intense pharmaceutical regimen supplementing two full-day operations. Not quite as easy as in an internet magical forced feminization story, but still, she'd made it through enough surgeries and could make it through more, if that's what it would take.

Maryam's body had seen so much renovation it reminded her of a gentrified neighborhood. She had had her first surgery at the age of 22, the "Benjamin Classic" as Lena called it. "Mild" breast augmentation came two years later, followed by vocal chord reconstruction, brow-bossing, and – her personal favorite – a buccal cell graft for her vagina. She had named each of her eighteen scars after poets. She called her favorite Mahmoud, but never told anyone which it was.

One year prior to the day of her surgery, she was sprawled out in her living room.

"Are you sure it's safe?" Maryam could see her mother's lips pursing into her iconic scowl despite the poor resolution of her Aug.

"Mom, it's fine. I've been reading the studies for years – "

"Ma'ashallah, my brilliant girl." Maryam huffed in response. After so many years, it still felt good to hear, but Maryam wouldn't let her know that.

"I know the tools they're using and they have the major risks covered. And I don't know when I'll get another chance if I don't take this one."

"Roohi, you know I don't know these things. They are not what make me worry."

"Everything makes you worry," Maryam scolded.

"Worry worry worry! That what you always say to me! Can't I have a feeling that is not worry to you?"

Touché. "Okay, tamam, sorry... what is it then?" Fatima scowled silently.

"It's about baba isn't it?" The mention of her father immediately registered on her mother's face.

"I wish he were here for this, too," Maryam continued. "But it's been two years now and I don't want him to be the reason you can't be happy for me."

"Astaghfiru lillah! He would have been so proud to see you have a child. I am proud of you. But he would not have wanted you to do this alone, and I do not either. Maybe you can wait a little and get married first? Wouldn't that be good?"

"Oh no no no no, are you trying to use baba to guilt trip me into getting married right now?" Maryam was enraged. "This is a once in a lifetime chance, I'm not about to lose it because I want to wait for a man. And I'm certainly not about to believe that he would have let his feelings trump mine about my own life. Do you remember what he said to me when he saw me for the first time after being released from detention? He said, 'ma'ashallah, habibi'. I know it's not what he wanted for his only son, but he never let it on."

Fatima couldn't respond, but Maryam could not enjoy her victory for even a second before guilt set in.

"You're right to have your feelings. I just wish they could be happy rather than scared."

Her mother's voice softened. "It is being a mother, habibi. I can't help it."

Her mother had always been fond of saying this; Maryam had never been so fond of hearing it.

"Are you eating well? Should I send you more food?" Her mother always turned the subject to food when she didn't know what to say. Maybe she'd been a little too hard on her. "Actually, I just tried making maqluba at home the other day."

"You are becoming such a cook, ma'ashallah!"

"I'm trying, mom. I promise I'll make you some next time I see you." Maryam chuckled as she heard her mother spitting on the other end.

"Good. I had better be impressed. You'll be cooking for my grandchild soon, inshallah."

"Inshallah."

"Oh shit."

It had been almost six weeks since Maryam's operation with no sign of a period. She had been told to expect the first cycle between one and four weeks after surgery, and she couldn't have been happier. She went on a spree through the feminine care aisles at all five Duane Reades in her neighborhood. Maryam couldn't count the number of times she had been condescendingly told how lucky she was to never deal with periods. Had she been keeping track, she would have known it had been 294 times.

When the fifth week ticked past with nary a spot, she finally called her doctor. She knew she should have called sooner, but that would have been admitting that something might have gone wrong. She had mostly been feeling fine, otherwise, or at least as fine as someone can after a 10 hour abdominal surgery.

"I've mostly been feeling fine, otherwise, or at least as fine as someone can after a 10 hour abdominal surgery."

"Haha, very true," Dr. Ojumu said, snapping on a pair of gloves. "Any sexual intercourse?"

"Seriously? What's that supposed to mean?"

"Just a standard question, I absolutely did not want to imply anything. I'm guessing that's a no?"

"That's a no."

"And... you haven't been drinking?"

"Nope, only water." She was lying, but not so much that it would really matter. Right?

"No drugs?" Maryam could swear he raised an eyebrow at her. Arrogant prick.

"No, no. I swear on Nancy Reagan's grave. Wait, she's not dead yet, is she?"

This was why she ran through therapists faster than romantic partners.

"Umm, yes..." he said ambiguously.

"You know you're really making me wonder what kind of impression people have about me."

"Just trying to rule out possibilities. Now get ready, this is going to be *cold.*"

Maryam flipped through her phone while ignoring the jerky robotic camera that was investigating her. She tried striking up a conversation about the connections between the CIA and the recent military coup in Saudi Arabia, but it didn't stick.

"OK, OK, I get that you don't want to talk about government leaks, but can you at least tell me what's going on?"

"You're sure you haven't been sexually active since the surgery?"

"I really hope so. Why?"

"I can't be 100% sure until I get a blood test, but I think you might be pregnant."

"Shut up! How the hell is that even possible? I'm barely healed up enough to be moving around and you said my hormone levels haven't completely straightened out yet and and and I haven't had sex in what... six or seven months?"

"Your guess is as good as mine, and I don't say that often. Go home and get some rest for now, try to relax." Dr. Ojumu said in the closest he could get to a reassuring voice. "Is the medical port giving you trouble?"

"It pinches sometimes when I'm sitting. Mostly I'm just pissed that it never fucking shuts up. Does the voice mod really make it work better?"

"No, just an excuse to charge the insurance companies more," Dr. Ojumu betrayed a chuckle. "For the love of God, Maryam, just keep your head low and think of the baby."

Under the circumstances, God's love felt as absent as an immature boyfriend's.

"Maryam"

?

"Maryam"

The voice was faint, but soothing. She couldn't tell whether it was a single voice or a chorus.

She had picked the name Maryam as an homage to her late maternal grandmother, but hearing it now those phonemes felt like *her*. She slipped into the Mar and breathed the Yam, saw the word wrap her body in strands alternating the sharp corners of Latin and the sinewy smoothness of Arabic.

The sun mother laughing flight youth light light light

Light. So much damn light, she could even hear it and taste it.

Maryam jolted up and immediately vomited. She did a quick recap of her previous day to make sure it wasn't her fault.

Her stomach groaned and she heaved again... and again... and again...

An invasive test or five later, Maryam's medical team had a few answers to work with. The baby was indeed Mary's. The father, on the other hand, was a mystery. They checked every legally accessible genomic registry in North America and few less than legal ones, with no luck. All their attempts to narrow down the father's geographic or ethnic origins were met with an unending maze of inexplicable gene combinations. Dr. Ojumu claimed, with an adorable air of unexpected solemnity, that the baby seemed to be from everywhere and nowhere all at once.

Three-and-a-half weeks later, Maryam was waiting in Dr. Ojumu's office for the seventeenth time. She was upset.

"Why the hell does a lawyer need to be present for a medical check-up?"

"As you know, Ms. Jalaali, the Walker family is threatening legal action. We can help make this whole situation blow over without a fuss. *If* we can rely on your cooperation."

Esmerelda Sanchez shuddered on the inside as she said those words. When she had taken her job with the foundation, it certainly wasn't to act like some corporate enforcer, but here she was anyway.

Maryam jerked her gaze away. "Look, I've made up my mind. I just wanted to consult you to figure out the safest way of going about it."

"Maryam, I *insist* you reconsider. We only have your best interests in mind."

"Uh huh, *my* interests. Last I checked, I'm the one carrying the baby, not FUQR."

"That may be true, but the foundation is the whole reason you could be pregnant at all. And, under the contract, you have obligations to aid in the research process."

"No way, I didn't sign up for this. I had all the tests, complied with all the procedures. I didn't apply for the trial expecting, well, *this*."

"Having a child is *exactly* why you applied for this, Maryam."

"Yes, but... not this way, not like this. I wanted the *chance* to get pregnant, but I sure as hell never applied so you could get me pregnant without my consent."

Ms. Sanchez's expression didn't waver for an instant. "You signed up to have a successful pregnancy, and right now you have one."

"Yeah, but I wanted to be a mother, not a surrogate. When I did it, who I did it with – it was all supposed to be my choice. You fucked up and took that choice away from me and now you want to take this one away, too?"

Ms. Sanchez wriggled in her chair. "Well, Maryam, I assure you that we empathize with you, and we're prepared to offer very generous compensation during and after your pregnancy. However, *if* you want to know about the legal ramifications of your 'choice', termination of a viable pregnancy is an explicit breach of the contract you signed, which would make you liable for medical costs plus damages. If you are unable to pay, you could be on the hook for jail time, up – "

"Do you have any idea how much all the experimental technology that went into this project was worth?" Dr. Ojumu shouted. "Do you know how many different corporations have their next fiscal year's outlook riding on your uterus right now?"

"And *there* it is. Some honestly finally, alhamdulillah!"

"Maryam, there's no need for this tone. Please don't do anything you might regret later."

"You've got a lot of nerve telling me what I will or won't regret. You don't know me. Women like you are always telling me how to be a woman, as if your experiences of it are *anything* like mine."

Ms. Sanchez looked aghast. She exchanged glances with Dr. Ojumu, but couldn't find the words. Maryam hopped off the examination table and started grabbing her belongings.

The calm in Dr. Ojumu's demeanor finally broke.

"Are you kidding me, Maryam? This baby is a breakthrough and you are not about to fuck yourself like this."

"Oh, of course, I'm so fucking sorry for not thinking about how this thing inside me makes you feel. Fuck you, go ahead. I know plenty of lawyers."

"As I was saying, Ms. Jalaali," Ms. Sanchez continued. "According to the contract, you are carrying quite a bit of proprietary intellectual property inside of you. The foundation quite literally owns a substantial portion of you. Damage it and you could face upwards of ten years."

Over the following year, this statement would culminate in Esmerelda Sanchez quitting her job to start an ultimately highly regrettable stint on a collective farm. But in the shorter term, it got the job done. Maryam agreed to carry the child growing within her.

Maryam's FUQR handlers took control of her personal feeds and confiscated her Aug. It was like she was back in the 20th century. Through media surrogates, they dismissed the "seemingly unusual" circumstances around her conception by shifting the blame to Mary and muddying the waters with allegations of mysterious foreign lovers. Authentic and fabricated reports fought tooth and nail in a furious networked battle that left popular opinion unsettled and bored. With the PR situation under control, Maryam was now ready for her glorious non-consensual apotheosis as America's Mom™.

The vast majority of the first month's media flood was a quaintly oh-so-turn-of-the-millennium back and forth on whether researchers were "playing God" – as if they did anything else anymore – or were righteous pioneers. Among queer people, many of whom were Maryam's close and not-so-close acquaintances, this took an eerily similar guise as a feud between Third Wave holdovers claiming Maryam was an unabashed gender assimilationist, cyborg feminist techie queers who viewed her with a disturbingly divine level of reverence, and everyone else who just desperately wanted to sign up.

Maryam's first commercial offer came from Matrilax, a synthetic baby formula brand owned by a tertiary subsidiary of Cold Spring Holdings Group, who wanted Maryam as the spokesmodel for their new ad campaign, "Matrilax: When Nature Isn't Enough." The slogan made no sense to her, but $100,000 seemed a fair price for having her picture taken holding a bottle and clutching her stomach, something she had never shied away from in the past. The novelty of the ad campaign was a moderate success, albeit not sufficiently to keep Cold Spring Holdings from dropping the Matrilax brand and integrating its facilities into its far more profitable weapons production interests.

On top of her commercial offers, the FUQR-aligned non-profits that had lobbied the NIH to fund Maryam's surgery came calling as well, shuttling her through dozens of media events, upper class galas, and fundraisers where there was more free booze than she had ever thought possible and nobody was allowed to give her a drink. She was the face of LGBT family life now, and they couldn't have her acting like some irresponsible queen at a night club, now could they? No, I suppose not, Maryam would say, before pardoning herself to bum a smoke off a busboy.

Her ratty furniture was replaced with ergonomic alternatives, her cabinets filled with dubious pre-natal nutrition supplements. The piece de resistance was the baby's room, now festooned with garish Technicolor rainbows and a creepy portrait of the original Matrilax Baby (who, unbeknownst to Maryam, had sold her cocaine in DC a few years back). She was set up with classes like "Mommy Yoga," "Cooking For Two," and one especially for LGBT parents, "Gayby Talk". "This is why I could never believe in a merciful God," she muttered. God remained mercifully silent.

Maryam could not have been happier when the mainstream news media lost interest a few weeks in. "Don't worry," her media handler said, "they'll be back in about six months."

Fourteen weeks pregnant, they gave her Aug back so she could do an interactive live feed. These could attract thousands of participants and millions of viewers. She was immediately surprised at how much she'd missed the Aug's feather light weight tickling her brow, the fuzzy glow of its overlay lighting up her vision, the feeds' million voices flowing in gentle rivulets around her periphery. It was the closest thing to good drugs the new picture of American motherhood had had in months.

Faces and voices started to fly into her field of view, dropping their questions and dissolving into thin air like soda fizz bubbles.

Would you rather fight one Horse sized Penis or 100 Penis sized horses?

"Wow! Off to a fast start, huh?"

Isn't it dangerous being pregnant so soon after your surgery?

"A little, but being pregnant is always dangerous? My doctors are being really... attentive.... They're always thinking of the good of the baby." Her handlers would be proud of her diplomatic response.

Will you marry me?

"No?"

MJ, you should totally check out my feed! @ShtStayn69

"Uhh..."

You should be ashamed of yourself!

"I usually am, but you're going to have to be more specific."

Have you gained weight?

"That's how pregnancy usually works, right?"

Do you know the seven secret steps for boosting your brand and monetizing your feed? I found out and am making more credits than ever!

"Good for you."

When can I get it????

"The researchers are still getting the next round of tests together."

You're so hot, do you still have a dick?

(Aman Allah, who are these people?)

How do you feel?

"What?"

Yeah! What does it feel like! Can you feel the baby yet???

...

How does it feel?

"Ummm, it feels strange, I guess. Different. Nauseous... I'm vomiting a lot. And, no, I can't really feel the baby. Well, not exactly, anyway? A lot of my abdomen is still kind of numb... I mostly just feel sore and bloated."

Who's the father? Is it true there is no father?

"Sorry, the lawyers say I can't talk about that one."

WHORE OF BABYLON, BURN IN HELL. My God would never allow a terrorist harlot with a stolen body to carry His only son!

Whore of Babylon? Who is this guy?

DON'T TALK ABOUT GODDESS MARYAM THAT WAY!

'Goddess Maryam'?

The percolating human foam started churning as the crowd's attention turned. Virtual faces now crowded every last bit of visual space in her apartment. Maryam's earpiece crackled. The overlapping voices blended into a harmonious static.

MARYAM OF BETHLEHEM, HEAR ME!

Maryam instinctively shut her eyes.

HEAR ME! BEHOLD!

Maryam slowly opened her eyes to see the blank walls of her apartment glowing like a picture from a professional home décor photo shoot. The faces were gone, but the static of the voices remained, albeit much fainter. She grasped at her face to see if her Aug was broken, but her hands found only skin where there should have been plastic and metal.

HEAR MEEEEEE!!!

"Fucking... I hear you, OK?! Who the hell are you?" Maryam shouted.

I AM!

"Yes, you exist, you've made that crystal clear already. Who are you?!"

I AM WHO I AM!

Maryam collapsed to her knees. She had gotten the gist.

I GAVE YOU LIFE AS YOU ARE TO GIVE IT.

The voice had softened enough for Maryam to truly hear it. The voice sounded like a massive chorus, booming lows and piercing highs in total harmony. Not a man's voice or a woman's, not even both. All, none.

"Why are you speaking to me?"

I CHOSE THE WOMAN.

"You chose me?"

I CHOSE THE WOMAN.

"Why me?"

WHY YOU?

Maryam struggled to decipher whether she was being mocked or asked for her genuine thoughts. Maybe even threatened?

"Yes, 'why me?'! Why *this* woman? Why not some other woman? Don't you want someone chaste, someone maternal? Someone who actually believes in you? Someone who had a uterus before her thirties? A real woman..."

I CHOSE THE WOMAN ABOVE THE WOMEN OF ALL NATIONS.

"I don't deserve this!" Maryam reeled in confusion at her own thoughts. 'Don't deserve this?' What kind of self-hating bullshit was this? Maryam had left that behind years ago in her youth, right? Her body, her rules, right?

Her knees buckled and she slumped to the ground. The static grew louder and her vision blurred. She thanked God she hadn't eaten much that morning, because her stomach was forcing it up now. She wondered what Allah would think about being puked on.

Eat a dick, faggot!

"Allah, did you just tell me to eat a dick?"

Maryam's could once again make out the human catastrophe that was her live feed. Now appropriately overwhelmed, she ripped the Aug off her face and vomited in front of exactly 4,928,701 live onlookers, a new personal record. If God was laughing, it was in silence.

Dr. Ojumu said her blood pressure had crashed from the stress of the live feed. Her handlers resumed control of her feed, citing her need for bed rest. But, they assured the eager public, they would be continuing to update the feeds with new information and promotions.

When she got home from her three day visit to the hospital, Maryam would have gone straight up to her rooftop and screamed her soul out at the New York skyline in a beautifully cinematic gesture were it not for the fact that she despised hearing the sound of her voice.

What had happened to her? Ten weeks earlier she had been a blissfully morose woman whose biggest problem had been dealing with her replacement of alcohol and drugs with fertility hormones and anti-rejection medications. She used to have friends, get fucked, feel alive. It was a dull, dissociated kind of alive, but at least it felt familiar, predictable, real.

There was that word again, "real". She clung to it like it was a rope over a deep chasm of religious delusions. Yes, delusions. She was a committed nihilist and atheist. And in all the religions of the world, she'd never heard of a God open-minded enough or with a sense of humor dark enough to make a holy virgin out of a hot messy, cut-up tranny.

If they were delusions though, they weren't only hers. Just the week before, she had received an invitation to a Virgin Maryam theme party. She was memed as a Madonna with child, a Goddess for a new queer age. Punks were writing songs about her, there were shirts, comics, zines, tarot decks, you name it. There was even a fundraising effort for a fan-made video feed about her that was keeping the foundation's lawyers very busy.

And there were the dyed-in-the-wool religious zealots. Most had concentrated around an ascendant fringe group known as the Church of the New Nativity, hard right-wing millenarians with white power leanings, centered in Oklahoma City, but now cropping up almost everywhere. Like countless other niche militants, they had expanded rapidly since the Crash of 2019 and the onset of the Iranian War.

Members of the group had, like most of the rest of the world, latched on to the bizarre legal battle surrounding her baby's paternity. As it passed through the warped bubble of the white power internet, though, the debate soon got very, *very* serious. A 42-year-old dentist from Poughkeepsie going by the delightfully vintage "SturmReich83" wrote a 36 page Biblical exegesis demonstrating that she, Maryam Jalaali, was carrying the Second Coming of Christ. Ninety-nine times out of a hundred, a screed like this would have died a quick, quiet death in the depths of the internet's collective memory, but, unfortunately for Maryam, this wasn't one of them. Maryam had received a few boilerplate death threats that she printed out to use during a Gayby Talk scrapbooking tutorial, but this was different.

Hoping to safeguard their investment in this lucrative but chaotic environment, the foundation lobbied a gay senator to help provide an armed detail for Maryam. Soon, two well-armed light drones – Zahra and Farooq, she named them – followed her from 30 feet in the air. The buzzing was incessant, but Maryam tried to find songs that synced with it. So far the best she'd come up with were Tangerine Dream and Bad Brains.

She did not take well to her de facto incarceration. Maybe things would have been different if she could get a weed delivery, but Farooq was, let's just say, a bit sensitive about the mother-to-be's health.

She looked around her apartment thinking of options. The kid wasn't even hers, and beyond that, she couldn't stand all of these suits and their robot minions telling her what to do. It's not going down like this, she thought. No part of this has been mine. She fished a mini-bottle from her bathroom stash and drank it on the toilet. Fuck it, if you're really the son of God you'll be fine anyway...

She traced a finger along her hips, holding for a brief second the hope that it would feel like *real* skin, warm and untouched. Her fingers found only craggy, lifeless scars and the cold plastic of the medical port, which lit up in response to her touch like a puppy thinking its master wants to play. "How may I assist you today?"

She wondered how many women could say their uteruses talked to them. This was what she'd always said she'd wanted, but in that moment she thought she might have given it all up just to feel the heat of her fingers along her scarred abdomen. She had wanted a body at peace with itself, but no, she thought, that wasn't it. What she wanted was a body that had never known struggle.

She was a far cry from little Sharif desperately trying to grow into manhood like it was one of those oversized suits his mother always bought him as a teenager for special occasions. A little boy who would try to picture himself as a grown man, a father, the whole neoliberal packaging of masculinity that fits in a commercial break but infects you for a lifetime. She was a woman, carrying another life inside her, but choosing to value herself first. And, per tradition, she was going to put herself first by pandering to a self-destructive whim or two.

She flipped through her messages, and briefly pondered calling her frantic mother before deciding it was the wrong kind of self-destructive.

"False alarm," she responded to her abdomen. "Good night."

"Good night," the port said, drifting off to sleep.

Maryam put on her jacket and left the house. The wind bit at her.

"STATE YOUR DESTINATION," the drone, Farooq, exclaimed like a drunk Dalek.

"Excuse me? Where the hell did you go to finishing school?"

"STATE YOUR DESTINATION." Farooq was a real asshole, not like Zahra, who at least knew how to mind her own business.

"I'm going somewhere to get drunk and make bad decisions." Zahra interrupted her rhythmic up-and-down bob for a few seconds.Maryam got the eerie sense that she was laughing, but reading a drone for humor was about as useless as reading her mother.

"PLEASE SPECIFY."

"Fine, I'm going to my sister Leyla's apartment."

"VERIFYING. VERIFYING. LOCATION VERIFIED. WALKING IN THE STREET IS INADVISABLE. REQUESTING TRANSPORTATION."

Overbearing as he could be, Farooq had that tender side Maryam just couldn't stay mad at. The car drove up in minutes and, not wanting to be rude to her knight in matte gray carbon nanotube armor, she stepped inside.

Everyone seemed to stare as her car sped by, but she tried to pay it no mind. She had been cooped up so long, she'd forgotten what it was like to be in public without her Aug on – it felt good slipping past people like a ghost, a dark blank spot in the fabric of everyone else's shared reality. Given how many mini-bottles she was packing away, it's not surprising that it took so long to dawn on her: they weren't staring at her, they were staring at her menacing new friends.

As the automated car zipped mechanically through the streets, the thought of dealing with her sister's attitude made Maryam uneasy. Leyla's matter-of-fact disposition and controlling brand of maternal instinct could sometimes – *sometimes* – be useful, but at this moment one of Leyla's lectures would have only killed her meager buzz.

Maryam put in her earpiece to listen to some more Bad Brains. She slid her last bottle out of her purse and drank along to the beat, but something seemed off about the music. She looked out the rear windshield to see what her metallic minions were up to.

"Pause music."

Nothing.

"Farooq? Zahra?"

She heard a faint whoosh behind her as she saw an LED flashing beside her. Someone was making a direct link.

"Jesus, Lena, was that really necessary? You couldn't have just disoriented them for a bit?"

"Honey, you might treat them like puppy dogs, but the last thing I need right now is a bunch of terminators sniffing out this line." Lena Serrano was tall and slender, a beautiful, classic kind of trans woman's body that had become rarer as puberty suppression early in life became more commonplace. Her matted dark black hair and shaky hands made her look like she hadn't slept for two days. Even over the digital link, Maryam could tell her apartment was oddly neat – either she'd started dating again or was finally listening to her therapist. "Still got the parasite, querida?" Lena asked.

"It's a fetus. And yes, I still have it," Maryam replied. "For now."

"Girl, you needed to get that shit out of you last week, deadass."

"Lena, it's not that easy… I've got punks worshipping me, racist jackboots calling for my head, doctors who won't stop prodding me—," Maryam pulled her sleeve up, revealing a dozen puncture marks, "—and literally millions of people paying for my every move. My handlers barely even let me leave the house anymore, and when I do I've got my 'puppy dogs' nipping at my heels."

"Fuck that, you've got friends who could smuggle you in some pills."

"No way, no pills. With all the transplant drugs I'm on, Plan B would turn my blood into toxic sludge within 24 hours."

"Shit. What about MVA? The machines can fit in a small box. Have someone wrap it up like a gift for you."

"I'm too far along. D&E's the easiest option at this point, and there's no way anyone's getting a rig that size to me unnoticed."

"Then find a way to get to the clinic. Your family can probably find some reason to take you out for a day or two. I've seen the feeds and I know you could make more money than Beyonce for an exclusive stream. All those cis people falling over themselves to get a piece! Then you can funnel the money to all the liberation armies you want. *So* cute." Good old Lena.

"Get the fuck out!" Maryam leaned over to her Aug. "I DO NOT NOR HAVE I EVER FUNNELED MONEY TO TERRORIST ORGANIZATIONS!" she yelled.

"But seriously, why would you pass up the chance to be the first trans woman to have an abortion? You'll be taking the biggest step forward for trannykind since we stopped using the asterisk."

"Do you think what they're saying is true?" Maryam muttered. "About the baby."

"You're asking me whether you're carrying baby Jesus? You born again or something? What the fuck happened to the Maryam who'd do drugs in church bathrooms with me?"

"Nothing really... it's just..." Maryam didn't know how to finish, but those mini-bottles she'd had on the way over had put her in an honest mood. "It's just that I've seen visions."

"Visions?"

"Yeah, visions. Light and divine voices and everything."

"Really?" Lena furrowed her brow. She started rolling a joint.

"Yes, really," Maryam answered with some agitation. "Well I don't know if they're *real*, you know? But I really saw something. At least twice now. The last time was right before I got... sick... during my live feed a couple weeks back."

"Holy shit!" Lena shouted. "I saw that! That was *amazing*!"

"*Anyway*, God spoke to me. Told me I was 'to give life'. Told me I was chosen."

"And what did you say?" Lena now seemed genuinely interested.

"I said I didn't deserve this. Can you believe it? Face to face with omnipotence and that's the best I could come up with."

"Bitch, you kinda asked for this, no? Did you ever honestly think people would take the news of pregnant tranny calmly?"

"No... I mean, yeah, I figured people would probably lose it. But that's not how I meant it...," Maryam was ashamed of the explanation she would have to give, and besides, time was running out on the secure link.

"Anyway," Maryam continued, changing the subject. "Just think, what will the Nativists think when they find out I flushed God down a tube?"

"LOL! Oh, they'll definitely try to kill you. I would suggest fleeing the country."

"I have been wanting to see my parents' village in Palestine. Might be appropriate given the circumstances, you know?"

"I meant somewhere like China or Brazil, not the middle of a military quarantine zone."

"Maybe I could live out my days as a guerilla."

"Bitch, don't get sentimental on me," Lena said. "Your puppies will be waking up soon. I've got to go. Promise me you'll call your family and get your damn abortion so I don't have to see you on a fucking piece of toast."

"Fuck off, don't be jealous." Maryam blew Lena a kiss with both hands. It was the last thing she did before blacking out.

"Hey, I think he's coming to."

'He'? What the hell did they mean, 'he'? There had better be another unconscious person in here with me. Is that smell *gasoline*?

Maryam looked around what she guessed was the back of an old van, plastic draped all along the interior. A child could have pieced together what was happening. "I'm being kidnapped, huh?" she said groggily.

"Yup," replied one of the men next to her. He was white, a skinhead, on the large side, with a distinctly military aesthetic.

"Wait, what the hell? Is she *driving?!*" Maryam screamed.

"It's OK, she knows what she's doing."

"Are you fucking kidding me? She's going to get us all fucking killed!" The last time Maryam had seen a human driver outside of cheesy throw-back vids was six years earlier.

"Don't think for a second that I'm not tempted" said the woman.

"Cut the shit, Olive," the man retorted. He felt really proud of that one.

"Olive? That's kind of a cute name for a deranged fascist. Were your parents old school hipsters whose ironic love of Hitler and Jerry Falwell took a wrong turn?"

Olive reached back and slapped her across the face.

"Watch the fucking road, you maniac!"

"Hey, my brother was diagnosed with manic depression, that shit's no joke," the second man said. He was tall and lanky, and his smiling, deeply tanned complexion helped break up the creepy Aryan Nation vibe.

"*Pedro!*" Olive snarled, reasserting control of the situation, "what was the condition of the tin cans we torched?"

"Both down, one totally smoked."

"Good, get her sedated and start prepping. We should be at the lab in about ten minutes."

"No way, she's pregnant. We've got to wait at least another hour before we give her any more."

What lab? What are they going to do to me? Maryam's mind raced as her knowledge of biomedicine hurled into her vulnerable consciousness.

"'Totally smoked'? What are you, fifty?" the white man chimed in, about ten seconds too late. As he cackled at his own stroke of wit, his jiggling bald head and tactical turtleneck gave him the distinct look of a circumcised penis.

"*Lieutenant* Jackson!" Olive snapped back, sounding rather like a burnt-out teacher who had lost control of her class. "Did you manage to salvage anything good?"

"I only had time to salvage one of them. Picked up about a thousand armor piercing rounds and twelve L-type power cells. Should be enough to power the EMP generator for at least three days."

While the zealots' stream of military acronyms filled the van, Maryam looked around frantically for anything that might help her figure out where they were going. Pedro had linked what looked like a trans-vaginal ultrasound device. It had to be at least fifteen years old; set against the backdrop of the van, this museum piece was grotesquely medieval. There was a beige box she guessed was a mobile rapid PCR kit for genetic testing. Gleaming forceps. Abdominal syringe.

"I can't for the fucking life of me understand why *my* God would put his faith in that *thing*. That beautiful Child was meant for a *real* woman, not some sinful, butchered mental case," Olive growled, snapping Maryam back to attention.

"How the fuck would you know? Have you ever talked to God?" Maryam snapped back. "No? Well I have."

Jackson abruptly slapped Maryam across the face. His joking, self-satisfied smile had twisted into anger. "God doesn't talk to people like you," he barked. Olive smirked in the rear-view mirror.

"You love this baby so much? Why don't *you* take it, Olive?" Maryam saw on Olive's face that she had struck a nerve. "Go ahead, Jackson can cut it out of me right now with that knife hanging off his belt. Do you see me stopping you?"

"Just give me fifteen minutes," Olive whispered.

"Military comm chatter saying the nightly tin can patrol is on its way," Pedro shouted. "Five... no, six blips incoming at... seventy miles an hour. ETA ten minutes."

"Run the EMP, we're almost there," Olive pressed down on the gas.

Maryam was hurled to the floor as they hit a pothole. As she looked up, she recognized the tenements of Jamaica, erected as a quasi-legal occupied ghetto for the city's Muslim population during the worst of the martial law years. The tenements were modularly constructed from used shipping containers based on designs submitted by a green architecture firm from San Francisco whose previous work included the world's first completely AI-automated high school and the largest carbon-neutral supermax prison in North America.

Maryam couldn't fathom what a bunch of white Christian terrorists would be doing trying to hide in the middle of over half a million Muslims. Then, she registered the towering husk of the abandoned Jamaica Hospital. Rumors abounded on underground internet streams in the post-war years about military experiments on human subjects conducted there. Maryam got as far as believing the stories of risky cybernetic neural pathway integration experiments, but drew the line at human-animal hybridization. Knowing that the stories were most likely myths did little to calm her fears.

"Holy shit, you're actually going to do it, aren't you, you psycho?"

"We're doing whatever it takes to protect the Child."

"You're more likely to kill the baby than save it."

Olive took her time responding. "God will protect the child's body. We're here to protect its soul. People like you ruined this country. Brought it down from grace. The Child will change that, but he can't be allowed to grow in sin. He needs to be born in righteousness and purity like he was intended to, before you stole him."

"And that's you? No offense, but I don't know if I'd exactly call this righteousness and purity."

"Better than the degenerate filth you can offer. I wish we'd nuked the security zones and wiped out you and your kind when we had the chance."

Maryam tensed up at this last comment. It wasn't as if she hadn't seen the sentiment a thousand times before on the feeds, but the sound of it coming out of a flesh-and-blood and definitely not an AI person made her stomach sink. To her surprise, though, she then felt her stomach jerk right back up. In fact, she felt herself lift off her seat for 2.3 seconds that felt like minutes as the van plunged into a twenty-eight foot sinkhole in the middle of the Van Wyck Expressway.

The media storm over the incident would spur an acrimonious debate over vital infrastructure spending in Congress that would lead to one mildly entertaining corruption scandal, one third of the Department of Transportation's recommended budget increases, and three years of silence on the issue.

Fifteen weeks pregnant and back in the lap of overwhelmingly monitored luxury, Maryam slipped on her Aug and try to see what she could glean from the feeds. The whole laundry list of federal law enforcement came down on Jamaica with all the subtlety one would expect. All mention of the Nativists' and Maryam's connection to the crash and the raids was suppressed. Maryam's corporate handlers flooded the feeds with stories that Maryam's car had been hacked by a member of a supposed Muslim terror cell. Police claimed that these terrorists set fire to the mosque they were allegedly based out of before any evidence could be gathered.

Maryam's mother and sister came to visit her once she was taken out of intensive care. Maryam and Leyla did not see eye-to-eye, and not just because Leyla's existence had precluded Maryam from naming herself after Leyla Khaled. Leyla was the smooth, polished counterpart to Maryam's... *eccentricity*. At thirty-seven years of age with three children, a benign husband, and a booming real estate business, Leyla's life looked like a clichéd vision board and she had an attitude to match.

"I need to get an abortion. I need your help," Maryam blurted.

"No 'hello'? You go straight to 'I need an abortion'? Are you fucking kidding me?" Leyla had all the emotional subtlety of a military AI.

"Amaaaan, do you not see my situation here? What part of this seems sustainable to you?"

"I think you're being selfish."

"Selfish?? What fucking part of this is selfish?"

"Do you know what my family's been through, what mom's been through, because of you?" Leyla shouted, with not a little relish. "People feeding every fucking move we make? Mom just mostly sits with her back to the windows and moans when we're not visiting you. Did she tell you that?" She hadn't, but it didn't take an Aug to see it written all over their faces. "And all so that what, so you could play out your little fantasy and then act like you never wanted it?"

"My little fantasy? Was being a mother just a little fantasy to you? Was planning your life and family just a little fantasy?"

"You want to be a mom? Step up to it. That uterus you got comes with responsibilities whether you want it to or not. Not that you've ever known anything about taking responsibility for anyone..."

"What about your child?" Fatima broke in sternly.

"It's not my child," Maryam snapped.

"It's growing inside you, how is it not your child?" Fatima wagged her head. It shouldn't have, but her unflinching lack of hesitation surprised Maryam.

"It's, umm... The doctors have run genetic tests and the mother is the woman who donated the uterus. I can't tell you anything about the father, but I am definitely not the mother."

"*Maryam*, I did not raise you to be so cold. What does it matter who the child came from if he found his way to you?"

"You're right, 'ami, I know. It feels like the whole world wants to use me or kill me. I'm so mixed up I'm half convinced that the Christian God is using me as an oven. I wanted my body to feel more whole. Uncomplicated. Mine. And now I'm the last person who gets to have any say over it. Allah, it sounds so stupid now that I say it, but it's true! I can't keep this body and hold onto myself at the same time, and if I have to make that choice..."

At this, Fatima threw herself on her unsuspecting daughter in a furious embrace. *Habibi... habibi...*

"Wait, mom, no... you can *not* possibly be thinking of helping her with this,"

"Leyla, look at her. Look at your sister," Fatima said, loosening her hold to look at Maryam. "She has decided for herself. She has always decided for herself. When she told us about herself and your father was gone, I said everything I could to convince her not to transition. You remember, yes? I could have stayed stubborn and lost my daughter, but instead I decided I would help her however she needed. If all she needs from me now is help, I will give whatever help Allah gives me the strength to provide."

Maryam smiled as she struggled to get her frenzied mother off of her. "I need you to tell my FUQR handlers that you need me for Eid ul-Adha feast. Once they let me out of the hospital – *if* they let me out – Lena can get me a car without anyone knowing. I just need to get out of here."

"If they say no I will yell until Allah himself silences me." Fatima replied with a profound sense of self-satisfaction.

"Yes! Perfect! Shukran, 'ami!" Maryam squealed with a delight amplified by Leyla's look of concerned resignation.

Eight days later, Eid ul-Adha, the holiday of the sacrifice, came to pass.

Is this it, that one final argument to shut everyone up? Including me? Especially me? No more Pinocchio syndrome, no more dysphoria, no more "you would understand if…"s. Ya Allah, how many more times do I have to be cut open before I get to be real enough to make my own choices?

The minutes she spent lying on the table she was overcome by how close her body felt to her. There was no distance, no lag in processing sensations into feelings into thought. She felt as though her heart were cycling through every beat that had come before – the gentle flutters of childhood; the slow, euphoric release when she hugged her father as he emerged from a federal detention center in 2025; the tight arrhythmias of her first love and her first assault, whose uncanny similarities dawned on her for a brief, terrifying, and glorious moment. The cool, stale air and buzzing ceiling lights took her back to the schools of her youth where she'd managed to eke out life-sustaining slivers of acceptance from the few kids kind enough not to call her a faggot. The doctor's fumbling motions and rapid-fire apologies as he placed the tube inside her reminded her so vividly of a particularly cute but awkward ex that she couldn't help but relax and laugh.

As the vacuum started, she felt her uterus clench. Despite it having come from another woman, its sensations felt more overwhelmingly direct than any of the others, even though the memories they brought were more difficult to decipher. With each contraction, she could hear her mother's screams, but they weren't the emotional tirades she was so accustomed to growing up. They were louder than any she had heard before, and pained, yes, but so eerily familiar, like it was imprinted deep in her marrow – deeper even.

Her body was hers. Her body was everyone's. It made the kind of fucked up sense to her that felt perfect.

A small part of her just wished the father could have been there with her to share it.

God could not be reached for comment.

Control Shift Down

PAIGE BRYONY

"Did you hear about Lynn?" Sissy asked me.

I blew across the top of my fresh coffee. I didn't want to be here and I didn't want to know whatever she was going to tell me. I didn't want to know Lynn either, because I knew her by Cherry – her work name – first. Cherry I admired, she was strong. Part of me hated Lynn for being Cherry's weak shadow.

"I cleared six-hundred pleb tonight," I said. I squinted at the dawn and put my back against the window side of our booth. Down the street the red lights of the curfew barriers stuttered dark, letting city cleaners pass through in APCs. They had sponsor decals from the same company that made my coffee. "That's rent," I said, not looking at her. I said "rent", but I meant "a fistful of null chips, which I could be jacking right now if you hadn't called me out."

Sissy whistled low. "Comfy government job," she said, and I heard the smirk in it.

I gave her a look. If she'd asked me there to bitch about my Class A license, I would give the city something else to clean up.

Sissy held up a hand. "Good money. But I asked if you heard about Lynn."

I just grunted. Cherry taught me how to do full service and be safe. Taught me how to keep my head on, how not to think desperate when tips were lean, how not to go nasty when the tips fell like rain. How to handle a skittish Rob, how to milk a spender, how to assemble and then conceal the full suit of armor you put on before taking off your clothes and slipping into the tactcam window. I was Class A half because of my own badass, which Sissy better not forget, and half because of Cherry. Cherry taught me how to be a shiftbitch and survive.

But meeting Lynn, for me, I guess it was kind of like what Robs feel if you let them see the armor. And maybe that makes me a bad person, but I didn't want to know that behind Cherry was a quiet, lonely, scared woman named Lynn. Just like the scrubs who side eye us for making top bank. I couldn't forgive her for it, even if the only reason I met her was because she let me stay with her so much last year. And no one can wear the armor all the time.

She could have been thrown out so many times, and had Cherry's license revoked, for letting me stay there. My null chip habit is like a payroll tax off the top I don't question even when it bites into food or keeping the lights on. But chipping is legal when two licensed tactcam whores sharing a room is not, and Lynn treated the risk of keeping me in from the cold like I treated my nulls. A cost taken for granted. I felt very cold just then.

"Alright, Sissy," I said. "What about Lynn."

Sissy wrapped her hands tight around her cup. "She must've got approved for the implant," she said and stopped suddenly. Sissy smiled thin and hard, like she was going to start crying, but just took a long swallow of coffee. "Didn't say anything to nobody."

"Sounds like her," I shrugged. "But then how do you know?"

"Made the news last night," she said. "Guys brought it up in my room, so..."

"Why the fuck would – "

"Because they thought it was fucking funny," Sissy spat. "You want to see? You want to fucking see? Because they made me look. They made me. Just—"

Sissy threw her hands up and shook her head. She held herself and stared at the coffee bar.

She didn't want to be here either, I realized. I scare her. Maybe she needed a friend, but that's not why she called me. Good. That meant I was safe enough to be forgiving.

"Hey," I tried. "Sissy, I'm sorry."

"I was hooked up," she stammered. "So I did a lot more than see it."

Her phone sat there between us. I picked it up and read.

Lynn had been saving the maximum allowed each month. Pleb is entirely digital and every transaction is tracked. There are many things you can't buy with it, and people like us aren't allowed any other currency. You can't buy a home for example, only rent, you can't set aside more than three hundred a month, and if you have more than ten thousand saved then any time you pay or are paid there are huge new charges.

So it takes impossible discipline to save up enough to get a womb implant. That's what Lynn had done. Sissy was wrong, she had told somebody about it. She'd told me, months ago. How close she was getting, how much it meant to her. That she was getting out of the business. There wouldn't be any more Cherry.

And we fought. "What fucking good is it to leave us behind? What shiftbitching done to you ain't never gonna leave you. Only thing now is you'll be alone," I taunted her. She stopped just short of sneering at me. Took the kind of breath makes you taller and your eyes tighter. "I never been here," she said. "Everything I taught you. and you never learned that first lesson. Don't ever be here for real."

I was hooked up sometimes twelve hours a day, and fucked up on null chips the rest of the time. I just wanted the numbers to get bigger, and I wanted to sleep without dreaming. I wanted the biggest cash out and the biggest check out. We fought and I left. I opened my own tactcam window and lived upstairs in a room that looked out on an armored mobile trash incinerator at night. My only company was remembering what she said, don't ever be here for real, and it was a lot easier to live by when I hit Class A and other bitches stopped trying to awkwardly include me in their scene.

Told myself that was the end of giving a damn about what happened next, to me and to anybody, let alone Lynn. She'd bought her new womb from Dr. Ventnor about two months after that. Top quality synthetics. Actual grown tissue was out of reach for anyone we knew, but Ventnor was reliable. Shiftbitches said she gave a damn. They'd ask her if there was anyone like us outside, and she'd make some noise about medical privacy, but smile and tell us about "trans women," and how they could go unnoticed, get married, have real jobs. Even be doctors.

One day, Lynn woke up with cramps. She contacted Dr. Ventnor who said not to worry, it's normal, she was just having her first real cycle. I hadn't thought about this in a while. Fuck Sissy for filling in the gaps of my carefully wrecked memory.

"How can they print this shit?" I wondered aloud, staring at her phone in my hand like a turd. "Like how do they even know this to begin with?"

Sissy didn't answer, just let her phone explain that the cramps didn't get better. Apparently Lynn was waiting for an interview with a public database, her first since quitting tactcam. She had discovered a long time ago that our license was roughly equivalent to lots of other low level government jobs, including something people used to call "librarian", and while no one we knew had ever tried, it was theoretically legal to apply for transfer. She didn't have the equipment for our job any more, but she could find anything you wanted from any data feed in a flash so there she was, in a stiff blouse and pencil skirt, sweating out the cramps and ready to try the impossible.

The pain got so bad she fled to a bathroom and security cameras in her stall alerted police there might be a junky in there.

She looked a lot thinner than I remembered. I muted the footage so I didn't hear her screaming. Officers stood outside her stall. Her blouse was open and her skirt around her ankles. Something put a fist through her belly from the inside.

I dropped the phone.

Sissy grabbed my hand hard. "So while you were off being fucked up about losing your hooker mom, some sick Rob was pissed that his favorite toy went off the market. Motherfucker already had all her IRL from backdooring her neurocase. He hacked her, Kira. Uploaded a wetworm and it replicated till it ate her from the inside. And he—"

She gritted her teeth and shook. My hand hurt. I wanted to jerk it away and hit her. I hated myself for it, for everything. I held her hand harder instead. I got up and changed seats to sit next to her, to hold her.

"He bragged about it in my room," she said through stifled sobs. "I was hooked up."

When you're hooked up, they're "in" you. Tippers pay to watch, but spenders, the Robs, they get your tactcam feed direct so you can feel their avatar touch you, hear their breathing. You'll feel what they want you to feel and vice versa. Anyone with half a brain knows that some motherfuckers want you to feel horrible things, so this was originally rolled out with artificial intelligence. Cheaper, less ethical problems, no human urge to lash out at the customer who hurts you. That lasted about a week before a hostile AI network nursed on a constant diet of piss play lobotomized a dozen users in a virtual dungeon. AI doesn't fear starving, or homelessness. Turns out people are a lot easier to rape than machines.

I let her sob into my shoulder and stared out the window. I thought about my numbers. My dealer worked a stand a block up.

"Hey," I said softly. "Hey, Sissy." I held my palm just under the table and showed her a chip.

"Kira goddammit," she pulled away.

"Alright, it's ok, hey," I took her hand again. "Look. You need to not work tonight."

She wiped her eyes. "Rent going to pay itself?" I could see the armor sliding on. "Can't just not work."

How much do I owe you, Lynn? She hates me and I offered comfort. Out of my own pocket. How much? Can't bring her to my place. Can't save her, there is no saving. How much do I owe and how do I pay? A life for a life?

That might work.

"No, okay, hold up." I made her look at me. "Not that, not tonight. You work for me tonight."

"Bitch please," she snorted. "You don't save fuck all even if you were for real."

"I got eight K," I said and stared her down. "I got eight K. And you work for me tonight."

That afternoon I bought three cheap nulls and a little something extra on the way back to my room to wait for Sissy to call. After our talk that morning, I'd taken her down to the benches in the alley next to the market where we could talk to other girls. They knew to give me my propers since I'd never made the mistake of being friends like I'd done with Sissy way back. I did her box braids up which took a few hours, and by the time we were done, we had most of what I wanted to know just from listening to the gossip. Schedules, specialties, that sort of thing. Sissy would get close to sobbing every time someone mentioned Lynn again, but I kept her calm.

I picked a handful of girls out who I knew were on my shift and competent. Girls who owed Lynn too. Gave sissy enough to flash at them and say I got a plan, ask if they want in. Let them know a Class A license might open up soon.

"So much for my 8k," I thought to myself.

But then, the bitter anger I expected to follow that thought didn't show. I felt nothing. It was like watching my leg just dangle after a reflex check instead of kick.

Maybe 8k was too big a hammer and I'd just wound up kneecapping myself, and this was shock. An armed customer service rep on the corner gave me the eye and I hustled across with my head down. "Fucking pimp," I muttered under the hum of his baton charging up.

And maybe it didn't matter, 8k, it was all going to go to chips anyway, right? Why did I start saving? I wasn't going to buy me a shiny new cunt and lose my job. If I wanted to blow it on day passes outside, I would have by now. Why pay to get moved from the kennel to the petting zoo for a couple days? So I could smell the people who threw me peanuts behind their avatars at night?

But I had saved. I had even skipped a chip here and there to work longer and save. I wanted nothing, and I don't mean just no "thing", or that there was nothing I wanted, I mean I wanted nothing the way other people want to be rich or want to be wanted. That there was nothing I wanted more than nothing. Intangibility. A chip gives me that, for a little while. I heard that if you upped your dose enough over time, it could hollow you out completely, painlessly. A soft way to go, and one they couldn't bring you back from, couldn't clone you out of because the copy would be as blank and unproductive as the shell you left on the street.

That was my retirement plan.

So I had no obvious reason to save. But I did. When my tracking dot blipped out, whatever was left of me would get recycled, the numbers would go down with me into the nothing. I wanted, when that day came, for girls I'd spent these years avoiding to say, "wasn't no one like her." The money, I wanted to buy credit in my name, from the dealer, the market, buy all the shiftbitches that meal they'd been making payments on, or one last high on me. I wouldn't just be gone, I'd be transcended, I'd be beyond, untouchable and nothing at all but a shared memory of one badass party for the richest bitch on the block.

But Cherry wouldn't be there.

Lynn had killed Cherry, and a Rob had killed Lynn.

So fuck it. New plan.

Yolanda was out on my stoop, swabbing a new girl's neckjack with alcohol. Someone cruel had sold the little raw thing on a 16 pin model, no doubt lying that bigger meant faster upload, and she'd be able to pay off the difference in a week. But at least she didn't look like she'd get an infection, even if the girl couldn't stop scratching the underside of her head where it'd been shaved.

"How you living?" I asked Yolanda as I held my eye up to the door scanner.

"Getting by," she yawned. "No younger despite best efforts. At least I try though," she teased.

I grunted. This was an old game. And I had been twenty-four for six years now. "You win," I said, entering my code. "I think I am done."

Yolanda's eyebrows near flew off her forehead. "I was playing, girl, no need to chip off into the sunset."

"Hear about Lynn?" I asked her.

Her face said yes.

"Who the fuck Lynn?" said the new girl.

"Know your place," Yolanda intoned, snapping her fingers under the girl's nose.

I lingered on my steps, looking at the new girl's neckjack. "I heard there's trans women outside getting stylists to do their hair like us now," I said.

"And I bet they don't pay pleb they earned for it neither," Yolanda snorted.

"It's the... fashion. The new thing," I laughed.

Yolanda licked her lips. "Mhm. Bet they stand real tall in them high heels ... on the other side of them walls."

I shooed the new girl away from my door, muttering. "I think I am done. Just with this side of it. Time I paid it forward. But tonight's about payback."

"Won't be no one else like Lynn," Yolanda shook her head.

"Yeah," I said. "But what we need is another Cherry." I shut the security door behind me and went upstairs.

When Sissy finally called I was heating broth in a mug and stirring vitacubes into it, watching the cat on the side change color with the heat and words form above it reading, "hot pussy".

When I was finally gone, the walls of my apartment would flash hot, sanitizing light for five minutes, and this mug would be the only thing left of what belonged to me.

Especially if I was really about to blow most of my savings.

The mug had been a birthday present from Lynn. Bought it while on day pass outside the decivilized zone. How much did that set back your plan, I wonder, I thought to myself and answered the phone.

"They're all waiting, Kira," Sissy said before I could say hello.

"Tell them I'll forward two hundred as soon as they log out. And breakfast is on me when we're through."

I hung up and opened the bag on my counter. The back of my mind calculated how long I could drift null before work and still half ass my way through, but it was just habit. I swept the chips into the drawer and grabbed the something extra.

Exodenizens, the people who mine water and ore out of asteroids, are the lowest class allowed to have and raise children. Whoever had me was three classes below that. Maybe I had siblings, maybe not, I'd never know. I wasn't even "born". I just showed up as a blinking red dot on the district curfew tracker one day when some distant engine of commerce told the world outside that labor was getting pricey. Not enough hungry motherfuckers out there to break their back for scraps? See what's able bodied in the cracks of the decivilized zone, give them a work ID, and suddenly they can be seen, be taxed. Instant human resources in the catastrophic event of a potential living wage.

So no I wasn't "born", but I was definitely a kid for a while, and when I was a kid, everything scared me. Didn't matter if it was real or not. If anything, the more impossible something was, the more it scared me. Other kids, they were scared of bigger kids, or their caregivers, or the cops, and I get that, I had a healthy fear of those things. But what kept me up at night was the impossible things in the dark. Scared of the fostervision screen coming on in the middle of the night and trying to eat me in my bunk while the other kids slept on. Scared of being flushed down the toilet. Scared of blood pouring through the vents of the group de-louser.

As I got older one big fear turned out to be a horrifying truth, that I would wind up looking like the older boys, sounding like them. That's the one I ran from instead of hiding under the covers, and that's how I wound up a shiftbitch. That's how I found out there was still one class lower than the parents who were not parents. The fear never really went away either when the others did, until I found nulls.

And now I don't even remember what fear feels like. Even looking at Sissy's phone that morning, it wasn't fear.

I let my robe fall off as I walk down the stairs. Nothing but thin lingerie and thinner walls between me and the window. I finish my broth and set it on the stairs and walk inside. I set my something extra in place between my neck and the jack and feel it there like a spider in the back of my mind. I can feel its fear as the light comes on and the street outside can see me through the window. Its legs tuck up underneath it and I think soothing thoughts to it, that I'm going to let it back into the dark soon.

With the jack in place, I can no longer feel the weight of my own body, the first seduction subroutine taking control of my muscles, a puppet while my mind scans the chat rooms of other girls. He's in there somewhere. I know what characters to look for. I idly moderate the rooms until, finally, I see the username in their feed. I play it out, encourage the girls to make him edge. He thinks he's leading them on, but we know his type, the ones who beg and never pay, who throw fits.

And when he's just about chewing his own tongue with lust, I give the word and a girl closes her cam.

Some people are really into that. "Edging" they call it. It's a thing. But it is not his thing, not at all. He's the instant gratification type. I dismiss the auto debit notice in the back of my mind that tells me I've settled up with a girl going by Jocasta. I am surprised by my own capacity for pleasure as I watch his avatar pop back into the lobby.

And by then the girls know I put my money where my mouth was when I told them my plan. He has a half dozen of them flirting with him like he's the last Rob on earth. I almost lick my fingers at the thought of snuffing their windows out like candles with one word, every time he gets close to making a deal.

I stalk him like this from window to window. Just like he stalked her. It takes me three hours to close the circle and with a thought, I let "Steph" know to send him to my window.

He can see me through the glass. I have my leg across my knee, leaning far back with my arms open. I turn off my auto-moderation, which would kick him immediately for certain keywords. I let him rant about the greedy bitches, even though I know it drives good Robs away. I won't see another Rob again after tonight anyway.

"Oh you poor thing…" I say, letting him come into focus through my window. I extend him an invite to a private free tactcam. A private, unregulated, tactcam. "Why not spend the night with me, lover?"

He's smirking, but incredulous. I can see his sweat. The stained t-shirt. He's so hungry for it he doesn't care how he looks when fed to my window. And he knows he's untouchable. No doubt miles away, maybe even off world, safe behind screen and jack and cozy in a room separated from mine by who knows how many walls and checkpoints and drone turrets. But right now all I care about is the distance between his hand and his fly.

"Free?" he asks.

"Maybe you come see again sometime, yes?" I say, giving him just enough of the whore he expects to make it credible for a fool.

A burst of static. "WARNING" a pop up flashes between us. "THE SECURITY CERTIFICATE OF THIS WHORE HAS EXPIRED."

The room glows red and though I am concealed behind the pop up to his eyes, I feel exposed. Now I'm sweating too. I see him flinch.

"CONNECTING CARRIES OF RISK OF MALWARE. YOU MUST DISABLE VIRUS PROTECTION TO CONTINUE."

I hear laughter. The watchers who almost left are now getting a different kind of show. "That he-she gonna fry your dick off, bro!" one of them howls. Robs don't like exposure. He's backing out as others come back in to watch. But he's still hard.

Fuck pride. I kneel down, try to remind him what's behind that warning. Let him see my breasts, see me wet my lips for him. "You want this," I make my body tell him. I turn off autoseduce and try to remember what it was like to be present for a fucking, to actively fake desire. I try to make my grimace a pout, make him know that he wanted this. "What's a five minute virus scan in exchange for an hour of bliss?" I coo up at him.

He grins.

Another howl of laughter from the mob. "You're not coming anywhere near my game lobby if you stick your e-peen in it," someone crows. And now he's angry.

"Fuck you, dude!" He's incensed and worse, he turns away. "This is government pussy, and you can't win on the ranked ladder without me carrying your fag ass."

I freeze. This can only get uglier. And even if I bring him back, now I know there's someone here who knows him. A friend. A witness.

"Fucking scrub, that's anything BUT pussy," laughs the witness. "Want to dip it in this freak and suddenly I'm the fag. Welcome to blockedville, Anon, population nobodyigiveafuckabout".

Anon? Ah. They're just usernames to each other, nothing more. Now I smile.

"I give a lot of fuck," I tell him and spread my knees.

He's watching me again. For several long moments nothing happens, but the goading gets louder.

"Don't worry about the watchers," I say. "Come on in and I'll make you a star."

And then I can smell his sweat too and know he's inside.

He can't see that my window's gone dark. Only my teeth and the whites of my eyes shine out from it to users outside—confused, disappointed little boys outside the old house, daring each other to knock.

"I like girls like you," he says, with that oh so charming ironic pronunciation of "girls" they always use when talking about my kind.

"I like men with a sense of humor," I say. "What do you do for laughs?"

"Oh... you know," he chuckles, uncomfortable.

"Yeah, I know..."

I reach inside me, where the fear was buried, open the palm of my mind and let the spider climb up. I give it my mouth to speak with. To eat.

The coffee could strip rust from an engine but does nothing for the foul taste in my mouth. Nulling leaves you numb, but a horrorcore is entirely different.

Anyone lost who doesn't need chips to get through a day, first of all, how?

Second... say you want to go ask Alice. All chips are basically wetware medicine that fail inspection and then go stranger after hitting the street. It's not legal to sell at the Tea Party, so the Caterpillar, (any licensed dealer), buys them off the companies in bulk, fucks with their code, and looks to profit selling to us. So he's sitting on a mushroom shaped motherlode of chips that'll take you anywhere, and Alice is like "fuck home, I get raped for a living, sell me some of that outer space shit."

I'm Alice in this scenario if that wasn't clear.

Jacking a null is like nibbling the left side of the mushroom, gobbling it whole in my case, and going to a sleep beyond sleep. Not unconscious, anti-conscious.

Then there are the endless unique experiences Alice could taste and live between that extreme and the other.

A "horrorcore" is the other. When Alice chips that, it cranks her senses to a sick, ultra human perfection, then drags everything she's ever dreaded out from the secret places of her mind and forces them front and center. Afraid of heights? Instant, gut wrenching vertigo. Scared of the dark? Everywhere you turn in your panic you see light strangled before it can reach you. Ghosts, rapists, bugs, whatever it is, it's there, and you can smell the death, feel the knife against your throat, count the hairs on his arm as he holds you down by the neck, or hear the chittering of a thousand mandibles eager for flesh. Take a little, and it's like going to a 4-d monster flick. Take a lot and it's a very scary unbirthday.

I hear the people who actually dig this like it the way some people like sour candy, but it's not my style.

The coffee makes me grimace, and I wave over a server since the girls already knew what they wanted. They wanted to know what I wanted, and that's why they were there. That and the two hundred I sent them all. No one's looking me in the eye, but their sideways glances at me all say now what? while they bullshit back and forth.

"Lasered my legs last night and wasn't THAT shit a long time coming."

"Smelled like a national park burnt down and I'm on the other end of the block."

"Says the bitch who set fires every time her thighs rub together!"

"Good thing ain't none of us can keep these legs closed then."

It's good, it's rowdy, and I'm outside it all. I've spent too long keeping away from them, being invested in them, for this to be natural and easy. They can feel me watching through the armor without speaking, but there's nowhere else to look but outside, and I have to just keep my hands busy rubbing a chip between my fingers under the table. Finally coffee arrives and I reach out for mine as a girl points her cup at me and says, "Here's to you," and I nod and do something with my face that apparently isn't a friendly smile when they reflect it at me.

I raise my cup to drink and another girl puts a hand over it. "Why?" she asks.

Now they're all staring openly.

I take a heavy swallow. "For Cherry," I say.

And some nod to that. But not Sissy. Sissy snorts and keeps scanning. "Fuck Cherry," she says. "This is about Lynn."

The laughter is gone and something else sits at the table with us. Something kind and quiet, and none of us know what to do with kindness, and its why they stare at me suspicious and why I can't speak.

And even though it's mistrust and discomfort, the fact that we're all feeling it is what matters. The pain comes again, my pain, their pain, it's all the same. With the pain comes the fear, the fear of losing any of them. Dying won't be so easy now.

I traded my funeral for yours, Lynn, I think to myself. You fucking owe me.

At least the food finally got here.

"God, fuck... I haven't had food, like food food, for a month," a new girl laughed weakly.

"Month of cubes?" an older girl asked. "Are you chipping that hard or what?"

"Fuck no, it's just rent, I'm clean, ok?" she stole an apologetic glance my way, adding "sorry."

"Rent's real," said another. "20% in 6 months? Not on government pleb."

"Hold up, we're rent controlled, is that a penalty?"

"I... don't know? Maybe. I can't follow all the penalties, there's alot."

"Well yeah, they're designed to be traps." The table's alive now, and this is my last chance to disappear if I want to, but for once, I'm interested. "They're posted 'publicly', but without a day pass AND a ride to city center you can't see them, so—"

"So you got to log in with your license number on the .gov," I say. "Lynn showed us how."

They look at me, and they can actually see me. I'm here. I cough, and ask, "Hey, uh... it's ... Rosa, right? Rosa?"

The new girl nods. "Yeah."

"Where is your window getting hosted?"

She answers and it raises an exasperated shout from the crowd. Rightly so, since she's getting scammed, and before long everyone's swapping trade wisdom. Everything Cherry knew and then some. I'm present. I remember more names. I remember we're strong and we survive, and that's not the worst thing that can happen.

I can be more than me if I stay here with them, I think. That's kind of like disappearing too isn't it? Death, he's the Rob that never logs out, he'll always be there. And here I was saving up so I could pay him myself for a ride I already got tickets for. Fuck that! I'm the one who gets paid!

I look out the window at an armed customer service rep. He looks nervous at the sight of us inside. Laughing. Comfortable. Numerous. I bet I could do his job. Make shit a little easier around here, let someone else get my Class A. We're strong, we survive, and we're pretty fucking smart. We'd just have to make sure your position was suddenly vacated, I think, smiling at the rep through the glass and watching him leave in a hurry.

Sissy gets a wicked grin and passes her phone around. Somewhere outside, a guy who used to be known as traphunter88 learned the same thing. Set his own apartment on fire, screaming where no one could hear him but his cam. Newsfeeds only got access to his last ten seconds of life. Even on her old phone we recognize the stained t-shirt. His voice, screaming "They're fucking inside me!" as he smashes at the safety lock. The coffee tastes much better seeing what's left of his face.

After The Big One

COOPER LEE BOMBARDIER

Payton hadn't been to the community center in years, but that night he attended the trans-masculine meeting. He walked the tree-lined streets from his truck to the warm glowing windows of the center. He wasn't unhappy in his life, not most days, just—so much of his life felt compartmentalized. He wanted to remember what it felt like to have all of himself in the same place at once. That sense of community he'd felt in his queer youth was lost to him now, everyone scattered to all corners, sticky little cottonwood seeds riding the wind.

Back then he was miserable and didn't like himself very much, but he had tons of friends. Maybe it was that he just didn't have time to hang out like he used to. There were plenty of younger guys who wanted Payton to be their mentor, their daddy, or the older guy they could work their shit out on, but he longed for peers, who could relate to being over 40 and more than ten years into transition, who were concerned about what came next beyond what letter appeared on their driver's license.

He took a seat on a folding chair in the circle, listened to the names and the pronouns – was he supposed to keep track of all of them? – and looked at the mostly young, mostly white faces. A couple other older guys sat in the circle. Maybe they could go out for a drink later? But then the facilitator announced that, in the spirit of being more inclusive, they now reconvened at a vegan smoothie parlor instead. Payton didn't want a kale-apple juice in bright lights. He wanted to sit in a dim bar with other adults and try not to feel alone. He was still grumbling to himself about all of this when it was his turn.

"Hey, Payton, he/his, I'm just here 'cause I want to connect with other guys like me." He glanced around the circle, smiling, until his eyes snagged up on some 20-year-old unicorn who shot him snake eyes.

"Excuse me," the baby unicorn lisped, their hand cutting a half-circle in the air, "we are not all *guys*! Check your misogyny at the door, okay?" This tiny creature seemed to Payton to be levitating off their folding chair with anger.

"No, pardon me your majesty, I do not believe I was hailing you as such," Payton boomed across the room, doffing his baseball hat. "Besides, where I come from, 'you guys' is a gender-neutral term, so don't gentrify my *vocab, okay*?" He stood up and turned to leave. The facilitator held up a pleading hand and Payton tucked his hat back onto his head and sat back down, surprised and embarrassed at his own outburst. He looked up around at the group through his eyebrows.

"Okay, Pie," the facilitator, "You've been warned before about cross-talk during the intro circle. It is not a place for your call-outs." The facilitator made air-quotes around "call-outs." Pie pushed out their pierced lower lip, and then reached down to fiddle with a rainbow-yarn legwarmer.

The group discussion went from restroom worries to letters for hormones, to a discussion about why this meeting wasn't a safe space for non-binary people. Payton sighed. He remembered dealing with restrooms, hell, he'd dealt with getting hauled out of public restrooms by security guards longer than half these people'd been alive. He just didn't remember being so snotty about everything. He had some important shit he needed to talk about, too. How do we live as adults in this world? Who is gonna love us when we are old? Where was a safe space to talk about what it felt like to fail, to lose something you put your whole heart in to?

Then one of the other self-proclaimed guys said: "What about the trans-masculine group being a safe-space for us, too?"

The facilitator stood up fast and clapped his hands three times. "Okay, y'all TEN MINUTE BREAK! Restrooms, including accessible restrooms, are down the hall to your right!"

Everyone in the room scattered to avoid the impending war. Payton grabbed his jacket in case he decided to peace-out the side door, before the baby unicorns all skewered the "binary-enforcing" transguys on their special sparkle-horns. He walked past another meeting room and glanced through the glass door. It was the trans women/trans-feminine weekly meeting. The place was packed. He wished that the two groups could meet as one sometime. Perhaps that would give the little brats some perspective: listen to all of the epic bullshit the ladies have to deal with every fucking second of every single motherfucking day. He walked to the kitchen area and poured himself a compostable cup of filtered water.

"'Scuse me," an older lesbian shouldered past him, giving Payton an air of friendly contempt that felt familiar. She wore impeccable biz-casual. He assumed, based on nothing other than his own defensiveness, that she perceived him as a traitor, that it should have been more important for him to maintain a life as an erotic placeholder, a desired object, than to ever figure out how to be happy in this world.

"Oh, pard'n me," he said, making his shoulders smaller and swiveling aside to take up less physical space. "You work here?" He tapped his own chest where a name-tag hung on her plum merino sweater.

"I'm the E.D." She, too, was defensive. He caught himself. She must have to work ten times as hard to be seen as legit when she had the triple-whammy of being a not-white gay lady. He now lived the bizarre existence of being perceived as having no empathy or experience with oppression. The unicorns saw him as just *The Man*, one rung below Dick Cheney on the oppressor ladder. He smiled.

"Well, thanks for all you do. It means a lot. This is a hard town to connect with others like you, you know? This place is like a beacon."

"Oh yeah," she cracked a thin smile, "the bat signal has been up for a few years now, people come here based on rumors about how queer-friendly, about all the resources we have. We've got to have a place for them to come."

"Non-profit work can be thankless. So, uh, thank you."

"Lisa." She stabbed out her hand.

"Payton," he said, and took it with warmth. A loud inhuman groan came from the open event room in the center of the building. Out in the street, car alarms blared and bleated into the night. Booms so deep they were almost inaudible, like someone driving past with the biggest subwoofers possible wired into the trunk of their car; the sound was felt more than heard.

"What in the hell—" The older woman's composure flickered. Then a screech, metal tearing. The floor rolled. Lisa and Payton locked eyes, he opened his mouth, and the cinderblock walls on either side of them shattered. The north wall of the building fell outward as the south careened inward, the community center folded into a parallelogram, cinderblocks snapped apart, steel I-beams wrenched, and a waterfall of shattering glass drowned out the screams of the trans meeting attendees.

Payton remained frozen in a small cave formed by a bank of cabinets and the Formica counter of the tiny kitchen. He waited for pain to consume him and then for everything to stop. What next, he wondered, how does death come? His eyes burned. Everything was covered in chalky dust he could feel but not see. His left arm felt wet. He listened for more of the sick deep groaning sounds, heard none, and inspected the wound. In the dim he discovered a deep bloody gash. He felt the rubble underneath him and found his coat, a red plaid mackinaw that belonged to a father he had adored and who had disavowed him long ago. He told people it had been a gift but in truth he'd stolen it.

He pulled the coat up close to his chest and coughed up a mouthful of dust. Felt in his pockets and pulled out a bandana. In the tiny triangle of space he wrapped a torn strip from the bandana tightly around his left arm, then wiped his face clear of dust with the rest of the cloth before tying it over his mouth. He moved to crawl free when he felt a shoe, and knew it belonged to Lisa. He found her foot, and followed her leg with his hands, brushing away shattered concrete, pressboard and papers.

He shook her torso. "Lisa. Lisa." He pushed a hand up onto her ribs. She was breathing. He crawled forward further, choking back a sudden urge to sob. Flashes of finding his mother sprawled across the kitchen floor. Little stabs of guilt for being so judgmental towards this woman. Not a time for feelings, he told himself. The microwave oven must have fallen on her from the top of the fridge. Payton felt her skull with his fingertips, gentle. It was bleeding like crazy, but it was intact. He let out a sigh. "Jesus-fuck-ing-Christ."

He remembered horsing around with his older brother in the woods as kids; he fell climbing a tree. He got a cut in his forehead and it bled so much his mother whisked him straight to the emergency room, only for the doc to discover a slice the size of a fingernail. Again he remembered his mother on the kitchen floor, his father looming. "Head wounds bleed all over the fucking place, Lisa," he said to no one.

He pushed the debris off her the best he could, pulled her sweater back down around her waist. He shook her again. "Lisa, we gotta get out of here before the rest of this shit pile collapses on us, 'kay? Wake up, sister."

"My head..." Lisa stared at the blood on her fingertips when she pulled them off of her forehead.

"We're both gonna be fucking dead if we don't get out of here, now." Payton stood, wavered, almost passed out. As a kid it was how he got to keep himself, willing himself to not black out no matter how bad the beatings got. He reached down and put his hands up in Lisa's damp armpits, yanked her up to her feet.

They picked their way across the destroyed footprint of the building. In the event area, the concrete floor was split in two. Posters depicting LGBT history were torn and folded over the busted blocks and beams. Ash everywhere. They passed where the trans women's meeting had been. Floor to ceiling bookcases were toppled in a logjam. Payton couldn't see anyone, but he noticed blood in the dust. The blinking white emergency light flashed.

He tugged Lisa forward. They reached the trans-masculine meeting. The room was open to the night. A great tree trunk lay like a heavy lintel across the space. Folding chairs were strewn around the rubble. It was break, so most everyone was out of the room, Payton thought. He thought about the other packed meeting. Not on break. They pushed on.

Payton spotted movement beyond a rough concrete chunk. A figure, bent over.

"Hey, is somebody there? We gotta get out of here!"

"Help me!"

Payton propped Lisa up against a jagged piece of standing wall. "Be right back, 'kay? Don't pass out on me." He scrambled over the debris and rubble and found a tall woman with lots of layers, raincoat over sweaters, skirts over pants, scarves wound in a cozy nest around her neck, all completely gray with dust, trying to lift up a steel beam.

"Help, quick."

Payton shoved a shoulder under the beam to hold it up. His blonde hair hung sweaty in his eyes. He groaned and pushed beneath the weight of the crushed support.

"Holy fuck, hurry!"

For a second his vision went black.

The tall woman stooped and pulled a body out by their rainbow legwarmer-clad ankles. The person was unconscious.

Payton stabbed his fingers at their throat, feeling for a pulse. "The unicorn lives! Long live the unicorn!"

"What?" The woman wiped the dust from her mouth and nostrils and glared at Payton. "They're alive. Let's get the fuck out of here."

She turned and strode toward the exit. When she reached Lisa, she scooped the other woman up in her arms like a kitten and marched out of what used to be a door. A power line hissed and crackled across the parking lot. Payton carried the young person, light as a duffel bag of laundry.

"What now, Bruce Springsteen?" the tall woman asked. She bent her knees and placed Lisa down on a grassy median. The neighborhood came alive around them as the ringing in their ears subsided. Chaos lit up in thin slivers of moon. Dogs barking everywhere. Occasional cries.

"We gotta get the hell out of here. If we're still around when the big one comes, we're fucked." Payton stared at the tall woman, and pulled the bandana down from his face. "Hey, how did you know that kid was under all that crap?"

"The other one, with dark hair, the *nice* one from the meetings? They were crying, saying they couldn't pull them out."

"The other one? Where are they now?"

The tall woman shrugged. She wiped her face with the elbow of her shawl. "Wait, the others? In your meeting?" Payton wasn't sure he wanted to know the answer. She shook her head, silent.

"I'm Judith, by the by. And you are?"

When she talked, she led her sentences with her chin.

"Payton," he struck his fingers off his chest in an absent tap.

"Anyway, they'd just called a break. About half of our group left to use the restrooms or to go smoke. Hope some of them got out. I didn't find anyone in the room...still alive." Judith's eyes welled but her face remained impassive. She pulled her torn raincoat tight, to ward off a cold that didn't exist.

"Pie, Pie! Are they dead?" Another young kid with a dark mohawk, probably in serious need of a shower even before the quake, ran up and shook the limp form on the grass. Tears had created muddy eddies on their dusty face.

"They're not dead," Payton said.

"Well, thanks for getting their pronoun right." Their anger hit the air like a fist. Then they softened. "Sorry. I'm Jazz. Thanks for saving my friend—"

"Listen, y'all," Judith said, casting a circle with her hands, "I'd love to stay here all night and have a coffee klatch with you girls, but Mr. Lumberjack here is right, we've gotta blow this clambake or we will so very much not be saved."

"We're *not* girls!" Jazz's mohawk seemed to bristle with anger.

Payton stooped to daub blood from Lisa's brow with his dirty bandana. The older woman whimpered. Blood caked on the crisp oxford collar of her shirt, and blackened the plum sweater.

"My truck, I'll get it, if I can. Stay here. Watch Lisa, make sure she doesn't pass out."

"Aye-aye, Captain," Jazz said.

Payton ignored the remark.

He turned and ran and everything hurt. The nearby houses had toppled but were clear of the street, not on fire yet. Payton wondered if the bridges still stitched the halves of the city together. He approached his quarter-century-old Japanese truck, pushed a tree branch off the side. It sputtered alive when he turned the key. The headlights illuminated a wide gap in the asphalt. He reversed away, swerved around a person who rushed out of the darkness, and headed back to the community center.

Payton and Judith lifted Lisa into the back of the truck and onto a foam pad under the canopy Payton used for camping. Judith tucked a musty sleeping bag around Lisa's body.

"I'll stay in back with her," Judith said.

Payton shut the camper shell door, picked up the limp form of Pie and placed them onto the bench seat of the truck.

"Get in," he turned to Jazz, whose crumpled cockscomb of dark hair listed to one side. How old could this kid even be?

"Where are we going?" Jazz climbed up into the truck and pulled the creaking metal door shut.

"Somewhere safe." Payton's eyes stayed pointed forward. It occurred to Jazz that Payton maybe didn't have a real plan. They didn't have one, either, so they kept their mouth shut. Just weaved an arm around the thin shoulders of their friend.

"East," Payton finally said. "Those were only the foreshocks. We gotta get east, up, now. Before the Big One hits."

East and up, east and up. A mantra that looped a crazy refrain in Payton's head as the adrenaline ebbed in his blood. His eyelids were made of lead and it took all of his might to keep focused on the road. Memories of last time forced their way in. Payton rubbed his eyes and repeated, first to himself and then aloud, *east and up, east and up.*

During the Cascadian Subduction, years before, the authorities had kept survivors corralled in the expo center. The same expo center that three generations before had held interned Japanese-Americans. Police shot people down in clumps if they tried to leave. When the aftershocks hit, everyone was drowned alive, dead tadpoles floating in a dirty pool. Payton's mouth went slack, remembering. *East and up, east and up.* He'd never sit still and watch shit like that happen again.

The highway narrowed in twists as they neared the limits of the city. No traffic, either direction. Somehow they were ahead of the crowd. Maybe the first bridge crossing had already been closed behind them. God only knows what people were doing when they got the fancy new emergency alerts bleeping on every damn gadget they owned. It wasn't gonna help.

"Wherearewe," Jazz murmured, cast in green and black chiaroscuro by the lights of the dash. They rolled the back of their head across the seat, one sleepy eye cracked.

"Almost to last city bridge," Payton said, grateful to no longer be alone with his thoughts.

Payton jammed the brakes. "Fuckfuckfuck..."

"What is *this*?" Jazz asked over Pie's slumped form.

"Shut it, just let me handle this."

Payton rolled the truck slowly forward. A couple of cars were pulled to the side of the highway, doors open. Two soldiers in full gear argued with a small group of people. Another couple of soldiers hauled a white and orange barricade into the highway. A soldier cradling a machine gun across his belly jogged up to the truck.

"Woah, there!"

Payton pulled to a quiet stop. "Evenin' sir," he said with utter nonchalance. Like he was a Mormon at a Sunday DUI checkpoint. He'd studied the language of dude long enough. *These are not the droids you seek, fucker.*

The soldier, probably even younger than Pie, rested a gloved hand on the windowsill. His right pointer finger lay straight out above the trigger. His helmet was way too big for him. Kid looked scared, too, Payton thought.

"Sir, the highway is closed on emergency orders. You'll have to pull along side them cars over there and your party will need to vacate the vehicle."

Payton glanced real slow over at those cars, then back over at the young soldier. "Okay, okay. Say, man, what's going on? I just want to keep my family here safe, you know?"

The soldier's eyes darted from Payton to Jazz to Pie to the camper shell. He squinted but couldn't see into the back on account of the window tinting. His mouth twitched. Payton noted each micro-movement. The other soldiers struggled to get a second barrier out of a camo-painted truck.

"Sir, I am sorry, but I cannot provide any information at this time. I am going to need to ask you to pull up alongside those other vehicles over there and exit your truck, sir."

Payton's hands gripped the wheel 'til his knuckles blanched. "Yes, alright then—"

"Scuse me, uh, sir? Sir?" Jazz said in a high, bright voice.

The soldier cocked his head and stared at Jazz. "Yeah?"

"Say, can I ask you a favor? Can you spare me a cigarette? I am dying over here. I'd owe you one big time."

The soldier stared. His index finger lifted a fraction and then pressed back down flat. He glanced quickly over his left shoulder toward his companions, who had finally untangled the barrier from a nest of others and were lowering it down from the truck.

The soldier walked over to the passenger side of the truck. He regarded Jazz, kid-to-kid, gender-something to gender-something else. He produced a pack of smokes from somewhere inside his massive armored vest, shook one out to its filter and tipped the pack toward Jazz. Payton swore Jazz batted their epic dark lashes at the boy, working their own nuanced language of gender, subtler than any he could decode.

"Thank you," Jazz said.

"Don't mention it."

"Sorry. A light?"

"Oh, right." The soldier fished through a cargo pocket and pulled out a brass lighter.

Payton was damned if the soldier wasn't blushing. Jazz bent their head down toward the offered flame and the soldier folded in to cradle it from the breeze, their heads as close as lovers, Jazz reached their left hand back and jabbed a pointed finger toward the barricades. Payton hammered the accelerator pedal. They screeched forward, leaving the poor boy soldier lost in a blue plume of burnt rubber and wasted chivalry.

"Hold on," Payton mumbled, as he careened toward the barricades. The two boys saw the truck bearing down toward them. They dropped the barricade held between them and jumped behind a truck. Payton's little truck shattered the wooden staves. Jazz swung around and looked back at the soldiers scrambling up from the ground, then sat back down and took a long drag off of the cigarette.

East and up, east and up.

"That fire back down there? What is that?" Judith said squinting and pointing into the distance toward the city.

"Probably the state line bridge. The feds probably took it out." Payton said without even looking.

"Now, why the hell would they do that, Han Solo?" She turned back toward him and the others.

"We've got to fill up these jugs with water," Payton said, "these taps are still working." He pulled water containers from inside the canopy.

"Who put *you* in charge?" Pie bristled, but the swell of anger only made their head ache worse. "And why do you have all of this shit in your truck?"

"Just be glad he does," Judith said, pushing a big square plastic jug into Jazz's thin chest. "Everybody, fill up the jugs. And drink. You too, Pie. Glad you're back on line here." Pie'd come to slumped over on the bench seat of the truck, alone, having no idea where they were or how they'd come to be in this truck that was way too butch for them. It was because of Payton's insistence on escaping the city immediately that they were probably alive at all, they now admitted to themself with great reluctance. But of all the people to get helped out by, gah!

Payton guzzled water and then splashed some onto his filthy face, carved away the layer of grime with his bandana. It left him with a raccoon visage, which made Jazz chuckle to themself. Payton dropped a big water jug to the ground with a thud.

"Okay, listen everybody. The cascade of these seismic events will activate every adjacent dextral strike-slip, subduction, or sinistral rift zone. ..."

Jazz made devil horns with one hand and turned to Pie. "*Sinistral*: our new band name!"

"What the fuck are you even saying right now, Mr. Dude?" Judith asked, forehead crinkled in confusion.

"I'm saying we should still get another 80 miles east to the other side of the mountains to be totally clear of the subduction zone. Military and law will have too much shit going on back there to come out there. And summer people are gone. I can drive you there, but then you're on your own, cause Pie here is right, I'm not anyone's boss." Payton bent and grabbed the water jug handle. "I've got a place to be."

"Like where?" Pie said, sharp and shrill.

It seemed patently ridiculous to them that anyone would have an agenda after a massive natural disaster.

"Not that it's any of your business, but I gotta go to my rally point."

"*Rally point?* Please." Pie folded their ropey-muscled arms across their torso and studied Payton with sharp eyes.

"My emergency plan... my girlfriend, Faith. We made a plan, before— if shit hit the fan, we'd meet up at this ol' fire lookout..." Payton walked over to the truck as he talked, and pulled a map out of the glove box. He stabbed at a red dot drawn on the map. "Here. I researched it, triangulated between her city and mine—it's far enough away from the epicenter of the Colossus' rift, far enough away from front country and other people..."

"You *knew* this shit was gonna happen?" Jazz glared at Payton. The guy looked seriously tired. And he kind of smelled.

Payton took a big breath. All his life he'd struggled to find a way to feel safe in his own skin, in his own life. His difference as a child seemed to magnetize to him both fondles and fists. He became obsessed with perfecting survival skills, making fire out of nothing, shelter out of wishes. The Colossus gave him something to work with, to prepare for.

"Well," he began, "After the Cascadian Subduction, the Pacific Plate went deep underneath the Juan De Fuca..." Payton stacked his grubby hands in the air one on top of the other. "Like dirty dishes piled too close to the edge of a sink—"

"But I thought the Colossus was a woo-hoo tinfoil hat story...like that giant brown dwarf comet that was supposed to come and smoosh us all," Judith broke in.

"Well no, you see, because the prior Cascadian weakened the Earth's mantle from the Denali Fault to the San Andreas..." Payton's hands jabbed the air, his voice grew more animated. Like he was channeling some public television science show, Pie thought. They fished a crooked cigarette out of a crushed pack and settled in for a mansplanation. Natural disaster, now, that could take a minute. Jazz handed over a rumpled matchbook.

"...And its upheavals deepened rifts as far east as the New Madrid fault and down the Mississippi valley. The shocks will reach the East Coast tremblors and..." Payton's shoulders deflated. He glanced around the others. He'd noticed this blankness drift across the faces of his old friends, and then of Faith too, until he trained himself to just stop talking about it to anyone. But it wasn't enough to make her stay. *You love an emergency more than you'll ever love me,* she'd said. "So what are we gonna do, sit in the mountains eating grass until the city is put back together, and someone remembers to come get us?" Judith dropped her hands onto her hips and looked at Payton like he was a stupid kid.

"Nope," Lisa said, her head back and eyes closed, calm as if she was working out the Sunday crossword. Everyone swiveled to look at her. She hadn't spoken for hours. "There is no city any more. Nothing to go back to. We're on our own, and we'd better keep moving."

The day after the community center collapsed, Payton drove til mid-morning sun cut in over the tips of the Doug firs. Pie kept turning the radio dial but found nothing but static. There was no reception on their cell phone. Eventually Payton turned the truck up the rutted gravel drive of a weathered ski cabin. By the time the women in the camper shell crawled out, Payton was already gone. Judith jogged around the gray, board-clad cabin, and found him ramming his shoulder into the back door.

"What are you doing?"

"Forgot my key," Payton muttered.

"Here." Judith pulled Payton back, cocked her leg up toward her ribs like a spring and pistoned her foot into the door, which cracked open around the lock.

"Jesus." Payton stared at her.

"What? Learned that in Krav Maga."

Payton cracked a weak smile. "Respect!" he said, walking through the splintered doorjamb. The cabin smelled of dust and stale air. A set of antlers hung from a nail above the large fireplace.

"Old family place?" Judith turned her head down to Payton.

"Somebody's. I have no idea whose."

"So—" Judith started to wind her thumb toward the broken back door.

"Here!" Payton pulled open a cedar chest. He yanked out several musty wool blankets. "We'll take these. I'll see what we got for jackets in the rooms."

"I'll check the kitchen for food," Judith said, adjusting fast to their new moral paradigm. They returned to the truck and each dropped a pile near the rear bumper, then walked back for a second sweep.

"Pie!" Payton came back to the truck and held out a green down jacket. "Put this on before you freeze."

"Ugh! It's *so* gross and seventies-old-man!"

Payton opened his mouth, about to tear into Pie, but Judith stepped forward.

"Look, you get hypothermia, the rest of us have to keep you alive. Put on the goddamn coat. You can still keep your legwarmers on!"

The small boulders of Pie's deltoids wrenched up around their ears. Judith crossed her arms across her large breasts and cocked her head. Jazz came over and steered Pie away.

"Good move," Lisa said to Jazz softly. She leaned against the chipped red paint of the truck, holding her head.

They loaded up the scavenged supplies: sleeping bags, two flashlights, winter boots, first aid kit, two old frame packs, and all of the canned food Judith found in the cupboards. She disappeared into the cabin one more time and returned with an old shotgun in one hand and a bottle in the other. The pocket of her raincoat bulged with a box of shells. She tossed the bottle to Payton, who held the 15-year scotch up to his eyes and swirled its contents in a slow circle.

"A little sumpin' for those lonely apocalypse nights," she said.

Payton's dry lips cracked in a big smile. Judith noted it in her mind like a rainbow: pleasant but fleeting, something she might not see again for some time.

"A gun? What next? Killing things?" Pie stopped loading things into the truck to glare at Judith.

"Maybe she'll use it to hunt down our breakfast tofu tomorrow," Jazz quipped. Pie's eyes blinked in shock. Jazz smiled softly into their shirt and continued stacking blankets.

Judith strode over to Lisa, whose office clothes were crumpled and caked in dirt and blood. She pulled up one of the blankets and tucked it tenderly around the older lesbian. "I didn't forget you on my shopping spree," she said, wagging a bottle of Advil by its cap.

"Thank you." Lisa tried to open the bottle with a flimsy grip. Judith took it from her and opened it up; shook three orange tablets into her palm, and waved Pie over with her other hand.

Pie sighed, and held out their water bottle to Lisa. No matter where Pie marked themselves on the spectrum, they'd never have anything common with either of them. To recognize having something in common with a woman (or man even) would mean to admit having something in common with an adult. When Pie thought about adults it was like someone was tying a plastic shopping bag over their head. They couldn't breathe. None of the options of how to be in the world seemed like good ones.

Judith inspected Lisa's wound. "Maybe I should dress this. Stick a steri-strip on it."

Lisa opened her deep-brown eyes and held Judith's blues in a steady gaze.

"Look up here, I want to check out those pupils of yours. I am afraid you are concussed, my dear." Judith held Lisa's chin up with her long fingers.

"You're being so nice to me," Lisa said.

"Why wouldn't I be? You're hurt." The sharp angles of Judith's auburn bob fell alongside her jaw. Lisa thought that Judith had the bones of Hollywood royalty, geometry that would only become more majestic with age.

"We're from different worlds." Lisa looked down.

"What, 'cause I'm all white and punk-rawk? Or 'cause you're so yacht club, is that what you mean?"

"Well, you do have white privilege. But also—I'm not trying to criticize you; it's just—not the same. How we came to understand ourselves as women."

Pie turned around from the tailgate of the truck and Jazz's head turtled out of the canopy. Their eyes searched Judith for an impending storm. Her shoulders came up by her ears then dropped as she let out a little sigh. She swabbed at the gash in Lisa's forehead with an alcohol wipe. It stung the older woman. Judith didn't apologize.

"Look, you don't have to believe that my childhood was a girlhood, honey. I *can* tell you with certainty," she enunciated the three syllables of 'certainty' crisply, "that is was not a *boyhood*."

"That's what some transgender women were saying on the land a few summers ago. They marched right in to our festival without a so much as a howdy-do and told us they hadn't been socialized as male." Lisa squinted up at Judith, who was backlit with sun, her expression lost in shadow.

Pie couldn't contain it any more. "Oh m'god! You're a *TERF!*" they screeched, cupping their hands around their mouth. "I knew it! TERF on the land!"

"Aren't we supposed to be using *TWERF* now, to highlight the fact that it's only trans *women* that the radfems *really* have issue with?" Jazz's painted nail poked the air.

Lisa and Judith stared at the two kids. Emboldened by their attention, Jazz dug deep and continued, "It's like the radical feminists got over the fact that trans guys were patriarchal capitulators because at least they still had vaginas and that mythical shared girlhood and even beards and balding are better than trans women to them because—"

Judith pivoted up from Lisa. "Thanks for your concern, but—"

Payton ran over and slid to a stop in the dusty gravel. "Where are they? Someone's on the land?" His chest bellowed up and down, trying to catch back some air.

"She is a *TWERF! TWERF on the land!*" Pie screeched.

"Jesus, Pie, I thought someone had spotted us!"

"But she is a *TWERF*, a hater, how can we be together if she is making the world unsafe for trans women—"

"Will you please just shut the fuck up?"

The force of Judith's voice made Pie visibly wilt. "When I need an entitled little shit like you to fight my battles, I'll just throw in the fucking towel. Jesus!" She tucked the tails of her scarves tighter into themselves and stalked off toward the treeline to the east of the property.

"This isn't Twitter, you two," Payton finished loading up supplies into the truck, "you're gonna have to think about something besides whatever feels good to spout off about in the moment."

"Uh, okay, *Dad*—" Pie started, but Jazz shot an elbow to their ribs. Payton tucked the embarrassment in his cheeks below the collar of his coat, hating that the kid was right. No matter how much he changed he couldn't seem to get his father out of his throat. A need to get out on his own bloomed in Payton and made his nerves zing with anxiety.

Lisa looked calmly from the overwrought man to the two kids. "Look, don't you all remember what happened in Portland after the Cascadian?"

Jazz and Pie looked at each other, then back at her, shaking their heads. They were in grade school. They remembered the drills and the cases of water bottles in the basement and the worried things their parents would say as they walked out the door for school.

"Well, it was almost complete anarchy until the feds sent in the tanks. All those people who killed their own neighbors over food? No thank you. We have to be careful of other people now. This world was never safe in the first place. And it is not getting any safer."

At first, Payton encouraged the others to make home in one broken-in-to ski cabin after another. He would be faster on his own, the supplies he'd buried would last longer for just him and Faith whenever she showed up, like they'd always said. She'd promised she'd follow his bug-out plan. He longed to see her again, disaster or not. But more than anything, he was afraid of being responsible for the others. Each time he brought it up though, everyone insisted on sticking together.

One place they broke in to had working solar, and they all stayed up late into the night playing Scrabble by lamplight. Payton got up from the table to stoke the woodstove. He squatted on his heels and goaded the flames with a poker, listening to the others, trying to place distance between them and his heart.

"She played ZA! That is *not* a real word!" Lisa flicked her finger across the table in Pie's direction.

"Is that a *formal challenge*?" Judith swiveled toward Lisa with seriousness. One part of this disaster was not having an official game dictionary to settle disputes.

"They use *they* pronouns. Not she." Jazz said with all the calm assertion they could muster.

"So, you two *don't* have genders..." Lisa asked with caution, fiddling with a tile.

"*Wrong.* We do have genders, and they're non-binary," Pie, too, was being careful. It came out sounding like they were speaking to a very young or a very stupid person.

Jazz piped up without a direct indication from Pie that they should get their two cents in.

"I reject the existence of the gender binary, so I am non-binary."

"Lisa," Judith said, laying out her tiles into the word X E N O P H O B E. "*They* don't identify as either male or female, masculine nor feminine. Isn't that right?"

"In my day, y'all would just been soft-butches," Lisa said, smiling. Pie wanted to leap across the table and chew her throat out, but forced a closed-lip smile back at the older woman.

"Shit, Judith you are slaughtering us all!" Jazz shuffled their tiles around.

T I E or T O E. *"Shit!"*

"It's not that I, personally, do not identify as masculine or feminine..." Pie began to explain.

"Really? 'Cause you kind of look on the more masculine end of things..." Lisa still smiled. Jazz squinted at Lisa. It was clear to them that she was not trying to egg Pie on, not intentionally.

"The gender binary is an artificial false patriarchal system which oppresses marginalized people!" Pie said, folding the worn arms of the green down jacket across their bound chest. A wash of warm rose splotched across their buttercream cheeks.

"Wait," Judith leaned back in her chair and held out her hand in a stop. "So, because I identify as a woman, I'm succumbing to the tyranny of the gender binary, is that it? And as for Payton here," she went on, enjoying taking up a devil's advocate position, "I suppose he's enforcing it! With all of that male privilege that just swooshed in on him," Judith winged both of her arms out and then up, like she was holding a golden trophy up to the heavens, "and now, our dear Payton, he takes up one end of the seesaw of gender, and I sit upon the other!"

Payton sat down on his butt on the cabin floor, looking weary. He pulled his ball cap back on. These sorts of conversations exhausted him—a waste of oxygen.

"Except aren't y'all are saying the seesaw doesn't exist?" Lisa tapped the table with her forefinger. She glanced around at the others, confused. "How the hell can Judith and Payton ride the seesaw if you're saying there is no seesaw!"

"That's not what we are saying," Jazz and Pie burst out in unison. Judith may have been fucking with them, but even Pie could see that Lisa was genuinely lost.

The younger two went silent. The world was going to hell in a handbag and the older people were crazy. Pie would have given anything, even their allotted can of food for the next day, to be able to tweet what these crazy old queers were saying. *Except*, they thought, *if they are crazy then we are probably crazy.*

"Maybe can we just dispense with the see-saw metaphor," Jazz said. "In celebration of our brave new world?"

"I just don't want to work with these categories that just feel fake and bullshit and oppressive to me," Pie said. Jazz slung a loose arm across their bestie's narrow firm shoulders and nodded at the others.

"Yeah, *none* of it works," Jazz said.

"Well, it didn't always work so well for me either!" Judith spat back. "But I found ways. Maybe you should see what gender can do for you!"

Jazz snorted. "You're hilarious."

"But seriously," Judith arranged her thick wrap of scarves into a snugger ring around her neck, "I don't want to be the only person utilizing a secret code for just me. I want to fuck up gender from the inside so that there's room for me. It's about where I fit and where I can be found. Not just what I feel like but how I want to be related to. Y'all can venture off the grid, children, but I like a map, even if I had to draw it myself."

"Maybe this is a stupid question..." Lisa began in her maple-syrup drawl. Jazz groaned and Pie swung around to shoot her death eyes. "But, what I don't understand is: if a person is of a non-binary gender, why are you always yelling at folks to tell them how they should experience you. If you are not of the binary, won't that just be obvious?"

She turned and looked to Judith for support, and continued, "I mean, people always called me 'sir' when I was in college and I had short hair, and

I am sure for some of Judith's life, or Payton's even, they were perceived as the wrong gender, or an incorrect mix..."

Lisa trailed off to the silence of the others, who stared at her with round eyes and mouths, but Pie didn't even volley back a retort.

Payton shuffled back to the table with reluctance.

"I don't know, everybody," Payton said, "I don't take other people's gender expression personally and how I express mine has nothing to do with anyone else—"

"But woe to anyone who tries to stand in the way of my gender—" Judith interrupted.

"Who stands in the way of your gender, Payton? As a man?" Pie shot across the table.

"I mean, just because I look like this doesn't mean I no longer have an experience of gender, of this one or what my life was like before. It doesn't make me "binary.""

"Pfft," Pie scoffed.

"Hey, Pie, at least now I have some fucking mental space for other things besides feeling miserable all the time—" Payton paused, unable to conjure what else consumed that mental space for the last few years besides preparing for disaster and trying to not feel like shit about Faith.

He pulled a hand from deep in his coat pocket and scratched his auburn beard, darker than his hair, thinking it through. "But every day it's like, how do I make space to be this man and be someone I am okay with? Being a guy doesn't automatically make someone the bad guy." Everyone stared in silence. It was the most Payton had said for days.

Jazz cleared their throat, the sound of a hamster sneezing. "I just— sometimes, like, I think we use all of these words, like, because maybe we're too scared or lazy to take the time to really see others for, you know, like, what they are."

Pie turned, seeing Jazz anew. They'd always thought of them as a newborn foal, wet fur and rubber legs wobbling to stand up, and now instead of bowing their head to examine their chewed cuticles like usual, Jazz turned and held Pie's eyes. The power of Jazz's loving gaze swept Pie's sharp comeback right out of their mouth.

"Well, maybe I don't quite get it all, but it kind of sounds like you all are fighting different battles in the same war," Lisa said, something clicking in place for her. "Like, maybe what you all want isn't really so different."

Payton stood erect and stretched his arms out and bellowed into the rafters of the cabin: "Well, maybe the gender binary is a social construct, but if so it doesn't matter, because *there is no fucking society anymore!*"

He sat down in a chair next to Lisa and let out a loud sigh. Judith started whistling the tune of *Ding-dong the Witch is Dead.*

"Did we already finish that scotch, Judith?" Lisa asked.

They camped several nights in high mountain passes and along forest service roads. The old rutted tracks narrowed, the woods healing over its wounds. Driving was barely faster than walking.

Jazz and Pie gathered kindling and firewood on autopilot. Jazz preferred the chore because it kept them from something more triggering, like cleaning fish or butchering rabbits. A few days of hunger eradicated Pie's staunch veganism. Jazz watched them gnawing a roasted rabbit leg with mouth agape like Pie was murdering a baby.

The pair crunched through the frost-crisped underbrush. Their exhalations made little white speech-balloons saying nothing in the air. Pie felt the altitude in their sinuses.

"You really think Payton's girlfriend is gonna find a way to make it down this far south?" Jazz asked over the chaos of branches in their arms.

"I don't know, I mean, how long can we live out here waiting for her? How does he even know she's still alive?" Pie's voice sounded tired. "He's *such* a drag, he probably doesn't even have a girlfriend."

"Why would you say that, Pie? He and Judith pulled you out of that building. You would have died." Jazz tried to keep a proud chest and eye contact with Pie. It was difficult because their breath kept fogging up the cold panes of their eyeglasses.

"Sorry, Jazz, he's probably a good guy. For a weird doomsday prepper."

"Okay, look, I overheard him talking with Judith about it when he thought we were asleep. I guess she's his ex. Sounds like she took off when he got all wiggy about the earthquake and making plans for it. I dunno, just makes me feel kind of sorry for him."

Pie paused, staring out through the pickets of white aspen trunks, black bands creating countless eyes on the thin white bark. "I just don't know what to think. Everything is probably gone. What are we supposed to do with that?"

Jazz placed their bundle of sticks down on the ground and entwined their arms about their friend's wiry-strong body. "I don't know how a person wraps their head around the end of the world. I don't know. There's no one to ask." Pie softened into their friend's arms.

"You can ask me." The two started at the sound of Lisa's voice. Her boots crunched frozen twigs as she walked toward them. "I came out here after Katrina. I lost everyone. The losing everything you can live with. It's the losing everyone that never stops haunting you."

Pie and Jazz stared at her. Pie's lip ring quivered and big tears plopped out of Jazz's near-black eyes, plop-plop, movie-star tears. The two stepped closer to pull Lisa into their hug.

Payton started awake, caught his falling body with his right palm into the near-frozen earth. Only he wasn't falling. Grunting, he pushed the clumpy bag away from his face. It was wet with dew.

"Payton," Jazz stage-whispered, shaking his shoulder.

"What the fuck?"

"Sorry, Pay—" Jazz took two hesitating steps back from the grumbling bear of a man. Payton's puffy eyes scanned the camp as he reached for his boots and his pistol. He noticed the dead fire's thin plume of blue smoke in the dark, Pie curled like a lost dog, and past them, two vacant dry spots.

"Where the hell are Judith and Lisa?"

"That's why I woke you! I was cold—s'gonna put more wood on, and noticed they were gone. I got scared—"

"Shh, shh, Jazz, alright? Let's go find them."

"What about Pie? Should we wake them?"

"No, let Pie sleep, we won't go far. Not safe for the women to go wandering off."

Jazz turned away, mouthing *not safe for the women* and hooking air quotes into the darkness. Does he practice sounding like an old dad in his spare time or what, Jazz wondered.

They walked delicately in the wake of the older man, trying to travel soundless and light through the woods. Payton stopped every few yards, listening to something Jazz tried but failed to hear. Jazz didn't get how his hearing could be so acute after all the loud punk and metal shows he mentioned he'd enjoyed going to long ago.

After about a half-mile of tiptoeing through the underbrush, Payton held up his right hand, his index finger pointed at the sky, his eyes looking to his left. How the hell were they supposed to know what this pseudo-military bullshit meant?

"Listen," Payton turned and spat a hoarse whisper into Jazz's ear. It tickled a bit. They remembered to be annoyed. Their eyes strained forward like that would improve their listening. A tendril of fear stroked across their neck. They longed to be curled up beside their best friend—but there, *that*.

"Yes," Jazz hissed, "Over there." They marched forward, chest broadened. They weren't going to let Payton be the boss-man any longer tonight. Though, if that wasn't what they wanted, they could have just left him the fuck alone, sleeping, and located Judith and Lisa themself. They spun around the coarse trunk of a large ponderosa and spotted the two women. "Oh!"

Lisa bent back against a mossy boulder, her bare legs aglow in the dark, her breasts free of her down jacket. Judith pumped her hand into Lisa, mouth clamped to her neck. Her layers of clothing contracted and expanded across her shoulders as if she were a blue heron contemplating flight. Jazz stood transfixed; the women's lust dropped a cool pebble in the bottom of their belly, a reminder of something they hadn't realized they'd forgotten. *Life.* Jazz felt the weight of Payton light softly into their back. He snorted over Jazz's shoulder. "Take a picture, it'll last longer."

Payton turned around and retreated. Jazz watched the women fucking for just a beat longer. Two beats, okay...three. When they turned back to camp, they smiled in the dark wet woods all the way.

"I want to go scout out past this ridge here," Payton swept the pad of his fingertip across a topo map. "Chance of a herd of mule deer here, and one will keep us fed for a while. We can smoke the meat so it'll last."

"I'll go with you," Judith said, looking up from mending the seat of Jazz's purple skinny jeans.

"You're needed here. I'll be fine, back before nightfall. There's another copy of the map."

"But how will you get a deer all the way back here alone?" Pie asked. "Let me go with you." Pie's sincerity surprised Payton.

"Hey, thank you. I'll work it out if I get lucky." Payton took Judith's purloined shotgun and the box of shells. He left the pistol with Judith, who placed it on top of her bag. He walked off toward the northeast ridge.

Judith stood back up as Lisa stepped near her. Jazz smiled, noticing Lisa give Judith's neck a drive-by caress. Pie mumbled something about nature calling and slipped away from camp. Payton's thin boot tracks remained pressed into the frost. Pie's own worn soles packed tracks along side them, then they veered off behind a dark mass of upturned tree root and squatted down to relieve themselves. Then Pie adjusted their clothes and kept moving.

They walked for hours, until a sense of time eluded them. The sun descended back toward the way they'd come. Barren snags of trees jammed their skeletal heights into the sky. The panic that Pie had reined in earlier began to whistle again in their throat. Their rainbow legwarmers were tattered and pulled, caught with burrs and tiny twigs. Pie had never been in a wild so vast, and now lost, alone, the majuscule landscape consumed their form.

Payton walked in soft fox-steps in a low lush valley on the far side of the ridge, lingered behind a scotch pine's lemony trunk and watched two deer. One stooped her long neck to take delicate sips from a tiny creek that rippled between small granite boulders. The other looked around in cautious sweeps, his black ears flicking.

Payton slowly raised the shotgun up parallel to the tree trunk and clicked the double barrel shut. Both deer started upright at the sound. Payton froze, the deer froze, and eventually he won. They resumed taking turns drinking and watching. He squeezed. The buck sunk into a tawny pile and the doe, black-glass eyes huge, skippered off into the underbrush. Payton knelt over the still-heaving ribcage. "I'm so sorry, buddy." He pulled a fixed-blade knife from his belt and gently slit the deer's supple white throat.

Far away, Pie heard the gunshot. It echoed back and forth against the ridge and beyond, one gunshot becoming so many ghost shots. They couldn't tell the direction of it. They'd never heard a live gunshot before.

It took Payton a good couple hours to gut and butcher the carcass to a manageable pile. He pulled a heavy canvas tarp from his pack, sought out some appropriate sized branches from among the deadfall in the woods, and quickly chipped off the tiny ancillary branches with his hatchet. He assembled a rough travois, loaded the carcass, and wrapped a flap of the tarp over the top. Then he stood, sighed, and tried to summon the energy for the long trek back .

An abrupt crunch sounded right behind him. A bolt of pain and a trickle of blood traced down the back of his neck. Payton's brain couldn't keep up with this new, immediate reality. He was struck again and fell from knees to belly on the pine needles and leaves. He could smell the pitch, the wet of the creek, his own body's musk. He wanted to sleep. The word "no" in hot white all-caps flashed across the blank screen of his mind. He forced his right eye open, saw a blur of boots.

"Shit, he caught us some dinner and even packaged it up to go!" Others (two? three?) bellowed loose-jaw laughs in response. "S'got a shotgun, see what else he got for us."

Payton felt rough hands on his waist, under his belt. His knife loosed from its sheath. He lay still, not wanting to alert them that he was conscious. He had no plan, no idea. He was fucked. Maybe the others would find their way to the lookout, to the supplies. Tell Faith that he tried. Sudden sadness surprised him. He wanted to stay. For them. These weirdo strangers. *The shit you ache for most comes in the strangest ways.* Tears burned in his eyes. He thought of them and smiled, the smile audible, almost a laugh.

"Aw, shit, our lil' buddy's wake now!" A shadow-form crouched low near Payton's head. He could smell the rancid tang of chew.

"Where are your people, pal? Got any others? Maybe some women?" He thumped Payton's ribcage with his boot-toe. "Hell, we'll take children. It's lonesome out here." The others guffawed. Payton tried to lift his head. The man closest to him sent him back down into the earth with the back of his heavy hand.

The voices in Payton's mind merged from Pie and Lisa and the others arguing over gender terms to deeper resonances and tones. Then a blip, like a swimmer breaking the surface of the water. He felt cold. Rough bark cut into his belly. The men had Payton bent over a deadfall Ponderosa trunk. His hands were bound so tight with the last bit of his own cord they were already swollen purple.

The men growled and cackled, he felt their greasy rough hands tugging at his belt and pants.

"We'll just find a way to pass the time 'til you tell us where your camp is," the tobacco-chewing one said, grabbing the hair at the base of Payton's head. "We're hungry, buddy." Another man yanked Payton's pants down, locking his ankles together.

"What the *fuck* am I looking at?" Another came over to inspect.

"What the—well, who the hell knows these days." The man unzipped his jeans and laughed.

Tobacco man came around to stare at Payton. "Fucking freak!" He kicked Payton's thigh, hard.

"Just kill him."

"We'll find the camp, with or without help."

"Well boys, a hole's a hole. Let's have at it 'til it fucking talks."

Payton saw flickers of blue-dusk sky, the clear gleam of Venus just making her way over the horizon. He heard the shuffle and the thud of the men's boots. Before they could reach him, hurt him, he tucked himself up in a faraway place, a spare white room cast in warm golden light and silence, a place he always kept safe and secret, away from the shell of a body that had hurt, could be hurt again.

"Oof," the man said, and collapsed heavy across Payton's back. A stone the size of a rugby ball thumped to the ground on other side of the tree-trunk. Payton could feel the man's erection pressed against the back of his leg. He rolled onto his side to slough the man off of his back, blanched when he saw the crushed back of the skull cutting jagged white teeth through hair and blood.

"What the fucking hell—who the fu—" shouted another man. A gun-shot silenced him. He accordioned to the ground.

The last man waved his hands in front of his torso; his sad little pink dick hung out of his fly. He glanced to the shotgun on the ground near his dead buddy.

"N- *no*- *no-no*, kid, no! You don't want to do that," his mock-gentle tone broke into his true voice. "*You little faggot,*" he hissed. Pie clasped the heavy pistol in both small, shaking hands and squeezed the trigger. The man looked down at his own chest with such sadness before he fell forward. Pie's lip trembled and they dropped the heavy gun. Payton scrambled over to Pie, and the two clasped into a desperate embrace. The valley held the echoes of the pistol shots close, keeping all that happened here from having any undue glory.

When they finally reached the fire lookout, Lisa gasped. A narrow ladder ascended up into a small room at the top of a spire of rusted steel girders, wrapped in windows. A few antennas poked from the top of the lookout, signaling out to dead airspace.

She turned in a full circle. With a clear sightline in all directions, the world was round, mountains in shark-teeth rows fading from purple to gray; there was nothing but the wild out there.

"Dear God." She buried her face in her mitten-covered hands.

"Hey, you okay?" Jazz placed a tentative hand on her shoulder.

"Yeah, yeah, I am. It's just—we're so alone out here."

"Well, we got each other!" Jazz said with a chipper up-note, until they let those words sink in for themself. Just each other.

Below the fire lookout tower was a small cabin. Payton smashed the padlock off with the butt of his hatchet and dug up his caches. There were water jugs, canned food, grains in airtight buckets, flashlights, a lantern, tarps, fishing rods, and a second pistol with a holster. They took watch shifts, collected firewood, set traps, cooked food. They played all the board games they'd stolen from the cabins along the way. No one would be coming to vacation up here next summer. They shared the small collection of paperbacks left in the lookout cabin.

Pie and Jazz built a shower contraption, but showering was something that still didn't happen too often. Jazz came up with the idea of everyone writing down things they were good at, and taking turns to teach the others. Judith taught them how to play poker, how to cheat at poker, and how to hand-sew. Lisa taught them grammar and the waltz. Pie taught them how to stick-and-poke tattoo and explained how to tweet and insta on a computer tablet they drew on a piece of paper. Jazz taught them how to tie the sailor's knots he learned from seafaring and how to spit really, really far. Payton taught them how to do sun salutations, how to meditate, and how to clean trout.

Often, the others would find Payton up in the tower, staring out toward the north, watching and waiting. Without any of them being aware of it happening, they coalesced into a unit. Despite their fucked up pasts or complete losses or disavowals, none of them could escape the gravitational pull of family that gently lassoed them in closer and closer.

Using A Treadmill, You Can Run Until Exhaustion Without Moving

SADIE AVERY

The cushion is making a rash on my face. I don't concretely feel it, but I'm aware its crisscross geography being carved into my cheek. It's like an alert blinking: *your face is itching and in mild pain. A rash is forming.* My body lets me know when something is wrong with it. Unfortunately for my body, I am drunk.

It feels like there are four or five of my body inside my body. This is an expected aftereffect of Greyhound jumpships, but knowing that doesn't make me feel any less awful.

It was worse back on the ship, where I wasn't entirely convinced that the fabric of reality wasn't on fire. My forearms opened and I could feel strips of skin tear upwards and blink into the sky. For a second I wondered if I'd accidentally blown all my credit mistakenly boarding one of the luxury cruises that fly up into the sun for laughs. I legit freaked out before remembering that, unlike the Henry Kissinger Martian Mining Subsector D Spaceport, those cruises would only ever be full of rich white people. In contrast, this ship was full of craggy-eyed riggers and a group of people with tattoos of eyes on their hands and big band instruments. One guy asked me if I wanted to hear a trumpet solo or buy a hack to let me gamble on my chip. And then we popped out of the jump: Mars. The Red Planet. The Really Big Apple. Etc. Between pulses of cerebral hammering and visions of dead stars

I wobbled and lurched here, this port-adjacent motel. When I stumbled in, the translucent-haired receptionist rolled her eyes, and you could tell she was probably thinking *Great, another first-timer, as soon as he's gone I'll have to pull out the ultravacuum and become closely acquainted with his vomit, which I'm sure he won't clean up, like a typical fucking idiot dude.* Probably.

Without my chip I can't project anything to watch, and I didn't bring a book, so there's not much to do apart from look out the window at ships tearing and booming into port. That and think, which predictably whisks me immediately into thinking about coming out.

I don't know why I'm so fucked up. They got rid of the last bathroom bill when I was a kid. Now it's taboo to have cis dudes play trans women on TV outside of universally groaned-at SNL skits, and there are a handful of trans women who can pass by TV standards who rotate around getting phoned in to play the trans coworker or whatever. They did that remake of RENT where they made it canon that RENT stood for "Really Everybody, No Transphobia!" Just a few weeks ago some guy who everyone says is the new Pynchon or DFW or whatever put out this interactive novel about a trans woman. Apparently before it became a staple, a lot of trans people were into the whole interactive novel schtick back in the old box-computer days, and he's paying homage to that tradition or whatever. I tried poking around to see if I could find any of the stuff he talked about, but I don't think any of it made it through in the big chip transfer.

But so yeah, it's common knowledge that, like, your problematic grandpa aside, basically everyone's cool with anyone being trans. Us rowdy gender fuckers have never been so aggressively tolerated in the history of ever. I really shouldn't be as worried as I am. And yet. Here I am. Cheap motel on Mars.

It would make more sense if I could say there'd been this long build-up of Gender Worry and Angst only relievable via adventurous space jaunt, but it was all pretty sudden and dumb. Last Wednesday after class I was getting day drunk with Leora. Leora's this gay cis girl from my Medieval History who's super cute, and like, we're both scared of boys, so. She said she hooks up with dudes every once in a while but tries to keep it lowkey because dudes are annoying. To be honest, I've been crushing. She's big into weird 'ios lo-fi pop and smoking weed and like, overalls. She does glitch art, that kinda shit.

I actually told her I was trans a few months back, which was kinda huge. She was cool about it, but I dunno, it was a bit weird. You could like see the cogs turning as I became The Trans Friend. It's been kinda simmering unspoken since then. I don't feel like she treats me any different, which I'm not sure if I should be thankful or angry about.

But anyway we're on the terrasse of some dive on St-Cat and she made this joke how being born with a dick is like an instant free ride for life. I was drunk and it hit pretty hard. I know that she's like, chill with trans shit and would totally apologize and be reasonable if I pointed it out to her, but I couldn't bring myself to do it. It's dumb, right, I'm sure she knows this shit.

I told her that I'd forgotten that I had work, slipped away, got another forty and plonked down in Carré Cabot. At which point, now unpleasantly, inescapably hammered, I felt less scared of sending a satisfyingly prolix good-bye-I-love-you-forget-me-immediately group message to all the big players in my life and finding my way into the Saint-Laurent than of maintaining continued interpersonal contact in flawless masculine performance. I sat in the mangy grass for maybe an hour then decided the next best thing was to modify my message to I'll-be-gone-for-a-few-weeks-I'm-safe-don't-worry etc, eject my chip, leave it in a ziploc in my locker, and hop on the next bargain ship from Montreal to Mars.

I can't help but wonder if coming here was worth it. I feel like I needed to get away from all the trash whirring around in Montreal to figure my shit out, but if there's an endgame in sight it's being blotted out by the two different arguments coming through the wall from the adjacent apartment and the constant sub-bass whirr of the mining drills all over the planet. Apparently when the drills start in the morning the impact sends up clouds of dust that tear across the planet at a few hundred clicks an hour. You hear stories of mine operators in puttsy little towns leaving their trailers and finding the whiplash from the dust coming through killed the family dog. There was a wave of labour protest a few years back because the clouds were turning into week-long dust storms that shredded up whole chunks of trailer parks. Then the storms died down and it became harder to be alive on unionless strike than it was to live in the flimsy housing allotted by the mining consortium that functions as governmental body on Mars. Night's coming soon and the drills will go down. Then I'll only hear the party next door.

One good thing, though, which delightedly surprised me at the dep built into the lobby in truest shitty Martian hotel form: to nMars whiskey is fucking cheap.

A few hours and ounces of whiskey later, I start butting my head up against the shit that brought me here. Like when a cat wants your attention: I brush my head against my pain, and then I back away.

I've tried looking for a genuine feeling to pin onto all this shit, and it's like trying to scuba dive in a bathroom sink: I can see everything clearly, but there's nothing to find, and I'm uncomfortably positioned in a very small space, and soon I will not be able to breathe. All the variables that should add up to me producing an emotion are sharply visible, but something along the way fizzles and the product is a white-eyed blank. Which presumably is all par for the course dissociation, a survival tactic from years of autosuppression re: gender, blah blah blah, we all took transsexual psych in high school. Still, it's busted. There's a layer of scary shit at the floor of my consciousness, and I don't know if I can crack it open. It's sedimented deep, and solid. Compact. Fossilized. Trying to dig at it flares up this whole deadening dissociative thing like being submerged in freezing, slowly-yet-implacably rising water, this whole thing completely antithetical to me being able to leave my bed or move or respond properly to stimuli.

I mean, holing up in the most unseemly motel this side of Olympus Mons is one approach.

I think for a second about getting a prepaid chip at the front desk to see if anyone's sent any really dire messages yet, but the interplanetary rates are always a few notches past obscene.

Instead I head onto the balcony. There's a hiss and a burst of steam when the thin commercially cool indoor air makes contact with the heavy sedimentary heat outside. Instantly damp, I watch the stars. They're all discoloured and spindly from the artificial atmosphere, but it's nice to think they're entirely different from any set of stars I've seen in the rest of my life back home. They seem to stutter against the sickly sky. After a while the rusty smell and the partying next door and the sounds of ships jumping into port like someone ripping a hundred pieces of paper at once fade into the background, and I don't even notice them anymore. There's not a single constellation I can recognise.

I am facedown on the carpet and the mounting rash on my forehead informs me I want to chew ice cubes. I like having those fuckers in my mouth because when I crunch them it feels like I'm crunching my own teeth to pieces.

The room doesn't have an ice bucket. The only container-type object I have is the now-empty 375ml mickey of whiskey I got from the dep, which means two things: I need to use an empty 375ml whiskey mickey as receptacle to fill with ice, and I need to buy another 375ml mickey of whiskey.

I feel scummy. The receptionist is on a chip call, saying "Babe, I gotta go, there's a customer—Rachel, I dunno what he wants, but it's kinda my job. Yeah. See ya later, dweeb." I catch her begin a smile which transitions to a glare when she sees how staggeringly hammered I am. She looks like someone who's actively trying to square her shoulders and project a don't-fuck-with-me look. I must look like the kind of goony drunk bumble-fuck who'll throw up on her floor or try to feel her up. I catch little streams of light filtered through her sky-cyan-dyed hair before she glares at me directly and I feel like dirt and look away.

Maybe she didn't really glare at me. Maybe seeming like a drunk aggro dude is more something I'm afraid of than something actually liable to happen. Who the fuck knows. There's no way I'm looking back at her to see. The ice machine is a small, off-pink cube on a classroom desk in the corner of the lobby.

The bottle holder at the bottom of the ice machine shrinks to the shape of the mickey when I put it down, contouring it, locking it in place. I push the button and there's a sucking noise and a smell like sulfur. It's one of the old models that generates ice from the air without spitting back out any oxygen to make up for what it takes in. They're outlawed on Earth to prevent shortages, but I guess either the consortium-government doesn't have oxygen sustainability high enough on its priorities to pass a law or it's illegal here too and this place just doesn't give a shit.

No ice comes out.

The receptionist is doing that thing where you wiggle a pencil and it goes all bendy, but also still pointedly not looking at me in that "you're not worth my attention but if you try to either steal that ice machine or pull any drunk shithead moves I will toss your silly ass out in seconds" way. It's pretty obvious I'm making her uncomfortable, right? I really really want to just get some ice and leave so I can stop putting this girl on edge.

I try the button again. Take two of sucking sound and sulfur smell. When I hold it down ice starts pouring into the bottle. When it's halfway full I let go, but the ice doesn't stop. I wait a bit, figuring the machine needs a second to wind down, but it keeps going. No slowing down.

I catch the receptionist's glance again. Her eyes are narrowed, both suspicious and scared, I think.

The mickey is like 200ml full of ice now. I click the button again. The sucking intensifies and the rate of the ice-stream doubles. We're almost immediately at 300ml and counting. I don't turn around but I'm certain the receptionist is watching me. My body blocks her view of the ice machine so I still have time to fix this. A few more frantic pushes of the button have no effect. The ice has now reached the part of the bottle that tapers inwards to the spout. It's rising exponentially faster and faster. I'm more terrified of making a fucking mess and ruining this girl's day than I probably am of dying. Ice cubes gather at the mouth of the bottle like foam. Fumbling, I cup my hands under the unbowed stream of ice. As my hands start to fill, I wonder if I can stretch out my t-shirt and hold ice in it like a pouch.

"Sir?"

The first cube to hit the floor bounces off the pile in my hands and skitters off towards the reception desk.

"Sir, are you okay?"

The next bunch come when I use one hand to yank the bottom of my shirt out and scoop the remaining ice in my hand onto it. In the second it takes me to pull this off, the bottle overflows. I instinctively put out both hands to cup the flow again and realize only with the crystalline sound of a dozen ice cubes hitting the floor that I let go of my shirt. I hear steps behind me and whip around, cupped hands still full of ice, to see the receptionist standing a few feet from me.

We make eye contact to the soundtrack of ice cubes cascading onto a tile floor. It sounds distant and faint, like the ambient low-volume roar of rain against the roof of a house.

I try to apologize, but instead my voice cracks. The sound made by the ice cubes pouring onto the floor could also be described as cracks. I realize I'm swaying a little. God, I'm *really* fucking drunk. In my peripheral vision ice cubes are pinging across the grimy floor. They look like cockroaches.

It occurs to me, ice melting in my hands, that one of the tools I read about online that's supposed to help with dissociation is running your hands under cold water and describing the sensation. Vaguely aware of the receptionist talking to me, I try to focus on the water seeping through my fingers, the pools of melted cubes in my palms. For the first time, I notice that the receptionist's nametag reads *Hi, my name is: Imagine,* and she doesn't look take-no-shit anymore, I can't even pay attention to what she's saying, but she looks fucking terrified.

We must make a funny image. This wasted goon of a boy-looking-kid holding a bunch of ice cubes and a puzzled-looking girl she—who is he kidding, *he,* the kid, the boy—sees from across the cafeteria and wants to talk to more than anything. Wants to compare notes, like do people give you and your girlfriend shit, what was it like before you came out did you ever feel so messed up all the time, is that normal or okay, please. They probably both think the other would win in a fight. He feels as though his entire nervous system is retreating and condensing somewhere just behind his skull. His face goes stony and stiff. The girl is shaking just barely perceptibly.

A pathetic attempt at a showdown: who runs away first.

It's me. Mumbling a *sorry,* I drop the ice cubes like the world's most halfhearted smoke bomb, grab the full mickey, and walk as fast as I can to the elevator.

As the doors close, I see the receptionist reach under the table and unplug the ice machine.

By the time the sun comes up (fuck, I should have gone to Venus, the days are like 120 days long there, I could drink all night for months), my drinking has hit the monologic stage. I'm back in my room, supine on the carpet, surprisingly empty bottle in my hand undecided if it wants to hold allegiance to me or roll for the wall. Once in a while I get this really intense desire to cry like a girl, by which I mean I'm crying, really crying, the kind of heaving that sends my whole frail bony torso thrashing, and someone's holding me who *gets it,* who believes that I'm a girl, like not-fucking-around actually believes me, not the half-assed shit where like, I dunno, I went to this queer poetry reading thing a while back and one of the coordinators gave a speech at the beginning about raising funds for ever-vulnerable trans women, but then later I overheard her wasted saying how she'd like to invite the big local trans lady poet to read, but she has a reputation for "being a dick". But whoever this is they're not like that, they get it and they're holding me, just barely keeping my thrashing body from flying away and saying *it's okay, you are a girl, you are a girl and this is normal it's okay* and I just keep going at it but it feels liberating for once instead of the kind of useless strained single-tear-and-then-two-hours-of-feeling-empty shit. I don't know anyone I'm not either afraid to come out to or afraid to talk to about occasional intense desires to cry. I really do wish I could have gone to Venus, beyond the tantalizingly long diurnal cycle—I read this book as a kid about these ragamuffin orphans carousing in its canals, and I've been in love from afar ever since. But then again, if I could afford to get there, a bunch of my other problems would already be solved. I looked it up once: the average income for trans women in Montreal is just shy of one-third the poverty cutoff. (There was something bad about housing too—I don't know. I forget. It was scary. I remember closing the application when I saw that. I asked about what jobs are like when you're out to this dude at the queer resource center at my school, somehow within a minute we were talking about something else, I don't know.) Ships to Venus cost like ten times more. There's a joke in the fact that my love for Venus is star-crossed. I don't laugh. The carpet is continuing the cheek-rash job started by the cushion with unbowed vigour. Most of my dreams take place somewhere in the vague fringes of a long war, without interruption, or ceasefire, or prisoners. When I meet my friends it plays out like: I say hi; they say hi, man; I fold inwards and stop paying attention to sensory information. Whenever I go into the student-run café at my school I'm thrown into panic by the hip tattooed queers that work there. I wind myself up taking too long to order or sitting with my legs spread too far apart and somehow ruining it for them. Their eyes gloss over me because the truth is straight boy customer #38457 is just boring. The rash means I won't be able to shave my disgusting stubble tomorrow. I invented constellations in the Martian sky but forgot the names I gave them. When I came in from the hallway, I noticed the laminated chart on the wall of mandated constellations on the bedside table. They had names like the Hotel California and the Ford Motor Company Star Quadrangle, and looked nothing like the ones I found. Excerpts from the argument being held in the hallway: "It's not your fucking money." "It's NOT YOUR FUCKING MONEY!" By the first definition of "to cry" in the built-in chip dictionary (to utter inarticulate sounds of lamentation), I have cried only once in the past year; by the second definition (to shed tears, with or without sound), several dozen. There is a specific technique to hiding your nail polish: form a fist, then tuck your thumb under your fingers. If the mirror isn't entirely and densely fogged, I don't get out of the shower, ever. Leora once asked if I hate my body, which I don't understand: it's not mine to hate. It never has been. It was decided for me that my body is the property of people who know better, like my parents, or doctors. In grade school I asked if I could do gymnastics instead of hockey and my mom laughed and said *I don't think you're quite flexible enough for that, love.* In the back of my closet at home there are two dresses (one fits), a women's cardigan I hate, a pair of high-waisted jeans, and a crop top.

Sometimes when I'm drunk I do this thing where I find the most dudebro-looking guy and walk up to him and say *Did you know I'm trans* and he looks confused for a second and I say *I'm a trans guy like I've had surgery and everything and now I'm here before you, a guy* and he goes *Oh, good for you man, what's that like.* And I talk about how rewarding it is, and how I love my new life or whatever, and how university is great. I make up uni programs to be in. *I'm in Reasonable Studies. Emotional Sciences. Interplanetary Geometries.* People ask if whatever school I say I'm in is accommodating to trans people, and I say *Yeah, totally* and then that I have to go to the bathroom. I distribute knowing winks as I walk confidently into the men's room. Inside, I fill my hands with cold water and wash my face, over and over again. My hands start to go numb, but it's a tangible numb. A numb I can feel. I leave the bar or party or whatever, bum a cigarette, and walk around aimlessly. I try to find hills to walk up or, if it's a residential suburban house party, I like to lie down in the street. Sometimes I puke in bushes.

The last party I did that at was the one Leora invited me to. I'm fucked up enough now that I think I can look this shit in the face. What does the face of my fucked up personal history look like, I wonder. If it has eyes, I don't think it blinks. There's an ice cube halfway to being a puddle under the bed.

A few weeks back Leora asked me if I wanted to see a movie then hit up a house party some friend of hers was throwing. I had weed in my backpack and I could tell that she wanted to get vaguely fucked up, so I offered to smoke beforehand, and we did. About half an hour into the movie, she'd been getting close enough to me that I could tell she wanted to hook up, so I put my hand on her knee and over the course of fifteen minutes, prompted by her leaning into me, I traced it up her thigh. We made out for a bit then I got uncomfortable in the theatre so I asked if she wanted to leave. I figured we'd go to a bathroom stall or something but when we walked out the door she stopped in the hallway to the theatre and started making out with me again. I could tell from what her hands were doing that she wanted to go further, so I knelt down and asked if it was okay if I went down on her. Honestly, the whole time I was mostly worried about someone turning the corner and finding us, but I dunno, she seemed into it and I guess it was like, what she was expecting, so I didn't stop. After a bit she said something about returning the favor but I managed my best wink and said let's save it for the house party.

We schlepped down to the party and lied to some people about being Illegal Commerces students from Brisbane, and when Leora said let's go to the bedroom I smiled weakly and finished my drink fast.

Memories about the night come up in two ways: either they drift up, slowly but not gently, and settle themselves over me, or else they ricochet out of somewhere unfriendly and embed themselves in my skin with a thud. I made the mistake of pressing up against my pain to figure out if I could see its shape and now it is awake, barreling down at me, spitting.

It's hard to put together any sort of timeline. I get images without much sense of causality. I sat at the edge of the bed putting my socks on, looking at my nail beds. I guess a friend of Leora's was there at that point because she asked what school I was in just before Leora took her by the hand and led her into the room's walk-in closet. The next memory is me in the bathroom realizing that what was on my shirt was probably just lipstick, but I felt like it had to be blood. I sat on the sidewalk outside and checked the shuttle times. I'd missed the last one. Leora asked if I wanted to get in a cab home with her and her friends, so I did. One of the friends asked how long we'd known each other. I said maybe about five weeks, and two of the other friends looked at each other and half-suppressed a laugh.

The next day, she sent a message: *Btw sorry for being a dick last night and hooking up with that girl. That was like just weird of me.*

haha no worries, you were drunk i cant blame you, I answered. I didn't want her to feel bad or whatever. I took a walk in the park near my house. Leaves were whipping around in little tornadoes. Leora sent back: *Also lets keep this sort of discreet don't need any gossip lol.*

Two thoughts floated up, bloated, patchy as corpses:

She tries to keep hookups with boys lowkey.

You Are Not A Girl, Idiot, How Could You Forget That.

It was shortly after that, for a period of about a week, I pretended I'd forgotten my own name.

When I close my eyes, I can still see shadows of stars from the unknowable future, and they are dead.

If you want not to die: you find out what people want you to be, then you perform it. People will let you know exactly what they want. You just have to know how to look. It's so easy. So ludicrously easy.

The drills start again for the morning with a subwoofer *whump* and a few seconds later a cloud of ugly dust slams into the window. Maybe it's just me, but I think I hear a whimper. I'll probably have to go back home in a few days. People will get worried.

Notes From A Hunter Boy: As Filed By Girtrude The Librarian

BECKETT K. BAUER

Hello bound book,

Well, I won you in a contest, and I promised to write so here I am. It was one of the contests we hold whenever a Man passes our camp and has time to stop in his wanderings. I think the Masters like to show us off, stir up our blood, remind us that what we learn in lessons matters in the world beyond our troop. This time our audience was a Historian. We didn't recognize the sign on his cloak but that's what he told us.

We played Tiger. First was Dhani, and of course I hit under his mask right away, then with Mattheu it was a simple matter of speed. Montiel was hardest – by then it was just me and the elder boys – but I jumped onto his back and grabbed his ears so hard I nearly ruined the mask. Commander Jee grumbled afterwards to be more careful, once I was panting on the ground, but under his angry eyebrows he was beaming at me. I didn't look Montiel in the face, out of respect, I mean. The elder boys are all used to me but it doesn't hurt to act modest. Instead I glanced at the Historian's bench and saw his eyes crinkled up, taking me in.

During supper he came over to sit at our stump. We squished to make room for him. He told us about his wanderings in long strings of words, so different from the secretive Merchants who last came through, or the Couriers who mostly just grunted.

He was coming from the mountains, and before that another boys' camp, just a regular one, with all kinds of Jobs mixed together. He said they numbered more than a hundred, and we wondered about their wandering, with so many boys, and so much to pack up. But apparently their encampments last more than a year, sometimes. A year, in one place! We all found this rather Womanish and said so.

But the Historian said it doesn't do to measure Manhood like that. He said apprentice Cartographers relocate every *morning*, does that make *us* Womanish? That shut us up. He also told us of a camp of young Diplomats, with entire libraries printed on rice paper so light one Mule could carry it all; and apprentice Astrologers, who have lessons in the dead of night, calculating with their Masters far from the lights of cities.

Someone asked what was he *doing* at all these boys' camps and he said, "Taking notes." "Notes for who?" The Historian said "Women" and we sat up even straighter. He said he was conducting research for some Professors at a university in Litentia. "I'm wandering there now," he said, "to drop off some scrolls," and our eyes got big, even though of course Litentia's just down the river—we've spent enough time memorizing maps and we know where the cities are, where Women wait, rooted in the ground, waving softly in the air. Not that it matters now, but we always know where the Women are.

We asked how often he visited cities. He said it depended. "How *long* do you stay?" someone asked, rather rudely, but the Historian just smiled and said, "As long as they need me." Some of us wondered if he was rather Womanish himself, but we liked him anyway and he answered our questions until it was time for bed. Everyone got up but the Historian pressed my arm and murmured, "I have something for you."

My prize! I was thinking of last time, when Jorj won at wrestling, and the Merchants gave him a green glass bottle that doesn't shatter. I'll confess when he pulled you out, with your smooth yellow sheets all bound in leather, I wondered if he'd made a mistake. "It's more for my benefit than for yours," he admitted, explaining he might collect it for his records some day. He said I should write whatever I wanted, everything was History, no matter if I was vanquishing Tigers or finding a tree to spit phlegm under.

"But I hope it can be a gift to you, too." He was looking at my face carefully. I told him thank you very much and somehow I wasn't even lying. I've liked writing reports and I like flexing new muscles and I'm curious, little book, about you. Don't tell the other boys. I'll try to chronicle more when I can.

Hello, book,

Something interesting happened, though I'll tell you the boring parts, too, since that's what the Historian wanted. The Ram's horn blasted us awake before the sun. I stood ready for Commander Bike while some boys were still lazing in their bedrolls. Then exercises, the elder boys in front, the youngins behind. Standing in the meadow with your teeth chattering, waiting, is hard. But once we start stretching I never notice the discomfort of the wild. I notice nothing but the feeling of returning to my body like porridge into a bowl, ready to run, to fight, all my muscles alive.

Once orange streaked through the sky I looked up at the Masters to see if it was about breakfast time. To my surprise I saw Commander Bike and Commander Jee with their heads bent together, looking straight at me. I blushed and focused on my form until the ending chant, but as everyone was filing away Commander Bike walked up to me. He told me to jump. I did, as high as I could go. He nodded and said, "Come with me," and we marched to the supply caravan.

I'll admit I wondered for a moment if he was going to grant me armor, like I'd dreamed – "you're ready to go off on your own, Malkim, the world's youngest Hunter!" Instead he pulled out an odd small shirt, with laces like a boot. He tossed it in my arms. "It's a calmshirt," he said. "You might want it soon."

We passed it around at breakfast and a few boys looked impressed but Dimitree examined it with raised eyebrows and then dropped it back onto the stump. "It's for your globs," he said, and some boys went "ah" and nodded. I put a hand to my chest. "What do you mean?" Zak reached over to pinch one and I slapped him away. "They're not much...."

"But they're gonna get big," said Dimitree, smirking, "big and dan-gly. Down to your knees." He mimed hunching his back under the weight of them, heaving them out of the way to catch an Animal, and some boys laughed.

"*I'm* dangly?" I growled, and to make my point I kicked between his legs, which he barely blocked. We dove at each other and he grabbed me by the chest—"Camel!" and I grabbed him back. "Snake!" Some boys pulled us apart, grinning, but I feel okay about it because I could have clobbered him.

I tried it on later in the tent and it was comfortable enough, helpful when I jumped. I suppose this means they'll swell more, like they do on some Men, even some elder boys, already—Yan. Portensio, I think. Herry? But theirs don't dangle to their knees, they do fine. Commander Flant had big ones, and he went off to hunt Elephants.I suppose they must get in the way sometimes, but then, so do turned knees and balls and shaky hands. Everyone has something.

It seems I'm racking up possessions! First you, now this shirt. I'd feel like a Woman about it but you're both small and easy to carry.

Dear book,

Today I misplaced my leather gloves and went back to the practice fields to look for them, and instead found Pytur and Franco groping each other beneath a tree. They were too engrossed to notice me, and I would have ignored them except at second glance it looked like their gens were touching. I flattened myself to the ground to watch, holding my breath for the catastrophe to rain down on them. Of course I was frightened, though I'll admit part of me was eager to see what happened so I could tell the other boys. Perhaps there would be an explosion. Or maybe it was just boils, like Dimitree says. Whatever it was, I wanted to know.

But nothing happened, besides the usual noises. Finally I couldn't stand it, so I straightened up and marched over. They saw me and sprang apart right away. By the time I reached them they were just lying side by side, arms wound round each other, no gens in sight. "What do you want, Malkim?" Pytur sighed.

"How were you doing it?" I asked.

Their guilty look made me certain my eyes hadn't deceived me. "Doing what?" they both said at once, and Pytur added, smiling, "Groping? *Surely* you know..."

"Your gens were touching," I said, but they denied it, said my vision was cloudy—hardly possible, with my performance at archery today. Finally Franco burst out, "*Malkim.* You might think you're an elder boy but you're not yet. Get your bony self out of here." I should have pulled him off Pytur right there and slugged him but I just left.

Later I told Zak about it and he also said I must've seen wrong. "Nobody touches gens," he said. "They wouldn't dare."

"They were," I said. "Snake in a hole."

"Then why didn't anything happen?"

"Maybe it's not actually dangerous."

"Of course it's dangerous."

"How would you know? Have you ever tried?"

"I'm not an Animal, am I?"

"So you don't *know*."

"What are you saying? That the Masters have been lying to us all our lives?" I almost said yes, maybe they have, then saw the look on Zak's face and we both started laughing. If the Masters were liars we'd have died long ago, from lightning or Beehives, Bears or bad mushrooms, and there'd be no more Men.

"But still," I said, "we don't *know*."

Zak said why do we need to know, when there's hands and lips and things that are so good for groping already. "Unless you can't get into that," he raised his eyebrows, and I scowled. Of course I can. That felt like the end of it, except then we stared at the horizon for a while. Finally we grinned at each other and he grabbed my head under his armpit and I fought him off and that was the end of that.

Dear book,

A troupe of Players wandered by this afternoon and gave us a show. I'm sure the Masters traded them well for it. We sat on logs under the cloudy sky until a bell rang to hush us.

A backdrop of green painted hills rolled down and a boy about my age, an apprentice probably, skipped in front of it. "The Tale of the Bear-Hunter and the Sweet Young Farmer!" he yelled. Then a Man paraded out, and I gasped because it was one of *us*, a full-grown Hunter, with the sign on his armor and everything. I caught Dimitree's eye, who was sitting next to me. "What's he doing here?" He whacked me. "*Think*, Malkim."

Oh yes, I remembered, these were Players, and skillful ones too. I was almost fooled again when a Player walked on who looked just like an illustration of a Farmer, made into flesh. She had the dirty coveralls, sign and all, and that strange floppy hat, and thick gloves, a spade, a wicker basket. She (he) couldn't have been a Woman but I was almost fooled.

She planted a seed into a brown wooden box and a sprout crept up – a puppet, sure—it got bigger and bigger, thick as my wrist, taller than me, and bubbled out ears of corn. She sprinkled blue water on it and danced happily as it grew. Somehow, this moved me, and my mind flew off elsewhere—to farms, to fields, and I imagined green things sprouting up around me, and then I imagined it slower, a green little hair one day and the next day a finger, or maybe a week later, because it takes so long, for things to grow. I imagined staying... and waiting... and going *home*, under solid stone, to wait... from now until my skin shriveled... pressing my feet over the same path always, shaping it... and never wandering away....

Luckily the play was so exciting I couldn't think like that for long. There was a Bear whose jaw really opened and closed, showing huge white teeth, and blood spurted when the Hunter killed it. He pulled the Farmer out and she gazed lovingly at him and then they kissed and ducked behind a screen and their shadows groped in a strange way.

When the screen came up the Hunter buckled on his sword, kissed the Farmer one last time and marched off without looking back, while she sighed and picked up her shovel. I suppose that's how love is between Men and Women. Then it was over. The Players bowed, beaming at our applause, and an older Man strode out who must have been their Director, though he was nothing like our Masters. He was an ornamental, with a long colorful gown that clung to his body, and strings of beads around his limbs and in the braids of his hair.

He thanked us for our attention and said the entertainment didn't have to end here. He looked at our Masters. "If you or your boys seek further pleasure, we invite you to our encampment tonight! Just across the stream. I'm sure we can work out a bargain." We perked up but Commander Jee declined with a grim smile. "I'm afraid our boys are a bit too young for your kind of fun," he said, and gave the Director a long look as the elder boys opened their mouths in protest.

I wonder what kind of fun we're too young for and keep straining my ears across the stream for clues. We've been guessing mad things – firedancing, Froglicking, Goatgroping – finally Kyro, sewing lining into his socks and annoyed with us, said it was probably just a bonfire with grog or shmuf or another of those medicines. "They probably just don't want us getting sick or acting fools." Killjoy Kyro, I suppose he's right. I'd still love to go but the Masters know best and anyway, I also like writing in you, in the blue light before bedtime, my pen stalking thoughts like Animals. Besides, my mind's still spinning with secret thoughts about Women on farms, Women in cities.

Dear book,

As it turned out, that wasn't the end of my night after all. Some time after I tucked you away and went to sleep I awoke to Zak's warm hand shaking my shoulder. I bolted up and grabbed for my knife but he jumped back before I could strike.

"Come on," he hissed, when I'd put my knife away. "The elder boys were allowed to go to the Players after all. I heard them leave. They're having a lark. Let's go!" Nervous protests entered my head, but Zak's eyes were gleaming, so I shrugged on my coat and better hose and off we ran.

"You didn't shake anyone else up? Dimitree?"

"They'd notice a whole fleet of us escaping, wouldn't they? Anyway, we're the most attractive." I snorted. "Or the oldest-looking, at least." I wasn't too sure about that, either – Zak has his crackly voice but what do I have? I thought about the calmshirt back in the tent and shrugged.

Soon we heard faint music, then could smell out the bonfire and follow its glow. A flickering orange mass writhed, and as we got closer it resolved into Men: dancing, playing instruments, sitting by the fire, yelling. All the Players were older than us, out of costume now, ornamental as their Director. We hesitated until we spotted our elder boys among them, then slipped onto a log by the fire.

Quickly enough a Player noticed us and shouted that we were out of drinks. Just as quickly steaming mugs were passed our way. It was grog, I knew that burning, so we sipped carefully, staring around, hoping the elder boys were too distracted to notice us. They certainly *were* distracted, but not enough. At the end of a song Yan stumbled over and said, "You're not supposed to be here." Zak grinned like he does and said we'd gotten special permission. Yan's eyes lingered on me, then he shrugged. "Be careful!" he called as one of the Players pulled him back to the dancing. "Don't be stupid!"

I didn't feel stupid, though, my eyes were open and my thoughts were jumping. I'd never seen so many ornamentals before, Men who catch your eye; I couldn't help seeing them as puffed Birds, as Animals (though of course some Animals are more like us). I noticed the globs on some of them, pushed up to the openings of their shirts somehow, a pleasant effect, soft pretty things instead of an inconvenience. Little moons. Some Men had chest hair, swirled into patterns as complex as tree bark. They had jewels

pressed to their skin, and beads, braids, paint on their faces, their fingernails, gowns that shimmered and flowed....

It looked like an awful lot of work. I wondered how long it must take
them to get dressed; how many supplies they needed, to stay so pretty.
Wasn't it all a bit Womanish? I asked one Player about it, and he rolled his
eyes. "Really? Don't you lot have a whole armory to lug around?" I blushed.
"Well, we're strong enough to carry it all." He challenged me to arm-wres-
tling and we strained but I beat him eventually. He was stronger than he
looked.

Zak meanwhile had finished his grog and possibly another. He tugged
me by the arm—"Malkim, let's dance!" We joined the group by the fire and
made fools of ourselves, but nobody seemed to mind. "Can you imagine if
we'd been assigned to this life?" Zak shouted, waving his hips in a clumsy
imitation of the Men around us. "Can you see me as a Player?" I grabbed
his hands and we giggled and twirled round. Sometimes we jumped to the
music and sometimes we partnered with Players who taught us steps.

Dancing, how marvelous! Like exercises but freer. Though we hardly
ever dance in the troop it felt very familiar. It reminded me of something
I hadn't recalled in years: a big bonfire like this one, the same huge black
sky, and figures with instruments, only in the memory they're faceless, and
much taller than me. And there are boys all around me and we're spinning
in circles—but it was so long ago, not this troop or kindercamp, so we must
have been *kids*, not boys, and Women at the instruments. I wish I could
remember their faces.

Another thing I thought of, especially when we paired off, was groping—hands on my back, mind relaxing, moving bodies with blood rushing through. There was one Man in particular who taught me elaborate
steps, grinning at how quick I caught on. He was pleasant to look at, a bit
older than the elder boys, with full globs and faint hairs over his scarlet
lips. But he was softer than any Hunter-boy I'd touched—his face shone
smooth, Womanish even, unweathered by the wild. I reached a thumb to
touch it and asked how he got so soft. "We have lotions," he laughed, and
then raised his eyebrows. "I keep 'em in my tent. I can show you if you like."

There was something in his tone so I asked, "Do you mean groping,
too?" He laughed again. "Well, yes, if you're interested. That's what your
Masters traded for, no?" I looked around and noticed Zak was gone, and
some of the elder boys; the ones left were pressed close to their partners.

Was this what the fuss was about, then, groping with Players? Strangers, ornamentals, grown Men? I thought with some annoyance of other things the Masters say we're too young for, guard duty, broadswords, when once I snuck into the supply tent and wielded one easily. "I am interested," I said to the Man, and he wrapped his shawl around my shoulders, pulling me close.

"I'm eggy, by the way," he said, as we walked. I wondered: Where had I heard that word before? He said, "Don't give me that look, you never can be *sure*, you know." I didn't know. He frowned at me. "This is the part where you say, 'I'm eggy, too, Samn!'"

"I'm eggy, too, Samn!"

He smiled. I saw a clearing with tents in the distance, lit up with lanterns, and shadows flicking inside. "What do they teach you Hunters? You've got to say it, *you* especially. You could be anything, you look so young." We drew near one of the tents, small enough for one Man. "Though I did guess. Glad I was right. Why mess with semmy boys when you don't have to?" He held the flap and I crouched in, and then we were sitting side-by-side on a bedroll, in perfect darkness. I thought of asking for some light, so I could see how Players lived, but then he drew closer and soon enough we were groping.

It felt a little strange, dreamlike, groping with someone I hadn't lived alongside every day since kindercamp. "He's not even a Hunter," I kept thinking, but I was having fun too. I could have learned a lot, tricks picked up from long wanderings, across lands I've never seen. But I'll never know because after only a few minutes I heard my name faintly, not from my Player's mouth but somewhere outside. "Mal-kim!" "That's me," I mumbled, freezing—"Malkim! Get out here this instant!" and then I could hardly breathe because it was Commander Jee's voice.

I didn't even think to say goodbye or thank you—I yanked my clothes straight and dashed out, only to stumble directly into Commander Jee himself. He yelped and grabbed my shoulders, stooping to my height.

"Malkim!" His eyes were huge, looking me up and down, and I waited for him to explode at me, but he just dug his nails in, breathing like after a hunt. There was a rustle behind me—the Player stumbling out with a lantern. We stood there with light on us as everyone took everyone in.

Suddenly Commander Jee did something very strange. He pulled me to his chest and wrapped me in his arms, so close I could feel his lungs shaking. He put his cheek on my head. I thought I must be dreaming. Maybe I was—when he pulled away he gave my arm a violent tug, turned, and marched us back to the bonfire, with no sign of tenderness on him.

Commander Bike was there, holding Zak upright, and exchanging heated words with the Players' Director, who was supporting the apprentice boy Zak had been dancing with.

"—unleash your boys with no training—"

"—I assure you, the ones we *sent* were all well-aware—"

"—no protection! If I hadn't caught them in time—"

"—but you *did*—"

"—do you think we have the stores to wander all the way to a city? We just performed our whole repertoire at Litentia, we can't go back—"

"—well, Goldcastle is just a bit—"

"—that's hardly the *point*, is it, we don't want to lose our youngest Player, we've been training him—"

"—not *lose*, you'd gather him soon enough, if you wandered back—"

"—oh, *well*, maybe you wouldn't mind letting one of your boys go through that ordeal, and so young, but in *my* estimation—"

"Enough," growled out Commander Jee, and everyone turned to look at him. He said he humbly begged pardon for the distress we'd caused – giving me another shake and not looking humble at all – but luckily we'd proved too idiotic to harm anyone. "Rest assured they will be punished," he said, "and receive the proper education. We had *hoped* it wasn't yet necessary." He said more to the Director I didn't hear because I was flooded with dread. A yank on my arm and then the horrible, dark, silent march back to camp.

But so far our only punishment was being excused from activities today, which was really more of a kindness. Zak's too ill to move from his bedroll and meanwhile I got to pour all this out. My hand hurts now, I think I'll get a bite to eat.

Dear book,

I've missed you and when my punishment ended last evening I was tempted to run straight in and write. Instead I made myself play Fleet Foot with the other middle boys, so I could prove Commander Bike was right, nothing has changed, I'm still one of them, a Hunter. He *was* right—they welcomed me back with happy shouting, and we had fun like always, *and* I got to be Chief Floot and caught more tails than anyone.

So maybe I'll take Commander Bike's advice and stop drawing lines in my mind between us. I've been staring around, at gens when they're out, and bodies if not, because even under our winter layers you can tell, sometimes, or guess, once you know the clues. I *know* the others' bodies, I see those shapes every day of my life; but now it's like they're whispering to me in a secret language, or like they're made up of *parts*, chopped up, instead of one solid thing. My own body too. And when I'm alone I conjure pictures in my head of every Man who's crossed my path, thinking back for globs (because they mean MILK!), or voices (I don't know why), or hair sometimes (though not on your head, and not the color, nor the color of your skin, as far as I can tell).

It got in the way of sleeping, and eating too, and lessons certainly, and eventually Commander Bike summoned me into his tent. I started crying and tried to hide it, but when he sat down across from me he stared. "What's all this for?" I blubbered out, "You're going to reassign me, aren't you?"

He was silent for a moment, then asked in a gentle way why I thought that. "Because I'm not fit," I mumbled, "I'm only good for... making... babies." The words sounded strange, out in the air like that. Commander Bike held his face very still.

"Because you're eggy?" he asked, and I nodded.

"Malkim," he sighed, "do you know how many eggy Hunters there have been?" Our own Commander Flant, for one. Sir Rourathon the Fierce, for another. "*Really?*" "*Yes*, really. *He* even birthed a baby, actually." I buried my face in my arms. "But you don't have to!" he said. "Malkim, there is a Job called Birther, but do you really think half our people should be assigned to it?"

I said I just didn't see how I was fit to be a Hunter if any stupid Human with an extra finger of flesh could make me fat, slow, delicate, perhaps even kill me, force me to a city and who knows if I'd return?

He pulled his lips between his teeth. Finally he said, "Listen. They assigned you to be a Hunter because they saw a Hunter in you. If you don't see him too," he smiled, "you're less aware than I thought, boy."

It was something to hear that from a Master, and finally I smiled back. When I was leaving the tent he clapped me on the shoulder. "Just be careful who you grope, okay?" *Not anybody, never again*, is what I thought. "Do your herbs like we taught you. Otherwise, stop thinking about it!" He patted my hair and that was that and I found I could sleep again, this was about a week ago, and I'm back to my usual self in lessons, a relief.

But a few nights later I bolted up in bed, horrified, because Commander Bike was wrong. How could I be a Hunter, or a Man at all, when this womb in me is just like a city with elastic walls, and all those eggs, Women waiting? And aren't seeds like wandering Men? I shook Dhani in the next bedroll and we crept out behind the tent, huddling in the cold, and I told him about it. His eyes grew serious and he said I was being silly. "They'll wander out when you bleed, don't you know?" He looked up at the stars, bit his lip, and then ventured that really aren't all bodies like cities, filled with skeletons and kidneys and things that never get to leave; but so much wanders too, blood and sweat and urine and breath, so aren't we all like Women and Men combined? Cities and the wild?

Somehow Dhani's mad thoughts, under those freezing stars, made me feel better, they often do. Anyway if anyone should be reassigned it's Dhani, who thinks like that and cried once gutting a Rabbit—he could be one of those holy Betweeners who make a home of a mountain, then wander to another years later. Next to him I remember, of course I'm meant to be here, a Hunter, a Man, to the ends of me.

So I'm feeling much better. What else has happened? A few days ago there was a Raven making off with some of our spelt and it swooped to claw my eyes out, but all I needed was one stone to kill it. I identified all the pawprints in our tracking exam. The winds are turning some fingers blue and the Masters are starting to plan our next encampment.

Dear sweet, clean book,
Some things seem to pursue you as soon as you find out about them.
It was recreational time before supper and I felt pleased with the day (I'd hit the target dead center twelve times). I wanted be alone, so I skipped off into the hills. I was doing cartwheels, fantasizing of a Predator to kill, or a lone legendary Hunter who'd show me his compass. I got to the thick of the woods where the light was grey through the clouds and greyer through the dead branches, and it was silent save for my footsteps padding.
I heard a noise and thought it might be a Squirrel. We just learned about the muscle-soothing qualities of Squirrel blood and I thought how

pleased Sir Cahill would be if I brought some back. I didn't have any weapons but I felt like I could wrestle a Squirrel bare-handed, so I stilled my body—*there* it was, a rustling in the underbrush. Then I heard a moan that didn't sound all too much like a Squirrel. I held my breath and crept forward.

And I reached a clearing and saw a Man, fully grown, too dirty and ragged to make out his Job. He lay on his back. His few belongings were spread around him, except for one round bundle on his belly that his arms clung to. I approached and he moaned again. From his noises and arched back, at first I thought he might be doing some kind of self-groping, and started to back away to give him privacy.

But then his moan turned into a scream and it certainly didn't sound like pleasure. His body twisted like a sweat rag being wrung out. I thought maybe a Snake had bit him, or maybe I wasn't thinking at all, maybe I just wanted to get as far as possible from the stain seeping from between his legs that was dark as night and maybe as blood, so I sprinted, I ran, back down to camp.

Sir Cahill was in the supply tent consulting with Commander Jee and when I told them a Man was bleeding in the woods Sir Cahill grabbed his basket and told me to lead the way. We all crashed up the hill; I recognized a mossy stone, a lightning-struck stump, an Ant hill, and then another scream. There he was. Curled on his side. The stain had spread.

Sir Cahill knelt by his side and roused the Man into noticing us, which took some doing. The Man murmured to ask if Sir Cahill was a Physician.

"I tend to the boys in our troop, but not precisely, no."

"Not a Midwife?" The Man looked fearful.

"Does this look like a city to you?" said Commander Jee sharply.

"We'll take care of you," reassured Sir Cahill, and ran his hands along the bundle on the Man's belly, "I spent some time training with Midwives," and suddenly I realized it was not a bundle at all. I must have made a noise because Sir Cahill glanced up at me.

"Thank you, Malkim," he said. "Go back to camp. Don't tell the other boys."

"Not so fast," Commander Jee growled out, and I froze. His eyes bored into me. "I think you ought to help." Sir Cahill opened his mouth but Commander Jee went on. "I think you ought to see. What'll happen if you're not careful."

There was some silence (the Man's groans had ceased) and then Sir Cahill said well, yes, he could use another pair of hands, could I get a cloth from his basket please. I knelt next to him where he squatted before the Man's outspread knees. I could see his gens, of course, saw he had a hole like mine although rather unlike mine at the moment; rather unlike anything that ought to have existed on a body, in my opinion.

Sir Cahill had me grind up an herbal paste which he spread onto the Man's tongue. "For the pain." He slurped it down and his body shuddered. Sir Cahill was clicking and squelching about but called out questions that the Man answered between convulsions. He was a Builder – "I... I keep up the aqueducts," he gasped – but he wouldn't say where his fellow Builders were or why he was alone, and far from a city, too, in this state.

"Thought you'd take your own self to Litentia, eh?" Commander Jee scowled. "Just lost track of time, did you?" and the Man mumbled, "Something like that."

"Do you know how long you've been this way?" Sir Cahill called up.

"I couldn't tell you that. I've been... I've been lying here... so long. I've been lying here a while." He clenched up and let out another wail. "Stars have passed... I've been lying here..."

Sir Cahill grabbed tools I wished I hadn't seen, busied himself between the Man's legs, then said, "Well, it won't be much longer now." He told him to get ready to push. Commander Jee ducked under one of the Man's armpits to hoist him and nodded at me to get under the other. I was sweating in the cold air, though not as much as this Man, whose body was strained taut, like a Deer hoping to rid itself of arrows.

Then the baby happened and I don't want to tell you because I don't want to remember all the things that happened at once, in quick succession, the screaming and the puddles bursting out and the Jellysquid tentacles and the stretching that I swear I could hear, like ripping fabric in the straw dummies when we get our spears into them, and did I mention screaming, and contorting, and Sir Cahill's hands outstretched, and my own body very far away....

I don't want to talk about all the things I saw that made me separate from myself, but what happened is, it was all over—the new person had fallen out of the Man and into Sir Cahill's arms, and Commander Jee and I (both of us shaking) lay the Man back down on the ground. He held the wet baby to his chest and shivered and cried and then Sir Cahill wrapped it in a white blanket and asked if I wanted to hold it. I didn't really. I wanted to run as far away as possible, or sink into the ground, but Sir Cahill passed it into my arms and I had no choice.

I didn't want to look at it. I thought of parasites, slimy Frogs, vile mushrooms that bloom up from nothing. A pathetic Wormy thing that could nevertheless rip you apart as bad as any Tiger. I thought of a creature like this growing inside of me and I had the urge to cast it on the ground.

But I was curious so I kept looking. The tiny eyes squinted open, and I saw silver stars poking out of that blackness, reflecting the sky. How long had we been out there? I suddenly realized how cold my body was and that this splinter of flesh was hot against it, so hot, maybe the warmest thing I'd ever held.

I felt Commander Jee stand next to me and all I could say was, "He's hot," with a laugh, and then I corrected myself. "She? It." I frowned and asked how it would get assigned, wondering if there was any way to tell, even now, at the very least whether it would be a boy or a girl. Commander Jee told me not to worry about it. I started shuffling through all the Jobs I'd ever heard of, trying to picture them, to match this bundle up to its future. But at that moment all the distinctions between Jobs, and even between Men and Women, felt very far away. Puffs of breath hit my cheek, wandered away, and returned again, and I thought, I don't know *what* you are, little thing; I'm glad it's not my Job to figure it out.

Now I'm in my tent, boys breathing all around me, and I don't know how to sleep with a mind that feels soaked with all kinds of fluids and screaming. I nearly saw someone die today and it did just what Commander Jee intended—the idea of ever giving birth makes my insides freeze up. But isn't there some beautiful mystery about it too? And isn't it true that you never know where your wanderings will lead you? No, I'll never give birth... but if I do, for some strange reason, way off in the future, I trust that I'll be Man enough to endure it.

TRANSLATOR'S NOTE

I don't enjoy speaking on the art of translation but my mailbox has been flooded with complaints so it seems I must make one thing clear. Vago Whipplesnap himself seemed almost in tears, to judge by the shaky handwriting—"Why MEN and WOMEN?? A scholar such as yourself!" When the Gostayan people, of course, have no concept of gender as we know it – or hundreds of genders, as some scholars argue, pointing to the Jobs that shape their lives.

But my specialty is language, not anthropology; and the Gostayan language poses a problem that can only be resolved with "he" and "she." The fact is, of all their society's distinctions, the only one that exists in their *language* – pronouns, word endings, etc. – is that between people who live stationary lives, in cities and farms and such, and people who wander the wild.

Now don't ask me to explain *why* they make such a distinction. Ask the historians, the biologists, geologists, anthropologists – or best of all, ask the Gostayans themselves, who know the answer so well they could never explain it.

All I know is that I listened to their language, which marked two categories; and translated to my language, which marks two categories. It's as simple as that. If I misled you, mapping gender onto an arbitrary distinction, so be it. Of course I have never met dear Malkim the Hunter-boy, but some of his descendants have assured me they find our distinctions equally arbitrary.

Themyscira

COLETTE ARRAND

What I know about my life before Themyscira comes to me in fragments: A hand on my shoulder, a favorite song on the radio, the perfume
my mother wore when there was a significance to things that, being a child,
I couldn't quite understand. My mother's perfume. I can't quite conjure it.
The brand she wore was a relic from a time beyond my memory, something
dark and husky, its color rich as it sat in the bottle. She was wearing it that
day, with a conservative dress and a pair of gloves. The hand on my shoulder. Her voice saying "Please reconsider."

From there, things are a blur. Her name, her face. Sometimes when
I dream I can feel the warmth of her hand enveloping mine as we walked
through an overcrowded street, how she squeezed when a man jostled her
shoulder, when a room was so tight that strangers pressed against us. I
never reconsidered. My mother was taking me to the docks, to an island full
of women who'd volunteered for relocation. There were advertisements for
it on television: wide open spaces and clean air, single-level buildings that
stood in contrast to the skyscrapers and apartment buildings that choked
off the sky where I lived, that struggled to contain the people of the city.

Like everybody, I arrived on Celebration Day. Themyscira never felt
right, never felt like a place I really belonged to. The women who came with
me on the ship were beautiful – taken out from the background of the city,
I was struck by the richness of human variety. But I was the only woman
with a penis, on the ship or on the island. Goddess, how long had it been
since I'd seen another woman's cock? It was Celebration Day, and I sat on
the dock waiting for a ship full of women to come in. The sun was setting

and there was nothing, not even a silhouette on the horizon. No ship that day, and no women like me. Just like all the other days I was there, really.

When I try to think about Themyscira it feels like it belongs to another world entirely, a different version of me who existed, who I can remember, whose impression upon my brain is distinct and indelible but nevertheless warped. Time passes and does that kind of thing to a memory. I watch old films sometimes and gaze adoringly at actresses whose faces are covered in layer after layer of makeup, creams and powders so thick the skin beneath it suffocates. They did that in order to better print the human image upon film, but film, as a kind of thing people store memories on, is like anything else in that it can degrade. All of those faces, faded. Hers, though, was different.

I found her while I was out spearfishing, weeks after a Celebration Day that never happened. Spear in one hand and binoculars in the other, I scanned the beach, the sea, and the sky, looking after my usual places on the beach, when I saw a black mass, rising and falling. It was a body. It was *her* body, face down in the sand and breathing like it could stop at any moment. I turned her over as gingerly as I could and she vomited on my feet. There was a piece of driftwood next to her and I tied this to my waist by a length of rope, placed her on it, and dragged her from the beach to my hut. She was so weak. I fed her water. I tried to keep her fever down. I stayed up all night wondering if she might die, not knowing what it meant that she was on the island.

I'm writing about her as a way of writing about Themyscira. The world was smaller then, or it felt that way – there was the island and there was the Mainland, and there'd been no contact between the two for months. Time trickled out slowly, the way time does when you're bored or in pain, but the lack of communication between our island and our former home had already broken a routine that had been established and carried out for generations – a ship, due to arrive with supplies and new women, was weeks late when she washed up; most of us had been panicking silently. There were other islands like ours, we knew. Islands full of people who'd exiled themselves to lessen the great mass of bodies choking up the cities. Our sacrifice, they said, was one that would be paid for again and again by those who stayed behind. This was the first Celebration Day any of us could remember where that hadn't been true.

Those of us on Themyscira understood each other as sisters, but as chosen families go, ours was loose. I went out to the beach every morning to fish, used my binoculars to look out as far into the distance as I could. I was looking for a way out, I guess. Or back. Back to the Mainland. I was tired of my kind of existence.

I managed to keep her a secret for two or three days. There was no danger, none that I could surmise, anyhow. She was a castaway, blistered and dehydrated. I cleaned her as her sores oozed. I waited for her voice to grow strong enough to speak in something more than a hoarse croak. I went out for shellfish one morning and returned to find my hut surrounded by my sisters. They murmured excitedly to each other about what was inside – a woman from the Mainland. Sick, maybe. Ill. Diseased. Dangerous. These words attached themselves to her freely. It'd been a long time since anybody on Themyscira had been ill, but you never knew with women from the Mainland. All those bodies, breathing – who knew what anybody had? Who knew where an illness could come from?

My sisters parted as I walked towards the hut. A pair of women emerged, carrying her on a stretcher. They wore makeshift gasmasks made out of pop bottles. There was another sister in my hut, wearing the same mask as the others, and I asked what was happening. "That woman is sick," she explained, spreading out her hands in apology, "and she came from the Mainland. We need to keep her away from the village until we know how serious it is." I asked to stay with her, and my sister asked why. I didn't know then and I don't know now. It was, I suppose, a kind of compulsion. She felt like my responsibility.

I was taken out to a hut further out on the edge of the village than my own. My sister, gas mask still tight around her mouth and nose, opened the door. Sunlight poured into the space, fell on her hair. She rolled over, shielding her eyes. She was still so red. So desiccated. I stepped into the hut and she began to cough. She reached for a glass of water on the nightstand and drank it. The door closed behind me, and we were alone.

The histories of places like Themyscira are lost much easier than is pleasant to think about. Men and women got onto ships and disappeared. Parents hugged their children and watched them depart like they were heading to university; four years, maybe five, in a place they knew existed but couldn't picture, time enough for the world to sort itself out, then they'd be brought back with stories of vanished continents, wild stories of hostile animal life and poisonous vegetation, vicious islands and the innocents sent there to die.

The truth is less cruel, but it's jarring to have your exile upset by the arrival of someone who isn't. Her voice regained its clarity. She told me her name and where she was from, but I wonder about the utility of that knowledge now. From Themyscira the world stretched out as a vast emptiness in all directions, and like Themyscira the country she claimed was home exists on no map I've ever seen. The maps I used to plot my own journey were castaways – countries were still Soviet. Countries were still countries. The Mainland, such as I remembered it, stretched out as a vast somethingness in all directions. There was land. There were buildings. There were people and stores and animals. I can remember my parents grumbling, in the distant past, about being forced to think of themselves as part of a larger whole than they'd previously considered possible.

I tried finding myself in others, but on Themyscira that was never quite possible. I was treated as a curiosity by friends and strangers – all those people on the Mainland and they'd never seen a girl with a cock before. They couldn't see how strange it was for me to live on an island full of women where nobody else had one. Life on the island was difficult and my sisters and I all wore the scars of that life, but I had ones that were older than Themyscira, scars from different struggles, and those I tried to keep hidden.

I saw her cock one morning as she changed out of her bedclothes. It was small, sticking out from a little mound of flesh. She'd had an orchi done, the scar faint, more like the ghost of a scar. On the Mainland I saw trans women so frequently that they didn't register. Nobody did. But here, after years of being alone, I was like a person wandering a vast emptiness, dying from lack, and she the realization of a dream. I said nothing. What could I say? That I recognized her, somehow? That I'd been on Themyscira for longer than I cared to remember, looking for myself somewhere, and that she was it? I didn't know how to say that. I didn't know if she'd find it rude.

I wanted to say something, though. I caught myself staring at her. She caught me staring at her. She was sick. She was coughing. She said I was so pretty that I hardly belonged on Themyscira at all, and I flushed, embarrassed. I frowned and she asked if she had said something wrong. She began coughing again, violently, and the fact of her cough took all of the space there was for conversation in our hut. She looked into her hand and frowned, wiping it into her runic. She said that she felt better, that she felt lucky to be alive, but how lucky were either of us, really? She coughed and cleaned herself with her tunic again and said she was going to sleep. When she did I listened to her ragged breathing and watched her chest rise and fall. More and more, her tunic was soaked in blood.

I asked her how things were on the Mainland, the things I missed by being here. She was confused by the question, like I was asking her to describe a neutral state of being. The Mainland was the Mainland. There was a flare up of some illness, there were still too many people in the cities, but it persisted because everybody believed it had to. She left in a depression – she mentioned a partner, "Dead now," the words popping from her lips like a bubble on the surface of a plague-ridden swamp. She volunteered to go to one of the islands because she couldn't stand their empty apartment. The ship was overcrowded, and it was obvious that some of its passengers were sick. It spread through them and overtook the crew. The ship's captain died first, bloody and feverish. They wrapped his body in a tarp and threw it overboard. Soon too many people were dying for any of them to be properly buried. Using what they had to filter out the germs as they breathed, the passengers were put to work throwing bodies overboard. She was part of a small group of people who weren't sick. It was her idea to leave the ship with those people while she could. They saw land and sent up a signal flare, but a storm blew the boat away from the island. The storm capsized the boat. Her party drowned. She found herself clinging to the piece of wood she washed ashore with, fading in and out of consciousness until she came to in my hut.

I reached out to put my hand on her shoulder, but she withdrew. How long had we been in the hut together? I couldn't tell. She was ill, we both knew, and I wasn't. We'd been left to ourselves and were both, in a way, waiting to die.

It was as horrible as she said, watching a disease go through the process of killing someone. By the time she reached the end stage of the illness, her breathing had become as familiar as the rhythm of a favorite song. It was a metronome that kept the time. It was white noise that I slept to. Its absence one evening was startling. I looked at her, still and withered in her bed, and cried. I thought to kiss her bloody mouth, my companion, but two sisters heard me crying, entered the hut, and saw her corpse.

I was allowed to return to my home. I tried to think of things as normal, but they weren't. I was changed, marked again, but by something more threatening to my sisters on Themyscira than the scars they didn't have. I kept myself distant. I wasn't sick, that much I knew, but I'd been touched by it, held myself responsible for what had happened. The island carried on though, her arrival, illness, and death processed and forgotten. Nobody on the island was sick, and Themyscira was Themyscira.

Before she died, she asked me what it was like to live in exile. I said it was no different from living on the Mainland except that I had my sisters here and on the Mainland I had my anonymity. I told her I preferred it here, where it was very beautiful and open. But I had closed myself off from Themyscira. I was alone. Were we in the hut together still, I would tell her that to live in exile is to live with an open secret that everybody knows incorrectly, that is repeated again and again until what truth you know becomes fiction. I wondered about this often: what was truth to a self-exile?

I began waking up in the middle of the night from dreams where my sisters hated me or loved me for reasons I hated. Dreams where the women on Themyscira were sick and it was my fault that they were dying. Dreams where a sister told me I was beautiful, but the word "beautiful" was hollow, like a tree gone rotten from the inside. Dreams where my sisters spat on me for my scars. When people ask me where I come from and I tell them, they can never quite figure why I left. They look around the city, sidewalks crowded by buildings and people, and say I was very lucky to be in a place that had trees and sand and a sweet breeze blowing in from the sea. They tell me the things they imagine themselves doing on a paradise like Themyscira and I believe them – for some people it's possible for ideas and places to remain unspoiled as long as they can't experience them for themselves.

I was sick though, or I thought myself sick when I wasn't, and nobody on Themyscira could help me. Where would they even begin? I gathered what supplies I had into a satchel and made for the beach where I found her. There were boats that spearfishers used to go out from the shore. I dragged one of these to the water with my rope. I had no plan and there was nobody on the beach to stop me. The tide pulled my small boat from the shore for me, I hardly had to row. For an afternoon all I saw was the ocean growing larger as Themyscira shrank in the distance. I fell asleep under the sun and dreamed about washing ashore somewhere, a different island, the Mainland, laid out on some alien sand and drying up like a jellyfish, hoping to be found. When I woke up, Themyscira was past the horizon. The stars were out and I looked at them, trying to divine some meaning from this new exile. I'm not sure I'll ever find it. One morning I woke up and slipped away from a world I had some small part in fashioning. Since then, I've been nowhere.

Cybervania

S Y B I L   L A M B

1

Sterile Amerika squinted at the nicotine-colored light seeping inside the garbage truck through the pneumatic cruncher that Gunk was always closing and she was always opening to get some damned air in here. The skies of North Texicoma were greasy from the second highest concentration of metal, plastic, and consumer goods recycling factories in the continent. After Oaxaca. Opening the door a foot let fresh grimy air circulate to their pile of 7 mattresses and ripped up rotten clothes and spiky boots and belts and old cell phones rigged for certain hack functions.

The only light in the 24 foot long dark greasy steel tank came from Gunk's collection of vintage cathode televisions, piled up in great columns around his 52" monitor work station. He also had a Nintendo 64, a 1982 coleco vision with 2 working paddles, a 1985 duck hunt gun, 2 blackberries, 2 pagers and a gameboy with tetris glued into the slot. He'd stolen them all when he had a gig unpacking the eWaste trucks, before he got fired for smashing another unpacker's face through the screen on a 2002 eMac, cuz he thought the guy called him a homo.

Last night he'd thrown himself into the garbage truck about 5 am whooping incoherent shit, delirious on rotary phone contact cleaner. The ensuing wasted jackhammer sodomy had left Sterile raw and farty. He said he was celebrating getting fired from his most recent demotion, a gig desoldering the batteries off old motherboards to make Lithium pills. Apparently he'd burnt a guy from ear to lips across half his face with a soldering iron cuz he thought the guy called him a homo.

"Well, he sure ain't no cocksucker," Sterile smirked to herself, lying on her plastic ass, scrunching a tangle of ratty black coats between her plastic tits and original, unmodified knees. She sucked her real, unmanicured, chipped-up-polish, broken nails and hash-stained thumb through her pillowy plastic lips, then stiffened as she smushed the least modified part of herself into the coats. Gunk would fuck her like a tennis ball throwing machine every night, but he'd only given her a kiss on her clit maybe 3 times all summer. She stayed with him for his quarter inch steel house and speedy bandwidth and cuz people just gave him drugs and mostly full cans of solvents cuz they were afraid of him.

It was still afternoon. Gunk was grumbling through his hangover, testing the four latest computer monitors he'd found, and coughing. As soon as he saw her eyes open he hollered, "I'm not here to make friends. It's called rock and roll and punk rock is supposed to be violent that's why it's good! That lil guy F.O.B. is a complete bitch in his gay fag mohawk he dyes with copier toner and his fake designer japanese biker jacket he bought with credit cards he stole using the weaknesses in older versions of outlook. Poncing around with his brand new welding goggles when everyone knows he couldn't even sweat a copper pipe. I am letting you know, not as my bandmate but as my main bitch, that I am waiting for him to side eye me or do any of his shit with acting like he thinks he's smarter than me. I am gonna punch him in the throat so he can't sing and break his two pointer fingers leaving him 100% unable to type."

Sterile nodded groggily, got up, popped ephedrine, methedrine, b-12, tylenol-4, and a gravol, and slung her Voltage Control Oscillator sequencer over her shoulder. She stood naked and dirty in the thin shaft of stained burnt sunlight in the back of a garbage truck with a guitar covered in knobs and wires strung low on her voluptuous plastic body, otherwise lean, with hungry muscles kept sprung by life in a crowded city-size scrap yard.

After waiting a practiced 13 seconds for the filaments in both amp and VCOguitar to warm up, she windmilled her arm and power strummed the selector toggles while doing the splits. An enormous screech riding on top of a bowel punch of underwater warbling erupted, sending the hundreds of tiny screws all over the floor vibrating in little circles.

Sterile and her goon boyfriend were actually noise rock stars. They mostly dodged work and mostly didn't get in trouble for their bullshit and free parties n stuff. It was a perfect shining future. It was an automated hi tech utopia. Sterile Amerika was lead "guitar" for SEXBOT, the biggest noise garage booty metal act in all of the impractical to find and ambitiously autonomous city state of Cybervania, Texicoma.

2

Every man and woman and both and neither in Cybervania was always amplified. To go outside without amplification would mean having to navigate a crowded lawless industrial settlement with no ability to communicate, your words disappearing beneath hundreds of other amplified Cybervanians and the ceaseless buzz, hum, hiss, and screech of thousands of computer speakers, fans and old overloaded power blocks. Right now, 3ight, the drummer from SEXBOT, was using a small child's megaphone run through a car stereo JFET overdriven with an 18 volt battery pack to explain a plan to steal some part of the spaghetti of blue and grey ethernet cables strung from shed to shack to RV throughout the town.

3ight was petite and tiny and most people understood her as a bundle of black hoodies and sweatpants with thick glasses and little skinny fingers sticking out in places. Inside the hood she had a toothy grin and a filthy mohawk dripping crankcase oil. She lived in a half ton camper-top hoarder's nest held out of the mud on a stack of tires. She had a bunch of expired birth control pills she would hook Sterile up with for cheap. Sometimes she'd get ahold of weird livestock hormones and throw hormone of the month club parties.

3ight was Sterile's oldest friend, they'd known each other for over 8 months. They'd met right after Sterile first hitched out to Cybervania on the eWaste delivery trucks. 3ight had spotted her jumping down from a pile of dead hard drives with her eyes glazed and the flesh of the back of her head still sealing shut around improvised cuts and sutures. 3ight ran up to Sterile and said just "hey." She flipped her hoodie down, flicked her greasy hair to the front, and pointed to the great nasty scar on the back of her own skull. Sterile had cracked a smile and within fewer than 36 sleepless hours they'd formed a band.

It was 3ight and Sterile's band, really. Gunk had only been added cuz he played a bass guitar made from a real battle axe that he had really chopped someone up with once, allegedly. Sterile did guitar and vocals. 3ight played an instrument that she'd made from a dozen cassette players hot wired to reel to reels and little kid pianos. She had awesome taste in untuned guitars and licked fingers touching bare circuits. 3ight got them maybe 3-5 gigs a month in addition to VIP status at the weekly ambient power noise party she hostessed. SEXBOT quickly became the hottest band in Cybervania.

Sterile spent like a third of most days or nights wandering the garbage piles with 3ight. Those two would stay awake for three days at a time rewiring radios and VCRs and stuff together.

Today, as they walked along narrow streets made of old forklift pallets planted in the mud, 3ight was babbling on and on through her megaphone about songs made of tiny songs and sounds made of interchangeable parts of sounds and the 5th dimension of music. She had some way she was going to build a device that could describe and manipulate that. Which was where stealing cables came in. 3ight was always trying to invent something she needed help stealing a crucial part for. Most of the time these plans failed but she seemed to neither notice nor care.

They turned a corner into a 200 meter wide clearing which opened onto the northern gate of Cybervania. Arriving trucks came here to be weighed. The clearing was defined by 4 meter high walls of old computer chassis. Near every case ever commercially available in North Amerika in the past 60 years was there. Sterile and 3ight joined a little circle of 7 or 8 other pickers waiting out the hot part of the day in a scatter of dust-covered automobile seats under an ineptly strung-up 60 foot tarp.

The ground under the tarp was more tiny screws and broken glass than dirt. Sterile lay back on her gear bag, carefully positioning her micro-shorts-covered bum on a softer-looking patch of tiny screws, and chain smoked something while watching little bits of half biodegraded silver antistatic plastic float around on the soft vortex of wind trapped in the walled-in lot.

After about ten minutes her rest was disturbed by a preposterously armoured school bus rolling through the gate and mounting the weigh scales. The original, intact 1980s STOP CHILDREN sign flipped out as the doors opened and a tall, scrappy, lazy-twitchy humanoid planted cleat-covered cowgirl boots on the oil-stained dirt and blinked light grey eyes through big 1969 granny glasses at the feeble nicotine-colored sunlight.

The humanoid wore knee high chuck knockoffs and the threadbare remains of black t-shirt and skinny jeans. A poncho woven of mostly blonde human hair edged with with little red microwires painstakingly unwound from dozens of tiny motors was wrapped into a cowl around their narrowed, narrowed jaw. They had the body of a whippet who moved like a flamingo, all tea-colored leather skin over long narrow taunt defined muscle, like all they'd eaten the past year had been pigeon and seagull eggs found by climbing hundreds of electrical towers looking for nests. 420cc round salines floated on on a chest like a taut crossbow. They had a shaved head, bleached and notched eyebrows, a whittled nose, a jeweled nose ring, a missing front tooth. They carried an enormous hockey bag over one shoulder, a bandoleer of phones and devices over the other, and a desktop pc under each arm. The Intake guys gave them a big wheeled shopping cart to push all the stuff in.

The flamingo-whippet pushed the cart into the clearing, then noticed Sterile staring at they from the couches. They narrowed they's eyes and pointed a long arm at her without breaking stride. Hair Poncho made sure they had Sterile's attention as they pushed by. They fingered those giant disco sunglasses while giving her the eye and a nod and singing "Beep beep beep! Boop beep beep beep!" They did not break eye contact until they disappeared around a noisy fan-covered trailer full of servers, off in the direction of the fenced-in giant humming transformer.

3ight smacked Sterile in the arm, "Holy Shit, QUEEF BITCoIN$ is back! " she gagged in a fuzzy treble screech through her PA system. Sterile said nothing, her PA was just the sound of breathing and an uncontrollable, poorly grounded feedback loop.

3

Over the next few days Sterile heard lots of vague, contradictory, distorted fuzz-squawking about Queefer Beef Bitcoin$. Apparently Queef had been recruited here a decade ago by the original founders of Cybervania, a coven whose 5 or so remaining members, all of them nearly a century old, were survivors of vintage "transsexual" treatments from back when operations had been done with unassisted human hands. Mx Bitcoin$ had rotated back and forth through at least 3 genders over the years. 4 if you count a best-forgotten attempt at "boy/assexual". Most people who had one of the 5 majority gender IDs called Bitcoin$ "her". Theys and Fluids declared "queef" to be queef's pronoun. The last time Queef completed any forms on the Cybervania network Queef'd given her gender as "-". But that had been 9 months ago.

Sterile smirked sourly, recalling how when she'd arrived here she'd written "IT" in the gender box at the Rations and Medical and STD center. If she still had a computer in her head she could have scheduled reminders in TASKS to await further indicators confirming Queef as a "her" or or maybe "pseudo-her" while postconsciously running response scenarios for engaging either an ultra-femme butch or an ultra-butch femme. With her ports empty and healed over she could only try to remember it in her brain, so she promptly forgot.

Over the next few days plenty of distracting things happened. There was a gang fight between Cybervania's Networks and Servers over DNS Name serv reroutes. The food store got in 3000 gallons of expired NRG drinks so everyone got ratchet on sugar cyanokablamamin. A truck dropped off thousands of hand-held FROGGER lcd games. Wifi was seldom over 3 bars. One of the independent data havens got a visit from some organised crime heavies and two developers with admin priv got stuffed in the back of a jeep and disappeared. For an hour afterwards the admin of Cybervania reminded everyone on Loudspeakers on poles all over the settlement that our main protection here was anonymity and our second line of protection was a 4 meter high wall of obsolete computer casings.

Then Sterile and 3ight went out to dismantle a battery rack next to an important server generator and got caught. Some guy started shooting at them with a shitty homemade taser. 3ight lit up with a crackling blue aura and Sterile threw herself over a barb wire fence and disappeared into a maze of buses from every decade there had ever been buses, parked backward and sideways with tin shacks and plastic prefab storage lockers on top of them. She ran over the tops of buses then dropped down between a tiny 2.2 meter rust-patinaed teardrop trailer and the fence around the main transformer field. She fell right into a hammock, next to Queef Bitcoin$, who was just chilling out and noodling on a child's crocodile xylophone piano.

"-" had on little else but her giant sunglasses, the remains of her jeans, and a stained cream-coloured push-up bra. A hand-rolled ditch tobacco cigarette dangled from her dry puckered lips, flicking ashes and squiggles of tobacco all over her amazing tits. "-" had been smoking a beat-up old va-poriser of BX09 crystals and was honey mello and unshocked by Sterile's appearance. "-" turned to Sterile and clasped a hand on both of IT's rigid shoulders.

"There you are! I've been looking for you everywhere!" Queef spoke without any amplification, her megaphone lay in the dirt attached to her messenger bag, charging off a chewed-up wire leading to the teardrop's utility panel.

Sterile blinked and shook IT's head. Queef embraced her delightedly tight and then pushed her arms length away again. "What's your name? I'm Queeferella Beefcakes Bitcoin$$ from Awesome Texxxas. I run chemicals back and forth across the country, been in a bunch of porns, I'm in a pretty neat rock band called BORN PREGNANT. I trade Bitcoins, I mix and dis-tribute BX pills and precursors. Yanno, stuff like that."

Sterile said that she'd noticed Queef's poncho that one time at the scales, but then couldn't think of what else to talk about. After a short, awk-ward silence she swallowed and turned her face to Queef and announced gravely "I just think you are my ideal most fantastically designed creature. You are too beautiful and it's driving me to madness. I can't live with you so beautiful yet so unpossessable. I have no other choice: I am here to cut your face up with my boot knife."

Queef studied Sterile, who seemed like she was waiting to Queef to agree with her.

"Um, no." was the first thing "-" thought to say after at least 13 sec-onds dumbstruck.

"I intend to be honorable and fair about this." Sterile continued, shift-ing her big plastic bum about in the ropey net and curving an arm around Queefs knees for balance. "I guarantee you to get one good slash of my face too. I know you have more beauty to lose than I, but attractiveness has only been formulaic for 100 years. For thousands before then it was all relative. Blow for blow is the most certain way to a kind of fairness when it seems that devils have chosen us for this unfair fight."

Queef leaned back and folded her long long arms behind her head. "I think I should get to slash you at least once more than you get to slash me me, cuz you started it." Her pale colourless eyes hid in dark smudgy narrow slits. "Where is this knife anyways?"

"I dropped it running from a security guard." Sterile gazed off at the distant transformers. "I thought we could just give it a run through tonight, since I accidentally figured out where you live. Y'know, so we don't get nervous and hesitate when we cut each other's faces for real some day"

"Oh yeah sure, yeah. Someday soon," Queef grinned.

They lay parallel facing each other from opposite sides of the hammock and Queeferella offered her the modded-out vape, held together by duct tape and oozing a smell like burning cassettes that got addictive really quickly. Sterile promised herself she'd just have a taste.

Queef launched into a wistful rambling story of hitchhiking and charming her way between other Cyberpunk enclaves hidden in the north and south ends of both coasts. She said she travelled between all of them at random moving BX crystal, and scouting bitcoin markets, and claiming the most interesting lovers in every port, occasionally surfacing in the world of normies and pinks to collect some coin.

"I'm working on my new band right now, BORN PREGNANT." Queef lazily bragged. "It's mostly me. My on-again off-again pansexual versatile boyfriend Fuk-o-Billy sometimes guests. Billy Fuk, he's kind of like psychobilly moog and tape glitch and power click, I'm more like riot girl electro acid trash-a-delic mumble rock, so like imagine those two genres together. His pansexual thing has kind of shaped me over the past bunch of years. like, these," she said, grabbing her 420 tits and shaking them at Sterile, "these are titties number 3, I've had a bigger pair and a smaller pair. I've been on crazy chupacabra progesterone, I've been on bull testosterone. If he's out to try it all, well then I'm prepared to be it all, and his predilections are a good way to gauge my cosmetic mods' success rate."

Sterile hadn't done BX crystal drugs in a few weeks and they were washing over her hard. She pet the lumpy scar beneath 8 months worth of dirty hair on her head and confessed she'd unplugged herself. She didn't even carry a mobile. She hinted at a past as a full service live sex doll in a Canadianian border town. Said one day she'd gone in for a semi annual upgrade and horrifically gouged out all her cognitive enhancements instead.

Then, she went on, she came to Cybervania and got with Gunk cuz he had a sturdy, robustly wired garbage truck and he was an exclusive top who "didn't do anything" and was strongly passive aggressive about her being a her. He was always passive aggressive with her, but he was respectfully never actively aggressive. When that happened it was only with other boys, as far away from home as possible, and he came home with their phones and cards and money and maybe splattered in their blood. The important thing was that it was probably no one you know so don't ask.

Queef didn't ask. Instead, from on top a stack of dead monitors piled up next to the hammock, she picked up a tablet that had been paused on last week's red civil war alerts and yellow toxic air alerts cartoon infomercial. Queef discreetly bluetooth paired it with the modest transdermal unit just behind her right temple, and began shuffling through a hundred pix of her with at least a dozen compound hybrid gender role presentations. Queef with ultra giant tittys dressed up as a rubber horse satyr; Queef with much smaller, leather harnessed tits, a close trimmed beard and 2 nose rings through nose job number 2; Queef with b-cups and a 1980s batcave haircut wearing nothing but 8 leather belts and a fishnet body suit.

"Miss Bit$, you've really looked like every Bit you ever mighta been. Its like you went into every possible time dimension and brought all of you back with you."

"Yeah..." replied Queef, and she stretched out "yeah" to make it sound as world-weary and snarky as she could. "I keep grabbing the wrong one and then I gotta go try again. Maybe one day I'll get her right."

"I'm just amazed that you had B cup tits then DDD tits and now you have C tits"

"Buh-Duduh-duC." Queef agreed, pronouncing all her old tits as a word.

"I mean, my tits are silicone D but then i got silicone injected on top of them going up a cup size every few years... it's not sketchy if you know people with a good reputation..."

"I don't even want tits anymore. Tits are stupid." Queef's inflection shifted so she sounded irritated and pissy and too tuff to be upset."They get in the way, and everyone judges me as a fucking sex robot. Every day i walk around with these tits people look at me like i'm one of the the mythical plastic people of the 20th century. Fake tits are like the signifier badge of the Shemale archetype, they announce to the world "hello I'm a fake made up person, everything I do is performative, my body is slave to my fetishes that are transparently rooted in self hatred. I don't want foreign objects inside me no more! From now on I just wanna cut stuff off or have it cut and pasted into different shapes."

Sterile, who was over 5% silicone by volume, narrowed her eyes at Queef, sneered, and said nothing.

"I hate my tits. I wish I could get rid of them now but Its like 4 or 5 bitcoin to even see a surgeon within 1000 km of here. I'd have to go to one of the cities for a few months ...."

"I know how to pop both tits out of existence for no money and no effort," Sterile snarked. "This girl I met down in Morteville Loueasyana told me some dirty nasty stories about the DIY surgeries in the girl's wing of Angola Penitentiary. I used to live on the border of Canadia, I've seen some wild frontier 1st aid kit surgery transitions."

Queef stared at Sterile but her eyes were actually fixed on something in another dimension. She drifted a few moments more then shook herself back into attention. "Hey look at when I used to live in a tree" she said and pulled up a pic of "-"self living in a tree house and wearing just filthy coveralls. Queef listed off a bunch of cool stories about her time in the treehouse and Sterile let herself get lost in listening to Queef's Texicomanian drawl.

All over the little porch of the teardrop trailer different mobiles and handhelds bleep blooped, too many notification sounds to count. The sky was a deep purplish brown with yellow mist gently swirling between the radio masts. All over Cybervania transformers hummed and fans whirred and thin tin walls let the blurred sounds of thousands of computer speakers out into the hot dry air. IT only zapped back to attention when "-" said "hey my boyfriend's home!" several times in increasingly frantic inflection.

Sterile followed her first startled gut reaction, which was to grab Queef by the legs and part them wide, gripping her ankles at arm's length, until Sterile could see Queef's Iron Man y-fronts through the remains of "-"'s skinny black jeans. They locked eyes; Queef was surprised, possibly amused, kind of maybe smirking, but mostly unreadable.

"Shit!" Sterile bleated, her face flipping indecisively through half a dozen expressions. "Y'know, I'm sorry, My best friend just got electrocuted by some asshole while we were stealing deep cycles. I totally forgot, This isn't some frigid cold feet shit, I totally forgot about this electrocution thing that literally like just happened... actually it might still be happening. I'm sorry, I gotta go deal with that."

"Yeah ok do that" drawled Queef, now affecting a politely bored tone. "My boyfriend is literally home. And I honestly really only fuck for credit goods or services, You must know how it is. But f'real, you falling off the roof on to me has really been a kick! Come see my band win battle of the bands next week."

Battle of the Bands? Against who? Sterile wanted to ask, but suddenly there was a guy in the teardrop trailer turning lights on and messing around.

"Hey Billy Fuk-O" sang Queefy and out walked FOB in his foppish psychobilly jacket, completely useless goggles and stupid toner-dyed mohawk. Sterile, her mind razor-sharp from Queef's bathtub party drug vape, stood for almost 10 seconds staring at him.

Sterile was agape. The revelation that Fuk-O Billy was FOB? She hadn't seen it coming at all.

She and FOB stood on either side of the hammock both too high on really shitty drugs to process, until Sterile solved the problem by climbing the barb wire fence into the transformer yard, her enormous plastic ass and titties cushioning her easily over the barb wire, and running off down a row of 10 foot tall buzzing green boxes.

FOB squinted through red eyes out into the darkness "What is what? Is? Bit$y?"

"Yeah, yeah baby yeah. Here," said Queef as she stuck the blue smoke gurgling vape in his face. He accepted and shortly afterwards they had sex that was mostly bad with 2 or three briefly really hot parts.

4

With BORN PREGNANT in town, taking all the attention, SEXBOT could only book a single gig the next week. They were due to play at Silo 13, which was a giant concrete room with couches and beds and cushions all over the bottom 8 feet of it. It was so echoey that by the third song you could still hear echoes of the first song. It wasn't even a real gig, it was more like a noise punk skillshare club. 3ight got anxious and neurotic and started blaming their lack of organisation and practice and group dynamic. Gunk called bullshit on 3ight, called her hoarder slut a bunch of times, and simultaneously said the problem with them not getting any gigs would be solved if he just beat the shit out of FOB.

The next day, Sterile was walking the boardwalks with Gunk and they passed Queef. Gunk started babbling about how he wasn't certain but if she proved to be a girl he would totally fuck her. Sterile ignored him, sent no signal to Queef but a lingering side eye. She wasn't hiding from Queef or spying on her. She would walk past her, make eye contact, nod, and even smile but with a practiced look on her face like she was off to some important cyber thing with 3ight or something.

With no gigs, SEXBOT had endless free time, which also meant Gunk went and got in trouble. He caught a ride on the eWaste trucks into OK City and hustled on a downtown street in his scraggle beard and tight little scrapper's body covered in jail tattoos and no fat, just hecka body hair. He went back to several guys' hotel rooms, and when they dropped to suck his dick he kneed them in the face and stomped them unconscious, took their wallets, devices and anything not tied down, and dumped the mini bar into a pillow case.

He did this like 3 to 5 times, before he accidentally picked up an off-duty officer and put him in emergency with his jaw bust in half and a crushed sinus. It hadn't been a sting or anything, it had been a cop who got off on blowing bad guys. Gunk had to shave his head and also his hairy arms and even his trademark unibrow but then put on a fake mustache, wear his secret pair of nerdy glasses, and not go outside for a few days.

Sterile had to smirk at the "irony". Actually it was more of a coincidental perceptual role reversal presenting an amusing symmetry. Or maybe it was irony. Language these days was mutating in weird ways.

3ight wasn't really much good for any weird phone pole climbing or router piracy satellite dish repositioning hijinx. Even days after the tasering she was getting these bouts of shaking her arms and rolling her head about. She spoke like she was quoting from a transcript of a meeting with visitors from the future that had been cut to ribbons and then taped back together at random. She couldn't type any sense either. All she could do was play drums all day.

"I had a vision while being electrocuted," 3ight explained, slow, jittery, and hard to follow. "I saw that time signatures are notes and each note is a folded composition. I'm going to unfold the sounds folded up inside sounds..." Her words scattered and jumbled, and she gestured her fingers wildly like ten fine tip 2014 wacom tablet pens, sketching out spiralling block diagrams.

Sterile smirked and said "cool".

The night of the gig at The Silo came. Sterile was jamming out on her VCOguitar. Gunk was shirtless and sweaty and gross, his disguise glasses rendering him half sightless, sweat dripping off his epic mutherfucker of a fake mustache, occasionally chopping up the couches with his battle axe guitar. 3ight was doing something with loop sequencers samplers and printer guts. Sterile stepped up to the big stadium announcers ribbon mic, rolling her head around, tripped out on the music.

The Concrete Silo was full of not quite a dozen strung-out Cyberpunks wearing headphones and listening to them through different filters. Sterile was about to improvise something to sing but only got out "yeah" before she noticed Queef, androgynous in a black toque, gas station attendant coveralls, and a pair of overly thick aviator sunglasses, looking at her. Sterile confirmed it was her by her cleated cowgirl boots. She looked at Queef. She confirmed Queef was looking right at her looking at her.

Sterile bleated out one more, longer "yeeeeah!!!" into the microphone and let that echo around. The room was deep under echo. Then she stopped playing and wandered away from the stage. Gunk and 3ight were deeply involved in showing off or noodling out and didn't really notice.

She went over to where Queef was sitting, flopped across the couch with her arm behind the back, and swung a leg up over "-"'s lap. "I keep thinking about when you had me over to your place that one time..."

"You broke into my place and then ran off. I figured you'd break in to my place again or something. Meanwhile you ignore me out on the boardwalks." She sucked at a mason jar that was empty but for melted ice. The Silo didn't have ice or mason jars so Queef must have walked in with it. "Y'know I used to be a transsexual too when I was younger. I can side eye you side eyeing me every time. This place any fun? They got drinks? Gas? Hash?"

Sterile eyed her considerably. It took her a while cuz she had been wasted since 2am. "Whats a nice "-" like you doing in a disused industrial space like this anyways? I thought BORN PREGNANT was supposed be the top party band of Cybervania now?"

"Well, if IT isn't my own favorite rockstar telling me how to rock." Sterile looked confused. "It's a David Gerrold quote," Queef explained. "He wrote that book where he time travels so much he has like 50 years of orgies with only different version of himself until he winds up mating with a female himself so he can have a boy and girl child of himself with fertility drugs to inherit time traveling and become him and girl him."

Sterile wasn't following at all. The two just looked at each other.

"I almost got castrated last year," blurted Queef, mostly blasé and factual. "I was gonna get it done by friends at Cybertopia, North California but I chickened out. These 97-year old 20th century trans witches do it." Queef lit a new smoke off her smoldering previous one.

"I mean, I need it to play with. I got 7 main lovers across the settlements and we are very physical and they all like me functional. I'll prolly wait till I'm 60 and just get a vajay. I'll still be hot for a few decades and I can bottom more often and mature into femininity."

Sterile cocked an eyebrowless eyebrow at her. "I got castrated for semi free 25 years ago in the wilds north of Motor City by a roving pack of feral trans. The deal was i just had to live with them and help them make clover estrogen wine and trim their pot fields, but when Motor City winter settled in, I ran away to the big city, rented my clit out by the hour, signed a lease on a loft, swallowed enuff dick to get fantastic huge credit limits. and after that I just did whatever made sense to keep it going."

"Where was your expensive loft?" smirked Queef.

"I don't remember" IT said finally, dismissively. "The important part is I personally fed my nuts to some punk's dog 25 years ago and today I still got a clit that'll core a hole through drywall."

Sterile waved down a little chubby waitress with long blue hair and ordered her and Queef both a Psychobitch tab.

"I'm fully funtastic cuz I'm on a cocktail of libido drugs. But I get em from Canadia on SilkRoad so it's usually less than 1 or two bitcoin a year. I can show you later."

"You been chopped for 25 years and still function." Queef's face was poker. "How old are you?"

"I dunno!" Sterile blurted in fantastic put-on outrage. "27? How old are you?"

Queef smiled sourly. "Twenty-seven," she hissed.

They both looked sort of twenty-sevenish. Their eyes and hands suggested neither was remotely close.

Sterile smirked as the pixie came back with their bitch powder. It was a mix of dextroamphetamine, methylphenidate, depoprovera, algestone, a micro dose of valium to keep your blood vessels from bursting, and secret ingredient diet pills from craigslist.

"Of course the past few months I've hardly had chance to use that libido. See my boy Gunk over there smashing the couch up with his scrap metal guitar? He likes to pretend he's straight so I play along for now. I enjoy having a knucklehead boyfriend who intimidates everyone, definitely, but a girl needs to get her clit wet now and then, you feel me?"

The blue hair girl knew Sterile and cut them nice fat lines of acidic greasy bright orange powder.

"That boy don't even lick my kitty clean. Some nights it's a waste of my talents."

Out of the corner of her eye she caught Queef looking at her, thinking' real hard about something.

They did the lines and laffed and laffed and cleared their sinuses over and over and next thing they had slipped out of Silo and into the back of PACMAN club. After less than a dozen songs they were in the center of the dance floor, doing erratic made up dances, paying close attention to each other's discreet detailing, and trading blow for every blow, their crotches barely separated by their rotten punk pants. They were sloppy and posthuman and dorky and full throttle, all scrambled into a pummeling flurry of hyper idealised body parts and skull and star tattoos. Then, out of nowhere, Queef broke from their embrace and looked Sterile in the eyes and nodded her head forward, body language for *about to break some news.*

All "-" said was, "I got this thing, I gotta go do a thing. I'll see you in battle. Right here, tomorrow." She wrapped all her fingers around Sterile's hand for 3 seconds, no longer, and then she ran out onto the boardwalks and took off towards the transformers.

"No, hang on, it's important cuz I really relate to your body, come back let's just talk!" Sterile bleated after her, but Queef was gone.

Everyone had seen them clash. Every tiny moment of clothes falling off of bodies too incongruous for clothes to work right on had been scrutinised to the picosecond, to the pixel. There were videos from every angle. And annotating every recording was a TL/DR of comments whooping and hollering and cajoling and ogling them.

5

The PACMAN Club was full to capacity, which was something hundred people. The air stank of freshly cracked instant beer, baking soda, and cigarettes put out in acrylic hair. Post-punk polyglamorous nerds from at least 9 genders lounged all over the bar, their bodies copied from dreams they'd had sleeping off cheap drugs. Their pheromones were turned up to maximum, and their emotions and energy and libidos had been picked out perfectly for the night on 256 sliders in their minds' eyes' settings panels. They draped themselves over vintage 1982 pacman table consoles that had been upgraded with cheap AI add-ons, making the ghosts about as smart as a typical 14 year old humanoid. They all had their tether cables plugged in and were having infinite eaten by ghosts orgasms.

The Battle of the Bands was a big deal and this tall tin barn was the closest thing to a real club in Cybervania. They had real cement floors, the 2 or 3 times it rained here a year the roof held fine, the lights had light switches and almost all the outlets worked. PACMAN had 2 chemical flush toilets and sold toilet paper at the bar for 0.0002 Bits. The only light, apart from the 13 tabletop PACMAN games, was from a 16 foot high neon sign from the abandoned RED ADOBE MOTEL, which was the last real building before the 40 km dirt road to Cybervania.

SEXBOT and BORN PREGNANT sat in booths on opposite sides of the club, but widthwise not lengthwise. There were so many opportunities to sit further apart that their shade seemed just for show. Queef was animated and bright, she held court with FOB and a dozen fans and groupies. Their conversation was buried under dozens of amplified voices and devices but Queef, all wry smirks and talking with her hands, sure looked witty from across the room.

Sterile sat between Gunk and 3ight as they shared a second BX and Hash cyber hookah-bong. Gunk was belligerent drunk, and 3ight was melting unrecognizable computer parts with a blowtorch and really intensely fixating on something only she could see. In the back of her head Sterile wanted to scream and shake them and tell them to be better at this and smarter and do organized stuff like they had a plan and the focus and drive and confidence to march out and take the prize. Why the hell weren't those two doing that? Sterile blamed herself for not even being able to think of what she was supposed to say to make everybuddy act like a winning band. She couldn't be hopelessly disappointed at her boyfriend and best friend. But nor could she hang any hopes on either of them.

Instead she sulked and slumped in her seat and watched Queef and crew toasting jars of sugar liquor and laughing like they'd already won. Sometimes Queef would pause between jokes and her mouth would tighten into a pucker and her eyes would go to her hands folded in her lap, then to nothing 1000 meters nowhere in front of her, and then finally after for-ever over to Sterile who'd been waiting to meet them for as long as they'd taken to land on her.

Then Queefer B. Bitcoin$ rose as if to step out from Sterile's gaze. She excused herself to her boys and glided into the open middle of the barn, through a crowd of people half dancing, half kicking about old computer keys and bits from the scrapping they did in here during the day. Sterile jumped up and strode over to her. Everybody not having cyber-sex with Pac-man watched closely.

Queef stood there with her body like she rowed and played hockey. She wore a buckle-covered catsuit with enormous villain collar, 20 cm wide utility belt, spiked knee pads, and spiked gauntlet megaphones in 20th cen-tury army green. Her head was cleanly shaved but for a tiny tuft of magenta on her left temple just opposite her implant.

Sterile, with a body like she played rugby, but encased in over 3 gallons of Dimethylsiloxane T&A, was poured into a minimal black merri widow with 8 garterbelts and stockings made from synthetic leather. Over her left shoulder was a shiny black megaphone, with steel braided cables running to her vintage rebuilt 1972 sports radio broadcasters headset and a collar of black clone-peacock feathers. Her collar was almost a foot taller than Queef's.

They met in the middle of the dance floor. For no reason they both put out and clasped each other's left fingers, and stood there, not 2 feet apart, holding hands and looking at each other. Somebuddy with a big throaty electric voice squawked "MAKE OUT ALREADY!"

"Wanna climb into the loft and throw monitors out of the loft doors or sumthing?" Sterile asked.

"Take off your pants!" squawked a fuzzy tinni megaphone somewhere.

The two clambered up into loft, a bunch of whooping behind them, including GUNK yelling loudly, "Hey Queef, come here, come here, Sterile, tell her!"

"Tell me what?" Queef asked.

"He wants to fuck you. But only if you're a girl. I been with him 5 months, honestly I can't recommend it. The sex is really only like 2 or 3 hours a week but he's gonna keep hanging out and making really awful vulgar jokes about bitches. He beats up city boys and gives me their phones.

He beats up lots of people but he'd never lay a hand on me. On good days he's kind of like a drunk pet mountain lion."

"I envy that." said Queef. "You have a normal boy-girl relationship. "

"Omigawd, that's horrible!" Sterile went over to an outlet, pulled a baby food jar with steel wool and wires and kerosene in it out of her shoulder bag, and shoved the raw wires into the socket. The steel wool spat white hot sparks and the jar of kerosene caught fire. Sterile lit a Cybervania ditch spliff – part ditch weed, part ditch tobacco, part speedy BX crystals.

"I envy you, Queef. Your body changes like a flowering plant; Like a plant that doesn't even have flowers, like flowers growing out of a gazelle with lightning bolts for feet, every piece of you designed. You look like no one else and no one can look away. Everybody is so amazed by how they can't grasp what you are that they need to be near you and be seen and liked by you to make them feel cooler. They treat you like a rock star and carry you from party to party over thousands of kilometers."

"It's all bullshit," Queef sneered. "It just means I sometimes go to the city to flog an old rich guy in a diaper to fund me transporting party drugs around the country. I just got what the FFS doctors told me computers told them I needed. At this point I feel like my face was cut off and covered in a rubber sheet. I'm not actually attractive. I just cut off everything that wasn't attractive and now I don't look like anybody."

"Queef get me outta here! Take me with you! I want just a taste of your life. Let me be with you, I know you enjoy me around, I know you get hot when my body is touching yours. Let me just be your sidekick for the next few towns until we hit either coast!"

"Look, obvs, you and me together is amazing. You and me dancing out got so many hits. The one video where you see our clits bump for like half a second got 104 thousand views in the first night. I do metrics on all my own personal sites' traffic data. When I see numbers that are like ten times my average, I know you are someone very important. But you gotta understand, I don't have just this life. I have a dozen lives in a dozen towns. Yes, you are smart and funny and weird and have great music chops, but so do most of my other half dozen lovers between Cybertopia and Cyberopolis. One of my other lovers also has DDDD tits, one of my other lovers plays VCO guitar, several of my other lovers break into my house without warning to molest me. You are cute and clever and we really connect, and I get off on just seeing our bodies together, but I already have multiple versions of that relationship. Sterile honey, this Bitcoin$ has full wallet. Maybe in another version of time things turned out different between you n me. At least we will always have that."

"What? No we don't! How can we share another dimension that we aren't even in? We hardly did anything! I didn't even pull off one single completed smooth move on you," screeched Sterile. "What happened to the fantastic party androgyne of legend from coast to coast, from the freshest leaked newsfeed to the deepest zipped archive?"

"That is not who I am! In this rotten scene you can't be surgically xformed into a sex doll without everyone thinking you owe them access. Like having your erogenous zones doubled in size means you've opted out of consent. Like they're allowed anywhere up to a hand's length inside my body just because I manifest as a cartoon of their fantasy. Gawd I hate being this fake bimbo mannequin I made up when I was a baby queer. Hey, you remember when you said you could get rid of these blow up doll tits? How?"

Sterile scrunched up her face and buried it in her hands. breathed twice deeply and looked up with her face ambivalent. She felt the knife in her boot. She took a huge pull of the spliff. Greasy blue smoke puffed out of her nostrils. "It'll cost you a syringe of hormones. You holding?"

"Sure. Easy. I got a Perlupe – the mexican power endocrinol." Queef took syringe in a box from her messenger bag and handed it to Sterile. Their left hands met again, Queef had 70% of a set of black acrylic nails and a 7.5 cm hose clamp as a bracelet on each wrist. She had to take them on and off with a screwdriver. Sterile's wrists and ankles were snared in long black silk ribbons tied round her arms in bows. The ribbons were ratty and speckled with food bits.

Sterile pressed the needle on to the syringe, uncapped it, and shot it in to her right hip. With the empty syringe still in her she passed the smoke to Queef. "Ok, you sure you are ready to undo your tits?"

"Tits are bullshit; I'm not bullshit; yes I am," Queef said, faking a smile.

Sterile thought this seemed the perfect moment. She pulled the syringe out her ass and jammed it 1.25 inches into Queef's left tit. Queef hardly even felt it until a pin hole size squirt of salty water came spraying across her field of view. She tried to spin away from the second jab but it was too late – it just landed crooked, and her second tit started to dribble salty watery blood.

Her face was trying to get upset, but on more than one level she was also still trying to find certainty that this was real. Trying to believe things had gone this far in a literal instant.

"Omigawd omigawd omigawd what the fuck have you done?!?"

"I totally just popped your tits. They will drain in the next hour or so. No need to head to emergency cuz your body is fine to absorb all that salt water."

Sterile was completely unprepared when seconds later Queef swiftly grabbed the syringe and plunged it into her right tit 1,2,3,4,5,6,7,8, times. On her ninth attempt she aimed for Sterile's left tit but Sterile caught it through the middle of her hand. She sprang up on her meaty legs and kicked Queef high in the chest, which made her fall backwards, while bloody salt water sprayed right in her eye.

"Blow for Blow!" screamed Queef, goggle eyed, caught in a fugue.

"Gawdammitm I was kidding around, trying to look tuff, it was a joke dammit!"

"You stabbed me in the tits for real with no warning!!"

"I came up here to make out with you while fondling your tits. This bullshit was your idea."

Queef, with a face that could have been furious or melancholy or delirious with glee equally easily, stomped over to Sterile and pulled her close by the shoulders. Sterile at first uncertainly grabbed Queef round the waist, then more certainly cupped a hand around to palm the top of the curve of her coccyx. Silicone and saline burbled down their fronts, their clothes grew sticky and slick, their giant sinking tits slopped across each other. Queef kissed Sterile, certainly and hard. Their very different post human lips combined in unknowable intense sensation for a few moments. Then Queef snapped her head to the side. Her narrow eyes fixed on Sterile's closed ones. When Sterile opened them, she pushed her away and climbed back down to the party.

6

Sterile spent at most 2 minnits total trying to stop her bloody gooey silicone leak at an old kitchen sink nailed to the wall in a narrow hallway with faded cybergutterpunks bumping past her to the 2 toilets. Silicone is both greasy and sticky. It was all over her hands and was seeping into her panties. She frenzied to fix her tits or even regain her composure, but before she'd even declared it a lost battle she got her 6th 2nd wind since she last had any sleep.

A new clarity washed over her like adrenalin and endorphins and shock. She burst out of the hall way back into the main room. Queef was already on stage 1, prepping BORN PREGNANT to go on. It was time for battle! Sterile grabbed the scribbled-out song list she'd written on a piece of cardboard and studied it, trying to remember her songs.

Gunk was in the back of the place, at the one shitty lopsided scuffed torn pool table. He was in some stupid argument with a guy in a holographic tiger shirt. They hadn't been playing pool; the table was useless for that. Rather, the guy had been showing Gunk SexThot tapes that beam hot sex VR right into your brain. Gunk had found a Thot of Queef Bitcoin$ but the guy hadn't forewarned him that she tops in it, or that the SexThot producers had made her clitty even bigger in post prod. Gunk was threatening to punch the shit out of the guy and accusing him of making normal chix with dix porn all fucking gay. SexThot guy was screaming back at him. He was half a foot taller than Gunk and seemed hungry to teach him how to really be an antagonistic asshole.

Sterile didn't have time for this. BORN PREGNANT were sound checking! She grabbed Gunk's drink and poured it on the pool table, almost all over the SexThot. The SexThot guy screamed and scrambled to save his gear. Sterile grabbed Gunk's Battle axe and started for the stage with it. "Hey don't touch that I just tuned it!" he scream-whined as he plodded after her. She plugged it in and told Gunk to just do whatever he liked a bit and try to punch BORN PREGNANT with bass or sumthing.

Then Sterile went over to 3ight, who was still in the booth, hovering engrossed over her giant tangle of wires. She grabbed 2 of the dozen or so switch and knob covered boxes and pulled. 3ight screamed like a cat in a cold bath. "Don't touch it, don't even look at it it, it's finely tuned to 5th-dimensional frequencies!" Using negotiation leadership powers she never normally had, Sterile talked 3ight down from hysteria and arranged a compromise: they wrapped 3ight's tower of gear in a whole roll of duct tape and then dragged the entire table onto the stage.

And so SEXBOT were ready. BORN PREGNANT faced them on another stage at a 60 degree angle. They had a boy version of 3ight with mutton chops but an otherwise shaved head. He was wearing a rotten sweater, playing something like a circuit-bent theremin.

They also had FOB, who was hopping back and forth from foot to foot and noodling on some weird guitar that had lasers instead of strings and squealing about how he was the laser shredder in high-pitched metal voice. Gunk screamed FUCK YOU POSEUR FAG COCKSUCKER and threw an instant beer bottle at FOB's head. It made a cheap plastic "tok" sound but did no damage. FOB was so enthusiastically self-absorbed he didn't even notice it.

And then there was Queef, standing with dripping empty tits at the microphone, drumming her fingers across the stand and looking right at Sterile with a cocked eyebrow and cocky sneer. Sterile mirrored her but cracked a smile for almost a full second before getting it under control. The first rule of fighting is that whoever starts the fight is most likely to end it.

We have to fight, Sterile thought. Everybody's waiting for it.

She shot the soundboard guy a look that made him drop everything and turn up all her channels. She plugged in 3ight's machines. The most weirdly complicated crystalline pitter patter splatter of sound came from the monitors. It sounded like crystal shards fighting over mating partners. She revved her VCO. Her big plastic lips grazed her pilot's microphone.

"♫♫ Let this be our battle royale ♫♪" she sang in a tone that might be snotty punk or nasal t-girl. "♫♪ SEXBOT gonna make your whole body shiver ♫♪ Leave you begging for more while I eat your eyes and your liver ♫♪"

Suddenly Sterile was full body punched by a rushing tide made out of the sound of a thousand double basses and violins and wash tubs warbling a strange minor scale. Queef's dirty chain-smoker's alto emerged from behind the churning, boiling froth of melody.

"♫♪ BORN PREGNANT don't care what you do ♪♫♪ Everyone knows who laid eggs in who ♪♫"

The battle was off. Queef and Sterile both stood tall with their shoulders back and the remains of their tits out, defiant challenging looks on their sanded-down little faux-delicate jaws, elaborately made up eyes narrowed to slits. Queef mashed her long strong nimble fingers across her plastic alligator keytar and made a noise like a wall of gargle-singing fish. Sterile clicked 6 switches forward and surrounded herself with the rumbling uneasyness of 100 death grind bands tuning up and sound checking. They sung as hard as they could. A single song began to emerge from the chaos.

3ight had easily overpowered BORN PREGNANT's percussion and was keeping time for their accidental supergroup. FOB had dropped the FX rack into the mix and was turning freakishly post-human harmonies into the most agonisingly mind bending soundscape. Gunk was brutalising his battle axe into delirium. The stage around him was getting smashed up and ripped apart in a slowly but certainly growing radius. He kept growling at FOB like he wanted to kill him with his teeth.

Then, swinging her skinny fingers high over her head, 3ight punched the large red button that activated her newest invention. It looked like 2 milk crates of cell phones daisy-chained together. Every other device of 3ight's had been sawn in half and had its guts run through the milkcrate stacks before reconnecting to the rest of itself.

Sterile felt her insides grab themselves in an impossible way. She could hear echos of the part she hadn't played yet but had been about to play. She heard herself sing all her songs better than ever before. She heard herself sing songs she hadn't written yet. She heard Queef doing the same. The two singers stood in the middle of a churning hurricane of garbage and smashed computer bits, screaming in unsensible harmonies at an amplitude that made people cry, cum, collapse, and wet themselves.

Boots planted firmly, amps turned to 11 and lungs on fire, their voices mixed into something beyond regular unenhanced human grasp. Around them, all of SEXBOT and BORN PREGNANT and also another something hundred people at the PACMAN club were writhing around on the floor, some sicking on themselves, some laughing uncontrollably, most in manic bliss. Only 3ight was still clinging to the decks. After 8 bars she clicked the switch to move from 5D sound to the 6-dimensional sound system.

Queef and Sterile's eyes locked and they grinned so wide it hurt both of them. They were at the very leading cutting edge of musical innovation and also dripping with chemical titty blood. They lent their voices to be surrogate to the demon angel they were singing to life. They reached for a high note.

Then there was a 66 foot wide lightning ball explosion and the battle was over.

Epilogue

Nobuddy was killed by burning wifi. Several people were killed hideously by sharp brutal 2 meter long tin sheets flying off of the exploding tin building and that was kind of a big deal for a few days. The next day when the fires were out and and many of the survivors had sobered up they'd found FOB screaming and crying, his fingers crushed to bloody shards by a battle ax that had been swung so many times it was now blunted to the point of being more of a hammer. Fuck-O-Billy would never twiddle knobs again.

3ight had seemingly been vaporised or time shifted out of reality or something. Her sweatsuit and glasses were found in charred pieces but not one skinny finger, nor even one over-processed 3 foot long hank of greasy hair was found. The only things in her pockets were dead batteries. The last thing anyone had heard her say was distracted mumbling. The only note she left behind was a few hundred pages of circuit diagrams.

Gunk was thrown clear in the explosion and ran away. This was testified to by an eWaste truck driver who Gunk stabbed in order to take his truck. He was gunned down 2 weeks later when the scandalous manhunt for the blowjob robber climaxed in a crowded diner in Baxton Rouge, Loueasyana.

Queeferella Bitcoin$ emerged completely unscathed besides for tiny stab wounds. "-" even had time to loot half the club's heavy-duty soundsystem before her north-western primary, FOG, drove down the north road. She jumped into his 1984 Ford Interceptor, tossed the PA in the back seat, and disappeared.

Seven hours later, long after everyone else had been found alive or had their body carted away, Sterile crawled out from the collapsed barn. She duct-taped her perforated boob shut as best she could, marveling at the slow spread of liquid silicone and infection and unwipe-off-able chemical goo she was lactating all over everything she still owned, which at this point was all fantastically filthy if not partially burned.

She clumped out of Cybervania's beige box festooned front gates and began the walk 40km down a lumpy gravel road towards the old interstate. She steeled herself to walk amongst the unevolved unenhanced unconnected idiot masses who had been too weak, too slow, too horribly human to properly surrender their will to superior algorithms and feel their cognitive processes ascend to enlightenment, leaving their bodies free to live out their days frolicing mindlessly amongst the power cables.

Under The Rainbow

JANEY LOVEBOMB

It's 11:30pm Central Daylight Time, on Thursday, April 15.

The gas tank has no lock.

Courage: Convincing yourself you can do something, even when you're not at all convinced.

Connor learned this from Grandpa, not from being a delinquent. Connor has never been a delinquent. Well, until now anyway. Falls, winters and springs diligently doing school, summers on the farm with Grandma and Grandpa, away from the city and the suburbs and the bad kids, away from all the kids. And now here's Connor, not a mile from that place of exploring fields and shucking corn, doing something devious.

Here's how you do it: put one end of the hose into the fuel tank, the other end in your mouth, firmly seal your lips around it, and suck. It just tastes like rubber at first; that's okay, keep sucking. You *reaaallllly* have to suck. Your mouth gets tired, but that's okay, because then you finally get it – a rush of spicy liquid in your mouth. Also all over your face and up your nose. A lot comes out of a Hummer.

Heart: not turning back when it's damn well too late anyway.

Connor falls on the ground in a rush of dizziness and nausea; the stars are blurry and spinning.

Brains: how many cells do you have to spare?

It's 9:30pm on Tuesday, April 12. The guitar is untouched in the corner for the thirtieth night in a row. Connor is drinking underwear-drawer whiskey and listening to Patty Griffin sing about growing up poor and without permission and learning to assert your own existence because it's all you have. This is the one thing that ever puts Connor in the mood to pick up the guitar or sing – to put on a white paisley dress from a Wichita thrift store and pretend to be Patty Griffin and sing.

And, of course, this is the one night that Mom comes in without knocking. Which maybe Connor wanted her to.

It's 11:45pm, Friday night again. The stars are slowing their spin. It's dark and quiet and big out here. Connor belches gas fumes. It hurts until it hurts less. Connor stands up, woozy. An Army Reserve base is no place for someone both drunk on and toting gasoline stolen from that Army Reserve base. The field is a dark lake of young wheat, seed tops blowing like foamy waves. Pulling the heavy gas can is like paddling a small boat.

Connor tucks the gas can into the bed of the truck and pulls onto the dark road, back into the gridded streets and lights of the Wichita suburbs. Lucinda Williams is singing about what a sweet old world it is.

Riley's dad's house, close to Connor's parents' house, 12:05 am. A neighborhood of 60s bungalows that are finally falling apart, just like the economy that made them. Riley's sitting at the kitchen table in an oversized, threadbare Pink Floyd t-shirt, with a bottle of beer and some old weird book about magic or something, listening to Cowboy Junkies. Everyone has a thing. Riley's is replicating magic symbols with found objects and dead stuff. "You're late, Connie," she scolds; "just where you been at this hour?" Riley likes to pretend she's older.

"I was just going for a drive," Connor says casually. "with my big can of gasoline from a Hummer, what else?" Connor has been practicing how to say it.

"Holy shit," Riley crinkles her nose. "You do smell like gas. You brazen miscreant, I didn't think you'd do it!" She tousles Connor's hair to get a blush, but Connor's face just looks pale.

"Hey you okay?"

"I think I swallowed too much gasoline," Connor mumbles.

"Jesus, Connie," Riley gets headache medicine and a glass of water. "Take these and drink that," she commands, "and when you're done drink some more." Connor swallows, then belches gas. It actually does feel a little better.

"You didn't think you had to, did you?" Riley asks. "Angelo can get money for gas, without risking his life and freedom."

"You know it's hard for Angelo to ask for money from his parents."
Riley sips her beer. "Boohoo."

"I'm tired of not doing anything." Connor's head is on the table. Connor can hear the old Frigidaire humming through the table, kind of pacifying.

"Dude we are doing something," Riley responds, "and it's gonna be *fun*. How about doin' stuff with *other people* more?"

Connor peels a red, wood-grained face off the table to pick up Riley's beer and take a swig. "Hey, this is pretty good."

"Anything'll taste good after gas," Riley swipes the bottle back. "Like you need more booze tonight; why don't you take a shower? God forbid Dad comes home and lights the stove."

"Where *is* Frank?"

"He had to work late."

Connor stares at the table. The grain looks blurry. "Okay, I'll go shower. Just because you said so."

"Connor," Riley says, watching Connor shakily stand up, then looking down at the beer bottle she's mindlessly peeling the label off. "I don't know what you got goin' on at home, and I'm not gonna press you. I'm just... I'm glad you're coming with us. It'll be fun."

"Me too," Connor says, looking down at the 70s linoleum pattern. "I'm going to do more stuff with you. And Angelo. Starting with this trip."

"Maybe you'll even move to Kansas City."

"Weirder things have happened," Connor smiles weakly and goes into the bathroom.

Connor opens the bathroom window and strips naked thinking *don't look in the mirror, don't look in the mirror,* but oops! looking in the mirror like always, seeing a body that looks as awkward as it feels, angular like a cubist painting, getting that wave of despair. Connor gets in the shower, lets it wash away, down the drain with the gasoline.

Starting with this trip. Things will be different.

Even in high school, Riley and Angelo were the friends Connor had the most intense feelings of desire and fear about. They smoked behind the school and poked at everyone's bullshit. Bullshit had kept Connor safe but now safety wasn't keeping Connor alive any more.

The water starts running cold. Connor towels off and borrows a robe hanging on the door.

Riley's passed out on her bed with the light on. She looks sweet hold-ing her book, like a kid who falls asleep reading bedtime stories. Connor turns her light off, and falls asleep on the couch.

It's unclear what time or day or year it is, but Riley and Angelo and Frank and Mom and Dad and Grandma and Grandpa are standing around a coffin where Connor is laid out in a suit. Connor yells "No, you're burying me in the wrong clothes!" But they just stand there as Frank shakes his head and shovels dirt on the coffin.

Which is strange, because then it's sometime in the wee hours of Sat-urday morning and Frank comes in through the side door. Connor starts to sit up and Frank soothes "No, sleep, sleep," in his deep husky voice.

It's 8:00am Saturday morning. Connor wakes up to a knock on the door and a splitting headache. It's Angelo, looking cheerful even in his cool leather jacket and dark sunglasses. He hugs Connor tight. "How are ya buddy?"

Instead of answering Connor opens the bottle of headache medicine. "Oh like that, huh?" Angelo sets his sunglasses down and picks up last night's beer bottle with half a label on it. He drinks the last bit. "Hey this is pretty good," he says. "How many did you have?"

"Gasoline," Connor moans.

"Aw man I think you're starting to have a problem," Angelo jokes. "No, Riley texted me last night. Hey, you know you didn't have to do that? I would've paid for gas." He puts his hands on Connor's shoulders and starts to rub; he's being gentle so Connor lets him. "Where's breakfast?"

"I fough' you were bringin' breakfaf, jerk," Riley sputters, coming out of the bathroom with a toothbrush in her mouth. Angelo squeezes her around the shoulders, then pulls out a bag of donuts. "Well at leaf' you're a fweet jerk." Riley softens and puts her free arm around him. She runs to the bathroom to spit.

"Did you get any coffee?" Connor implores.

"Shit I forgot. The donut shop has shitty coffee anyway."

"I would have drank it."

"I'll make some," Riley chirps, coming back into the kitchen, taking bites of a donut. Angelo takes his phone out to text. Connor picks up a cup and holds it close for comfort.

Angelo's phone chimes, the screen says "Tia M. 2 messages: ...bringing your boyfriend to meet me mijo?..." Angelo says, "Okay my aunt's ready for us tonight, she's making enchiladas."

"I love Tia Maria!" Riley picks up.

"She loves you," Angelo sighs.

"She loves everyone," Riley answers. "Especially you."

Riley and Angelo are on their second donuts while Connor's picking at the first and wondering if black coffee is really that good on an upset empty stomach.

"If we leave soon we can do a few hours filming in Las Animas," Angelo proposes. Everyone has a thing. Angelo's is doing apocalyptic film projects in abandoned houses. There's one in Colorado he wants to do on the way to his aunt's.

When they're packing the truck, Frank comes out in his robe. "Don't do anything I wouldn't do," he says with a fatherly gesture, then laughs. "That's not a very good guideline, just trust your better judgment." He hugs all of them and waves as they drive away.

Connor's still a little queasy, so Riley drives. Angelo sits in the back, feet up next to his film equipment.

Grain fields and silos and cow pastures roll by; the smell of dairy production hangs on the edge of the little red brick towns that have exactly one bank and one grocery store and one Dairy Queen. Connor and Angelo take turns sipping whiskey. Angelo offers to Riley who says, "Dude I'm driving." When they get out of range of the Wichita stations Riley looks through Connor's cassettes: Patty Griffin, Lucinda Williams, Jenny Lewis, Neko Case.

"Wow, you gotta lot of women acts in your truck," Riley says.

"So?" Connor says defensively.

"Nothing. Way to go."

Trees give way to wild grass scattered with little white and red prairie flowers, lines of cottonwood, and an oak here and there.

Connor wonders why people think this part of the country is empty. To Connor, the west isn't empty but open. It's a place to imagine things because it's not already full of things. Ghosts. Spirits. Buffalo skeletons herding across the wide land, people skeletons riding horse skeletons, yelling, chanting. Saying, *Connor, what are you thinking about?*

"Connor, what are you thinking about?" Riley asks. "When're you gonna move to Kansas City with us?"

"Oh," Connor becomes aware of the car again. "Um. I want to. I just... need to figure some things out first." Everyone has a thing. Except Connor.

"Like what?" Riley prods.

"Like... um... money? What I want to do with my life?"

"You can figure those things out in Kansas City. What are you afraid of?"

"I don't *know!* Everything? People? Getting stuck?"

"Aren't you stuck right now? There's more things in Kansas City. There's a scene. Maybe... maybe you could even get into school with us."

"I won't fit in." Connor stares out the window.

"*I* don't fit in. Still glad I'm not still in Wichita, like you keep saying you don't wanna be."

"You do keep saying that," Angelo agrees.

"I know. I just..." Connor looks at the landscape rolling by. "I just don't want anyone to get tired of helping me. I need to do some things on my own first."

"What's getting in the way?" Riley probes. "Besides being isolated?"

"I don't know. I'm confused."

"Hey Connie," Riley softens her tone. "I know what hardship is like. I'm a poor queer crazy woman. This world is fucked up. You got friends, Connie."

Connor takes the bottle and takes a swig and then says looking forward at the road "*I'm* poor. *And* crazy. *And* I'm...I'm..."

"And you're drinking too much, twerp." Riley reaches for the bottle.

"I'm not," Connor caps it and passes it to Angelo. "Okay, I'm done. See?"

"What were you gonna say?" Riley continues. "Are you *queer* too? I mean come on, you can tell me."

"I don't know what I am. I'm a college dropout."

"You dropped out of Fundie college. That's an accomplishment, actually."

Angelo leans forward and puts a hand on Connor's shoulder. "Connor, why don't you just move to Kansas City and stay at my house? You can get a job, tell the world you're gonna live on your terms from now on." He squeezes Connor's shoulder just a little too hard. Connor squirms.

"You're a great example of self-determination, Angelo," Riley says dryly.

"I determine my life, no one else."

"Uh huh," Riley says. "Hey, when are you gonna introduce Jonathan to your family? He keeps telling me he wants to meet them."

"When I feel like it."

"Yeah, when you gonna feel like it?" Riley is enjoying this.

"When I'm ready to do it on my own terms. I don't have super-cool tolerant parents, you know. Wait, you *don't* know."

"What part? Having an intolerant family or pretending I didn't need their money? Yeah, I don't know what either of those is like."

"You're a dyke bitch, Riley."

"You're an arrogant faggot, Angelo. And I love you so much."

"I love you too. And my folks helped some with grad school, that's all. I'm doing this because I believe in my art."

"Weren't you already doing your art?"

"Yeah, because I *chose* to do it, instead of feeling sorry for myself or waiting for the perfect place to do it."

"Okay. Glad you're so empowered. Like I said, you are a great example for us all."

"Thank you. Also by the way I'm not a faggot."

"Oh sorry. I know, *you just love Jonathan, you're not defined by that,* and also blah blah blah, something about individualism."

Instead of saying anything Angelo opens the bottle and drinks from it, sort of a lot. No one says anything for what seems to Connor like a long time.

The cassette player is singing *This tornado loves you, this tornado loves you.*

Riley finally breaks the silence. "Don't forget you have Tia Maria,". "She's pretty kick-ass and she loves you for who you are."

"Yeah, that's true. All the way from Pueblo."

"Hey, by the way, that's where we're goin'!"

It's 3:00pm, Mountain Daylight Time, and they are crossing the state line and the sign that says *Welcome to Colorful COLORADO.*

Riley is trying to find a radio station, going from static to *Double XL, Double XL* to *In these uncertain times, God's word is a beacon of* back to static again. "Hey where's that whiskey at?" she calls out.

Soon they reach Las Animas, and get off the highway. Angelo is sure they can get cheaper gas in Larr. It's a dry, dusty, run-down town, but the gas station is modern. There's an old woman behind the counter. "Ya'll not from around here are you?" she asks curiously.

"What gave us away?" Angelo smiles.

"Not enough dust on you."

"We'll work on it."

"What brings you around here?"

"Making a film."

"In our little town?" The old woman perks up. "Are you gonna shoot me?" She puts her hand against her gray curls.

"Aw I'd give you the lead role, but it's not that kind of movie. You know the Skilling Mansion? It's a little west of here."

A dark expression comes over her face. "Yeah I know about that place," she says. "Ain't no use goin' to a place like that," she says. "No good'll come out of a place like that."

"We'll take our chances," Angelo swaggers.

"I reckon you will," she says, handing over change. "You just listen to these gals with you, yeah? They look to have more sense than you."

Connor does a nervous lip-bite. "Yeah, *Angelo*," Riley pokes.

On the way back to the truck Angelo says "I better listen to a *gal like you*, Connor."

"Yeah. Funny."

"Don't worry Connor, I think she just sees that you're a sweet person with sense." Riley says. "You think she knows something about the house?"

"I think she's a crazy old lady," Angelo balks.

"Well someday that's what I'm gonna be," Riley retorts, "and I hope anyone ever listens to me then."

They drive through the short length of Larr. The town looks so dry. The people too.

It's 3:30pm, Mountain Daylight Time, and in the distance a large house stands out against the tall grass and dark sky. Closer, it looks like a castle, surrounded by squawking crows. Two round turrets frame the wall, and a cupola with a widow's walk points above the center.

Down the dirt lane, grass brushes under the truck with a gentle slapping noise. A ruined old Sheriff's cruiser is swallowed by grass on the side of the lane. "That's weird," Riley says. Then there's a rusted out Comet from the 50s. Every 30 feet there's a car that looks like it will never start again. Angelo rolls the window down and starts filming; it's windy, the air is heavy and electric. There's a 90s model that looks nearly intact. "This is weird," Riley says. "Why are there so many abandoned cars here?"

"People probably left them here to not have to deal with them," Angelo says, looking through the camera.

"Why not just send them to a junkyard?" Connor says.

"Because rednecks," Angelo says.

"Hey that's my family you're dissin'," Riley says.

"Mine too," Connor says.

"Mine too," Angelo says. "They're just pretending to be respectable."

They stop about thirty feet from the house. Its three stories loom in a faded green with bone-colored trim, rows of windows across every level, wraparound porch with loose boards. To the right is a broken wooden fence, and beyond it a corn field.

"I dunno, Angelo," Riley says. "Who's keeping that corn field? Maybe someone lives here."

"Come on, look at that house," Angelo replies. "Windows are cracked, posts are broken, it hasn't been painted in anyone's guess how many decades. We passed plenty of corn fields on that road; this is probably someone's around here."

There's a high-pitched humming, a chirping sound. The crows are diving into the corn field and black specks are popping out of it toward them. They are bullet-shaped bugs with wide-spaced red eyes.

"Ow!" Riley yells. "That stings! I'm getting back in the truck." She does, Connor does too. Angelo continues filming crows and locusts. There's more and more, soon a certifiable swarm is coming out of the corn, the sky is dark with them, they're smashing against the truck like hail. "That boy's insane!" Riley yells. She rolls down the window to yell "Get in the truck you lunatic!" but several bugs fly in so she rolls it back up. "This is crazy!" she says. Connor is staring into the swarm, watching it obscure Angelo.

The swarm passes, leaving Angelo covered in red welts and smiling. "That was amazing," he says, "Definitely using it."

Riley opens the door again. "You look like a fuckin' plucked chicken. And *that was a fucking sign.*"

"Aw, don't be superstitious, Ri," Angelo says. "We just disturbed the crows, which made the locusts swarm. It's the circle of life."

"What the fuck ever. Connor do you believe me?"

"Um. I don't know. I think they were seventeen-year locusts?"

"See," Angelo says, "Connor thinks it was just some locusts."

"That's not what I – " Connor is cut off by a rumble in the sky.

"Come on inside, I'll protect you" Angelo says. "Also I don't want it to rain on my camera." He pulls his filming bag out of the truck and walks toward the porch steps.

"Come on Connor," Riley sighs, then under her breath, "We're gonna wind up protecting your ass, you idiot bro fag."

"What?" Angelo doesn't turn around.

"I said *your sweet ass is gonna be my responsibility.*"

"Thanks babe," Angelo pats his own ass.

Riley and Connor run up the porch, past railings with vine-like braids and flourishes, to catch up with him in front of an oak double-door.

"Angelo, I know you are set on this but – "

Angelo brings his finger to his lips, then places it on Riley's lips, then turns the big brass door handle. It squeaks and clicks. Riley and Connor freeze, Angelo peers inside. It's dark and quiet and cool and musty. "I don't think this is a good idea," Riley whispers.

But Angelo is already going inside. "It's an abandoned building, Riley... this is... my turf," he says, panning and zooming with his camera.

"Hold on," Connor says, noticing, under a chair on the porch, a pair of old snakeskin boots adorned with shiny red beads, picking them up to look at them.

"Hey..." Riley exclaims, "those must... belong to someone..." and she rushes in after Angelo. Connor holds onto the boots and follows, closing the door. It's immediately so dark they can't see each other. "Angelo!" Riley calls out in a stage whisper, "Angelo! I think someone lives here! There were boots by the door!" Their eyes slowly adjust; they're in a big room with a grand staircase. There's no Angelo. There's a corner to the right; they turn it, and they're startled by the red record light of his camera.

"Come this way!" Angelo turns around.

"I think someone lives here!" Riley says again. Angelo keeps walking. There are paintings along the hallway, portraits and landscapes barely popping out in the dark against the patterned green walls. There are also photographs, of a handsome man in nice clothes, of his wife and children also in nice clothes, a few of a woman with dark hair.

"Angelo why do you think people would leave these pictures?!" Riley hisses.

"I don't know," Angelo says. "People's lives are broken. Their families are broken. They walk away leaving everything because the place has all the memories in it."

Angelo's camera light falls on a large painting at the end of the hallway. It's the woman with dark hair. She's leaning against a piano in a red evening dress with a high slit up one leg. She has high cheekbones and dark eyes and her dark hair falls in waves below her shoulders. Her expression is seductive and longing, like someone powerful caught in a vulnerable moment. Or like a singer might look for a portrait.

"Who would leave this?" Riley says. "This is *beautiful.*"

Connor walks closer. It *is* beautiful. The lady is mysterious. A singer. A chanteuse. Connor is filled with a feeling, that one, the one with the lady singers and the dress.

"Connor you're blocking my shot," Angelo says. Connor stays, not even hearing.

"Maybe you're right, Angelo," Riley says. "Maybe this is just a big abandoned house full of people's abandoned memories." She looks up. "I guess I know why you film in these. It's so sad it's beautiful."

"It's holy," Connor says.

"Yeah," Angelo lowers the camera. "This is what I live for." He puts his arms around Riley and Connor. "I'm kinda glad to share it with y'all."

"Hi. I don't mean to break up your moment."

Riley slowly turns her head to the left. A woman is standing there in a long black dress. The woman from the painting.

Riley jumps, which makes Connor and Angelo jump and turn.

"You like my painting?" the woman says tilting her head.

"Oh god I am so sorry!" Riley blurts out. "You live here! This is your house? I am so, so sorry, we didn't know anyone lived here."

"Please," the lady says. "You knew; I heard you saying it over and over." She looks at Angelo. "But this one wouldn't listen, would he? Typical, handsome."

Angelo squirms. "I..."

"Spare me," she says. "I heard enough about my sad abandoned life just a second ago."

"I'm sorry!" Angelo says.

"Don't be," the woman says. "Or you can be if you want, but apologies are boring." She glances at the camera. "So do I get to be in this movie or what?"

"You, um... *yes*," Angelo stammers. Neither Connor nor Riley has seen Angelo nervous before. He runs his fingers through his black hair. "You are the star of this film as far as I'm concerned, miss – "

"Brinda."

"Miss Brinda," Angelo says.

"Don't call me miss."

"Brinda. Got it."

Brinda flips a light switch. It seems bright at first, but after adjusting it's dim lamplight. The walls come alive with the vegetal patterns. Brinda looks at Connor, and Connor meets her eyes. They're intense. "Those boots," she says. "I have some just like them."

"Oh, sorry," Connor demures, "I found them outside and I thought... Here." Connor offers them to Brinda.

Brinda reaches her hand out and almost touches them, then says: "You know what. Keep them. For helping me with my locust problem."

"What? Really?"

"But first I want to see how they look on you."

Connor looks at the boots.

"It's okay, put them on."

Connor puts on the boots, which zip up the sides. Surprisingly, they are Connor's size. They're adventurous and elegant, like, like... a daring cowgirl's.

"Yes," Brinda says. "They should go to you."

"Thank you," Connor says looking down. "I can't believe how nice that is."

"Don't mention it," Brinda says.

"Damn," Riley whispers.

"Oh I'm sure there's something here for you too, doll," Brinda says.

"No I just..." Brinda is looking at Riley, fixing her with that uncomfortable gaze. She is too striking to look at and too striking to look away from.

For a second, Riley thinks she sees her mom on Brinda's face, which scares her even more.

"Why are you here?" Brinda says.

"For filming," Angelo says.

"Pretty small for a film crew. When are the rest coming?"

"It's just us. I'm independent."

"Why are you here?" Brinda says again.

"I just told you," Angelo says.

Brinda studies them and seems to soften. "Okay, come with me." She goes into a room. The three stand there for a moment.

"I think we should," Riley says.

The room is lined with candles, mirrors, altars, cushions, books and jars; it smells like incense and herbs. Two windows are cracked open. There's a wood stove in the corner with a steaming kettle. The gentle sound of steady rain mixes with the gentle crackling of the stove. Brinda pours hot water into a teapot, sets out four china cups, each a little stained, then lights more candles around the room until it's bright.

"Sit, please." They take cushions, as does Brinda. She pours and hands them each a cup of dark, earthy reddish-brown liquid.

"What is it?" Riley asks.

"My people call it tea," Brinda says, smiling.

"Oh. Ha," Riley says. She glances at Connor and Angelo to see if they're drinking.

"Are you scared?" Brinda says. They sideways glance at each other.

"Um..." Riley says.

"It would be reasonable." Brinda continues. "You walked into a stranger's house. You don't know who I am."

"That's true."

Brinda smells her tea, takes a sip. Connor and Riley and Angelo sip theirs; it's bitter and tannic but warming.

"Now. I need to know why you're here," Brinda says flatly.

"What more do you want us to tell you?" Riley says.

"Tell me what you want."

"We don't... want anything."

"I sincerely hope that isn't true."

"Why?"

"Who wants nothing is dead," Brinda says dryly over a sip of her tea.

"I don't want what most people want," Riley shrugs.

"That still leaves what you do want."

"What if you wouldn't get it?"

"Try me."

Riley sips the tea again. "*What if I want to live in a house by myself in the woods far away from anyone?*" Riley says. "Would you get it?"

"Oh," Brinda says. "That's *something*." She studies Riley for a moment. "What does that give you?"

"No one to not listen to me," Riley sighs. "No one to treat me like I'm crazy."

"Some people might think you're crazy for living in a house by yourself in the woods."

"I knew you would," Riley says defensively.

"Not me, child."

"Okay," Riley says, not quite believing her. "Maybe they *would* think I'm crazy. But they'd be where *I'd* have the power, so it wouldn't matter."

"Ah, you want the *power*." A sideways smile creeps to Brinda's lips.

"I mean no. Yeah. I mean – "

"There's nothing wrong with wanting to have power, Riley."

"How do you know my name?"

"I heard Angelo use it." Brinda smiles again.

"How do you know *my* name?" Angelo says.

"I heard *Riley* use it. You were calling to Angelo, afraid that you'd walked into someone's house, right, Riley? Someone who lives in a house by herself, far away from anyone, where she has the power?"

Riley sets her tea down. "Are you a witch?" she says suddenly.

"You are *just. Precious,*" Brinda says, sipping her tea down to the bottom.

Riley clenches her arms with her hands, not noticing that she's doing it. "Are you going to do something to us?"

"I'm going to give you what you want." Brinda smiles, pouring herself and each of them more tea. "Provided you know what that is."

"What I *really* want is to do some filming of your house," Angelo says. "With you. If you'll let me."

"Why?" Brinda asks.

"Because it's beautiful and mysterious, like you. Of course, I want to respect your privacy."

"You *are* a charmer, aren't you?" Brinda's smirk is intense, the way she narrows her eyes. "Why do you film in abandoned places, Angelo? Or places you *think* are abandoned."

"I'm attracted to them. Places a map or an address can't tell you anything about. Places you can't buy admission to. Places where all the rules don't mean anything."

"Where *all* the rules don't mean *anything*," Brinda drawls the words out.

"Yeah," Angelo says.

"Why do you make films?"

"Because I want to show people. I want to take them out of their comfortable world. I want to make them feel what I feel in these places. I want to haunt them and make it stay in them."

"And what does that give you?"

"It's my *art*," Angelo is getting frustrated. "It's... I don't know. It gets me recognition... it's my career... it's my *life,* okay?"

"Do you want to be famous Angelo?"

"I guess. *Yes.* Okay. Yes. So I want to be famous. Like any other artist. I want to be celebrated for my work. Is that bad?"

"Nooooo," Brinda whispers. She re-lights a candle and seems to be enjoying herself.

"Okay, I'm glad you think so." Angelo brushes his hair back with his fingers.

Brinda lights more candles.

"And you, dear," Brinda says to Connor. "What's your name?"

"Connor Morrissey," Connor almost whispers, but makes eye contact.

"You didn't think you'd slip by by being quiet, did you?"

"No."

"You're consistent, I'll give you that." She takes out a silver cigarette case and opens it, glances at the three. "You don't mind if I smoke?"

"I'll take one," Connor says.

"Gooood," Brinda smiles and gives Connor one and lights it, then her own. Connor breathes out a sigh, looks at the cigarette.

"Nat Shermans. You're a classy lady."

"I do what I can." She sets an ashtray between them. "So. What do you want?"

"You won't let me lie, will you?"

"No," Brinda blows a long, narrow stream of smoke.

"Okay. I want..." Connor looks at Riley and Angelo, then takes another drag.

"I want... I want to be like you."

Brinda gives Conner a scrutinizing look. "Riley wants to live in a house alone like I do," she says. "Angelo wants to film me, and you want to *be* like me in some way I can't wait to find out. You flatterers." She leans forward. "So tell me, sweetheart, *how* do you want to be like me?"

"I want to be..." Riley and Angelo, are looking at Connor, expectant. Connor looks down, takes a drag, exhales. Looks back at Brinda, finally.

"I want to be a *singer*. You're a singer, right? I saw the pictures of you, and the painting."

"You. Want. To. Be. A. Singer."

"Yes. A singer."

Brinda sits back and studies Connor, her cigarette up between two fingers, her other arm crossed. "Okay," she says finally. "We can do that."

"Wait," Connor says. "That's it? You're not gonna ask any more questions? You're not gonna make me explain why I want to be a singer?"

"No." Brinda says flatly.

Riley and Angelo are looking at Connor. They have the same question on their faces that Connor just asked.

"Okay you three," Brinda puts out her cigarette in the ashtray. "I'd like to take you upstairs and show you something special."

"Wait. Do you *really* think you can give us what we want?" Connor says incredulously. "Like grant our wishes? Like a genie or something?"

Brinda laughs out loud. "You are *so. Cute.* Of course not like that."

"Well then... what? how?"

"You're going to have to see for yourself what I have in mind. Now come on, I have other things to do today." She rises and gestures up with her hand.

"I don't know..." Riley says hesitantly. "We only just met you and – "

"Riley, do you really want to be powerful?" Brinda interrupts.

"Well. Yeah."

"There will come a time when you'll have to act like it."

"I. *Okay*," Riley stands and walks up to Brinda, looks her in the eye.

"Good," Brinda smiles. "You two, come on."

"Can I start filming now?" Angelo asks.

"Oh." Brinda seems to hesitate. "Yes," she agrees finally.

"Okay, then I'm in."

Connor puts the cigarette out. "I don't guess I have a choice."

"Yes you do," Brinda says curtly. "You can stay here. Or go wait in your truck."

"No," Connor says.

"I didn't think so."

"Just... tell us what it is first?"

"And spoil the surprise? I don't show this to many people, Connor. This is your lucky day." Brinda winks, and leads them out the door.

Now that the hallway is lit, many pictures are unmistakably Brinda: on a stage, on horseback, some with an older man, the one in some of the other pictures, a handsome, dapper man. In one picture Brinda looks much younger. At the end of the hall Brinda turns on a chandelier lamp above the staircase. There's a grand piano, rugs, polished floors, that green wallpaper everywhere giving the faint impression of a garden.

"It... really looked abandoned from outside... and in the dark," Angelo says.

"Keeps solicitors and nosy people away," Brinda grins. "Present company excepted." She leads them to the stairs. "Notice this," she says pointing to a gold-yellow carpet with lush geometric patterns on it. "Stay on the yellow carpet if you will; we're just going to follow this yellow carpet."

"Okay," Riley says. She and Connor start up the stairs behind Brinda. Angelo follows, catching a shot of everyone going up the stairway. It's broad enough for all of them to be side by side.

Upstairs, there's the same green plant wallpaper flanking the yellow carpet, doors and hallways on either side, a large stained glass window ahead.

Angelo takes a 360 while Riley and Connor pause at the first door, which is cracked open. Light and some sound come from inside. They peek through the door: just an old record player playing a cello conceerto.

"Keep up now," Brinda says briskly. "And keep to the yellow carpet, please."

"Brinda, who's playing that record?" Riley says. "Is someone else here?"

"Bach. I find baroque music relaxing. Don't you?"

"*I guess*," Riley says, perplexed.

The hallway splits right and left, and Brinda stops.

"The yellow carpet goes both ways," says Connor.

"Then we can go both ways, can't we?" Brinda says. She goes left and motions them to follow. Angelo sneaks a bewildered look to Riley and Connor, mouths, "*She's crazy.*"

Brinda stops by a door. "I don't show this to many people." She opens the door.

There's just some chairs facing a broad curtain against one wall. "What?" Riley says. Brinda walks over to the curtain.

"If you'll sit... and *cloooose your eyes...* and keep them closed till I tell you." She smiles. They sit.

"I'm feeling kind of weird," Connor says.

"Cloooooose your eeeeyyyyssss," Brinda singsongs. They all close their eyes, but Angelo leaves the camera on. And Connor peeks through one eye. There's the sound of a curtain opening,.

"Reaaaaaaady?" Brinda says. "No peeking!"

"YEEEESSSS," Connor says.

"Okay, *open your eyes.*"

The curtains have been drawn back to reveal a black screen. Violins play and a voice quietly says "I guess I know why you film in these. It's so sad it's beautiful." Riley grips her seat. A caption on a black screen reads "Winner: Best Picture, Sundance 2016." Another voice says "It's holy," and another "This is what I live for." Then the caption "*Haunting... moving... an inventiveness in narrative style* – Peter Travers, Rolling Stone." There's a flash of three people looking at a painting of woman against a piano. A flourish of ominous strings. Then the caption "From director Angelo Ortega." Riley grabs Angelo's hand. There's shots of them driving to the house, standing in front of it, a quick flash of the locust swarm with a panicked string section.

It goes quiet. There's Angelo opening the door with a loud click. Then "*this changes film* – The Austin Chronicle." Then shots of the three and Brinda: going up staircases, watching a movie of themselves, the caption "*turns the camera onto your secret dreams and nightmares* – Richard Roeper, The Chicago Sun Times." Then a shot of some village. The caption after says "*magical... meta as fuck* – Vox."

Then there's a stage with discordant guitar sounds, shots of running down halls, opening doors that go nowhere and doors that go to big open rooms. Then *"I'm not calling this film a tour de force, everyone says tour de force. Do movie critics ever look in a thesaurus? Anyway I've never seen anything like it and I'm pretty old* – Gene Shalit." The music crescendos on the silhouette of a tall, striking man. The screen fades to black. A smooth voice says "Tell me what you want."

The lights come back on and Brinda is looking expectantly at Angelo.

"What... what was that?" Angelo stammers. "Are you... filming us? Do you have people – "

"So suspicious," Brinda mocks. "So, what did you think?"

"I don't even know how to think," Angelo says dumbfounded. "How did you do that?"

"I didn't do it, you did, Angelo. It came from your dreams. It's what you want, isn't it? You can have it."

Angelo sits silently, looking at his hand on his lap. His other is still in Riley's. He looks up at Brinda. "How?"

"Know that it is what you want. Hold it in your mind. Keep your camera on, and keep filming to the end of this tour. Got it?"

"Yes," Angelo answers without hesitation.

"This is crazy," Riley says. "And creepy. Why should we trust you? Angelo why should we trust her?"

"It's not my job to make you trust me and you may go as you came: of your own free will." Brinda walks to the door. "There's more rooms. Coming?"

Angelo gets up with his camera rolling.

"Gonna wind up protecting your ass," Riley says.

"Thanks babe," Angelo says.

"Connie, stay close to me," Riley grabs Connor's hand.

"Riley I'm feeling weird," Connor says.

"Me too."

Brinda leads them down the hallway. Either from the number of doors or the sounds of their steps falling flat against the patterned walls, the house feels strangely huge, even bigger than it looked. Brinda opens another door, motions them to follow.

This room also has a broad curtain, but no chairs. Brinda summons them over. "Cloooooose your eeeeeeeyyyesssss," she says.

"Do we have to?" Riley says.

"Oh suit yourself," Brinda opens the curtains, reveals just the other half of the room.

"What?" Riley says. "Where's the screen?"

"For crying out loud, this isn't a movie one, Riley," Brinda snaps.

There's a set of French doors. Brinda opens them to a small balcony with stairs down to a garden; it's not raining anymore. She leads them down; time seems to pass strangely. Where there was only a fallow garden now there is a small village of cob cottages with gardens, full of art, surrounded by woods, with a grove and a large fire circle in the center.

Songs and chants rise through the trees. People are in the village, in lapsed time tending their gardens, cooking together, dancing. They make love freely and frequently, which seems part of the magic. Most of them are women.

The villagers gather in the center, around an effigy of a person on a stake over a blazing wood pile. Those at cardinal positions around the circle are holding a pentagram, a sword, a branch, or a cup; the one holding the branch is Riley. Each person speaks a magical phrase and throws origami shapes into the fire. It's a spell of protection. Village Riley says *May we burn from within and never again be burned from without.* The fire blazes.

"Riley, come on, back this way," Brinda says.

"I don't want to," Riley sniffs. "I never want to leave here again."

"You aren't even here now," Brinda says.

Riley wipes her face, sees just a small unkept garden. She looks at Brinda. "What did you do?"

"What did *you* do," Brinda says. "You want it?"

"More than anything."

"Good; remember that."

"I still don't know if I should trust you."

"You shouldn't," Brinda heads back through the french door. Riley looks at the empty, cloudy sky, sniffs, looks at Connor and Angelo. "Let's stay close."

Back in the hallway, Connor says "I guess the next one's mine? I mean, we don't have to... I already know what – "

"Shush," Brinda says. She leads them around a corner, stops by yet another door. Connor hesitates.

"What are you scared of, Connor?" Brinda says. "You saw nothing bad has happened so far."

"I just... I don't know..."

"You're free to turn around. Maybe you're fine with just having other people's visions."

"You still have those cigarettes on you?" Connor asks.

"Not on this carpet," Brinda says.

Riley grabs Connor's hand, Angelo puts a hand on Connor's shoulder. "We're with you, Connie," Riley says. Connor doesn't say that that's what's scary.

This room has a large curtain like the other two. "You have a real motif going," Connor says.

"Ready?" Brinda says.

"Yeah," Connor says.

"Cloooooooose your eeeeeeyyyyyeees," she says.

Connor sighs and closes them. "How long do I have to do this?"

"You three don't understand fun," Brinda says.

They open their eyes. There's a bar and a stage, and a bunch of people standing around. Connor orders a whiskey sour. "Connor what the hell?" Riley yells over the crowd. No one's on stage, but there's a country electric guitar on a stand.

"You're a good bartender," Connor says to the handsome bartender in a nice suit. "The best damn bartender from... where are you from again? Portland or something?"

Someone takes the stage; it's hard to see them but the crowd cheers.

They play unrecognizably distorted chords. Riley and Angelo plug their ears and hold their heads. Connor winces and tries to see who's playing, but the crowd is trying to rush the stage. Connor catches a glimpse of red boots and a white paisley dress. An awful, deep voice sings, warped and distant and wobbly like a broken record.

I knewewewewewewewewewewew you'd lovelovelovelovelovelove me as loooooong as you wanwanwanwanteeeeeed.

Riley and Angelo are getting trampled in the rush. Connor is slumped to the floor by the barstool. "That ridiculous fuck should kill itself," someone yells. The echoes of singing combine in interference patterns to become a single, dissonant scream.

Connor stumbles through the angry crowd until they aren't there anymore, toward the door.

"Stay on the yellow carpet!" Brinda yells.

Connor runs down the hall, head pounding, the hall itself constricting and dilating like Connor's pulse. Connor runs and runs for a long time until there's a door, slams it shut, and slumps against it, breathing shallowly.

It's 11pm on Tuesday, April 13 in Connor's room. *I'm never leaving again,* Connor says and sits on the bed, then falls down onto it. *It hurts too much it hurts too much it hurts too much.* There is a hole in Connor's chest, Connor's heart is exposed, squirting warm blood all over the bed.

I'm gonna die right now. I'd like to die in my country girl dress like a real poor redneck trash tranny. Then Connor is wearing the dress, struggling with bloody hands to reach the guitar next to bed and pick out a song:

young girls in their bare feet cigarette smokin' lookin every which way wishin and a-hopin...

Connor drops the guitar and fingers the heart-hole. I'm gonna die and this is what my life comes to. *Better off dead than alive anyway.*

That's true, says a voice that sounds like everyone's.

It's some unknown time of night on Friday, April 16. The hallways are echoing with songs that come from nowhere. The walls and floor and ceiling are wailing and howling faintly. Riley holds her head. Brinda leads them around a corner. The hallway stretches, shortens, wobbles in dimension. The lights dim, brighten, fade green, red, yellow.

"I'm gonna throw up," Riley says, then does.

"My carpet!" Brinda says, then "never mind, come on." Angelo helps Riley up and they run down the hall together. Brinda opens a door. There's nothing but a black expanse of space.

"Well it's not this one," she says. The hallway echoes *I go out walkin' after midnight, out in the moonlight just like we used to do.* Brinda sings back, "*I'm always walkin' after midnight, searching for you.*"

"Fuck this," Riley says and starts limp-running, yelling "Connor! Connie!" The hallway stretches on and on. Riley notices it stretches farther than she can see in both directions and there's no one else there. "Connie?! Angelo?! Brinda?!"

Angelo's voice echoes from somewhere distant.

It's September 1, 1995, at a big public elementary school in Wichita. Riley's mamma went away. Daddy is too sad to go to work and he drinks too much. Riley is outgrowing her clothes. People make fun of them.

"Angelo?"

The hallway goes on and on and it's too big for Riley's little legs.

It's a sad, sad world, and you're a sad, sad girl...

"Stop it!" Riley yells.

Nobody careeees.

"Angelo!" she sobs. "Connie!" The lights are glaring, bright and fluorescent. Big legs walk by while she sobs on the floor; some of them stop and face her.

What a pitiful little thing, they say.

Riley's hands are covering her crying eyes.

No mother, not much of a father, tsk tsk tsk.

"Shut up!" Riley yells.

No discipline. The child needs discipline.

It's October 15, 1995 and Riley is in the back of a car. "Where are you taking me?" she cries. The man wearing a suit turns around. He has big, bulging eyes. He only looks at her with them and turns back to the wheel. Riley starts punching and kicking the back of the seat. "No!" she yells. "No! No! No!"

When she opens her eyes there is no seat, just a padded wall, and three other ones just like it, and a bright white light.

You're going to hurt yourself. Stop doing that.

Riley hits the wall over and over, then takes out her pocket knife and stabs it. Bright white fluff rushes out of it and covers her, wraps around her, pulling her arms back. Now she's in a straight jacket and she can't move. "Leave me alone!" she sobs. "Fuck you!"

We didn't want to do this; this is for your own good.

"Let me out!"

There is no getting out. You might as well calm down. You will be here forever.

"Fuck you!"

It's April 16, 2016, and Angelo follows Riley down a hallway through a doorway. The door slams shut behind him. "What the fuck!" he yells. "Riley!?" There's another doorway and another. Angelo keeps running through halls and doors, each one exactly like the last one. "This is crazy," he says. He turns around; the last door he ran through is shut. He opens it, and there's nothing. "Where the hell am I," he whispers to himself. He opens the next door: Nothing. "This can't be happening." The darkness is cold and it goes on forever.

It turns into shiny black mirrors that reflect him. He is naked. He has nothing but his camera. "Let me out!" he yells.

He drops his camera by the strap and pulls his hair. "I want to be out!" he yells. He runs at the mirror and it shatters into his flesh, into a million shards, a hundred million, infinite shards.

It's February 4, 2004, and Angelo shoots up in his bed panting. The alarm clock says 4am. It was a bad dream. He lies back down, the sheets wet from sweat. He's almost asleep again when he notices the red light of his camera where his alarm clock was, bloody carpet where wet sheets were. And there's a screen. A movie of Angelo bending his legs back over his shoulders to suck his own dick is playing for a million people. A hundred million people. Infinite people. And the score goes *It's a small world after all, it's a small world after all.*

"Shut up!" Angelo yells. "Shut up shut up shut up!" He throws the camera through the screen, puncturing a hole to nothing but blackness. Around him is nothing but an audience watching a screen where Angelo is sucking a hole of the blackness inside of him and hating himself.

It's some horrible time on April 16, 2016, and Angelo props up Riley where she is on the floor next to a knife in the wall.

"Angelo," she cries, "where are we?"

"I don't know," Angelo says, "a nightmare."

"I forgot where we were. Where's Connor?"

"I don't know."

"This place is trying to separate and confuse us."

"We need Brinda."

"I don't trust Brinda."

"She's all we have."

"We have each other. Somewhere we have Tia M. with her prayer candles lit for us to make it to her house safe."

They get up and run together two more rooms down, where Connor is on the bed.

It's 11:00pm on April 16, 2009 at the secret cabin in the woods. Everyone has left the party except Angelo and Riley and Connor. Connor has stayed because they said they wanted that and Connor wanted to believe them. Angelo and Riley separate molly and mushrooms into three doses and they wash it down with juice and vodka. The air melts into warm liquid. They start touching each other. It's the most intimate any of them have ever felt.

Riley kisses Angelo. Then Riley kisses Connor. Then Angelo kisses Connor. All their boundaries have melted. *Can life ever actually be like this? Connor asks. Can I tell them I love them? Can I tell them everything?*

A dark shadow is in the doorway, barely noticeable at first, like it might go away if they ignore it, but growing. It's smoke. Someone has lit the door on fire and scrawled SATANS FREAKS on it in sharpie. They put it out with pillows. Riley is crying. Angelo is looking outside to see anyone. Connor is crouched in a corner, rocking back and forth, saying "it's not safe see it's not safe" over and over.

It's 6:66 on Friday, April 16. There's a dark figure in the doorway. It's Brinda. Connor, Angelo and Riley are all in a room in her house, they remember.

"Someone hated us," Riley says with tears.

"I ruined it," Connor says. "I made you unsafe. If it weren't for me..."

"What do you want, Connor?" Brinda says.

"I don't want anything."

"Who wants nothing is dead."

"Okay, I want to be a fucking girl. Not a tranny one. A real one. A safe one." Riley and Angelo look at Connor open-mouthed.

"You all need to come with me right now," Brinda says.

"Why should we listen to you?" Riley says.

"You don't have a choice anymore."

"Did we ever?"

Brinda stands there looking at them.

"Did we ever?!" There's a pitching moan of wood and the light dims. Brinda leads them back around the corner to where they started, only now there's a staircase going up.

"Are we gonna die?" Connor asks. Brinda doesn't answer.

Upstairs, there is a single hallway forward in the wavering light. There's an audible, tangible beating sound. It opens to a room of people facing a man in a regal chair on a podium. The people turn as they approach. They have hollow, empty eyes and it sounds like the rustling of dry corn husks when they move.

"Who are these people?" Riley whispers.

"They aren't people anymore," Brinda says. "Don't look at their eyes."

The man is the one from the pictures downstairs and from the bar. He is radiant, not only as in good-looking, but also as in his skin is glowing through his three-piece suit. He looks as suave as Lucifer himself.

"Hi Daddy," Brinda walks up to him and kisses him on the lips. She sits on his lap and caresses his neck. "I brought you these three. Their desires are strong."

"Come forward," he says in a voice like black suede with rhinestones in it doused with Old Spice. "Tell me what you want."

Riley steps forward. "Hi I'm Riley."

"I know that."

"Who are you then?"

"You can call me the wizard of desire."

"You know what I want, wizard of desire? What I really want? I was thinking and I figured it out. I want to always remember that I am strong, and smart, and resourceful. I want to never forget how far I've come or who I've come with. I wanna take some slack for my dad and for us three loving fuck-ups."

"What about power?"

"Yeah, like I just said."

Angelo stands by Riley. "Hi wizard. After all this shit, what I want is to be brave enough to let these people know how much I need them. If I get any other wishes, I want to get to keep making movies and be proud of who I am."

"I thought you wanted fame and fortune?"

"Well, yeah. But those other things first."

Connor steps next to Riley and Angelo. "Look wizard, I don't know what you're offering but I just wanna feel my heart. I wanna find somewhere in all that scar tissue the willingness to risk my safe nothing for my life. I wanna show these people I love who I really am."

Brinda says "Go ahead, Connor; tell him what that means."

"Oh. I wanna be a woman."

"Oh *really*?"

"Yeah."

He smiles. "I knew that already, but I'm glad you told me. It's so *easy*. Come up, my darlings. I'll give you more than what you asked for."

"Umm...that's real nice," Riley says. "But I think we don't actually need your help. I think we got this."

"But what about that land?" he says. "The land in the woods? Or Connor, how would you like it to be as though you *always were* a woman?"

"I want that so much," Connor says.

"Connie, whatever he gives us, I don't think it'll be real," Riley says.

"It will be better than real, Riley," the wizard says.

Connor stands there caught.

"Connor," Brinda says. "Come here, please. I need to tell you something important."

Connor gets up on the podium. There's a circle symbol like some kind of ritual seal in front of the throne. The wizard looks at Connor's feet as she steps up to it.

"What are those boots doing in my house?" he pushes Brinda off him. "I told you *never to bring them in*."

"I didn't," Brinda smiles. "Connor, stand in that circle."

"Connor, don't listen to what she tells you," the wizard says. "She wants your dreams, like she took all of those people's behind you. She's the Witch of Deceit. You should know her tricks like I do."

"Connor, click your heels together," Brinda says. She brings her lips against her father's ear and says "I've got you now." His eyes go wide. Connor clicks her heels together.

For a second, time stops. Then in what feels like either eternity or three seconds, there's a flash of white and purple light in all their heads. There's a collective sigh of all the corn husk people tumbling to the floor. The wizard lunges for Connor's feet; his hair is white and he's frail. Brinda pulls him off. Her hair is gray; she looks much older.

"Understand this, Dad. You're in *my house* now and you're going to behave yourself like a good boy. Aren't you?"

"Yes," he says defeated.

"All of you help me with these sad heaps."

They all take armfuls of desiccated skin and clothes wrapped around bones. Riley has one in a Sheriff's uniform. Brinda leads back to the stairs.

"Brinda, who were these people?" Riley says.

"It doesn't matter now," Brinda says. "They were dead a long time ago."

Outside it's clear and the stars are out. They throw the remains in a pile on top of some corn husks Brinda gets from of a shed. She douses them in gasoline and lights them up.

"Take the boots off, Connor," Brinda says.

"Oh..." Connor says sadly, and takes off the beautiful boots. Brinda takes them. Brinda and Connor and Riley and Angelo look at each other in the red firelight.

"Now get the hell where you were going," Brinda says. "And don't come back."

"But my shoes are in there," Connor says.

"My camera and phone are in there!" Angelo says.

"My knife is in there too," Riley says.

"You'll get new ones," Brinda says. "Go live your fucking lives. If I find out a year from now you aren't, and I *will* find out," she looks at them dead serious, "I'll kill you while you sleep."

Riley grabs Connor and Angelo by the hands and pulls them toward the truck, Connor looking at Brinda's face in the firelight, Angelo looking at the house. She opens their doors and shoves them in, starts the truck, peels out in a circle, and goes 30 on the dirt all the way back to the blacktop.

Heat Death Of Western Human Arrogance

M TÉLLEZ

She turned to me with half-lidded eyes, her mouth turned upward like a cat's face. Her hands rested on the worn wooden surface beneath her congregation of plants. We needed nothing to see with, just the full moon's cool blue cast. The slopes and lines of her shoulder and hips and chest shifting under the distant light made me feel calm and welcome. I thought about how many seasons would pass before I could be with her again like this.

"I'm thinking about killing myself, kid. They're going to send us off to Mars. And all these plants I live with? They'll *die*. The atmosphere can't shield us from the radiation, which of course they're lying about. You saw the leaked data dumps."

"Yeah." I was unsure of how she expected me to participate in such a topic.

"I'd rather end my life ritually than get sold off and shipped out to die in pain from harsh radiation of another" – Her voice rose sharply – "of a whole other fucking planet, kid!"

She faced me in full. Tendrils of thin cascading palm leaf brushed her cheeks and shoulder. I looked at the fear set through her body – the tension holding her up – a live individuated Earth organism.

Yes – how could they send Earth organisms like Loma to Mars with no provisions for integration with the Martian noosphere? I felt scared for her and didn't know what to say. What could I say? She is dominant in verbal language and I am not. Yet another layer of difficulty one encounters as a third generation Slow Stepper™. We were not engineered to be talkers but we have to be now that people think it's too cruel to leave us shriveled up on Mars. I've heard rumors that the versions after me will have improved speech facility. My skin is pigmented like a dying purple seed husk and slightly iridescent. Every third season I leave Earth to grow the Martian irrigation network at Garden City. The radiation doesn't transform me in the ways that Loma fears.

My name is Inri.

Loma's generation fought for organisms like me to have individual autonomy rights. I'm not so sure Loma foresaw this outcome, where I am contributing to a structure that will usurp her way of life – maybe, it is still all conjecture, this "shipping out" business – I feel perplexed.

"Loma," I start, holding out my arms, "Why don't you come to me and I can stroke you. There is a lot of tension."

Her face contorts angrily then fills with woe. She plods over. I enjoy the rustle of the plants as she leaves their embrace and comes into mine. She wears a sweater knit from recycled fibers, whose loops stretch across many small provocative rips. Her skin smells pleasant with the musks that her glands produce. She is soft with hair. She runs her fingers and long nails along my arms. She calls me serpent because that is how my skin feels to her. I have no hair. I have no decisive genitals either. For Loma I wear a prosthetic. She likes it when I use my mouth on her. My generation has tongues and interior ridges like teeth to vocalize language. My generation does many things compared to our predecessors. We are very different. But through our shared cell memories I can know their experiences. It upsets Loma how different the generations are in the few years we have existed, and yet here we are in this predicament.

"Ugh, you're so special, Inri. You're so beautiful and special," she laments into my shoulder.

"Because I am yours?"

"No!" She recoils. "Mine? I'm not – nobody belongs to *anybody*. You're free to do as you wish and I count myself lucky to have you *in my life*." Her voice rises at the end again. I do not point out that no one ever asked my generation if we wanted these individual freedoms. These personal autonomy rights. She fought for us to have that. I know.

My favorite with Loma is her body writhing against the genital prosthetic I wear. She engorges herself with it. I love Loma's body and I love the sensations she experiences on it. Human-identified Earth organisms put out so much rich sensory information they don't find valuable. What Loma values is my height (I am tall), and my size and my heft and musculature. She says I have a perfect balance of male and female energies (I do not know what being either of those is like so I cannot say).

Loma values the way I do whatever she asks of me. I value her attention. I value the heat exchange of her body's life processes interacting with mine. It frenzies and ebbs with thousands of generations of existence on abundant Earth. There is nothing on Mars I interact with that is as aggressive.

So I wonder what her death might feel like.

"Loma, would you still prefer to die than be shipped to the node, even if I would be there with you?" She sighs loudly and says she looks forward to the release from the prison of her own body in this mortal realm, the joining back with the cosmos. And I do not tell her I used to know that too before she fought for me and my rights.

"It's just so complicated, Inri. There was no *way* I was gonna stand by and watch the creation of a lifeform made entirely to support the colonialist expansion into space. Okay? And there's no way I'm going to let myself be carted off for another sick attempt at capitalist consumption." She looks at me with a determined scowl as I wonder, isn't that what happened? I was created and here we are. She sees I am thinking and squeezes my shoulders for attention.

"Look, if we don't resist we'll be eaten by the machine!"

Loma says this often and I am never sure what she means. Even with hormones and protein regimens that endow Loma with heightened sensory perceptions of her environment (holistic integration, her friends call it), her behavior and her speech are dominated by a kind of selfhood. She seems numb to the feedback from her cyborg body. She describes herself as alienated even though she is part of many symbiotic geographic and cultural systems. She uses group words but doesn't explain who her groups are, and is rarely willing to learn me when I ask. Maybe this kind of isolation works for her in resisting the machine. She has not answered me.

"Are you serious in your desire to die, Loma?"

"If they try to ship us to the node, yeah." There is a determined twist in her brow. I am not so sure that she is prepared. She exhales a clouded sense of revulsion and lays her head against my chest. Her long fingernails graze my bare back and it excites me. She feels good – her heat and her smell and her attention. This is her way of grooming me to play. We spend much of our time playing. Often she invites me over to have space in the room like one of her many flourishing plants, and I like that. I think Loma considers that I am in love with her in a human way. There are non human-identified humans that talk about love and they say 'mutual survival,' and I love Loma in this way. But she does not seem to want mutual survival because she wanted me and now she wants to die.

"Inri, it's the full moon tonight. I want to please you."

Sometimes I hear Loma talking to her friends about how beautiful I am when she pleases me; what sounds I make, the way I react. There are how-to sexual relationship guides that Loma and her friends have made. Small pamphlets that describe our bodies and how to touch them and what to expect. Having a relationship with a serpent like me is desirable as *an alternative to the non-consensual, consumption-based lifestyle expected of mainstream human society.* That's what her pamphlets say. I get confused by the words *mainstream* and *human* and *society* put together like that. I have trouble understanding why Loma describes our relationship in the terms of a society she doesn't want to belong to. How does our relationship have importance among the non human-identified societies? And the other systems of life organization among the microbes and plants? And the subjugated peoples too who aren't even allowed to participate. They live and die powering the machine Loma hates with their labor, and I am confused why she and her friends do not also fight for their autonomy rights.

"You blossom like a flower when I touch you like this, Inri. That's why you're so special," Loma coos over my supine body. Her two hands have splayed me open where my legs join my torso. She strokes me over and over. Develops a rhythm. The room fills with the scent of my musk, which Loma inhales slowly, deeply. She loves to smell me this way. I wonder what the other plants in her room sense under this beautiful moonlight in this warm space. My predecessors were never so deliberately stimulated. They had very low interaction rates with higher energy peoples. They relied on chance encounters, looking attractive, and mutual cohabitation. They were initially conceived as a modified rhizome that would have a symbiotic relationship with dormant bacteria of the Martian soils. We did not have a bipedal form until the second generation's twelfth version. Now we look more acceptably human and people want to touch us. We like that.

"I love fucking you," Loma breathes across my ear. In this moment I think, I may have confused her attachment to me. I think I have misunderstood her grammar this whole time. Maybe I am also misunderstanding what she means when she says she wants to die. I feel sad. I feel alarmed. I cannot tell what her plants feel because using words has distanced me from them.

The moon was setting when I gathered myself to leave in the morning. Loma slept and I felt uneasy because she could not leave her bed to see me off. Times before I spent whole days curled up around her, comforting and being appreciated. Perhaps she forgot now I would be leaving for a long time. Maybe she was too sad because she would die and I wouldn't see her in this form again. I watched her sleep. When I said, "I have to go, Loma," she pushed herself up wearing her cat's face and stretched her arms around me. She was hot from rest and her breath and breasts and hair were all I felt. One last blossom, she said into my neck. She inhaled me deeply and kissed me below my ears. Then she let go and slid back amidst her sheets, leaving her sweat smell on my body.

"I'll come back to you if you want, Loma," I said in the sleepy room.

"I'll miss you, Inri..." she said from her covers.

I return to Garden City for the growing season.

My generation collects in our familiar Martian crater, by a mountain very few people on Earth care to know of, and with our engineered life processes we encourage the redevelopment of the fourth planet's latent ecosystems.

We do not use words to speak and we do not have the strong body heat of Earth organisms. Surrounded with each other, rooted in cooperation, we share. Those of us who met lovers have much to exchange: Human-identified love relationships are pleasing. We learn about intimate behavior from our partners and that's beneficial. But they do not seem mutual. We compile the non-mutual interactions, trying to sense the greater network of forces affecting them and why they occur. Then we must let it be.

This growing season is a critical stage and we are here because we want to grow. We do not concern ourselves with any reality beyond the present. Besides, we do not have the energy to expend. My feelings for Loma go dormant.

As the planet turns I enjoy the sheer undulations of the sun, the microbial exchanges, the slow shifting pleasantness of existence, and I am not again confronted by the human word concepts of *work* and *rights* until I have detached from the rhizome and boarded the transport where there are human-identified earth people manning the craft.

This is what I think at first: *Are* they human identified? As they secure me for the voyage back to Earth, something about them strikes me as different. These humans speak slow, though they speak. More than I do. Maybe they are new hybrids. Maybe I am so freshly departed from the rhizome that I have forgotten how humans can look and I am projecting my expectations.

When the operator checks my security harness, I think I see their clay colored skin shimmer as their hand draws away. Iridescent like me? Loma's lamenting body appears from my sleeping memories – this is a new generation of slow steppers? A new version? I am unsure why we would be changed to also man spacecraft...

The iridescent person will not make eye contact with me.

I do not feel well, so I sleep.

When I am released from the specimen collection and sterilization wards and into the Earth public environment I am so enthralled by the heat of the ground and the intensity of color that I release my scent from the stimulation. It draws several bugs close to me. I laugh. It is just past the summer season. The air is cool. The weight of the gravity is comforting. Rain is falling. The twilight moon is a crescent shrouded in veils of swiftly passing storm clouds. There is so much information everywhere. I have not spoken except to pass through my clearances from Mars, and as I venture to form words between my ridges and tongue, what comes out is *Loma*. I liked to say her name so much – it felt so pleasing to form and vocalize – but this time it feels like a word that means leaving. I stand still because I realize I have left and I am not sure what I am supposed to connect with now. I feel so disoriented. I wish I could root to the Earth for comfort from these sensations, but I was not made to do such a thing here. I am alone.

I am back in the city enclave by the sister rivers, near the communal home where I am provided living space. I am waiting on the trolley platform and it is rush hour. There are young children wearing book bags everywhere, laughing and bumping around, seeking the attention of their parents. I realize today is the customary half-day that precedes tomorrow's holiday and that's why there are so many small children in abundance. Normally at this time of day there are only workers and the teenage indentured. The children give off good energy. They are very aware, maybe because they are not yet strong with language. They look at me with large eyes, daring or shy or unsure, depending on how their parents regard me.

I do not believe that Loma was shipped off from Earth. I did not encounter any humans while I was growing, but there was also no reason that I would have. We do not experience time on Mars in the same ways we do on Earth, and we only interact with what is in relationship with our rhizome. And there are hardly any habitable places for humans on Mars yet, not with so many growing seasons to come.

The trolley pulls up. It is a full car and we are packed in shoulder to shoulder. It feels comforting. The children are having fun – they seem to enjoy the density like I do. Having their presence fill the air makes me feel good. There are not many children or families where the home is. My little home. Where Loma lived there were a few but it seemed as though her neighborhood was changing from the old families to the new political collectives like she belonged to.

Loma...

The trolley is making its way through her neighborhood. The stop-bell dings and a fresh stream of people board and leave. I remember leaving at this stop many times to see her. This time, I find a seat. I feel a pang of longing for my rhizome on Mars. I would be connected to all these people if they were part of my rhizome. But here everyone is a free individual. They stare ahead and do not make eye contact. I am like them now. Free and autonomous. Loma fought for my rights.

Thieves and Lovers

EMMA ADDAMS

There were three Bogarts but only two Bacalls tonight. Some unlucky Bogie would be going home alone, unless they were all feeling adventurous. Most everyone came trying to recreate the famous couples and movie pairings, except the Brandos, who tended to sulk and rage in corner booths all by themselves. Sylvia imagined they were mostly just interested in fucking each other. And of course there were some like Mike, the bartender, he worked as Monty Clift and was happy with whatever bed he landed in.

If she was being honest, though, the flickering holograms were bumming her out tonight. She was growing tired of the way everything got blurry at the edges, moved a half step slow like the whole bar was underwater or the audio was out of sync. And having to look out from her own little false Lana Turner as she batted away the roaming hands of too many James Garfields with their innuendos about ringing twice was making her hate old movies. It had been a year since she got hired on at the bar, Rick's American Café, and for the last couple months she refused to watch any movie in black and white.

One of the dishwashers, the new kid, was dragging the garbage out back when Sylvia went on her break. He was a handsome kid, with slicked back hair and a dark little mustache that he seemed proud of, *probably because he was about fifteen and these were the first hairs he'd ever grown,* Sylvia thought. He held the door open, a big bag in one hand, and waved for her to walk out. She thanked him in spite of his lingering eyes on the grey-toned digital skin of her chest.

Sylvia turned off the box on her hip and the image died. The boy threw the trash in the big dumpster and when he looked her way his stare wasn't absent the lust. She was trying to remember if he'd seen her before, actually seen her and not a black-and-white Lana Turner, and whether he knew she was trans. He certainly knew now. He was giving her the "I want to fuck you but you're a monster" look that she got during the day, which had made a job that hid her face sound so great.

She had four texts from Andy. He was making progress on his book, or so he claimed. This was a belief that he held for a few nights each month, but when she'd last read it the whole thing seemed like a mess. It was supposed to be this gritty memoir of being trans and on the street. Of course, "the street" was a series of couches that he slept on for half a year while being a punk and dumpster diving with crusties in his early twenties. Now Andy was considering taking time off from work to get the book done, but both of them knew they couldn't afford that.

Sylvia put out her cigarette, turned Lana back on, and headed back to work. She was behind the bar when the night's tenth Marilyn Monroe showed up. Sylvia couldn't help but laugh. Seeing them all doing their best not to acknowledge one another was too funny. *I bet Marilyn would've killed in a comedy about clones,* she thought.

"How much would you wager that none of them have ever watched a Wilder film?" a man at the bar asked her. She didn't know who he was supposed to be. The grey glow around him was muted, meaning it was an expensive box. "No doubt half of them are college girls with a poster of Marilyn up on the wall." He spoke in a light theatrical British accent, something clearly affected.

"All looking for James Dean in a black and white bar, I'm sure."

He laughed. "Yeah. I mean, not that that's a bad thing though. Nothing wrong with knowing what you want, even the improbable." His smile was made of pure charm. It was easy to be dashing when you wore the face of a movie star. "Could you get me another gimlet, please?"

"Sure thing, hon." She went down to the middle of the bar where the gin was kept and began mixing.

It was getting late and the crowd was thinning. The Marilyns now made up almost half the remaining patrons. One of the waitresses, Alana, asked Sylvia to make a highball. She mixed the two drinks – everyone always ordered liquor or fancy cocktails at the bar, they didn't even have any beers on tap anymore.

"The guy over at the end of the bar," Sylvia said, slightly nodding her head at the man she had been chatting with, "you know what he's from?"

"Looks familiar," Alana said. She'd been working there for several years. She was the one who told Sylvia to apply, way back when, after they met at a picnic. "American?"

"Lilting British type accent."

"The skin is amazing. Almost no buzz. The clothes even move with him," Alana said. She took the drink and, through whatever magic it was Alana had, found just the right Marilyn on the first try and gave her the highball.

Sylvia brought the man his gimlet. He sipped it and said, "Excellent," then lifted the drink to Sylvia, laid a twenty dollar bill down and walked away. She watched him walk towards the door, take another long sip from his drink before setting it down at a table and leaving it behind. He was gone. She was watching the door for a moment more before one of the Marilyns snapped her fingers in Sylvia's face and said, "What's a gal gotta do to get a martini around here!?"

When she woke the next day at home, it was just past noon and Andy was giving himself his shot. He always closed his eyes as the needle went in, but his face didn't show any other sign of pain. The notebooks and old journals Andy was constantly digging through for his memoir were strewn about the coffee table. He had a theory that the rush of T would drive him to find key details, though this hadn't proven true yet. It was Sylvia's theory that the same rush was the reason there wasn't a sense of cohesion to what she'd read. Everything was rushing from one momentous insight to the next, like he'd been running around that whole time having epiphany after epiphany. The best sections, in her view, all came when he wrote mid-week and had a clear mind. Those parts he was funny and laughed at his naivety. He was a good enough writer that he could let the moments shine for themselves, but he kept over-explaining stuff, like his story about the, in Andy's words, "literally life changing burrito". She had tried telling him this, but he just argued that it was Sylvia's bias against testosterone.

"I made you some coffee," Andy said, without looking up from a spiral notebook that had a bunch of faded and peeling band stickers all over the cover.

"Still in search of a turning point?" Sylvia asked.

"How were the movies?" Andy asked, not rising to the bait.

She didn't answer, going instead to the kitchen and pouring a cup of coffee.

She sat next to him and gave Andy a kiss on the cheek.

"I mean, it all went sour on that trip to Reno. But then Joshua tree was so amazing. It doesn't really work in that order though," he said.

"I don't get why you don't just switch them then. How many people will know? Five?" Sylvia asked.

"It wouldn't be the truth. It wouldn't be honest."

"What were you so excited about last night?"

"I put the Catholic stuff back in, with the visit to my mom's. I thought it helped. But maybe I'm wrong."

"Can I read it?"

"Not yet. Maybe later." Sylvia nodded but didn't say anything. He hadn't let her read anything for a few weeks now.

She could tell he wanted to get back to work. She left him and headed to the bedroom and turned on the TV.

Sylvia had a text from Alana, who had apparently gone home with a Cary Grant last night. This led Sylvia to thinking about the man from last night. She started looking online for him, scrolling through classic film tumblrs, but nothing with him showed up. He wasn't popular enough for random reblogs, apparently. Sylvia thought of the man: debonair, British, slightly effete. He was practically the picture of a Hitchcock spy movie villain—James Mason or Claude Reins.

That's how she found him, third billed, in *Foreign Correspondent.* The actor's name was Herbert Marshall. She dug through his filmography until she found a still image that matched exactly the man from the night before.

The film was *Trouble In Paradise,* and Marshall played a gentleman thief, Gaston Monescu. It was a pre-Hayes Code film, 1932. After convincing herself that she ought to watch it for research, to help her with banter and tips, Sylvia found a streaming site and began watching.

It was a screwball comedy, one of the very first. It still had all the marks of the theatre in the dialogue and banter, none of the movie timing that came with later films. There was the continental adulthood of it, a maturity that was able to poke fun at itself. Something about the hazy picture quality, the lack of a running score, the quietness of the scenes, drew Sylvia right in. The movie was a dream and Sylvia was thinking of all the late night movies she'd watched growing up in Fresno, the black and white screen drifting her to sleep, the glamorous starlet she'd become in her dreams.

The whole second half of the movie she had her hand up her skirt and was stroking her cock. While she hadn't disliked the look of the man in the bar, she hadn't particularly found herself attracted then. But now, watching the film, she was imagining herself in the elegant ball gowns of the star, having her necklace stolen by his hands as he grazed the nape of her neck—

Andy walked in right as she came. He crashed onto the bed, seemingly oblivious of the fact that she'd just finished. The bed rocked with his weight and the clear cum ran down the side of her stomach and onto the sheets.

"Shit," she said, trying to wipe up the sticky mess but mostly just rubbing it into the sheets. She grabbed some tissues and cleaned herself up. Andy had fallen straight asleep. It was only four and Sylvia wondered when he woke up, how long he'd been working. She hadn't asked.

After cleaning herself up more properly, she got into bed with Andy and cuddled into him. There was a wet spot on her hip, but she managed to ignore it and fall asleep. She dreamt in black and white and it was about the man at the bar or the actor or maybe both.

The man didn't return that night, or the night after. Sylvia had never been one to look out for a customer's return, not even the big tippers. She kept her head down, flirted with customers enough to not seem bitchy, and got through her shift. But now she was looking to the door every time it opened. She'd watched Trouble in Paradise four times in the two days.

The first time through she was mostly watching Francis Herbert's character Gaston and thinking of the man from the bar. But the next few times she found her attention drawn by Kay Francis, one of the two leading ladies of the film. She had the sort of casual glamour that reminded Sylvia of being thirteen alone in a theatre and staring up at the screen and pouring herself into a film, losing herself, back when Sylvia's pain would stop existing and be replaced by flickering pictures on the screen for two hours at a time. Before she even knew she was a girl, Sylvia imagined herself a leading lady. Before transitioning, movies had been her whole life.

She had a few hours until work and Andy was wrapped in his writing, maybe even making something like progress, and so she went to her room and turned on the film again and began touching herself again. She hadn't finished since that first night, but it was still nice to feel something like a libido return. It reminded her of being sixteen and hiding in her room in a way that she hadn't imagined could carry nostalgia. And when Andy came in she began pawing at him. He yawned and stretched. She began kissing his neck and he didn't push her away. She was excited and engaged in a way that hadn't happened in months. She kissed her way down his torso. As she was going down on him her mind went to the movie and the actor and the man who came into her bar and she found herself pausing to moan in pleasure, muffled into Andy's thighs.

She looked up at Andy, staring up the path of hair on his stomach up to his fuzzy little chin. His head was still arched back on the pillow. She wanted to ask if she'd been bad, for him to tell her that she was just some dame and he couldn't get caught up in her trouble. She wanted him to be Humphrey Bogart and to sneer at her before they kissed. Or at the least for Andy to run his hand along her cheek and look at her with a Cary Grant smile. *Make me feel like a girl*, she thought and wanted to say to him. But when he caught her eye and saw the lust, he slid out from under her, patted her on the head like she was his kid sister, and went into the bathroom. She heard the shower start a moment later.

That night the man returned. Sylvia was shrouded in the digital ghost of Lana Turner and pouring highballs for Grants and Bogarts and Hepburns. The shimmer of their holographic skin made it seem like they glided as they moved around the bar. She wanted to be drawn in, like watching the movie earlier had done to her, yet she couldn't help but imagine the pasty skin and receding hairlines and dull eyes behind every one of their false faces. And her mind kept coming back to Andy turning away from her.

Then Gaston walked through the door.

He was making small talk with some Rosalind Russell, and he must have told a funny joke because she was laughing. It was in that moment that Sylvia watched him steal the pocket book.

There was a very clear protocol for what to do. She would get Tom, the manager, and he would get whoever was working the door tonight, probably Joey, and they would escort him out. There were too many thieves in the movies for them not to be prepared.

Instead, Sylvia mixed two cocktails and brought them to Gaston and Russell. As she was setting them down she slid the pocket book out of Gaston's coat. He felt her do it. He made eye contact with Sylvia that let her know that, but he didn't react.

Sylvia bent down and pretended to pick the pocket book up from the ground. It was a vivid green and looked alien in her muted grey hand. "I think you dropped this," Sylvia said.

"Oh my. Thank you so very much. I am in your debt, ma'am," Rosalind said, fully in character.

"It's really nothing," Sylvia replied.

"What splendid luck!" Gaston said, clapping his hands together. "And thank you for the drinks." Then, turning to Rosalind, he added, "My treat, of course. On my tab please."

"Of course," Sylvia said.

As soon as Sylvia walked away the jollity returned. The Girl Friday was having a ball, even if her Cary hadn't shown up. She watched as the two continued chatting, and in between taking orders did her best to keep an eye on Gaston, but if he had made a second play for the pocket book she didn't see it.

It was about an hour later while she was in the bathroom that she found his card. He had slipped it in her pocket without Sylvia noticing. It was a fancy embossed piece. On the front it said, *Baron Gaston La Valle* and on the back was printed an address in the hills and a phone number. When she came back out he was gone.

The next day she spent the afternoon convincing herself not to call him. She wasn't working until eight, and Andy was entertaining a friend from the trans group he facilitated once a month. Sylvia had gone to one of their social events and by the fourth time she heard the word "problematic" she made an excuse and left. The only trans person she regularly spent time with now, other than Andy, was at work with Alana. Sylvia knew she shouldn't keep hiding out in the bedroom, that she should help Andy be a good host, instead she just kept turning Gaston's card over and over in her hands. She had her phone out and was looking at the blank screen when Andy poked his head in.

"Hey. How's it going?"

"Fine. I'm just reading."

Andy took a long, slow breath, and said, "Listen, I don't want to be a jerk, but it's kind of rude if you just hide in here until they've left."

"I'm not hiding, I'm just feeling antisocial. Also, that's kind of a jerk way of asking me to come out."

"Just say hi quick. They're great."

Sylvia didn't want to. She wanted to call Gaston. But she got up from the bed and went with Andy.

"Jace, meet Sylvia. Sylvia, meet Jace," Andy said. Jace was sitting on the couch and didn't bother to get up when Sylvia came over, just offered their hand. They wore a denim vest and chain wallet and pinstriped fedora like they were the drummer from a 90s songs cover band. Behind their glasses – black box frame Weezer style – their blue eyes had the hint of wrinkles that betrayed Jace's otherwise youthful looks.

"Oh hi! Andy's told me all about you."

"Hi." Sylvia sat down on the armchair and Andy took the seat on the couch near Jace.

"So, you work at a black and white bar?" Jace asked.

"Yeah."

"Oh yeah. I used to go to anime cons and stuff. I liked playing as a boy. You ever watch *Cowboy Bebop*?" They kept talking before Sylvia could answer, "I had a really sweet hologram I'd wear. I stopped doing that once I came out as queer. It was a good hiding place back then, I guess. Let me fuck around with gender. Still, wouldn't want to still be hiding like that. Probably feels pretty fake. I'm trying to be more real, you know?"

"That's wonderful," Sylvia said.

"Sylvia loves the old movies. She used to make me watch them, when we started dating. I always just fell asleep though," Andy said.

"I have a hard time watching older films. So heteronormative. And totally binarist. Damsel in distress and some big man to save her," Jace said, with a smile. "It's all so regressive." The whole time they said this they stared straight at Sylvia, not once looking in Andy's direction.

Sylvia rolled her eyes. This is why she only ever said she was a waitress whenever queer people asked.

"It's of the era. And some of them aren't so bad," Andy said.

"And the race issues. I couldn't stand to go to one of those bars. Just so much privilege flying around, you know," Jace said. "No offense, of course," they added, only then looking away from Sylvia and over to Andy. "I guess that's just LA though. Everyone is so fake here. In New York I was part of this collective of dykes and fags and trannies—"

Sylvia got up. "I just remembered I'm supposed to go in early tonight. I have to get ready. Sorry I can't better entertain you. No offense, of course." She went to the bedroom, closed the door before Andy could follow her in, grabbed up her purse and then headed straight out past Andy and Jace before either could say a word.

She was sitting in her car, parked on the street, still fuming. Andy had followed and he was crossing the street now. He jogged up to the car and knocked on the window, but Sylvia didn't roll it down. So instead he came around and got in the passenger seat. She could have locked the door, but didn't.

"Hey, I'm sorry about that. They were just trying to show off. Everyone's always trying to be queerer than thou, you know. I mean, they're white and use the word woke unironically." Andy laughed at this, but Sylvia didn't. "I wouldn't take what they say too seriously."

"Fuck that little shit. Part of a 'collective' of trannies! Who the fuck do they think they are!"

"I'm sure they didn't realize what they were saying. They were just trying—"

"And like I don't know tons of old movies are racist, or that it's fucking heteronormative. And that whole fucking authentic self shit. Ugh!"

"Sorry. They're really sweet, really. They were trying to show off, probably nervous." It was warm in the car and Andy rolled down the window. "They're just like newly out as trans and are trying to like prove their credentials you know. It's just insecurity. They've talked about that a bunch with me." Andy waited but Sylvia didn't respond. She was staring straight ahead and not at him. "Come back up. They'll apologize, you'll apologize, it'll all be cool. Please. For me?"

"I have to go to work. Okay. I'll be back home late. I'm closing tonight. Now please get out of my car."

Andy stayed seated a moment longer, but must have decided the fight was over and got out. He didn't say goodbye and neither did she. Sylvia watched him walk back to the apartment building and disappear into the hallway. He hadn't looked back.

Sylvia didn't have anywhere to go so she went to a coffee shop near work to wait until her shift started. She had a couple hours to kill, and the book she'd been reading wasn't holding her attention. Andy had texted and apologized and told her she was being childish. She didn't respond.

Instead she called Gaston.

The phone rang four times before he picked up. "Hello," he answered, in his Gaston voice. She wondered if he had a special phone for such a thing or just always spoke in that voice.

"Hi. This is—" she realized she hadn't told him her name, "I work at Rick's American Café, the black and white bar. You gave me your number."

"Of course. Lana Turner."

"Yeah. Hi."

"Hello Lana. How does this evening treat you?"

She imagined he didn't want to hear all about her relationship drama, so instead she answered, "Just fabulous. I'm about to go on for my shift. Can I expect to see you tonight?"

"Unfortunately, no. You see, my business requires me to be elsewhere."

"And your occupation, is it gentleman thief?"

"I'm no thief, though I wouldn't pretend I come to money in any honest manner. What you witnessed last night was, how shall I put it, just a little sport."

"I could have you banned from the bar, you know."

"Yes. I am well aware."

"I saw the movie you're from the other day. *Trouble in Paradise*. I really liked it," she said.

"I am quite happy to hear that," he said, still with the accent. He had perfected the stilted cadence of early talkies, she'd give him that. "I wish to ask this delicately, so as not to be taken in the wrong way, but I would love to see you again, outside of your work."

"I might like that," Sylvia said.

"There is, well, more." He paused. "I am looking to live out a scene and need a leading lady. In all the clubs like this and the meetings of people,

well, people like me, I've yet to meet my Madame Colet. Or a Lily, for that
matter."

"Never?"

"There have been Miriam Hopkins, no doubt, and a Kay Francis or
two. But never a Madame Mariette Colet. Never a Lily. In my weaker moments, I have thought of abandoning my quest and trying my luck as Wil-
liam Holden or some other star. But then, when you stole back that purse, it
struck me. If I cannot find one, I ought to make my own Colet."

Sylvia stared at her coffee, thinking of this man and his futile quest.
This was exactly the sort of pitiful search for the perfect girl that Andy would
laugh at, but Sylvia thought of this Gaston walking into different bars over
and over and looking for his Colet and felt a pang in her heart. And more
than that, more than the sympathy, she wanted to be his Madam Colet.

"If," he continued, "you were to come, wearing a skin I procure for
you, to my manor, I assure you it would be to your gain."

Rather than answering, Sylvia bit her lip. She had, in the years working at the club, never gone home with a customer. She was with Andy, and
even if she wanted to go home with some man, she knew the truth was that
she feared what might happen when someone reached under Lana Turner's
dress and found Sylvia's cock. Or the look in some guy's eyes when the projection was turned off and her face was left staring at his. She hadn't dated
a cis guy since high school.

"Well, shall you be my Colet?"

She paused, but only for a moment, before answering, "Yes."

"Excellent! Expect a package tonight at your bar. Do you work tomorrow?"

"Yes, but I can trade shifts."

"Please do. On my card is my address. Please show up at nine in your
finest gown."

"And pearls too, no doubt," Sylvia said.

"It would only be fitting," Gaston replied and then hung up.

When Sylvia came in for work she smiled at all the lost starlets and
leading men, and this time it wasn't just out of professional politeness.
She didn't even turn her box off during breaks, for tonight she was all Lana
Turner and forget the rest. She bantered with a John Garfield, trading innuendos, and was rewarded with a nice tip. Her thoughts drifted to *Trouble*

in *Paradise* and Gaston, and she messed up a couple drink orders, bringing whiskey to a Bogart who'd ordered a vodka martini.

After a few hours her feet were getting sore and she was reminded of reality enough that her spirit finally drifted back down. She then thought of Andy and the fight and her anger bubbled back up. She kept checking her phone, expecting to find a real apology for not sticking up for her, but the only text she got was Alana asking to trade shifts next week.

It was right there. Alana had Thursday nights off, and all Sylvia had to do was ask. Instead she texted Andy. "Hey u up?"

He replied ten minutes later: "im working"

After that Sylvia texted Alana and they agreed to trade shifts.

Early the next evening, while Andy was deep into rereading his journal from the Reno trip, Sylvia was busy getting ready for her date. She'd put makeup on and was wearing her polka dot dress. He barely looked up from his notebook.

They hadn't talked about the previous day or Jace. All morning whenever she came into the living room or kitchen he made an excuse to go to the other room. He was being childish, and probably so was she, but Sylvia didn't want to fight this time. So she let him avoid her. At least she wouldn't have to look at him while she thought about what she was planning that night.

She tried the Kay Francis skin on around five. It had the matte glow of an expensive box. The eyebrows were plucked thin and the hair parted in the middle leading to short curls. A debutante with a touch of flapper style. It was always odd to have gray skin in a room full of colors, but she couldn't help but find herself smiling as she twirled and the skirts of the holographic ball gown billowed out for her. It was, without a doubt, the best box she'd ever worn. Maybe the best one she'd ever seen, for that matter. *God I'd be swimming in tips if I had a Bette Davis one of these,* she thought.

Sylvia turned off the projection and found herself staring back once again, she still felt a touch of glamour and twirled once and felt her skirt lift up around her, brushing her fingertips. She then heard the front door open and close. Andy had left.

A few minutes later it was Sylvia's turn to leave. She didn't spend much time thinking of where Andy might have gone as she grabbed up her purse and made sure the door was locked behind her.

The drive up through the hills brought her away from the beat up apartments and strip mall nail salons in her neighborhood to the posh Beverly stores and old Hollywood mansions. She drove past them and further into the lush greenery. The whole drive up she was debating in her mind how and when to tell him she was trans and whether she shouldn't just turn around and forget this idea entirely and call Andy.

When she found the address and pulled into the driveway, a gate parted for her as if in wait. The not-quite-wild trees that lined the street were the front for a fashionably disheveled front lawn and hedges. She parked her Civic in the driveway. She might've wished she'd driven a better car but she imagined anything short of a classic Bentley with a chauffeur and Norma Desmond in the back would've looked out of place.

Before getting out she turned on her Kay Francis box. Her hands were shaking and she fumbled with the button before closing her eyes and taking a deep breath. She then pushed the button and let the gray skin overtake her own. It was dusk and the color had mostly bled from the world in that moment before night truly began. This time her black-and-white appearance didn't feel so mismatched with the world.

He answered the door himself, already wearing his Herbert Marshall skin. She realized then that she had hoped he would answer as himself, ease the tension by letting her know that he was just playing a part and had a face of his own to share with her and she would reveal hers, and then she'd know what to expect. They could lay out the terms of their fantasy and she'd know what to do. But of course he hadn't.

"I am so glad you decided to come. I had feared you wouldn't."

"This box is amazing. I've only worn the work ones before."

He took her purse and placed it on the table next to the door, letting her leave behind the darkened red leather so out of place on her gray arm. Sylvia followed him into the house. It was filled with 30s-era art deco pieces, art and furniture both. She tried to not be too obvious as she stared and gaped at the walls. "It must be very nice to live here," she said, finally. It sounded stupid and she felt poorer in that moment than any time she'd been late on rent.

"I feel as if I don't really know the house, honestly. My business takes me many places."

"Like Venice, Baron." Sylvia flashed him what she hoped was a starlet quality smile.

His eyes softened. "Yes, like Venice. Madame Colet." He took her hand in his and brought it to his lips. It was the type of affected gesture that Andy would have done ironically and followed with an exaggerated bow. But the man did it with sincerity and a suaveness she knew was practiced. Her hand felt calm and still in his. His lips were soft and there was a hint of stubble she felt along his bottom lip as it brushed the back of her hand, though of course the face he wore was perfectly smoothly shaven.

They shared this moment while standing before double doors, and afterward he opened them with a flourish.

Inside was a black and white scene she recognized at once. It was the dinner party and she could see all the principals moving about. There was the Major talking with the character Giron, and Lily, wrapped in fur, regaled a crowd of men in tuxedos.

"This is amazing."

She entered the room, black and white and toned to match her box precisely. The chatter of guests had the distinct movie feel of unreal noise. Nothing was being discussed but the noise never stopped.

Actually, something was being discussed. It took a moment, since Sylvia was at the wrong end of the room, to realize what it was. But the voices of Giron and the Major were clear and sat above the din of the room. It was dialogue from the movie. She recognized that at once. She walked over to the men. Along the way she brushed one of the projections, a background actor, and felt a small pressure push back. None of the solidity or warmth of flesh, but not the empty projection she'd expected.

"Hard light," the man whispered. She hadn't realized he was at her side. "There is the hint of matter. Quite technical."

Sylvia pushed at one of the characters' arm, her fingers gliding through as if in a thick gel or maybe like fog you can feel but dry to the touch. She pulled her hand back, the man seemed unruffled and continued to chatter empty noises to fill the room. She looked around at all of the actors, all these empty faces. Were they all empty?

"So then they're all projections? Everyone?"

"Yes. It has been quite the undertaking, making this little scene."

She wanted to ask if she was the first person to be in here, or if he'd shown others. But there were two possible answers – she wasn't special or he was probably really lonely – and she didn't want to know which was true.

Instead, she joined the party. After all, she was Madame Colet. This was her party. Her ballroom. Her manor. It was Gaston that was in love with her.

The projections went through their paces and delivered their dialogue and Sylvia did her best to match. She had seen the movie a half dozen times, the last couple times as background noise while she was getting ready, so she could aim in the right direction, even if she probably didn't get any of the lines quite right. It was an odd sensation to be the center of the party amongst all these ghosts who couldn't hear her and only ever responded according to the script.

Sylvia was cornered at that moment by Giron, who was something like a business manager in the movie. She wasn't quite sure about that part, something of the era and how the world worked just didn't translate ninety years later.

"Madame Colet, I must have a word with you," he said.

Sylvia searched her memory for the scene, but whatever this was about she didn't remember.

"You misunderstand me, Madame. I mean only—" Giron stopped midsentence, clearly cut off by whatever line Sylvia was failing to say. She wished she had a script to study.

He nodded and left. As he walked away, Sylvia tried to grab his arm and felt her fingers slip through the fog again. She looked at all the characters in the room, all these empty suits walking around. She felt crowded and all alone.

Sylvia then began looking around for Gaston again. She was feeling lost in the scene swirling around her. She bumped into someone, a young woman in the background, and slid right through her and a shudder ran down Sylvia's spine. This was like the moment that a pleasant buzz turned to a bad high. She could feel her heart begin beating too fast and Sylvia needed an anchor.

Then she saw him. Gaston was having a hushed conversation with Lily in the corner. She knew this scene. She had her footing. Everything looked right again and she wasn't lost. Lily wanted to rob the safe that night, not wait, but Gaston was falling in love with Madame Colet. With Sylvia. He turned away from Lily and headed towards Sylvia.

"Madame Colet, I am afraid I must pull you away from your admirers for a moment. There is an urgent matter of business."

He led her through a drawing room and up the stairs, a grand staircase. They were out of the party and away from all the hollow bodies. In the foyer and the hall everything was in black and white. Sylvia wanted to pause, to take it in. How many rooms, how many sets did he recreate? Did the full film play out here? Was there a phantom Colet before Sylvia had arrived, having her purse stolen at the opera and returned by Gaston. But the show went on and she followed her Herbert Marshall, fully in character, up the stairs and into a bedroom, her bedroom.

The next line came to her as if she'd rehearsed it. "When in a gentleman's room, where does a lady put her jewels?"

He smiled, which technically wasn't in character. Then he followed Sylvia's lead. "On the nightstand, I imagine."

"And what if I don't want to be a lady? What then?" He looked slightly embarrassed and did not respond. Sylvia went on. "I have a confession to make: you like me. In fact, you're crazy about me."

They embraced. It was a full kiss, their mouths pressed together, but unmoving, a stage kiss.

"I can hold back no longer, Mariette. I love you," he said.

Sylvia couldn't think of a line and so she answered back with a kiss, hoping it was close enough. She began getting hard and hoped her tuck wouldn't come undone.

"But I must admit, I have not been honest. I am not the Baron Gaston La Valle, but Gaston Monescu, the famous thief."

At that moment the door opened and one of the characters exclaimed, "Madame Colet that man is a crook!"

Gaston turned to him. "There is only one crook in this room, your advisor Giron."

The moment had been so lovely but the movie kept playing and Sylvia wanted to go back to the kiss.

Giron had his finger in Gaston's face. "This criminal—"

"I, sir, may be a wanted man, but you are a rat. You have stolen millions from the Madame. If you wish to assert otherwise, I am sure that the police will gladly listen to your story." At that two police officers in old French uniforms arrived and grasped Giron's arms. "I have given them a full report of all your activities, along with a detailed account of the ledger books of Colet and Company. Farewell, monsieur Giron."

The officers left with their man. Gaston closed the doors behind them.

"I must leave," Gaston said, turning toward the window. "Giron will convince them of my identity, and they will return for me."

Sylvia knew her line. "I know that, but for tonight you will be mine."

This was the fade to black moment, the editing trick that let the viewer fill in the details. But Sylvia was still here and so was Gaston. There was no director to end the scene, to call cut. She put her hands on his chest and brought her mouth to his. This time it was not a stage kiss, and they did not part their lips except to fall on the bed.

As they groped one another Sylvia kept waiting for his hand to reach down and for everything to stop. She knew she shouldn't let it get there, that she needed to be safe, but instead she gave herself over to the moment. And when she unzipped his pants and grasped his cock, a protrusion of pink flesh in their grey world, she stopped thinking of what Sylvia should do altogether.

She was Madame Colet in her Paris manor. She was Kay Francis on set. She was with Gaston, the gentleman thief in her bedroom. She was with Herbert Marshall with a film crew looking on as she brought her mouth to his cock. She was on screen for thousands in darkened theaters, watching as their matinee idols fucked in the scene that never was allowed to make the final cut. This was the fulfillment of every innuendo and knowing glance. And when he was finished and then reached down to return the favor as a gentleman does, she didn't stop him from reaching up her skirt.

He paused, and in his eyes she could see the sudden realization of what he'd found. His hand stopped moving. He was looking at her, and his face behind the black-and-white mask was unreadable. His mask was unreadable. Sylvia felt herself pulled back to her own life beneath the hologram. She had fucked up and now it was over and she couldn't breathe. His hand was still there, limply resting inside the band of her panties.

He wasn't moving and she wasn't moving and it felt like neither of them knew how to move anymore.

Say something. Say something. Say something. Run. Run. Run. Sylvia's head couldn't form a plan. She needed to get out to get away from him. But he still hadn't moved. Hadn't acted. Then something shifted in his face and his eyes came back from Sylvia's crotch to her eyes, but his hand remained under her skirt.

This was Gaston, the gentleman thief, and he was not so crass as to let an unexpected cock stop his fun. With his free hand he tore open her gown.

She was pretty certain her actual dress had torn in the process. The brightness of her shirt and the redness of her overheated chest was like a tear in the hologram, bleeding color. The box tried to catch up and glitched before finding a pattern to respond to. Even still the dark blue of her bra stood out. It really was an impressive model.

He brought his mouth back to hers. He was tweaking her right nipple with his left hand. She came with a moan and an arched back, her toes and fingers a mess of nerve endings too sensitive and numb at once.

Gaston took a handkerchief from his pocket and wiped off his hand. He kissed her once more. He took her chin in his hand. There must have been a drop of cum he'd failed to wipe off and she felt the wetness press into her chin. "I am afraid I cannot stay the night."

"Please do."

He sighed slowly. "It could have been marvelous."

Sylvia said, "Divine."

"Wonderful... But tomorrow morning, if you should wake out of your dreams and hear a knock, and the door opens, and there, instead of a maid with a breakfast tray, stands a policeman with a warrant, then you'll be glad you are alone." She wondered again, how many times had he rehearsed these lines.

He left the room, looking back at the door. He reached into his pocket and took out a string of pearls. Sylvia felt at her neck, of course they weren't there, not that she'd have felt them anyway. She smiled at him and he smiled back. Then he left and the doors closed behind him and she was alone in the room.

Sylvia's purse was still on the table at the door. As she was coming down the stairs she had worried he might have stolen that too, but he was a gentleman thief after all. As she fished out her keys from the purse she found three one hundred dollar bills in her wallet. In the driveway she saw an old car pulling away and leaving out the gate. She couldn't see Gaston or Lily, but she knew this was the final shot of the movie. The two thieves and lovers comparing their stolen goods as the screen shrunk to a small circle amidst the black until nothing was left. The iris effect.

She was floating the whole drive home, a heady mixture of afterglow, exhaustion and the joy of having three hundred more dollars than she'd started the day with. She was wondering if she should call him again and replay the scene. How long would she need to wait?

It wasn't until she stopped to get gas that she thought about Andy and what she'd say to him, what they'd do now. When she came home he was asleep on the couch. She got a blanket out of the closet and draped it over his shoulders. They could talk in the morning.

She washed up quickly and got into her pajamas. She was tired, but couldn't help herself, so instead of getting straight into bed she pulled out the Kay Francis box and played Madame Colet one more time. "It could have been marvelous," she whispered. "Divine."

Matchmaker

DANE FIGUEROA EDIDI

SEVERAL YEARS AGO

Somewhere in the underworld where the illusion of the absence of time is a common folly, where dreams are devoured as readily as memories, somewhere, in the broken structure of a universe warring against extinction, is this day. This day of the wedding of two spirits that even death could not separate; spirits brought together by shell, and bone, and lifetimes. This day set in the meadow of ethereal bliss. Cascades of sunlight spill into a verdant field. The Living and the Dead weep tears filled with stories of laughter, stories of lost love.

And there's me, dressed in a leather dress that hugs the curves of my hips, dyed the most decadent of hues. In the crease of my cleavage lies a tattoo of an azure phoenix, resting its head on my right breast. My chestnut skin glistens even in the golden brilliance of Elysia.

Standing on high heels, adjusting my brimmed hat, and placing on my glasses, I offer a smile: *A Matchmaker's job doesn't end just because both parties were killed. Even beyond death, souls can find their truest loves, particularly when it wins me a one way ticket to resurrection...*

Now

Tabitha elongates her body as I come through the door. Darkness upon darkness, her hazel eyes blare amongst the unseen. With a guttural purr, and a flicker of the lights, I scoop her into my arms, stroking her body sweetly.

I live in a small one bedroom apartment; *alone*. It is flooded with golds and reds; a black sofa rests close to the window. There is wooden table ornately carved with images of dancing women joining hands in an unending spiral of exaltation. I release Tabitha and breathe in the smell of street-bought oils, handpicked sage, and nag champa.

My name is Angelique Dayton, daughter of Margarite Dayton, granddaughter of Melicente Dayton, great granddaughter of a wise woman named Ruth. I am the first Matchmaker in a whole line of hairdressers and information dealers, minor witches who made wages by selling and bartering information. The *Rituals of the Hair* is one of the oldest forms of fellowship. My sister Vanessa has a shop in Baltimore. She is renowned for her ability to garner information on any topic she desires. Since I was a child I enjoyed other things, namely men and love. I always found pleasure in connecting friends, Matchmaking, not realizing that my witch grandfather had a latent aptitude for Matchmaker magic: magic of the blood, of the heavens, of the soul. Through bone, or shell, or card, or vision I have never been wrong. If a person wants to find a loved one, a Matchmaker can use their blood to do it.

It's morning, and as the sun kisses my cheek I feel the tap of Tabitha's paw. I shift away. Last night I decided I'd rather binge-drink than actually heal. It's exhausting, always having to engage broken dreams. This mother had come to me wanting to find her missing son. I couldn't reveal I'd helped him to run away with his new bride a month before. All these people who just don't have the tools to function in a relationship! It pisses me off.

Now of course, you're probably thinking, isn't she a Matchmaker, don't most Matchmakers feel bubbly and joyful about connecting people in love, etc. Truth is, while I take great pride in my abilities, sometimes people just get on my fucking nerves.

Wiping the exhaustion from my eyes, I sit up and open my laptop. It seems I don't have any human clients until later in the week. I tap the screen, feeling a tingling in my hands: electricity dances from my finger tips and an older woman in a pin-striped suit appears. Her short hair is slicked back. She is translucent.

"Martha," I say to the hologram.

"Mistress," she replies.

"Do I have any magical clients?" Martha closes her eyes and on screen a name appears: "Adrian Antos". The House of Antos, an old and powerful family, half vampires and witches. He has come behind his mother's back to find his missing brother through blood magic. He is willing to pay. I grin as I shuffle to the kitchen, collecting herbs from my cabinet for a Divination Spell. The hologram of Martha reappears.

"You have another request mistress," she says.

"I'll get to them later, this one is too good to pass up."

"But—" I tap the air beside Martha and she disappears. I place a pot of water on the stove.

While I wait, I open a bag of cat food and nonchalantly scatter it into Tabitha's bowl. She exclaims, turns her head and walks to her food, staring at me. Like she's angry it ever touched my hand, "You're a cat Tabitha."

"And you're still as awful as I remember. No wonder you're single."

The voice is deep, like a penetration. I turn to see a half moon smile on thick lips.

"And you're still mad I didn't fuck you that one time at Calafia's," I say evenly. "Which was ages ago, we were teenagers, but for some reason you have issues with rejection." I turn off the stove, pour myself a glass of water, and flop on the couch. I can smell the scent of expensive cologne as he sits on the arm. The crease in his black pants remains unwrinkled.

"You still hate men?"

"Not men, just you motherfucker," I say, grabbing the remote, "Now, what you want?"

"To hire you." He pouts a little. Reginald, son of a Soul-Broker, works for the government in a secret department very few know about. His job is to monitor witches and protect our secret from mortal awareness. His sister Calafia and I once belonged to the Order of the Azure Mother, a coven of trans Witches dedicated to finding the First Mother. But the less said about that fuck-up, the better.

Reginald and I may not have slept together at that party, but we did for the whole year prior. Involuntarily, I smile at the memory.

He waves his black hand in front of my face. "What are you daydreaming about?"

"Nothing," I lie, rolling my eyes. "Now, what scheme you have cooking?" I turn to him, tilt my head, and frown. "And no, I ain't selling ass, so don't ask me to fuck one of your government friends." He is about to object and I raise my finger to the air: "oh don't act like you haven't asked me that before."

He leans into me and smiles, revealing two perfectly pointed fangs. His eyes gleam silver. "I need you to find someone."

"Who?"

"An agent named Veronica."

I ball my fist, mutter a curse and, an electric hiss dancing around my knuckles, I strike his jaw. He falls to the ground. I stand over him as the rise and fall of my chest becomes sporadic. "You hired her?"

He gets up, rubbing his jaw, but he maintains his composure. "She is a powerful witch."

"And you are my friend!"

"I am a guy you used to fuck."

"For a whole year."

"There's a difference."

"For some people." I flop back on the couch. "Why?"

"She stole a talisman from our archives." He digs into his suit jacket and produces a piece of paper that looks worn. He unrolls the scroll and places it on the table. Tabitha, with newfound curiosity, leaps onto the table. On the paper is a drawing of a necklace, on its end a crescent moon cupped in the hands of a naked praying Goddess. "The Talisman of the Crescent Heart," he says.

"And?" I finish the water and walk over to the cabinet where I keep my wine.

"A little early to be drinking, isn't it?"

"And?" The wine makes a swishing sound as it falls lullfully into the glass.

"The talisman can generate natural disasters."

"What of it?" I wave my left hand as if shooing away a fly.

He stares at me, his mouth agape, I see a fire dance in his eyes, then a look of uncertainty. I swirl my glass. "Am I supposed to say, *oh no, not a natural disaster!*"

He snatches up the parchment and rolls it with a ferocity that makes his hands turn red. "What happened to you Angelique? You were always a fucking bitch but now you are heartless. Are you miserable because that wandering priest who doesn't like to wear shoes picked that white cis woman over you?"

"A white woman who you hired, and allowed to steal a powerful talisman." I take a drink and try to suppress my memories, of a verdant field, of a couple, of two spirits joined in love, of a man who knew me from many lifetimes past, of a waterfall of joy, a wandering of tears. Aaradash: my love, *a wandering priest who knew not his destiny before my kiss.*

Reginald stares at me with clarity in his eyes. He taps his hand on his head. "I'm sorry Angelique." He walks towards me and I back away, his hand reaching for the glass, my own trembling with fear.

"You don't get to come in here and save me," I say, my tongue an arrow of bitterness. He stops.

"The Earth can't take any more strain. Humans are already destroying her. If Veronica leaves the talisman on the Dais of Sol she will trigger a global disaster."

"Let the world die. You and I both know death is better than this cesspool."

"Angelique—" I turn away from him, the round shape of my hips swaying as I march to the kitchen. The echo of my bitterness is the slosh of wine in the glass. As I drink, he stares at me and shrugs. "Let me know if you change your mind." I watch the darkness gather him into its embrace. He leaves the parchment behind. I decide to take the bottle back to bed with me.

"Angelique." My eyes dart open and my hands, hot with anger, release a fireball. How many men plan on invading my space today? By its light I can see it's Aaradash. Speak of the devil. He leaps away, a look of surprise on his face. "What are you doing?"

I scramble to my feet and spin a dagger of azure light at him. He blocks it by shifting his staff to the left, then conjures several glowing balls of energy. They rush into the floor around my feet, and stretch into bars, forming a magic cage. *He's been doing that spell since I met him. So predictable.*

I strike the cage. It flickers and I see him flinch. I strike it again and it shatters, the shards dancing around me, changing from gold to azure. I can feel their heat against my thoughts. "We were lovers for ten years. You thought I would forget your tricks, priest?" Crossing my hands and flicking my wrist, I freeze the shards in mid-air, then send them darting towards him.

"Using your Matchmaker powers to tap into magical vibrations, Angelique? Clever." He raises a hand and holds the shards suspended between us. I can feel him pressing against my thoughts. attempting to re-establish power over his magical spheres. The shards shift from azure to gold then back again.

"You won't win, priest." I feel the fibers in the carpet singing to me. I smile and stamp my foot and the threads unravel and wrap themselves around him, pulling him to the floor. The spheres disappear and my daggers fade. I walk towards him and bend down, close to his face. "Did you really think you could best me?"

"It is not me that will best you," he says with sorrow in his eyes, "but your own arrogance."

I feel a searing pain rush through my body. The wind is knocked from my lungs. I fall to one knee, my limbs exhausted, my fingers aching. The carpet falls away from him, tattered. I *sacrificed a good rug for nothing*.

With strong arms, he lifts me and places me into the bed. My head begins to ache. I try to swat his hand away. It doesn't work.

"You don't get to hurt me and then feel good about taking care of me, you selfish asshole. You ruined me. I was so happy before you. Now all I do is make other people happy. Then I come home to this apartment with that fucking cat that gives me the worst side eye in the history of animal companions. Even the cat thinks I drink too much. And it's never enough to exorcise these memories of you, your ghost heavy against my skin, your laughter poison in my ear. I am sexy, full figured, curvy. Men fall at my feet. And I sabotage them because of you." I am whispering now, tears refusing to fall. I realize I am slurring my words,

He doesn't respond. He simply sits down. Over the scars of his chest surgery is now a tattoo of words, written in a language I can't decipher. He wears a skirt that made him appear to be dancing as we fought. His mouth, that mouth that once filled me with delight, that mouth with its snakelike smile, is bent in a frown. I yell obscenities at him, tell him he pushed Veronica to become evil. And when my rant has reached a fevered pitch and my throat burns...

"Stop it right now!" A deep voice, a symphony of tones. Both Aaradash and I turn to stare at Tabitha. She stares at us.

"Mama?"

"Yes," Tabitha says.

"You've been spying on me through my cat?!" I'm too tired to be angry.

"Yes," she says, "and if you were not buzzed all the damn time you would have sensed my presence by now."

Flashes of images race through my head, flashes of encounters, I gasp, "Wait, were you watching me when I was—"

"No girl," Tabitha says shaking her head, and looking at Aaradash, "I have no desire to watch my daughter engage in ruining her life further."

"What is that supposed to mean?" Aaradash asks blandly, "You sent me here."

"Both of you shut up please," I push against my pain and sit up in bed. They ignore me, their bitterness drowning out my demands. I close my eyes, their voices become a hum against my own; I start singing. Aaradash says something about how overbearing my mother is; my own voice becomes a low whisper. My mother says something about him being a hippie unable to commit. *Focus on the blue, hear the chorus of the Ancients, voices coated in love, in the colors of DNA.* He tells her she is a snob, and that is why she couldn't keep a husband. *His peace is fragile in the face of my mother's shade.*

Hear the air around me begin to dance with sensation. She tells him his mama was a ho, his daddy was a ho and he a ho. *Block out the image of a grown man arguing with a cat that sounds like my mother.* I grimace, a little, and my nails begin to stretch. I open my eyes and claw at Aaradash's arm.

He screams, but too late. I murmur words in a tongue mortals have never known and few witches remember. His blood forms strings at the ends of my nails. The vibrations of his affections pound against the air as he bites his lip to stop it contorting in pain. I wiggle my fingers so that the blood, a silken web of red, begins to dance. Images appear on each strand, flickering like a movie. I ask the blood to find his truest love. And...

I see myself. Smiling, as I was on that day, and him, his lips dancing on my own... in Elysia. Tears rip themselves from my eyes. I look for Veronica. He does love her but not like he loves me. Her image seems lost in a flood of desire, and familiarity. With a wave of my left hand, my body becomes pleasantly warm. The piece of him that cares for her flies from his blood and forms a tiny light. I close my eyes and feel my nails become smaller. His blood liquefies and seeps back into his body. The wound repairs itself.

"The Seeker Spell is done," I say rising from the bed and going to turn on the shower. "Reginald contacted me about finding Veronica and an amulet she stole only this morning. My mother must have heard and sent you here so I would read your blood to find that thing."

"She was always very manipulative." Aaradash is staring down at Tabitha, who now seems to be free from my mother's spell. She leaps into his arms. She is a traitor, but what can you do? Aaradash smiles and stares at me, a confused look on his face.

"You're seriously gonna take a shower before we save the world?"

"Veronica doesn't even know where to go to do what she needs to do," I say, sensing Aaradash's lover's confusion in the air. The Seeker Spell is strong, "Right now she's in Virginia in some glade trying to dig up another artifact to locate the Altar of Sol. So, yes, I am going to take a shower."

Adorned in a black skirt and white sweater, I drape a dark mini cape around me and step into black and white striped heels. I adorn myself with a brooch made from the laughter of a rising goddess—mortals call it a diamond. Snatching a brimmed hat from my closet, I place it on my head, and grab a small wand crafted from the bark of a fallen oak. I tap the air and watch glitter burst from the tip. I walk into the living room. Reginald is here. He must have got my message.

"Where my money Reginald?" Tabitha, still free of my mother's mental control, is rubbing against his legs, purring.

"Always to the point huh?"

"I really don't care about the world or this bitch, but I do like my bills being paid."

Reginald places a thick envelope into my hand. I raise an eyebrow, he's paid me more than he promised.

"Veronica would never do something like this," Aaradash says, the golden bracelets lining his arms making a gentle noise as he shifts his arm. "I still think she's being controlled,"

"If you need to think she ain't evil because you have to rationalize why you left me for her, go right on ahead," I say flippantly. "Now, do that thing when the lights come out and teleport us somewhere for something." The seven spheres flick into existence and a waterfall of gold bathes us in its light.

When the warmth from the teleportation seeps away and the disorientation fades, we are in the field from my vision. The ground seems untouched by spell or tool.

Reginald sucks his teeth and waves his hand, causing the winter chill to soften. He stares at his palm, reading some information, information which he always neglects to share. My ex-lover—well, they are both my exes—Aaradash takes his staff and sweeps the air with it. Bells chime and coins jingle. He stamps the noise into the earth. Both of them begin mumbling individual incantations. The small white light of my tracing spell dances beneath my feet.

"She's still here," we all say in unison. I sneer, but before I can say another word, there is a great wailing and I am falling, the updraft speeding past my face. I am falling and the ground is getting nearer.

"Float!" I scream in fear. "FLOAT!" The abrupt activation of the spell jolts me. I close my eyes and imagine the world filled with light. When I open them I can see I am in a room, torches lining its walls. I feel the energy of the float spell turn me and lower me to the ground. My heels echo with defiance as they hit stone.

The room is alive with hieroglyphics, On the ground is a carving of a wheel within a wheel. On the walls, a man lying on a stone tablet, awaiting the knife; of a woman offering a heart to a rising sun. So far, so legends of the dying and rising god. But while in the standard myth the sacrifice is accepted, this time the Sun chooses to hide his face at the woman's offering. And in the next image the sea rushes to find the hidden sun's light but drowns the earth in her journey.

Umm, how the fuck did a temple like this get in Virginia? The air heats and my companions appear around me.

Aaradash rushes to embrace me. "Are you alright?" I step away.

"I am fine," I murmur, turning back to the wall and retracing the narrative. What seems to be the first image shows the same woman embracing the man gingerly. Both Aaradash and Reginald are talking but I'm following another thread. In the scenario of the year-king, the sacrificial lover-king, after his ordained period of power and adoration, gladly embraces death. But here I see trickery, and here, a parting of lovers true. I gasp, turning to Aaradash: "Get out!"

"What?".

"She is going to sacrifice you! That's why she's interested in you! To take your heart. In order to activate the relic she needs a sacrifice. So, you have to go."

I wave my wand, trying to teleport him, feeling his weight resist. Aaradash lifts his staff, blocking the spell, and it fizzles, my intentions discarded.

"I am not going to leave you."

"Don't be an idiot!"

"I am not—" The room shakes as dust begins to fall, and a huge stone moves.

"Listen lovebirds," says Reginald. "If you can't do your job. Go back home. No one has time for this shit." He begins to walk through the door. Aaradash and I look at one another. I step in front of him. He moves out of the way.

Through the door is a hallway, damp and full of the sickeningly sweet smell of mold. It gives me a headache. The corridor shakes as another door opens. The light from my tracking spell dashes ahead of us.

Veronica! I remember the first time I met her. She was Aaradash's yoga instructor. She had the dullest blue eyes I had ever seen. I guess her hair seemed luminous. She was using ancient glamor spells. Perhaps she could have been considered beautiful, but it was her innocent grin that really swayed people. When Aaradash began to delve deeper into the practices of his ancestors, he chose Veronica to guide him. For the life of me, I never understood why.

I recall the timbre of his voice, assuring me that they weren't lovers. I recall him weeping at my feet, insisting I had somehow imagined the stolen glances and bartered giggles. He wanted to lie to a Matchmaker. A witch that knows when new love has taken root. And eventually he left, to sojourn, to find his godhood. And now, here he was.

"Angie," I hear Reginald call, "Snap out of it."

I shake away the echoes of an earlier time. We enter another room, carved with a spiraling serpent whose head juts out from the wall and rests neatly in the middle of the floor. I can feel the pulse of life vibrating from the walls around us, although the room isn't moving at all. I look down at the serpent's head.

"That's alive."

"What do you mean?" Reginald whispers.

I close my eyes and cast the Song of the Heart, a spell which reveals the essence of objects. I open them. The dead and living have become a tapestry of colors. Reginald is a brilliant light blue, pale, *unimaginative*, half succubus and half witch. Aaradash is a blazing gold, his light threatening to consume the room. The Serpent too has vibrancy, a tantalizing red. All three dim and pulse with life. I close my eyes again- they've begun to itch- and after a moment I open them, now seeing the world without the assistance of a spell. The smell of mold is stronger and my headache is getting worse

Reginald waves his hand, turns his palm towards himself to read what he's gleaned. My head begins to throb. I watch as Reginald's eyes bulge. He places a finger to his lips, then points to the hallway. Aaradash begins to start back. I do too, but then my hand rushes to my head. The smell of mold is overwhelming. I turn to Reginald as the light from my tracking spell swirls around us.

"Get out," I groan. I feel my knees buckle. Aaradash takes me into his arms.

"Angelique, are you alright?"

"Not mold," I murmur, "Veronica, spell."

I can hear Veronica's piercing voice. Her laughter is a cacophony. The air turns green, and darkness falls.

The black sea of possibility swirls over me, hands gripping my limbs, lips touching my breast. I collect dreams. My body is a lexicon of possibilities, webs of passion finding lines through me. An incantation kisses my flesh. A cup of past lives dripping the wine of the ethers through my heart. I part the doors of awareness. A tender azure light bathes my nakedness.

"Mother?" I ask, and my thoughts become a puddle of petals.

"A mother, but not your mother of blood. The age has come, The Father will lose. The time has been born. You have worshiped me, your Sisters have worshiped me. The realm of the Dead is bleeding. I am awakened. Believe once again. I am your Goddess, I am the Lord."

Before I can decipher her words I feel the rush of images bombard my eyes. Me as a young girl making a friend's blood dance into the air as I read her fortune. A teenage version of myself mistreated in school, my body seen as a betrayal to my truth, my foolishness in asking mundane creatures to affirm my magical being. My first drink, the first time I received affection, the first surgery, the last. Death, resurrection. I scream: "Aaradash!"

I wake up. It is night. I try to move, and find my body bound by some magical force. Stone beneath me. I am on a large dais. My back aches. *It is cold as hell!* I hear breathing to my side. The air feels thin, we are on a mountain. *It's fucking freezing!!!* "Aaradash?"

"He's still waking up from the spell." The voice is Veronica's.

"Let him go!" I say, fighting my disorientation, an effect of her sleep spell.

"No," she says.

"But he loves you, Veronica."

"You must think I'm an idiot. He loves you."

"Is that why you are doing this?" I ask, "Jealousy?"

"Things are all ready," I hear Reginald say, "Oh, Angie, you're up!"

"Reginald!"

"Sorry love, I had to get both you and Aaradash here so we could complete the ritual," There is a smile at the edge of his voice.

"You are amazing, sir," Veronica says. And then I hear the sound of lips touching.

"So, not only does she work for you, you fucking her too?"

"I was never good at keeping my hands to myself."

"You are appalling Reginald," I say, "and now you'll be a murderer too. Why?"

"We are simply going to localize a natural disaster to one specific little place in Africa. Did you know there are a bunch of European countries still receiving colonizer coins from certain countries? If we create a natural disaster, I can advise the president to authorize a military occupation under the pretext of relief, strengthening our presence there."

"What about all those innocent people?" Aaradash asks, his voice groggy.

"The innocent sometimes have to die in order for us to get what we want. And while there, we will have a direct pipeline to some of our friends in certain other parts of the world."

"You are violating the Witches Council agreement of non-engagement. Even the other countries' Witch Conclaves will not tolerate this—" I stop mid-sentence, my thoughts become a cloud of knowing, "You want to start a war..."

Veronica laughs, "Let the mortals fight. Let them kill each other. Send their children off to war. Blame it on some false prophet terrorist and when the world is bleeding out itself then we, righteous and saintly, shall intervene to usher in a new age of The Witch."

"Witches are the parents of the humans, we can't kill them."

"We can't wait for those idiots to evolve either—and anyway, when did you start caring about anything other than gold?"

"You can't do this," Aaradash says.

"I won't let you hurt him!" I scream, struggling against their spell.

"Oh dear," Veronica giggles,"Aaradash will be fine. It's you we're going to kill. You are his heart, dear. The thing that grounds this little Blood God to his humanity. Without you he will turn his face away, and with it the Sun's light."

"You want him to go mad..."

"No!" I hear Aaradash yell, and the ground beneath us begins to tremble.

"Restrain him!" Reginald orders. And I can feel Veronica shout. Perhaps she is stumbling, yes, and that is all I need because I feel it, below the vibrations of her magic, a bubbling song, hot, disjointed. *I can smell her blood.* There must be a little cut somewhere on her body. *Just a nick, that's all it takes.* I begin to hum, a sweet tune, something full of delight, something that allows her blood to dance with my intentions.

With a push of my body I leap into the air. Reginald stares in surprise.

"I cannot believe I ever fucked you!" I move Veronica's limbs as if she were a marionette. She attempts to resist but my will is stronger. She runs to Reginald. My other hand forms a fireball, which I throw at him. He deflects the spell towards Veronica. And Veronica has no defenses, because she is under my control. She catches flame. The stench of her burning flesh assails my nose

"You're killing your own comrades now?"

"Like you, she was easy to manipulate." Reginald says, lights spewing from his hand, "To be fair, I did tell her that her hatred for you would be her undoing."

I expand my awareness until I can feel the flight of birds. I imagine their wings as my own. I shout and a wall of feathers appears in front of me, and transforms his light into air. "You've sunk so low Reginald. Once you were invested in helping the world."

"The humans are parasites, they need to be controlled for their own good."

"Spoken like a true government official." My skin billows as wind forms behind me. It sounds like a sword slashing the air. I fling the wind sword towards him, He raises his arms to block the spell, grimacing when it slices his arm.

"The world doesn't deserve us, Matchmaker. Look at you. You help people find love and yet you hate them."

He blocked my attack. No matter. His arms are cut. I see his blood. I feel the song of his blood, the hiss of its loss. My thoughts seep into his limbs. But before I can *smile my throat* tightens, and I try to gasp for breath, my fingernails clawing. *He poisoned his blood somehow so that I couldn't take hold of him.* I fall to my knees, my heart pounding. *Oh my God I am going to die.* Tears begins to pour from my eyes.

"Your puppet master spell won't work on me. Fuck the ritual. I have wanted to squeeze the life out of you since the moment you chose this sad excuse for a God over me!" He balls his fist, the hold around my throat tightening. I look to Aaradash. He's unconscious again.

"Oh... the... fragility... of... men," I try to chuckle but the only sound my throat can produce is a sad gurgling sound, "You... are... not... a... god..."

"No!" I can hear Aaradash shout. And my throat loosens and I feel air fill my lungs, my gasping is not in vain. Reginald is pushed back against a rock that has somehow jutted up behind him in an instant. The rock forms into hands, grabbing him, squeezing him so hard that his mouth contorts.

I laugh. Aaradash's eyes glow with an eerie red hue. His normally calm face is taken by a sneer as he moves his hand and shifts the rock, piercing Reginald through with shards of stone. I race to the makeshift altar which houses the Talisman of the Crescent Heart. I grab it and can feel a surge of ancient power course through me. Reginald is on the ground, blood dripping from every part of his body. Aaradash stands over him, his staff raised to the air.

"Aaradash," I run to him, placing a gentle hand on his chest, trying to match his breath to my own, "Please, you are not a killer."

"He deserves to die," Aaradash's voice is laden with thirteen others, "And as I am a god, am I not supposed to administer punishment?"

"Beloved, please," I say my voice lighter, sweeter, "Remember when we met and you saved me from the depths of the underworld. Remember what our love felt like."

Reginald screams as the ground beneath stabs him once again.

"He wants to destroy the world," says Aaradash.

"He won't," I tell him. "He needs a Matchmaker, one that has the heart of a Child of the Sun. Please beloved, spare him, don't become what you worked so hard to free yourself from." I begin to stroke his arm, humming a song that I once sang to him as we lay by the river Styx, "I read your blood, I know how much you love me. I know I am still there in the secret parts of you. I know why you had to leave, and now why you can return. But if you kill him those three years away from me, those three years of finding yourself, won't mean anything."

The tension in his arms lessens and his eyes return to their beautiful brown hue. He smiles, his staff hitting the ground as he leans on us both.

"Reginald, I will call the Witches Council to come and retrieve you. As you poisoned your blood so my spell wouldn't work, I poisoned your blood so you wouldn't be able to recover quickly. You won't have time to escape."

"He'll never love you," Reginald laughs, coughing blood, grabbing his stomach, a smile on his face, "He will always seek enlightenment, because he is a god who doesn't recognize his own godhood. He will leave you always in search of fulfillment."

I walk to Reginald and lift my leg, hearing bone break as I bring my foot down on his face. He passes out. I tilt his head so he doesn't drown in his own blood. Clutching the talisman in my hand, I can feel it opening the air behind us. It will take us home.

TWO MONTHS LATER

"So take this charm," I say holding out a small ball of red marble to a round-faced woman who is staring at me with excitement in her dull eyes, "and keep it under your pillow and in seven days you will find your lover."

"Oh thank you so much!" She exclaims, snatching the marble. She giggles and races down the hallway. The lights in the room brighten, and I can feel strong arms wrap themselves around me. The scent of patchouli, nag champa and vanilla touches my nose. I rest inside those arms, turning my head to receive a gentle kiss on my lips.

"You are such an amazing person," Aaradash smiles.

"Thank you," I grin, "We should go to the room, you've been gone for a month and I really want to see what you learned on your travels."

"Well, I could show you here, I don't know why—" As what I am suggesting dawns on him, he begins to laugh. Taking off the few clothes he wears and rushing to the room, he turns to say "Oh amor, I heard Reginald has been punished by the Witches Council. Did you give back the talisman?"

"Yes," I lie, feeling the pulse of the talisman in a safe in my wall. Its warmth dancing on my flesh. I shove away its beckoning and allow my dress to fall languidly to the ground. Naked, I walk to the bedroom, my hips a hymn of seduction. I paint a cat-like smile on the edge of my face. "It's so nice to have you home."

Schwaberow, Ohio

BRENDAN WILLIAMS-CHILDS

Uncle Ray's alarm goes BEEP. BEEEEP. BEEP. BEEEEP. Doesn't stop. BEEP. BEEEEP. BEEP. Doesn't stop. Won't stop. He sleeps for five minutes while the noise continues. I look at the ceiling. There is a crack in the shape of a rabbit. It's only a rabbit in the morning. At night, it's a dog. In the day, I don't see it. It may be something else entirely. Maybe it's a spider. This is how people describe cracks in ceilings; a crack in the shape of an animal. When they look at them too long, anyway. I am five minutes looking at this rabbit now. Uncle Ray hits the alarm. Now it blasts the news. "COMING UP THIS HOUR: DAN MATHERS DISCUSSES THE CHANGES TO THE BEST PRACTICES REGARDING NEUROBIOLOGICAL BEHAVIOR-AL MODIFICATION IMPLANTS AND THEIR USE IN DELINQUENT YOUTH REFORM. REPORTING FROM CINCINNATI–" Now Uncle Ray is cursing. Now nothing. Every morning, the same noises from Uncle Ray. The alarm, the cracking of his knees and spine, the cursing. Every morning, the same noises from Aunt Marianne. She makes no noises. Nothing. But this is always the same.

"Up, pup," Uncle Ray says. He slams a fist against my door. It falls open. Falls is the right word. The upper hinge is broken. Every night, I re-set it, place the door back in its frame. I could fix it for good, but Uncle Ray broke it before I moved in, after my cousin's funeral, and I think it might be rude to cover up this crooked memorial.

"Up," I repeat. I am. Now I am sitting up and keeping my shoulders back. Posture. Shoulders back and head high. Alive, awake, alert, and en-thusiastic. "I'm up."

He's already gone. It is eight steps across my bedroom to open the window. On a good day, anyway. Sometimes there's a mess. A lot of my cousin's things got left in the room so now our combined stuff makes a low fortress of boxes. It takes five tugs on the blue string to roll the shades up. There is fog on the beans outside, dew heavy on them. Uncle Ray tells me sometimes how many pounds of beans our land produces. I forget. Aunt Marianne tells me sometimes how I am worth less than the beans. I remember. The line of the oaks at the end of the field glow yellow-green when the sun rises behind them.

I put my socks on. Left first, then right. Left, right, left. Right. Then my clothes and a hat, thick wool with flaps to cover my ears. Heavy fleece gloves. I hope there isn't another dead hen. Last month one froze laying an egg near the edge of the henhouse. Last month the air was a physical property. Not now. Out the back door and into mist. Through the back window I can see into the house. Aunt Marianne rising in her thick purple terrycloth bathrobe that's gone soft at the ends, the sleeves. Uncle Ray popping his back again. Next to the coop, the pigs are asleep.

The rooster is crowing when I get there. I tell him to shut up. He does. Then he starts talking again. I tell him to shut up. He doesn't. I tell him he's going to taste delicious. He doesn't shut up. I collect the eggs from the hens and tell him he'll never know his children. He's quiet. I tell him I guess I'm a little sorry. I'm not. I sit on the ramp and count the eggs. It takes three minutes. There are sixteen. One of them will break on the way back in. Usually one does.

My phone buzzes. I move to the far end of the coop where a plastic bowl full of submersible heating wires is making a low electric whistling. I lean down, stomach on hay and shit and feathers, and pull one hand free next to the heat. The message is from Rebecca, a friend from the internet. Well, from Chicago. The Chicago part of the internet.

REBECCA 05:50: oh my GOD i just woke up and u would think that Diana

I don't actually swipe my phone to unlock I because if I did that I would feel like I had to answer the message and it's too cold out to get the latest gossip about Diana, who used to be our friend from the Milwaukee part of the internet until she started dating a guy whose younger brother got neuropsycho behavioral modifications last year and now Diana believes that "in severe cases" just sticking a fucking wire in a kid's brain is okay.

She doesn't think it's like mobile institutionalization at all, which is what Rebecca says. So we're pissed at Diana. It's too cold to be really angry right now though.

I go back to the house. Put the fifteen eggs on the counter. Aunt Marianne is listening to the radio. She's not looking at me and sometimes, when we're very still, I like to pretend that she likes me and that she'll be smiling when she turns around. She won't be. Aunt Marianne is listening to the radio in her big nightgown and stirring grits. Instant grits. Which still take five minutes. "Looks like Thompson's shoring up the nomination," she says.

"Oh," I say.

"Wasn't talking to you."

"Oh," I say. I didn't think she was. But she was talking. I was there. Uncle Ray is in the bathroom shaving. Cousin Tim is dead for a few years now. I'm here, and I hear my aunt. Her and everyone like her who isn't talking to me.

"Yep," Aunt Marianne says. "Got a damn robot wife, Thompson, wires and chips and all..." She lowers her voice. "Ought to put a chip in the thing's head."

She is talking about me but not to me but she does this often. I am not thinking about myself. I am not thinking about the chips she wants to put in my head that she thinks would turn me back into a girl, maybe even a girl who isn't "some kind of autistic," and instead I am thinking about Thompson and how I have only ever seen one picture of Thompson's wife. Haleigh.

Haleigh Thompson doesn't look like a robot. That's what makes her so scary. There are robots working the farm over. They look like robots. Square and metal and not smiling. Their faces, if they are faces, flash different colors sometimes. Titanium and halogen. Help harvest the crops sometimes. Don't let their husbands run for president. Don't have husbands. Are "real" robots.

Okay, technically, Haleigh Thompson is not a "robot." The proper term for Haleigh Thompson is "user of robotic prosthetics." Sometimes "cyborg." But there are only so many ways to dress up someone who isn't organic anymore.

"I wouldn't want chips like her," I say, but I don't think Aunt Marianne is listening to what I have to say about what she says when she thinks I'm not listening but I am. Always.

Aunt Marianne pours out her grits for herself and leaves the rest in the pan for me. She shakes her head. "Walt. Go take a shower." She tries to sound enthusiastic when she says, "Your mother is coming by."

"Why?" I ask.

"Damned if I know," she says. "Ray told me soon as I woke up. Damned if I know a thing about what your mother does, child."

Good answer. I go shower. Uncle Ray keeps shaving as I do. "Walt," he says, while I'm washing my scalp. "You be nice to your mother, now, you understand?"

"Nice," I repeat. "Yep."

"She'll be here for the week."

"Why?" I finish and get out, dry myself off. Ever since I shaved my head showers don't take much time. Showers were a point of contention when I moved in but eventually Aunt Marianne conceded: I can in fact shower with Uncle Ray in the bathroom because we're both men, regardless of how we got that way. Uncle Ray doesn't care that I'm still saving up for a dick and anyway there's only one bathroom in the house. So we're efficient.

Uncle Ray is still shaving. Using a long-handled curved blade. His arteries stand out against his Adam's apple. I think about his neck, about the neck of the last deer we shot, now in the freezer, with a wind-pipe nearly as long as my inner arm. All thick and white and hard to hold but easy to crush. I cover my own neck with my hands. How easy it would be to cut open, like my chest was. I don't have to cover my chest any more. The deer we shot was a doe. Shot her through the heart. Tore her breast open the way I did mine but nobody stitched the doe up and started taking her seriously. She was dead. My father is dead, too, but I took his name and I'm alive and well and scarred and taken seriously by doctors who decided to "make concessions" because "she was clearly serious."

Uncle Ray is putting toilet paper on a nick by his chin. "I posted her bail," he says.

"Oh," I say.

"Petty theft," he says.

"Yes," I say. I know how to do it better than she does. Well, I don't do it anymore. I do know how. I don't do it. I live with Uncle Ray and Aunt Marianne now. No. Head up, shoulders back. "Okay."

"So have some pity."

"Yep."

Uncle Ray waves his hand in front of my face. Sometimes he does this. I follow his calluses with my eyes. This scared me when I was fourteen. But I'm eighteen now. This no longer frightens me. He's treating this like a joke, like it's something funny that he has to keep checking to see that I'm alive. I blink. Blink once for yes. Blink twice for no.

"I can't ever tell with you, kid," Uncle Ray says.

"Me neither," I say. He laughs, so I must have done something right.

Mom's in jail in Lima where she tried to empty a register while the cashier was taking a piss, so Uncle Ray and I pile in his two-tone Bronco and go get her. I stay in the car because the only people I like less than doctors are cops. The texture of the holes in the passenger seat where Aunt Marianne has accidentally smushed cigarettes is good. Smooth plastic bubbles like polished glass. I run my fingers over it over and over until Uncle Ray brings Mom out of the station and knocks on the door and I have to crawl over the center console into the back.

"Hi, baby," Mom says, not buckling up. Mom always calls me baby. "Baby" is a stupid nickname. Babies can't take care of themselves. Mom is wearing overalls. She looks like a scarecrow.

"You look so different. All grown up. How long's it been?"

"A year."

"A whole year?" she asks, and pats my head so hard that my scalp tingles. "All grown up." She's said this since I was fourteen, when the state moved me in with her brother.

"Grown up," I repeat and shrug. "Maybe."

"Where are you going to college?" she asks.

Uncle Ray just laughs. I laugh even though it isn't funny. "Walt dropped out last year," Uncle Ray says. I was at Northwest State for electrical engineering technology. It was a long drive.

Everyone wants to see people like me with chips in their heads.

They thought they were better than me.

The drive is half an hour and Mom doesn't say another word to me. She talks to Uncle Ray about my grandfather in Cleveland and about my Aunt Susie in Oregon, where Mom is moving, apparently. Uncle Ray nods all the way home and when we're home he opens the door for her. "Come on, Maddie, come in, let's get you set up."

"You know what, baby," she says to me as she swings her purple backpack over her shoulder, conspicuously empty, "I think I'm disappointed in you. About college." But she's not looking at me. She's following Uncle Ray into the house.

"Oregon's nice. Susie's place is real nice, it's got a big yard for being in the city," Uncle Ray says, and neither asks why I haven't moved so I assume that it's fine that I am standing still in the driveway, looking at the road where nobody ever drives except us and the neighbors.

Sometimes tourists or people visiting their great-extended-family end up here. They get lost outside of Wapakoneta, looking for their grandma's house or the Neil Armstrong Museum. They can't pronounce Wapakoneta. We have one movie theater. They call us quaint. I used to slash their tires for fun. Quaint is a word for people who don't have knives. A word for people who shouldn't exist. There is no should in my existence, not even the one the doctors suggested there might be; one with wires and codes. One where they could stop me from stimming and being trans. They couldn't. Statistically, someone has to defy *should*.

"Did you hear, baby?" Mom is asking, leaning in the doorway.

"No," I say, because I didn't hear anything at all. Maybe the sound of the chickens rooting behind the house.

"Baby. Robert Thompson's coming through while I'm here. The campaign trail, you know. Back in Lima. You wanna go see him?"

"He doesn't support corn subsidies," I say, which is easier than saying I think he hates me. If I say that then Mom will just say he doesn't even know me. But he doesn't need to know me.

"Is that a yes or a no, baby?"

"Go with your mother tonight," Uncle Ray says. "We'll watch the speech on TV."

"Okay," I say. And then there is a silence. So then I say, "What will you do in Oregon?" Even though I don't care. Mom starts to talk and Aunt Marianne's cat comes down the stairs from the attic and we look at each other until I have to look away and Mom is still talking and the cat walks silently by and nobody acknowledges it at all except for me. Outside, the fog is lifting from the fields and the mice are starting to wake up and tonight the cat will sneak back in.

When noon rolls around, and Mom is still talking, Uncle Ray's daily noon alarm goes off with a BEEEP. "Dang." He looks at me. "You want to run some errands, kiddo?" It's one of those questions that isn't a question at all but actually just a statement about what's going to happen next followed by a question mark. But he's making the face that I think means *this will be better* and I trust him this time.

Errands might be boring but boring is better than painful and boring is better than awkward and nothing is more awkward than being in a house with Aunt Marianne and my mom, both of them looking at me and thinking about the *children they lost* when I'm still alive. "Okay, sure."

Aunt Marianne herds my mom into the kitchen, both their feet sticky from the old linoleum. It sounds like someone whispering while chewing gum. "You have a good time, now, baby," Mom says. "Bring us something good to eat. Get us some road snacks so we have energy for the rally tonight."

"Good," I say. "I'm up."

"What, baby?" Mom asks, staring at me. Aunt Marianne looks away quickly, like if she doesn't look then my Mom will be spared my awkwardness, also. Like not looking at me makes me go away and be the ghost girl they want.

I look Mom in the eyes and then, after a minute, when Aunt Marianne has lifted her head, I look her in the eyes, too. I blink once. I'm alive. She doesn't have to wave her hand in front of my face. "I'm up," I say again, and follow Uncle Ray out the door into the spring air.

Village Market and Deli is the only grocery store in New Knoxville. Village Market and Deli is actually a gas station. It smells like diesel and grass clippings even if nobody's been mowing the lawn. Uncle Ray parks by the big outside ice-box. The penguin on it is dancing and wearing a hat which is stupid, because I don't think penguins have ears. Aunt Marianne used to have a little song for the penguin, and when I visited, when Tim was still alive, she would sing it for us both. I don't remember any of the lyrics but I could still hum the tune if I wanted.

I follow Uncle Ray through the aisles. I used to be better about grocery stores. When I was little, when I was stealing, I had a good system for not getting overloaded. I would focus on one color. I don't know what changed. A lot. Since I was little, I guess. A lot changed. Duh. My phone vibrates and I have to stop following Uncle Ray to read the text.

REBECCA. 14:03 [three pictures of her face, three different shades of purple lipstick]

14:03: Which do you think is best?

I tell her the second color. I don't actually see a lot of difference but I'm glad she thinks my opinion is important. Then I type, "Sorry I forgot to respond to your message before. My mom's in town."

14:04: Oh shit dude I'm so sorry.

[And then a picture of her face. She's frowning. She has big metal eyes because her parents thought it would be less frustrating than glasses for her when she was a kid. Glasses mean yearly checkups. Last year she started wearing frames over them anyway. It was kind of a big deal in the /r/ antirobomods community because Rebecca is beautiful so other people pay attention to what she does. Most of them don't know she's also active in /r/ diytrans because she uses a different account there. I don't have to because I'm not beautiful.]

"It's okay. I'm gonna see Thompson tonight. Rally in Lima." I type a lot better than I talk. Growing up, my dad had a palm pilot that I would type on. The stylus was smooth and clean and I chewed up the end to hell. I don't know why he had a palm pilot. He should have sold it to a museum to pay our rent. He had a lot of stuff like that. Old technology because the new couldn't be trusted. It was good sometimes, though. Typing on the palm pilot was the thing that convinced the first set of doctors that I wasn't some kind of total idiot.

14:04 [a gif of her making a shooting motion, her fingers a little gun. Her tongue is out. Her hair is in a braid. She has purple eye-shadow, too.]

I start laughing. "Okay," I type, "as long as I can stay at your house after I do it."

14:05: Absolutely! I always wanted to be Mary Surrat. I mean, I really wanted to be Emma Goldman but you know.

"You can be both."

14:05: Porque no los dos.

"Yeah. I'll let you know how it goes."

14:06: I'll see it on the news. Good luck!

"Walt?" Uncle Ray puts his hand in front of my face. I can't tell if I appreciate this more or less than if he had put it on my shoulder. Either way he's snuck up on me. "What are you laughing at?"

I have to ground myself for a moment. We're inside the grocery store that isn't a grocery store. I can hear the fluorescence, the squeak-thump of a work boot on a soap-sticky tile. The walls are grey. Green. White. Somewhere in between the three. "Laughing?" I guess I am. "A friend."

Uncle Ray makes the face he always makes when I talk about my friends. But he doesn't ask the usual questions about how I met them or say the usual things about how I should be careful. He's deviating from his script. He doesn't know he has one. "I'm buying a bag of ice. Grab one and wait in the truck?"

"Okay." I start to go.

"You want anything special?" he asks as I start to go. He's looking at the Little Debbie snacks. "For your trip tonight. Getting your mom a Nutty Bar."

That's her favorite. When we lived in Cleveland, when my father was torn between building a signal jammer around our apartment or letting the doctors cut my brain up and fill it with wires to stop me from "making a permanent mistake from a dysphoria easily alleviated by deep brain stimulation," my mother mostly ate Nutty Bars. We didn't have a lot of money. Nutty Bars have protein. Peanut butter, at least.

I can't tell Uncle Ray all of this. Maybe he already knows. I just have to answer the question. "Okay. Star Crunch." I make myself smile.

"Star Crunch it is." He actually smiles.

When Uncle Ray can do something he thinks will make someone appreciate him, he'll do it. It's why he took me in, I think. Because Mom appreciates it. Uncle Ray externalizes. So does Aunt Marianne, I guess. But she externalizes in a way that's supposed to hurt. In a perfect world, she would internalize. In a really perfect world, her son wouldn't have died and she wouldn't have to internalize or externalize anything.

The bag of ice is cool against my legs, melting all the way home where Mom greets us at the door and I keep the bag between us. Her arms around me and the solid block of frozen water.

"Did you get snacks?" she asks.

Robert James Thompson thinks he's charming. Thinks he's kind. He thinks that the fact he's made of flesh and blood makes up for the fact that he fucks a woman more metal and silicone than human being. He talks so well. He talks a lot. His hair is parted to the side. His smile is fixed and bright. His eyes are blue and shining on the big TVs in the auditorium. He has cufflinks made out of petrified wood. He talks like he knows us, like being from Chicago and having once eaten a cheese curd makes him truly, deeply Midwestern. He isn't.

Behind him, Haleigh Thompson stands, smiling. She met with orphans or something earlier today. Her legs are bright and toned and I've seen the pictures in the magazines of the way the metal works into her bones, the way her nerves connect to the wires that connect to her brain. She is like one of those fancy metal eggs I saw in a National Geographic once. She's not real. But here she is. And she's smiling, like she isn't the inspiration for a million doctors to do the things they did to her to the rest of us. Or try to.

"I know you feel like we've failed you in the past," Robert Thompson says, "And you deserve better. And I'm going to make it up to you. I'm going to ensure opportunities for every young person in America. I'm going to make sure that this is really a country where a kid in Idaho has the same chance to be a cop or a doctor or a CEO as a kid in Manhattan." His shoes are polished. I want to set him on fire. He says something about inclusion and enforcement and takes Haleigh's hand and raises it high and she waves and she looks beautiful I guess and the entire crowd begins to clap so loudly that my ears ring and my eyes hurt and I feel an anger in my chest that's almost like choking. I curl up on the bench and wait, with my eyes closed, until all I'm paying attention to is the dark red of lights shining through my eyelids. I could stay this way forever. But I don't.

Now Mom is doing her makeup in the car. Using the rear-view mirror to fix her lipstick. We are sitting in the parking lot of a McDonalds. There is a cup of sweet tea with two straws in the cup-holder. "Well, baby," she says, "I think Oregon will be a nice change for me. Your Aunt Susie already has a place ready for me to crash for a little bit until I can get an apartment. You can come visit when I'm set up. I hear they have good fancy beer there."

"I don't want him to be president," I say.

"Hmm?" she stares.

"I don't want him to be president," I repeat.

"Then don't vote for him, honey," she says, "I think he's cute. Too bad he married a cy-babe." She laughs.

I don't think it's funny. The car is making a rattling noise. Metal likes speaking. More and more anyway. It's just rattling now, but I've read reports. They make cars that drive themselves, think for themselves, alert pedestrians to their presence in voices that are supposed to sound like people.

"Of course," I repeat. "Cy-babe."

"Baby," she says. She touches my neck. Her nails feel glossy like a magazine. "Do you have a single original thought in your head or do you just parrot back what people say?"

Sometimes she sounds like my father. I wonder if she knows.

"Parrot?" I don't parrot, I process. I have to make sure I'm hearing everyone right. When I was a kid, the doctors all said that this meant I was stupid. I could be so much smarter. They could program me to be smarter.

"Baby, you're not helping your case by saying what I say, you know." She re-adjusts the rear-view mirror for me. Bright red and white neon McDonald's signs now reflect where her face used to be. "Are you happy with your Aunt and Uncle?"

"Ha-" I stop. Think about the words. Shaped in loops like the arches behind us. "It's... okay." I don't know how to explain that it hurts but it's not painful. It's like a bruise but not like a cut? It's like a sunburn? It's like I want them to love me but I think they already do but it's not really *me* they love? It's okay.

"Would you want to come to Oregon with me?"

I don't even have to think about it. "No."

"Are you sure, baby? It must be boring as shit out here for you. I bet they've got support groups for people like you in Salem. It's a city, you know. Not like this." She rolls down the window specifically to point at it. "I know I was bored as shit growing up here."

"Uncle Ray..." I focus on the words again. My foot taps against the brake. Stop stop stop but I can't stop myself. "Told me. About how bored you were."

"I bet he did." She snorts. She takes the lid off the big iced tea and eats an ice-cube. It cracks between her canine teeth. "Shit. I couldn't make a single friend in this fucking place."

That wasn't what Uncle Ray told me about her. But I bite my tongue and don't mention all the friends she made. Friends like my father. "But I- I have friends. I don't need to move to Oregon." When we lived in Cleveland with my father, our apartment was full of bugs and sometimes mice. Our neighbors were always threatening to call people who would have erased me. I guess they think they succeeded by sending me to the country. Like a dog. That's the euphemism. Send him to a farm. He'll have a good life.

"How did you make friends out here, baby?"

"Online. And I'm not." She's staring at me. I clarify. "A baby." I can support my own head.

"You'll always be my baby," she says. Scripted. In juvie, they said I was scripted, too. That it was why I didn't fit in, why I stole things, why I *acted like a boy*. Because I had *learned her behavioral scripts from her father*.

The best part about the people who hate social scripts is they don't realize what they want is for people like me to be even more scripted. There are kids like me but not like me. Kids like me who got the wires. Those things are full of code. And that has to be scripted. A script to erase a script. Doctors don't even realize how clever they are about trying to undo us.

I take the car out of neutral. I take us out of the parking lot and soon we merge onto the interstate. I'm glad to be out of the city, from eyes I can't look back into. I'm glad to be done with Robert Thompson. It's misty out. I think about fog on the beans. About every individual pod. "Not really," I say finally.

"What do you mean?" She doesn't look at me. She keeps her eyes on the road.

"They put a chip in Haleigh Thompson's brain when she was a baby," I say. "Did you know?"

"Everybody knows, baby," she says. "And they fixed her legs up. Lots of babies get brain chips."

"Not me."

"Well, no, baby, your father..." she stops.

My father. My father now dead. My father now dead in prison for putting a knife into a cyborg's synthetic heart. My father who wouldn't let them touch me with their wires for so long. My father, who hated robots and cyborgs until it turned out that maybe making me into one of them could stop me from being trans and then, well, anything was worth a try right?

My father, who probably held that hope in his heart when he killed a man who was like what I could have been. "Was smart," I say. "About the robots anyway."

Mom just laughs. She laughs for longer than is necessary. She laughs for a long time. I wasn't kidding.

BEEEEEEEEEEEEP. Uncle Ray's alarm. Relentless. He slams his fist into it. The news. Relentless. "...FOLLOWING THE COURT'S DECISION TO ALLOW DOCTORS IN COLUMBUS TO USE NEUROBIOLOGICAL BEHAVIORAL MODIFICATION THROUGH DEEP BRAIN STIMULATION ON CASES DEEMED "IRREVERSABLE" IN LONG TERM ASSISTED CARE FACILITIES." I am awake before he is. I am in his bedroom to turn the machine off. It is pounding in my head.

Robert Thompson is on the radio and his voice is as slick as his shoes were and his voice is as loud as it was at the rally and he is saying "WHAT WE'RE SEEING HERE IS A REMARKABLE APPLICATION OF NEW TECHNOLOGY TO DIRECTLY BETTER PEOPLE'S LIVES. THIS IS THE KIND OF WORK I INTEND TO SUPPORT ONE-HUNDRED PERCENT IF I'M ELECTED. THERE'S SO MUCH THAT WE CAN CHANGE ABOUT A HUMAN BRAIN FOR THE BETTER-"

I fumble with the radio. It burns me to touch, so loud and venomous. Aunt Marianne smacks my hand. "Get the fuck out, Cassie," she says. She sleeps naked. When she wakes up and yells at me, sitting up in bed, she is obscene. I think that someday my own body will be this old and frightful but it can never be obscene. Not like that. Obscene in other ways. I should be upset that she calls me by the wrong name but it feels like I don't even know who Cassie was. "Ray, get your fucking kid out of here." Sometimes I'm *the* kid. Every time I'm fucking up, I'm Ray's.

Uncle Ray throws the tiny metal Christmas angel, next to the picture of Tim on his bedside table, at me. Underhanded. It still hits my forehead. He makes an expression like he just stepped on the cat's tail. I can feel myself not reacting at all and he's still looking like he's done something wrong but the longer we look at each other the more it's okay, the more he can just keep metaphorically stepping.

"Your alarm," I say. "Is bad. Change it." If he wants me to say anything more, I don't. I leave. I am already dressed. All I need are shoes. I wait a moment outside the door when I hear Aunt Marianne.

"Ray, I'm going to put a goddamn neurobio what the hell ever chip in that child's brain."

"We don't have the money for that." He's laughing. He's always laughing. Even when he shouldn't. He's like Mom in that way. Nervous laughers.

"Well, how do we get insurance or something like that?" Her voice breaks.

I'm the one with a bump on my forehead but I can tell she's in pain. At least she sounds like she's in pain. What am I supposed to do about that? My father used to beat people up outside bars for their money, my mother once stabbed a man in a hotel room and took his wallet. I know what it looks like to hurt someone. It doesn't usually look like just existing. But here I am, watching Aunt Marianne's cat drag in a mouse from outside, and I'm hurting her, I guess.

Uncle Ray answers her question very gently. The same gentle voice he used when I was adjusting to living in this house. "Vote for Thompson."

He's not laughing anymore.

There's no point in listening to Aunt Marianne's response. I move down the hall towards my chores, measuring my steps by the sound of my voice in my head. Efficient, measured. Robotic. I'm aware of my own existence as irony. I'm aware of my own existence as a joke. Neurobio-what-the-hell-ever. Neuropsycho behavioral modification. Neurobiological behavioral modification implantation. I have never been laughing. They have never actually made a joke. I'm up.

Uncle Ray and I drop Mom off at the airport at the end of the week. She's got a new backpack full of clothes. Maybe they fit her, maybe they don't. Either way, thanks, Aunt Marianne. The airport in Columbus is shaped like an orange cut in quarters and turned sideways and the inside is a big tunnel and there are too many people. I focus on my shoes as we walk. I almost walk into all those people but eventually we get Mom to the ticket counter.

"Are you sure you don't want to come to Oregon, baby?" she asks. Her hand is on the side of my face. She runs her fingers over my stubble. I don't know if she thinks it'll fall off or what.

"You gonna buy him a ticket right now?" Uncle Ray asks, hugging her.

"No, I'll just smuggle him on in my luggage." She sets the backpack down and starts to put my hand in.

I don't have to think about this. "Nope." My hand is mine. I take it back. Put it in my pocket. I don't say sorry.

"Okay, baby, well..." She looks at me but I can't meet her eyes. I don't think she expects that anyway. She kisses my forehead. "I love you, baby. Stay tough out here, okay?"

"Always." Like I have any other alternative.

In the car on the way home, Uncle Ray lets the Classic Country and Bluegrass Tunes station play Johnny Cash, which he wouldn't do if Aunt Marianne was in the car. Her son was buried to his version of *Peace in the Valley* and after that she hasn't listened to any Johnny Cash at all. I was fourteen when my cousin Tim was hit by a truck. He was ten. Aunt Marianne always calls him "our first and only boy" whenever she thinks I'm eavesdropping.

I guess Uncle Ray was just happy to have any boy he could get. We don't talk on the ride home but when we stop for gas, he buys me a Star Crunch without asking. He watches the road. I sit in the passenger seat with my knees curled up to my chest, pressing against my scars.

The thing about the brain chips is that they started out supportable because every horrible thing does. Doctors used to say that I was too obsessed with patterns, that I saw them everywhere. But sometimes there are patterns. Like history. History is a pattern and eugenics used to be supportable. Then they had to change the name. Then they invented a wire that connects to the brain stem that cures Parkinson's and Asperger's and depression and then... Sometimes when you're on a roll it's hard to stop so why stop with depression?

They didn't want to cure me of being trans, to start. They wanted to cure me of having PDD-NOS. A wire, some electricity, a little code. Stop me from stimming, babbling, thinking too much about patterns and colors and textures. It was just an added bonus, they said, that it would stop me from transitioning. But they're cutting out the middleman now because a life on medication, one that requires more than one surgery, is expensive to an employer and The State. Like anyone gets health insurance anymore. But, for anyone who does, it's not like there's coverage for surgery anymore whereas *Gender Dysphoria Alleviation* is covered up to 60% on most insurances. Thompson wants to get it covered up to 80%.

Which is why, today, on Election Day, I am packing to leave. Tomorrow I turn 19. Today, now. 12:01 AM. I have four sweaters, six shirts, three pairs of pants, an extra pair of shoes. Five hundred and twelve dollars –

stolen, earned, begged, never borrowed. The cat is watching me from the hall. I would take it, but cats don't travel well. The shirt I'm wearing is itchy. Every unpleasant sensation is still a sensation against flesh. I am made of flesh. I checked, this morning, last night, just to be sure. There is still blood in my hair. I'm not going to wash it out. I am human. I bleed. I will bleed on anybody who disagrees with me. I am human and I am leaving.

There's a picture of my cousin Tim in my room that I never had the heart to put away. It's sitting on the bookshelf, right on the top, next to the aerial picture of the farm from the 1950s. I put in my own picture, one from my fifth grade graduation. My mom had it in her backpack and I took it from her, but I don't think she'll miss it. It's pretty crumpled, but it looks fine next to Tim. We're both awkward big-eyed kids with bowl cuts and overbites. Easy to mourn.

I thought about writing a note but I don't have anything to say. A note like *sorry I'm leaving I didn't want to hurt you with my existence* would be stupid. At least over-the-top. Also a lie. I'm leaving because I don't want to hurt myself by living in this place anymore.

I'm not going to be minimized. I'm going to be. Just not here.

The door creaks. The pigs are asleep. The chickens are asleep. Uncle Ray and Aunt Marianne are asleep. I'm up. I make my way across 200 acres of soybeans. I take some for memories, some to eat later. The highway is empty as usual. 14 miles to Wapakoneta. The first car that sees me picks me up. An old woman with long, curly hair. She's tanner on one side of her face. "Where you headed?" she asks.

"Where are you headed?" I ask.

I don't need an original thought in my head. I just need to answer the question.

"Chicago," she says.

"Chicago," I say. "Okay." I'm going to need to let Rebecca know.

"You going there?"

"There. Yep."

It's Called Fashion

KAJ WORTH

You got a lolly for me

What's this can't you see I'm pissing. Give me some fn space.

The knee-to-upper-thigh area, the face were bright, and basically im-mobile.

Who even are you, why do you think I'd have a

Soph told me you would.

Soph who the even fuck is Soph

The person gestured: tall and thin in a weapon-like way, ass to audi-ence, loitering.

Wait I thought her name was like Tracey or Morgana or something like

Her name's Soph.

The voice was scratchy, deliberately high-pitched and aggressive as fuck. The shorts were a sickly green and rimmed with gold binding. The rest was adidas.

So what you got

Nothing, I told you, I don't deal, I don't do—

What you got

This interaction is going literally nowhere. There's like a shittonne of lolly dealers find your fucking own, I'm just waiting for a train pissing in peace all right?

This is our station you're pissing behind, girl. Our hill you're pissing on.

The person re-angled their trainer, which had protruding from its sole long, bouncy blades, to let the stream of piss pass between them.

Ours.

E shook the last few drops from her dick and pulled down her skirt, which was leather, but, like, shimmery.

Now get your health goth ass out of here.

The person leered. Their stance was that of a bullfrog, E thought; their hair an uneven blue. Soph or Tracey glanced back, her eyebrows pasted with some sort of high-end gold make-up that shone under the LED street lights which no one had yet thought to disconnect. She dropped a lolly stick; it floated, for some centimetres, down the piss-stream, which had just reached her shimmering feet.

Bby where you been?

Having an ˜encounter˜ with some queers in rick owens x adidas springblades

—

—

I got you a lolly.

They mimed head with pink mini milks: E measured, dexterous; L liquid and enthusiastic. The train, improbably, arrived.

> [...]
> ∫:   fuck can I
> #:   yes just let me, yes yep
> ∫:   fuck, yes[..]will you, can you grab me, like, yeah put your
> #:   oh[..]i just love it when you, when you're looking down at me, your hair like
> ∫:   ha-ha well i love looking down at you, you're so fucking angelic, your hair looks white, or like shining[..]please fuck me[..]yes, yep
> #:   please[..]can you, can you like hide me with your hair
> ∫:   what like
> #:   yeah[..]oh fuck
> ∫:   I feel full of affection for you bb

§: yes i feel like a krispy kreme like the caramel not the more
custardy ones this sort of stickiness is pooling all the
way from my dick to my heart

§: is this good for *you*

§: is this good for you

§: if I ask then it probably is like if it weren't I would prob just
do something else without asking[..]can I, maybe if I, yeah
right

§: like that

§: like that, yeppp[h]

§: L i'm about to come do you want me to come do you want
to come

§: I'm like nearly there, just please keep fucking me

§: where can I, where do you want me to come

§: oh anywhere, just sort of, here, just, just cover me I want to
see you come

§: will you come

§: I'm coming

[...]

[...]

§: You're a fucking lovely kitten. You're delightful. Fluffy as
fuck.

§: Two kittens in a nest. Snakes in a heap. Let's do the dishes
and think sad thoughts about how it's nearly winter.

[...]

Yeah but I have absolutely had the fuck enough with hi E with, with
that precise sort of silliness we're just in the end trying to eat, trying to, to
make coffee and tea and make the best of things right so they can literally
fuck off E don't you think

What

Those you know

Here the girl broke off, walked from the counter to the window of the
Plot and swept, with affected disdain, the horizon. The street outside was
quiet and the grey walls were tagged in exuberant layers.

Where've you been hiding anyway E you lot from the treehouses never come down here these days

Hm yeah but we were all busy we have been building quite a bit. Like—

But you realise that we need your help—

The other person, short and dark with a rattail and plenty of tattoos, turned to look at E.

We don't need their help. If they want to go off and sit in their little huts then to be fair we don't need them

E knew her from art school where her practice was deconstructing performance poetry, which had required, as was fortunate for most of the rest of them, very little space and equipment. E left the two in conversation, the taller with her coloured hair alternating between phrases of conciliation and accusations of insufficient solidarity, towards herself, for one, and towards the treehousers, as they had come to be known. E took a look in the fridge and idly washed two plates, scraping the untouched-looking hummus into a jar. Before, if you did at least one shift a month at the Plot you got 10% off and a say in the monthly collaborative redraft of the safer spaces policy. The Plot was no longer vegan.

The girl with the rattail came over.

What she means is that there's this weird hierarchy you know, it just seems all wrong is what I'm saying—it's not that we need your help, like all of you, all of your help that is, it's just that well you've all been drifting, since before, and while the men the cis men have in the end done us all a favour by wandering off to hang out by the river there's just something, well you know, off. Unsolidary.

E gave a slightly panicked look. The girl unwrapped a cola chupa chups and held it out.

We I'm sorry but we have to share I'm kind of running out

They passed it back and forth, E rolling a joint in between licks.

So how's L?

Fine. Good, even. Summer's nice. We're making a film.

Yeah you should bring her down now you've stopped hiding away. We've been organising so much cool shit it's so nice here, everyone helps out, you know? Like, people leave their egos at / the door

Right.

What. They do!! It's totally different now, I'm telling you, like—

Behind them, something had happened. A boy in a striped tshirt and denim shorts was crying in sulky hiccups. The girl with coloured hair was giving his elbow little strokes with one hand while fussing at something on the counter with the other. When E got there she could see it was the large jar of fermenting kombucha that had taken the place left empty when they no longer needed a till. It now lay in pieces. The liquid, splashed across the counter and dripping to the floor, gave off a sweet, yeasty, acid smell.

Mate you can easily do another

Yeah but it's the principle of the thing isn't it, they absolutely did it on purpose, I can't believe they would target me, what have I done

They?

E looked out onto the street. On the opposite corner was the person from the station, and in their hand was a catapult of lolly sticks bound with coloured string. They were bent over in a show of uncontrollable laughter, which, as they turned, allowed a flash of arse-cheek to be seen by all those in the Plot. It was not clear if this was deliberate. Their shorts were, after all, very short.

The day was grey, anticipatory. They walked into the corner shop at the station, the only one still open in this part of the city. It was stocked almost entirely with fragile towers of the various consumables people had brought to barter with.

Uh so can we have 2 mini milks please, the like ivory ones. Vanilla.

Hey man I'm sorry they pulled the power for the freezer.

Ah wtf??

E looked towards L, smoking clumsily in the doorway. L nodded.

Uh 2 drumsticks then. No make it 20. Pink and white not those gross orange ones.

What've you got?

E handed over a film canister of home-grown in exchange; unwrapped, for L, a lolly.

They chewed; paused; slobbered.

How many we got left E

Bb now is no time to be fretting about supply. Like, it'll be winter soon. Right.

—

Then: a hand on the respective shoulder, E left, L right.

E looked down; back; down again, like a sparrow, or like she was vogueing. There they were: the person. A pair of almost steampunk sunglasses; some sort of phallic object hanging from a chain, leaking slightly around the sternum; once again the two-tone shorts, this time trimmed with a vague neon ruffle, which looked like, in fact was, merely the person's boxers emergent. Well.

Me and Mechtilde told you. This is our station. You got to pay for access.

—

So I'll be having those—

Wait you sicko you can't

The person had whipped the drumstick, now cratered and elongated, out of her mouth, and licked it in a way that must have been intended to be salacious.

That's fuckin minging and you know it—

An elastic thread of sticky pink and white saliva had extended along with the stolen lolly, then snapped and draped itself lightly on L's chin and upper chest. She took a step back with her glittery arms spread, a reaction of disgust that glid, gracefully, into a gesture of challenge. The person took a step forward, placing the right trainer's front two blades precisely on L's plimsolled forefoot.

The sensation was ˜unusual˜.

The person then gripped L's shoulder, and, starting low, allowed the dangling spittle to coil on their tongue, with which they drew a line from chin to mid-eyebrow. L stopped inhaling but smelled the sickening sweetness of the person's breath as if passively and felt, curiously, weak. The person returned the lolly to their smirking gob.

I hope—this as the train pulled in, E and L blundering backwards and pulling each other into the open carriage—you get hep fuckin B!

I've been IMMUNISED—this, as the doors closed, with a cackle and a double-handed v-sign, each formed of a middle finger and a drumstick.

The saliva, drying, was tacky like cheap lube. A plain clothes conductor produced, morosely, a hand-held ticket machine.

You need a ticket?

You still exist??

The conductor moved on. Each passenger refused them with uninvested politeness as they might before have a beggar or newspaper-seller.

The conductor leant at the end of the carriage hands-free against a pole, working the machine like a gameboy, printing tickets which emerged in a perforated chain until, upon reaching a certain weight, the chain, like a white, feather-light turd, broke free and floated to the floor.

L and E drank coffee from their mugs and sat squished in at the top of their ladder. There were maybe 30 treehouses now, some dearly elaborate, others plain. There was a vibe of warm activity to the small corner of the park they had taken over, and, they felt, of majesty.

So what's the news re the gang

No news really. What even is it

It's basically Bette then and that other one, the short one. What's-their-name.

Who's Bette?

You know her. Tall, eyebrows, everywhere.

Wait I thought her

E paused.

Ok, Bette. Go on.

That's it. They just hang out and piss people off. Shorts and knee socks. That's how you can tell.

E pulled her knees to her chest and her fishnet tshirt over her knees. The sun was setting and the pink of the sky matched the pink of her lipstick.

L. Let's go hang out at the Plot more yeah? It'll get cold soon anyway. And they're bored and edgy as fuck.

Ok babe I can do that. It's good though, here.

Yes.

E put her hand on L's, which turned to meet it. The black was peeling from their nails.

The one-carriage train paused 20m before the platform, then continued through without picking them up. E ground a roach under the flashing soles of her trainers. They played pat-a-cake fretfully, trying to tuck the other's hair behind her ear on the off-beats. They had a sick haul: tinned meat; teabags; vegan haribo. They guarded their gymsacks with their toes like penguins.

The person didn't take long to show up. There was Tabitha, her eyebrows bronze and formed in flame-like arabesques, and there were three or so baby queers with knee socks sagging, butt-cheeks and bulges improperly covered by hotpants too hastily plundered.

They squared off, E and the person to the front, L between E and the booty, baby queers as back-up singers, bouncing on their new bladed soles, Tabitha skulking, sharklike.

E began:

You think you're so tough but we all know your mum worked for ofsted

You calling my mum??

The person pulled out an opinel that had been decorated with, it seemed, cunts passing themselves off as flowers. It snagged slightly against the wood, from rust or from the heat, but locked, at least.

Oh put your picnic set away; looks like you need to get some sandpaper on that couldn't cut camembert

The person darted forward; swiped; slashed E's forearm at exactly the point where she already had a tattoo of a slash, which itself covered a scar.

This confusion of layers was enough to stall everyone's response for a beat, including that of the person.

—

Wtf

—

It had, it seemed, started.

Do we let him in yet

They had seen the boy a few times before, casing the treehouses, but then he'd disappeared, probably to the warehouses near the river, an enclave of cis men and bad speed. But the last week or so he'd been there every day. He had a navy tartan shopping trolley and a Nike gymsack. In the torchlight he looked 15.

Mate you got a dick or a fanny

He looked up, startled but overplaying it, as if he hadn't been waiting for them. He'd chosen well; theirs was def the best treehouse, with an extension, and a lintel painted in pink glitter.

She's joking; we don't give a shit, just, like, watch / out—

E dropped the ladder. The boy half scuttled, half tripped up to them, dragging the trolley, which clinked regularly against the rungs.

They stared at each other in a daisychain of sizing up. E took in L's dark, bouncy hair, pointed shoulders. In the last year the fat in her plump cheeks had redistributed itself upwards; they were all apple. The shadows from before had filled out. In the treehouses everyone got enough sleep. What did the boy see: the implants, the monobrow? The glitter tattoos? He had nothing but an indistinct brand on his thumb. His eyebrows were very silky. A mosquito bite on his leg looked nearly infected but he clearly brushed his teeth.

What you called then

They call me the Rat

E and L both laughed. What a noob. Then a second reaction fired: the sort of compassion at a kitten who stumbles and looks, momentarily, foolish. They laughed some more, but felt bad about it.

Lol mate p sure all boys are called the Rat round here. Better pick some other rodent.

Degu?

Uh—

Or what about Badger?

What???? You haven't got half enough meat on you for that. Ferret. Weasel. That sort of / thing.

Then: the Weasel.

Or, in full, the Least Weasel.

The Least Weasel.

So: what you brought us, Least Weasel?

Sardines, spam, I even have cockles, corned beef. Fucktonne of / tins.

Ah you fuckin beauty

E and L helped him unload the trolley. The haul was glorious. L made a video of it on her phone. They displayed each can, the end-dates not even passed, the labels barely ripped.

What dyou want, Least Weasel?

Can I sleep, for a bit? Can you watch out for me?

Too much speed?

No I don't—no it was just, crowded.

Yes

Too many people

Yes

And dogs. Dogs and parties, posturing.

Yes

I just wrote instead.

You just wrote. Of course you just wrote.

Yes

Well look—E pulled up the ladder and opened the hatch to the exten-sion—this is yours. It gets kind of hot but if you think about winter it feels better. Sleep tight little weasel; least weasel.

Yes.

The Weasel was a total lightweight which made him an appealing houseguest. One toke and he was done. His eyes were all different colours, which is the sort of thing you only notice in a lover or a really intense youth, and E and L were strict lesbians. He'd been everywhere. The other cities sounded shit though, barely a change since before. They ate sardines and oatcakes and spinach from the garden. He'd been in love but the other had wanted to stay, a job, money, so he'd left them to it. E and L taught him which hole was which on the latrine, how, in general, to compost. He sometimes sang himself to sleep, which was sort of precious, but maybe he was too young to realize. He masturbated quietly, and always into his palm. They started calling each other 'sister' about which he seemed equanimous, with which he seemed on board. They dyed his hair, previously *Sally Can't Dance* blonde, zoo-flamingo-pink. He looked, all the treehousers agreed, like an angel.

[...]

§:   hey love

#:   hey

§:   hey[..]I'm just going to take these off

#:   well in that case I'll take these off[..]you don't think, where
        is the weasel

§:   nah he's off foraging we're good

#:   you're good

§:   *you're* good [...] fuck you're good

#:   ah you can I please lie you down, can we be a bit horizontal

§:   we can be totally horizontal do you want to be more
        horizontal

#:   no no I want you to be more horizontal [...] like that [...] you taste so fucking good[..]ok you taste weirdly good, what is this, you secretly filled your cunt with i don't even know what, salty rosemary honey

∫:   nah it's just you've not had a smoke for enough time for your sense of smell to return

#:   i'll never smoke again [...]

[...]

E's slice had hardened to a shiny red line. The Plot had enveloped the arts cinema on the one side and the pop-up burger place on the other. In the cinema they showed compilations of porn gifs; in the burger place people experimented with fermentation. Basically everyone worked there now, taking turns making tea and reading Kathy Acker. L was stirring lentil soup. E was washing up: long. One of the Plot regulars, who was wearing a sleeveless denim waistcoat covered in homemade patches, came over to dry up.

I heard what happened with the blue-hairs. That shit is ridic. Why do they have to ruin things for us.

They nearly got their hand stuck while drying a jar. E noticed the washing up liquid was being stretched very thin. Might more be found? It was hard to know what was left and what had already gone.

Well I'm glad it came to nothing. Or you know nearly nothing. Utter silliness.

Do you really think they're silly?

Oh man totally, like I know some of the younger ones, they were in the year below me at school.

They carried on trying to reach the bottom of the jar.

... Girls' school

You went to girls' school?

Yeah haha. Look at me now.

E looked at them. They were younger, she realised, than she'd thought. Eighteen at the oldest, still round at the chin, with stubby, paw-like hands.

I wouldn't have been able to tell.

Thanks. Lol. Yeah.

They wandered off. E washed until the rack was full and her hands felt slightly slick with the untroubled grease. L called her over.

Bby they want to screen our film

What the postporn one? What here?

No like outdoors. Down by the warehouses

I mean yeah cool ok I guess

They want to do something, like, before winter

A small pack of teenagers with blue hair and septum piercings had begun to gather outside. The most self-identifyingly outré had strapped gold cocks to their crotches or thighs.

P heavy-handed

You think they'll

Nope they wouldn't dare

No I meant, like, will this last?

—

—

Will—what—

The Weasel came chirruping up the ladder.

I fucking did it !!

What

What

I fucking got into ikea !!

Ikea was the holy fucking grail. No one had cracked it yet.

Fuck yeah!

Kyeah!

The route was, it turned out, simple. In through the skylight in the underground warehouse grotto bit, then climb down the stack of garden furniture. It was paradise. They filled themselves with gooseberry frogs, stale mini daim bars; they found sealed kegs of sparkling apple juice and tub after tub of fried onions; they painted with congealed ketchup on the deserted breakfast bar. They dived in a wire basket of plush rats; they walked down the one way escalator; they sat, cross-legged, in the middle of the space, larger even than the gallery that was now the home of the largest poly constellation in the city, and as such really off-limits.

Weasel. You did it.

E. Why has no one been in here though. It was so easy.

Lol no imagination. This lot have no imagination here. Any more.

The concrete was hard and cold under the mesh of their skirts – tutus found in the children's department – and they found themselves wishing for the Weasel's large denim shorts. Denim though. Not really a look for the treehousers.

Shall we get the others then? Like it's maybe not as good here as I want it to be but there's a shittonne of wood and no splinters.

Mate they are going to love this. Fucking love it.

L hoisted herself back up to the skylight and trotted back home. E and the Weasel tore themselves frogs and strawberry shapes off the large sticky lumps that had formed and made music on toy xylophones. The Weasel had a good ear. They sang, nonsense rhymes mostly, but where E's were hard and hip and gleefully macabre, the Weasel's were terrifyingly fresh. They stopped and gathered soft toys.

You're quite into mammals, then? From the looks of things.

The Weasel looked down and swirled his hand around the rat basket.

What are you into like reptiles then?

Noooo birds. And insects. L's more into birds I think, I'm into bugs. But, well you know, shiny fluffy things right. Got to match your interests to your outfits.

Ok.

The pause was not very long.

E do you have thoughts on the afterlife?

Uh well insofar as it's not a thing, that's pretty much my thoughts, my, like, thought.

Do you think you get to say whether it's a thing. Or not.

I said I *thought* it wasn't a thing. Not that it absolutely wasn't. Although we might be talking about different uh things. Or.

I I was just thinking about reincarnation.

Oh Weasel. Of course you were.

He smiled with wide, endearing eyes, and placed a rat crookedly on his head, then on hers.

And is that thought—a good one, is it, are you imagining what animal you'll be or something.

It would just make a change—

They decided to make themselves useful: they wrote lists with mini pencils of what could be made to function as what, sitting now on pre-made garden furniture in the centre of the warehouse. L was coming: they could hear her high, excited voice. The Weasel was shining, almost, in the torchlight. The treehousers began to arrive. So it was a group of 15, maybe more, who were standing, some carrying packs of tupperware, others bright, stiff fabric, others stacks of coffee, and discussing how best to transport things home, with the Weasel, blowing faintly into a coloured recorder, the noise like the distress cry of an unearthly bird-ferret hybrid, with a furry hood from the 'Lattjo play for all ages' range slightly cockeyed on his head, at their centre—it was this group, mostly in pink and black leather, glitter tattoos at the bases of their throats, who were there to greet the person, who had climbed through the skylight and was silhouetted, cock trembling, at the top of a pile of billy bookshelves.

It's the fuckin tweehousers!!

The insult seemed a bit under par and so no one bothered to reply, instead illuminating the person, and the ring of blue-haired youths on the roof behind them, with their torches. The person gestured to the back-up, who handed down a long, thick cylinder with a headlight attached. The beam swayed as the person slowly descended the ladder of flatpacks. It ended on the Weasel's face, which contorted in the glare. He was still blowing, distractedly, on the recorder. Something about the person changed; their timing was out, they found themself suddenly touching ground, had to look, momentarily, away from the group, check their footing.

What the fuck is that

The treehousers moved protectively around the Weasel, who was now getting the full force of the beam. The person twisted a dial which focused the beam exclusively on his face. They drew around his features, outlined his hood, his form, which, in its studied indistinctness, marked him out. He gave another bleat; lowered, slowly, the pink recorder. Everything that was glow-in-the-dark began to show on the shelves as the back-up crowded round the skylight to see.

The person was visibly not able to cope with the Weasel. They – this seemed the only term for it – writhed. The cheaper torches blinked. The backup awaited instruction. A plush crown-shaped pillow toppled from a wire basket. One of the figures began to descend, its contours twitching slightly, as if yanking at the lower edge of its shorts. From the height and the way that she approached the cringing person, i.e. dead on, no deference, it must have been Miriam. She linked her arm with that of the person, led them in a stumbling circle back to the shelving. The two of them climbed carefully upwards, Miriam taking the home-made spotlight under her arm. The last flatpack they kicked away, trying and partially succeeding in causing an avalanche, certainly blocking the route but qua act of revenge it seemed half-arsed. The Weasel went to grab the crown-shaped cushion. The treehousers, nonplussed, let him lead them out of the hole and into the greying afternoon.

The fuck, E thought, just happened.

The sky was pink and open as they walked down from the treehouses to the station. It was a week til the screening and no one knew if the weather would hold. They each had a translucent mac tucked into their kitbag, although E now took hers out and L made a video of her posing and bending. They were late for the train but another came almost at once. It was driven, they noticed, by the conductor of the other week. It stopped as if despite itself.

They got off at the other end of town and found, almost immediately, a corner shop they'd never seen before. From the outside it was completely dark but when they pressed their faces against the grubby window they could see movement. The bell sounded as they pushed the door.

The man turned from where he'd been stacking instant noodles.

What you here for

Dunno well we were

I've no lollies if that's what you want they're all gone sorry

Ah yeah hm k

Sweets and chocolate, lots of it, look, but nothing with a stick. Fruit salad blackjacks refreshers, all of that.

They conferred.

Apple tiger tongues?

Strawberry?

Done. How many for this?

E handed him a wooden ornament one of the treehousers had carved. It was of a vaguely mustelline figure on the back of a clumsy, manic bird.

The shopkeeper looked at it and rolled his eyes.

Yeah, ok, fine.

He shrugged. There was a funny draught as if the person had entered and they huddled, L throwing a protective arm around E's crinkly mac.

You k ??

Yeah yeah let's just / get

Yeah

Shut the door will you ladies it's getting cold

Yep sure have a good day !

E caught his eye as she pulled the door carefully to and saw that he wouldn't.

In the street it was warmer but they walked on closer together, E's bony arm tucked around L's neck, L's strong, tapering arm around E's waist and tucked on the other side into the patch pocket of her pleather skater skirt.

God how shit to be straight

What if he's not. What if they stay because they're / not

No no I could tell he was lonely. And also did you see his clothes

No I

Well exactly.

But listen bb it's not just straights that are lonely—

—

—

But L. But I mean but we're not lonely

No: but we see no one but ourselves do you not think

We have LW—

He's 'ourselves'—

By the river were three or so Plot people. Four-to-the floor came from the warehouses, each one somewhat out of sync with the others. They went to the sound person, whose moustache had definitely thickened since last year, who was chewing fervently on a sweatshirt-sleeve and looking at the sky.

Can you er do you think they might keep it down when we do the film do you think

Ha ha L yes no we can ask but also, good luck with that

The girl with rainbow hair from the Plot, the one who wore polka-dot dresses or ones with mexican skulls on, was pacing the distance between the warehouses. The paces varied between approximately 3 and 5 Doc Martens in length.

Think this gap here is the best if we set up the screen here like there and there no girls you tell me—

E and L shrugged. It was weird to have attention, the final say.

You know I think it's fine yeah, just, will the sun be in the right place

The sound person gave a number of quick, jerky nods and carried on staring at the sky. The girl with rainbow hair had a think.

Huh. From here I think. Well we should just wait until dusk given it's not that late now is it. That good?

A boy burst out of one of the warehouses and swerved into their group.

Oh it's you lot sorry!!! Didn't realise you were here!!

The red afro was stuck in part by sweat to his forehead and he shook it free and rubbed his eyes and beard, which was also dyed. Through his sheer tunic they could see the geometric shapes of tattoos, abs, pubes, against which his penis seemed oddly irregular.

Hey are you two living with that boy now?

What the Least Weasel?

What that's what you call him? Don't think he had a name here. Someone wanted to call him The Kid but he like didn't fuck and it seemed wrong.

He's a good'un.

Oh yeah he's a good'un ! yeah ,

Lovely Weasel—

Dear Weasel—

As they spoke in unison E and L smiled at each other and tugged the other's body with their arms, still draped around each other. How they knew each other! It was like melting, their thoughts were one creamy pool.

A taller man, naked but for a leather hunting waistcoat, had followed the boy out of the warehouse, and now grabbed him and kissed him. There was a lot of tongue.

What more do we need to do then

Uhh one hope it doesn't rain two hope those weirdos don't show up three make a screen four tell everyone think that's it

The rainbow-haired girl laughed.

But you two made the film so you just do the first two we'll do the rest is that good with you, how do you feel

Feel, wow I dunno so it's the first film we've shown with our actual bodies in and our actual voices it's kind of weird

And we've not even yet finished it

What L what don't tell them that !!

Lol to be expected I really don't care. Well good luck. Seriously though people will love it, they get enough of this, they want more—

This with a gesture to the taller man, who was now sucking off the red-haired boy, the sheer tunic stretched and draped around his head and upper body, rippling as his hands grasped and fingered the boy's arse. The boy's eyes were closed and his hand, clutching a piece of piping attached to the warehouse wall, was pale at the knuckles.

L stood behind E and reached around to cover her eyes. E could feel her breasts against her back and the crumbs of sugar from a tiger tongue against her eyelids. She jiggled her bum, which L gave a good squeeze.

The girl with rainbow hair raised her eyebrows. She had famously just broken up with her favourite lover and clearly felt she had to perform distaste.

Right lasses we are done here

Go on go on have a jiggle with us.

They all wiggled up against one another, each following the beat of a different warehouse. L was smiling so hard. E wanted to shake her to the point that she lost all form and they would shimmy into one. Then the wind picked up and so they gathered their gymsacks and walked back up to the station, playing I-spy for unlooted buildings, useful or lovely debris.

The Weasel couldn't cook or even, really, make tea, but he washed up unusually well. E and L were transferring the film using a feathered USB stick. The Plot had emptied out into the back yard, where they were grilling fake quorn burgers that were made of minced spam. The air temperature dipped as someone with a tom of finland print headscarf opened the cellar door and carried out a box full of novelty hot sauces. At the same time the person, somehow, appeared. In one hand they were holding their phone to their ear, but sideways; it was playing some sort of scissor sisters b-side. In the other was a chocolate minimilk, which was beginning to melt in creamy trails down their hand. In between them and E and L, who had not yet discovered the double significance of the chill, was a woman playing chinese chequers, and her wheelchair, which had nails welded to most parts the woman herself would not have to use. The noise of the person climbing onto a table was the only warning E and L got. They grabbed hands. The person leant over and let the melted lolly drip into E's hair, flicked it into L's eyes. Their kneesocks were lumpy with the almost caricature-like outlines of knives and arrows. The skin of their upper thigh was goose-pimpled, which in the context looked more like armour.

Is it just cold out or are you—

What the fuck is that thing you have

In genuine bafflement, E looked at L.

That thing—

The person pointed towards the kitchen, where the Weasel was singing a Jewish-cowboy-era Dylan song and sort of swirling at the water.

It's just a boy, wth is—

He's going to fucking get it. You keep him close. Or else:

The person did the whole drawing a finger across their throat thing.
It was very GCSE drama.

Then: the woman playing chinese chequers had had the fuck enough.
She gave her wheelchair a nudge which dislodged, domino-like, the neigh-
bouring chair, knocking in turn the table on which the person was standing, torso at 75 degrees. They lurched forwards; out of instinct both E and
L reached out a hand. L got the less pleasant right, that is, lolly, hand; E
the phone-as-transistor left. Perhaps it was just the combination of this unexpected touch, the surprise and rage in the person's eyes as they looked,
briefly vulnerable, at first E and then L, and the sicky smell of old lolly on
the person's breath, but they both felt, for the first time, the cold sink of real
dread.

The girl with the pornographic headscarf had come back in as the
person was leaving.

Ok what the hell was

Like they're just twats

The woman with the spiked wheelchair went over to the door and
wedged it shut.

E wasn't altogether sure they were just twats.

Well it finished uploading at least—

L gave the laptop a little tap, curt like the drop of the terminal ball of
a newton's cradle.

[...]

§:   hey will you come w me

#:   what to the toilet??

§:   yeah I just need you to

#:   to—

§:   to—[..]ah fuck i've missed you

#:   ha-ha dear i've been gone half an hour

∫:   yeah but I've been thinking all day about your face, your
            hands, let me, can I [...] oh fuck your hair feels good

#:   thanks bb did it myself

∫:   you're not really feeling this are you

#:   no I, yes, I mean [...] let me just

∫:   yeah let's just, wait was that knocking

#:   fuck em

∫:   is it ok if I go down on you

#:   fuck yeah [...] sorry for before I was just—like, idk surprised

∫:   yeah

#:   but this feels good

∫:   mm

#:   fuck L you feel good [...] [...] this feels really fucking—

[...]

[...]

∫:   can I ask you something

#:   jesus what a question

∫:   E what will we be

#:   when

∫:   well

#:   exactly

∫:

#:   we'll just love each other a lot

∫:   yes. it will be wonderful

#:   yes.

∫:

#:

∫:   will we make more films

#:   yeah our films are fuckin sick we will make loads more

∫:   and eat lollies

#:   and eat lollies

∫:   even when winter comes

#:   even then

∫:   good

#:   you

∫:   you

#:   you
§:   I fucking love you
[...]

They had a picnic, E, L and the Least Weasel. They had a picnic basket from IKEA, and loads of zebra print fleece blankets. The Weasel had his head in L's lap, who was propped up against E, tearing off bits of grass and putting them on his lightly pimpled forehead and watching them fall into his stiff pink curls. E rested her head on L's and let the wind arrange her hair like a veil of pink fluff in front of L's eyes. There were grey clouds but moving quickly by, and shafts of irregular sunlight lit them, were reflected by the tattoos and their fluffy silver jackets, passed on. E brought out the last three drumsticks.

To postpornography!

To tonight!

To well I was going to say to the future, to, to as much of the

To the future!

They unwrapped and chewed slowly. The Weasel stopped, swallowed, looked up.

Where did the whole lolly thing come from anyway?

Oh idk, twitter probably.

There was a pause, and as the next burst of bright, late sun fell on him, the Weasel asked:

And where did the blue hair thing come from?

E and L looked, automatically, to the other, but whether this was to pass the task of explaining, and whether either were up to that task, nobody could tell.

E, looking up:

Well I spose some things just come into being. But—

But what I don't get (L now) is why they're afraid of you. You Weasel that is.

E squinted into the sunlight and felt her heartbeat rise, a layer of cold sweat forming as if on the inside.

Do you need to understand?

LW come on don't you want to understand?

But why do you need to understand?

—

You know how you're always going on about winter
We don't go on about it!
—

But like Weasel that's when shit is you know going to get real.
Is it.
E rejoined the conversation, the cloud of panic having sort of dissi-
pated.
Things will be different, and difficult, and it's unclear in what respect.
Do you think we shouldn't think ahead? You're like the grasshopper. Or was
it the ant. No it must have been the grasshopper.
E squeezed his shoulder and he brought his hand up to meet hers and
grinned.
Lovely grasshopper.
He looked ahead through the unmown grass of the rec at the rippling
line of poplars. If you crossed your eyes slightly they became one. E did so.
It was soothing.
The Weasel wriggled and then lay still. Looking back at the poplars,
he said:
I suppose they don't like how I'm not one of you.
What that's fucking ridiculous you're one of us, how can you think
that, look at your hair. You're with us.
But.
She could see his fingers searching for grass to rip up, but the grass
was no longer the sort you could rip up, was stiff and cylindrical and entire-
ly its own thing.
I suppose they don't like how I am one of you.
L came in.
Weasel. What do you mean now. I'm getting lost.
I'm sorry.
He hopped up to a crouch and started bouncing and nuzzling them
in the manner of (E assumed) a puppy-grasshopper chimera. His face as if
bound in the centre, grinning, he repeated sorry in a high pitched voice and
they ruffled him and curled up together in a pile. There they lay, all three,
warm under the zebra blankets, as it began to drizzle, which they weathered, but then, when the fleece and their curled fringes were rimed with
rain, and the temperature dropped, and their arms were asleep, they stirred,

separated, trudged away from the hollow, the tiny crop circle, that they had made on the old field.

The treehousers had constructed a large frame from salvaged flatpack furniture. It joined two of the warehouses, the one where the few men with actual technical skills had a workshop, and the quieter of the darkrooms. The screen had been unrolled. It bulged lightly as the wind came off the river. There were yellow sweat stains as if tie-dyed on the sewn-together sheets, cum stains like faint batik. On both sides the mawkish political grafitti of the warehouse walls; all around the chefs, the toilet-cleaners, wall-writers, the tea-pourers and skulkers of the Plot looking variously more or less ill at ease with being crap at whatever they thought they might be doing to help. L escaped for a joint; found E. They sat and patted each other. They were nervous.

Where is LW

Doing a little dance in the twilight idk.

Is he ours, lovely kitten?

He is ours.

Yes

They pressed their faces together, each grasping the head of the other in their glittery hands, thumbs before ears, fingertips brushing through tickly hair. Their mouths tasted dry.

Let's do this then; let's fuckin do it

We're just pressing start, right. No chat, no faces.

We'll squat at the back

We'll hide our eyes

It's cold, E

Their matching iridescent a-line skirts only hit mid-thigh, and the white fishnets underneath were nothing in the breeze. They unfolded a plastic-backed ikea blanket around them like a crinkly tartan sepal. They walked back round to the screen. People had vaguely settled. Treehousers had ikea deckchairs; others had pallets, crates, in an affected post-apocalyptic aesthetic. Some hugged their knees with only sequins between their ass and the cracked concrete. No one had blue hair.

The screen held a rippling facsimile of someone's desktop. The background image was a pastel unicorn. Really? It belonged to the girl with rainbow hair who made bad coffee but had agile fingers. The .avi file was opened. E and L felt sick.

We good?

Yep yep do it

The girl with rainbow hair pressed play.

It was fucking hard for them to watch. To see what was theirs opened out. E looked left, L down at her feet, ignoring her own voiceover. Their knuckles brushed. E tried to stay very still. From the warehouse to their right they heard a rustle, a set of gasps. A black cloth was pinned at the entrance under the fire escape, but it had got caught on one side, and L, small and fidgeting, saw, suddenly and through the gap, a flash of pink. Grabbing E's arm she pushed the curtain up with her head. The interior was cavernous, with a network of wooden rooms not unlike the treehouses built around the walls. A circle of men, some still carrying tools, had formed in the centre of the room; behind, the articulated metal door was rolled up. At first, they could still only just see a triangle of pink. It was being lifted, though, and as they approached they saw, slumped on the back of a man in a green hulk t-shirt, the Weasel. The man's hair was matte red in the warehouse flood-light; they did not realise at first that this was blood. Fuck. The man swung the Weasel into his arms—E and L now up close, alternately silent though wanting to make some, any, noise, and making some, any, noise, fuck and no and expulsions of air, wanting, however, to stay silent. The Weasel's torso was clothed in a rippling sheen of blood. His face looked like someone had turned up the contrast on his usual acne, the flecks beautifully round and clustered around his mouth, which hung open. They looked at his eyes. No. The men crowded, jostling E and L who stood still and could not talk.

The fuck Rob

Those fucking blue hairs got him

What, those fucking hipster kids you are fucking joking

The FUCK

Yeah I was there w Michael just hanging in the bushes and then I see this kid just like walking towards the empty building carrying some shit, metal and stuff and we know him from before and know he's a bit weird like, grubby and that, but like essentially harmless and that girl the tall black one with gold eyebrows appears at the entrance and he drops the stuff and goes towards her either like a zombie or like he's on a mission, just like in a straight line, he has this weird hat on, we stand up bc like the blue hairs don't come here usually and something's *up* right, and he was just about to go in the building and suddenly this fucking swarm of blue hairs comes at him and that was fucking it

Where's Michael

Vomming somewhere idk but look you think he's gone, this one?

He's dead, dear, that's for sure

That's insane why the fuck

E and L felt light. Ok. They backed away from the group, the lights of E's right trainer spasming. At first, they hardly knew where they were going. As they walked, each knew without looking that the other's hand was searching for theirs; and the time between knowing and the relief of finally holding seemed infinite. They walked through the wide mouth of the warehouse and onto the scrubby expanse behind, for reasons neither of vengeance or martyrdom. The blue hairs were waiting around in the bushes, around the edges of the wasteland. Halfway to the maw of disused building they saw that they were surrounded. They stopped; held hands paw in paw like children. The air around was blue, the sky blue, like church-school uniform blue not the shades of cyan, kingfisher etc. of the hair, which grew like a fire or a dawn as they approached. Behind them, they didn't see their film playing, the images more distinct in the dusk, but reversed. The voiceover was inaudible, the soundtrack pitchless tinny beats. The blue hairs had probably raided a john lewis; how else to explain such a stock of sharp knives in jazzy colours and unnecessary but practical features. E held up her palm, which the closest blue-hair high fived desultorily, before slashing at her shoulder.

It felt like burning, but then actually it didn't. It both felt vaguely pleasant, and didn't feel at all. E and L looked at each other. This wasn't right. Then came more. Nothing hurt. There was, by now, no noise, just various shades of blue in the flesh or in the blades' dull reflections. Now both warehouse doors were open, and men were coming forward, in green body-paint and harnesses, in pairs and groups, and now also the people from the Plot had left the film, which was still playing, were joining the men behind the screen, watching. A cloud of blue and clammy legs. E and L were only sort of visible; they were upright still, propped by thrusts perfectly met from behind, from in front. From the building the person strolled out, strawberry mini-milks like blades between their fingers. They licked them left to right in turn.

Everyone was just waiting, now.

And what was this great light? The blue-hairs fell away, the person turned and fucking ran. As it came closer, which it did, but slowly, too slowly, E and L could see that it was stacked like a sound system, but what was behind was still hidden. They both knew this was dying. They both stopped knowing, at all. It wasn't dying. What was it come for? They were, they with their hands as if glued and their hearts and skirts warm and still, ready.

Gamers

IMOGEN BINNIE

Samara was a gamer, although she would rather not have been. Gamers on the Internet—trans woman gamers, cis woman gamers, deeply enlightened boy gamers, game journalists and Shigeru Miyamoto—would protest. They'd worked hard to separate video games from maleness, to make clear that it was gamer culture that was hypermasculine, not the games themselves. But Samara couldn't separate gaming from a boyhood spent confused and disappointed about boyhood. A feminist trans woman on the Internet would have demanded that she call her childhood a girl-hood before logging off twitter to play a deeply unsatisfying text adventure game from the avant garde of Trans Women And Games. But that was not Samara.

She didn't think about it much because if she thought about it she'd have to admit how boring she was: she liked Marios and Zeldas; Halos and Mass Effects; Metroids. Cutting edge experimental new school video games felt to her like feminism and punk rock: intended for people who were, on some fundamental level, cooler than her. She could have articulated the fact that "cooler than her" was on some level code for "whiter than her," but it didn't assuage the feeling that despite having transitioned almost six years earlier she could in some fundamental and shitty way still be boiled down to a boring fat guy who played a lot of video games. Despite having a sweet job and a long-term girlfriend, an apartment and enough money to order dinner in just about every night, she felt like some important part of her—the exposed part of her that would strobe yellow and red and be shot with arrows or lasers by a player character if she were the boss of a dungeon or castle—would always be the self-hating slob, divested completely from her own life, who she'd been in high school.

The unisex khaki and red polo Verizon uniform she wore every day—was wearing right now—didn't help. At twenty-five she might as well not have had a body; she had transitioned well before getting this job so she'd never had to talk about being trans here, which meant the only time she was aware of having a body at all was when someone used the correct pronoun for her and it took her by surprise. But today, especially, she might as well not have had a body. Last night she had stayed up until her brain was so exhausted it became incapable of forming new memories, playing Zelda.

For months now Amy had been obsessing over the first Nintendo 64 Zelda game, Ocarina of Time. She was doing a thing where she found every Skulltula and completed every side quest without using a walkthrough. It was all she really talked about, besides the usual Tumblr-inspired outrage at everything, but it seemed like it was also kind of fucking her up. Like maybe it was the bad kind of obsession. Samara was no psychologist but playing the same game on her own computer, like as a couple, seemed like some kind of a solution.

To something.

She would not have used the phrase "saving their relationship."

Samara had drunk three Mountain Dews before lunch this morning. She wished she was cool enough to have acquired, at some point in her life, a taste for coffee, but instead she was a cliche. She was exhausted already, and since there was nothing going on at work, all there was to do was chug soda to try and stay awake. On her lunch break, she left the brutalist Verizon office building in the Jersey side of the Philly suburbs to take a nap in her car so she could hopefully survive the afternoon.

It had been a sunny morning but now the sky was dark. Surreally so, in fact; it looked like the sky above the version of Castle Town Market that's in the apocalyptic future from Ocarina of Time. The only inhabitants of town at that point are called ReDeads, these desiccated muddy-looking zombies that move really slowly until suddenly they lurch at you, latch onto your back, and start trying to pull you apart. Some of the stuff in that game was goofy, but ReDeads were legitimately creepy, and Samara felt a chill thinking about them. Aware that it was ridiculous, she looked around herself in the parking lot to be sure she wasn't about to get jumped by a monster.

Before she had even turned her head, though, she felt an inappropriate weight on her back, pulling her toward the ground; then there were slender, dried-out forearms tightening around her neck. Her first thought was that she was big, that she was strong, that she could tear these arms off her neck, that she should do some judo throw or something to get what was obviously a ReDead off her back. But she didn't know judo and her second unbidden impulse was shame: even though it would have been absurd to think that not fighting would somehow be better, it was dude bullshit to resort immediately to violence.

While she was equivocating, the arms wrapped even more tightly; they felt almost reptilian. They were tight enough around her neck that now she couldn't breathe. She felt an appendage pushing against her right shoulder as another twisted her head toward her left. As if suffocation wouldn't have been enough, this monster from a video game was going to pull her head off, too.

It did. First she felt vertebrae grind against each other. The tendons in her neck pulled past their capacity, and then the rotation was disorientingly frictionless: her head just came off. As it spun and fell she saw that the thing on her back had been a ReDead with Amy's face, watching with Amy's usual expressionlessness as Samara's head thudded to the asphalt. It landed painfully with her face to the sky. Her last thought was how strange it was not to be able to turn her neck: that she was pointed at the dark-clouded sky and she could move her eyes but she couldn't turn her head.

Of course, she woke up in her car. According to her watch she still had ten minutes of lunch break left; her subconscious hadn't even let her have a whole nap. She had been tired enough to drop directly into REM sleep, which of course meant vivid dreams and which normally would have meant a feeling of restedness which right now she did not have.

Sleeping in her car on her lunch break felt like somatic time travel back to when she was younger and hadn't figured out that taking care of herself was something she could do, not just a thing other people did. This was how her body had felt when every night was an opportunity to stay up until you couldn't stay up any more, grinding for XP and eating the kind of food that made you feel a kind of bad you had not yet learned to acknowledge. An obvious message from her subconscious, informing her that her relationship to her girlfriend was killing her, was not something she needed right now.

The last few months had been shitty.

Amy had been having delusions: specifically, while she had been playing Ocarina of Time, Amy had been having Ocarina of Time delusions. Anxiety and depression had kept Amy from being a productive member of society like Samara for as long as Samara had known her, but Zelda delusions were new. Previously Amy's mental health stuff had always seemed like normal white girl trans angst depression and anxiety, but this new conviction that there was a little pixelated dead kid dancing his way through the yard, if you could call it a yard, behind the duplex—or the conviction that Dampe the graveyard keeper had hanged himself outside their window but that if one of them went over to check, his washed-out rictus would pivot on a splintering, mossy spine and smile.

Neither of them did much. They were not the kind of girls who got beauty rest or had conversations about combination skin; Samara's attitude toward their unswept apartment, with wires everywhere and overhead fluorescent lights, was the same as her attitude toward being a gamer; the same as her attitude toward her life. It was fine. She didn't hate it, but she wasn't excited about it. That might have been her relationship to Amy, too, although she wasn't in a place where she could admit that to herself. For one thing, Amy couldn't work; if Samara didn't buy her food and pay her rent, who would?

Years later, after they had broken up, Samara would understand that during the time when Amy was having delusions—which would turn out not to have been delusions at all—their caretaking and its corresponding dependence were a cycle, an ouroboros. But in the Verizon parking lot, as Samara actively refused to acknowledge that she was unhappy in her relationship with Amy, all she felt was that she was the center of the universe and that it was her job to make everything okay.

As she walked back toward her cubicle she could not help but look over her shoulder for monsters. The sky HAD become overcast.

If you read it as a metaphor for being trans, the plot of Ocarina of Time is pretty intense. What happens is, you start out as an eleven year old human kid who's spent his whole life in a town of forest fairies; you're already an other. You kill some stuff and save some stuff and then you learn the Song of Time, which warps you seven years forward in time—but not as a kid. In the future, you are yourself as an eighteen year old; because you're a video game character and pretty hollow in terms of personality, the game doesn't engage with questions about what it would be like to be an adult without having to go through the horrors of puberty, or whether your eighteen year old mind is developmentally the same as your eighteen year old neural anatomy.

The problem is that back when you were eleven, this evil wizard—the same evil wizard from every Zelda game, Ganon—stole some powerful shit, kidnapped Princess Zelda, and ruined everything. Seven years in the future, the world has turned dystopia: all your friends are dead, the town is ruined and full of ReDeads, and everybody is sad; the atmosphere is this stately and almost resigned sense that everything is over. You collect magic and items and stuff in the future; you travel back in time to when you were eleven, but like, when you're eleven you can't use the grownup sword. When you're eighteen you're too mature to use the deku sticks you used as a kid.

It's pretty ingenious. The atmosphere engulfs you, the story is compelling, it's really hard but not impossible, and pretty much everybody agrees it's the best game for the Nintendo 64, if not for every system ever. Samara has been calling it her favorite game since she was a kid, even though she hasn't played through it in years. When Amy mentioned downloading it a few months ago, Samara immediately thought about playing it too; but between Steam games and humble bundles and managing to score a beta tester spot for Final Fantasy XIV, she hadn't gotten around even to having Amy Dropbox the ROM to her until last night.

Her unacknowledged reluctance to play Ocarina of Time was consistent, too, with her unacknowledged reluctance to engage with anything. Because the thing you cannot help but think as you play Ocarina of Time is: what if I could go back to being eleven. Samara's father had been a professor, her mom a literal Marxist; from the time she was tiny, they'd supported her in any interest she'd even mentioned, and when she had finally overcome her internalized shame and fear and come out to them at nineteen it had gone better than she could even have imagined. Imagine playing the song of time and telling yourself at eleven what you know now. Imagine having that information while you were digging yourself the twin ruts of male-coded videogaming and shame that you'd spend the rest of your life trying to dig your way out of.

Samara had come out long enough ago to know that torturing yourself with what if questions was exactly the best way to ruin your life; that it was maybe the definitive trans woman self-flaggelation tool. And it was, in fact, the sort of thing that Amy did instead of leaving the house or finding telecommuting work or something. Anything. The sort of thing Amy spent most of her time doing.

And it was the kind of thing that worked so well as a torture device specifically because there was no right answer: if you could go back in time and come out at eleven, whether it went well or not, you'd eliminate this timeline. If she had come out younger, Samara would probably never had met Amy. If she hadn't spent her teen years with games and computers, she wouldn't have this job. What would she have done with her time as a young brown trans girl? Somehow... not computers? Even with middle-class parents, what's the economic outlook for a young brown trans girl who DOESN'T know computer shit inside and out?

Of course it's just another set of hypotheticals to stress about. But these are HER hypotheticals.

But last night she had gotten sucked in. She'd played through the first chunk of the game, had saved and passed out sometime after Link had learned the Song of Time and become a teenager. Now something like eight hours later she was having hyperrealistic Zelda nightmares and worrying that the sky in the real world looked like the sky above dystopian future Castle Town?

She did not want to break up with Amy.

She did not want to beat herself up for not coming out as a kid and she did not want for her body to feel tired and flop-sweaty like it had at age eighteen, and she would not let herself connect one to the other and then to the other; would not let herself connect any of them to the fact that it was not her job to take care of Amy; that there was nothing she could do to save Amy from Amy. To understand that she was enabling Amy's self-indulgence would have been to understand that in order for either of them to feel less fucked up, the foundation of their relationship would need to be reassessed. Amy had been loudly in crisis when Samara had invited her to move in; their Relationship had followed not long after that.

It would take Samara years and three or four more breakups before she really understood the fact that you don't need the Song of Time to reassess the foundations of a relationship, that all you need is enough love and trust to be honest with yourself and with your partner. And by that point, in this timeline, Amy would be long dead.

One of the most groundbreaking things Ocarina of Time did was called Z-Targeting. When you hold a controller, your fingers wrap all the way around it, and the N64 had a button on the back, where your fingers rested, called the Z button. If there was a monster or something to look at in front of you and you held the Z button, the controls would change modes: Link would focus on the monster or whatever and jump left or right relative to it, strafe, dodge, or- if you pushed up and B- swing his sword over his head and do a jump attack that did twice as much damage as a regular one.

When Samara came home after work the night of her lunch break nightmare, hollowed out but jittery from two more Mountain Dews, the first thing she thought about when she opened the apartment door was that overhead jump attack. She had a very quick series of thoughts:

That is a Dead Hand.

Its hands on their eight-foot long arms are sticking out of the floor of our living room and one of them is holding Amy by the face.

This is not real.

No, this clearly is real.

Whether or not this is real, it is happening.

A Dead Hand is a slug monster that lives at the bottom of a haunted well, except it's sort of humanoid—it's got a skull with a face, although its jaw is grotesquely long. If it stood up straight it would probably be fifteen feet tall, but it hunches way over like a question mark, leaning forward to bite your face with its horse teeth. The two truly fucked up things about it are that its skin is chalky white with these patches of red or brown that look like blood or scabs or tumors, and that it's got these arms growing out of the floor in its room. What you have to do is let one of the arms grab you by the face, so the monster will wiggle-creep its way over to you, and then you shake yourself free and then hit it in the face with your sword. But it did not look like Amy was luring the monster. She was struggling, but weakly, like she'd been doing a lot of struggling already before Samara got there, and the monster itself was gnawing on her shoulder. There was gore and Samara could see something white that was probably bone; her first thought was that she wished she could Z-target the thing and do an overhead jump attack with a knife or something.

The kitchen was to the side of the front door and without any further thought on the unlikeliness of the situation Samara found their biggest knife—still shiny from never having been used; they didn't cook much—and dove in, chopping at the arm coming out of the floor holding Amy's face. She had a moment of vertigo thinking about this happening in the game: you were always one person in the game. You were never going to have a chance to have some other Link occupy the monster while you hacked away at it. It was gross work, cutting through tendons and trying to snap bones by kicking; she was bad at it. But eventually she'd cut through it and it let go of Amy, who fell to the floor. A gross amount of blood spilled everywhere and Samara thought queasily that she didn't know how much blood you could lose and still survive, but it was probably not much more than this.

Normally you'd have to wait until the Dead Hand leaned its head down to bite you in order to hit it, but they were not at the bottom of a well, they were in a cheaply constructed suburban apartment; the ceiling was too low for the monster to pull its head away, and while the thing was gross, it was slow. Samara slashed away at its face for what felt like an almost hilariously long and vulgar time until it whipped its head back, hard, and fell forward, crashing against her shoulder and knocking her to the side. The hands in the floor wilted and disappeared. Samara knelt next to Amy, immediately problem-solving. Could you tourniquet an entire shoulder? Would she lose an arm?

"A haunted fucking ROM," Amy said, laughing.

"What?" Samara asked, even though she got it immediately.

"A haunted fucking ROM," she repeated. She winced. "It's like a scary story written by an eleven year old: I was feeling fucked up and weird and couldn't sleep and I got to the point where everything was a blur and the sun was coming up, downloaded a ROM from some forgotten and haunted corner of the internet—which apparently is a real thing—and that ROM was fucking haunted. Or something."

She started an ironic MWUAHAHAHA cartoon villain laugh, but it turned into a cough. Her eyes were brighter than Samara had seen them since they first started making out.

"So what do we do?"

"Well," Amy said, "I guess we get our shoulders chewed off by imaginary pixel monsters."

"Polygon," Samara said.

Amy scowled and then smiled.

"Look," she said. "I need some fucking heart—"

She choked on the word and her eyes started to close.

"Oh, fuck, no" Samara said. She slapped Amy's cheek like a paramedic on TV but her eyes were closed.

Samara looked around the room. In a Zelda boss fight, there would be pots to smash and get hearts from. Or grass to cut down. But there was nothing: just computers and DVDs, game cases and their enormous flat screen television, vintage video game consoles pulled to the floor by their wires during the confrontation. By the time Samara figured out that Zelda rules probably applied - that now there were probably hearts inside the computer monitors - it was clear that Amy wasn't breathing.

Once again Samara was problem solving. It did not matter if she was crazy. If Dead Hands were fucking real then Ocarinas of Time were fucking real and magic time travel songs were real and so once she had stopped punching Amy's chest as hard as she could, in a manner intended to approximate that of paramedics on TV, she plugged the plastic guitar into the PS3 and turned on Rock Band. She started it up and turned the sound all the way off on everything but the guitar, then started playing notes. She could pull the Song of Time from her memory, but in Rock Band the notes seemed to be relative. They changed depending on the part of the song, and soon she was frustrated and teary—not to mention the fact that she felt like an asshole, fucking around with a plastic guitar next to her girlfriend's chewed-up corpse in their smashed up living room, fully convinced that there were more monsters lurking outside the windows, the front door, in the bathroom and the bedroom. Through tears and appalled at how unpoetic the process was, she set the difficulty to easiest and chose the most straightforward song she knew.

"Low Rider."

Same shit the whole way through.

Finding the notes to the Song of Time and repeating them was uncomfortably similar to establishing a rhythm, during sex, that will lead to orgasm: she found herself rocking with the beat of her own song, swaying back and forth in time and going into a rhythmic trance. Soon she could actually see white light swirling in a circle around her. She kept playing and she felt the room around her dissolve; then she felt herself dissolve.

Then she was in her childhood home in her childhood body; she was, of course, eleven. She was holding a Playstation 3 controller guitar that would not actually exist in the world for over a decade and she wondered, briefly, whether that would be complicated or what. But then her mind went into problem-solving mode. Of course her initial impulse was to run to the kitchen, where the smell of vinegar meant her mother was making sushi, and come out as trans, right now, deep breath and rip off that Band-Aid. But then she thought about her life at twenty-five, about Amy: worried immediately about the horrible things that might happen to Amy if Samara never showed up to take care of her. But in the timeline with Amy, Amy died.

She thought for a second about playing the Song of Time and going back; nothing was set in stone. But then she realized that the guitar wouldn't work, wouldn't plug into any game systems that existed when she was eleven. And then she realized with horror that she wasn't sure she could remember the tune of the Song of Time; there was no pause screen to look at to refresh her memory.

And so she made a decision.

"Mom!" she yelled, heading into the kitchen, surprised that her pre-pubescent voice didn't feel weird. "Mom I want to do kendo! I need to learn to fence! I want to learn to fight with swords!"

Imago

TRISTAN ALICE NIETO

The lifecycle of the butterfly contains some of the most dramatic examples of holometabolic metamorphosis in the Animal Kingdom. Each developmental stage is highly specialised and distinct. Despite this, some Lepidoptera, such as Manduca sexta, *have been observed retaining learned behaviours between larval and adult forms, making them one of the only insect species to preserve information across different stages of metamorphosis.*

I

Everything to her was colour. Her wild, vibrant hair in tight curls that flowed down her back like a river, crashing over her spine and bleeding into her illustrated skin. Lips aflame with blood and passion. Irises that changed colour like the ocean, from stormy green to clearest blue. And then there was me, pale as a ghost, bone white hair in strands of silk. The only colour in my whole body was the rainbow behind my grey eyes, reflected off the microsensors that replaced my retinas.

These little moments used to mean so much to her. I was always so focused on the day ahead, the greater plan, the deeper meaning, that I often missed these fleeting glimpses of perfection. In the tepid light of winter morning, I stroke her brow, and try to part my sleeping eyelids.

In an instant, as if by some orphean curse, everything vanishes into shadow. I try to blink my eyes, to reset my vision, but the darkness only becomes harder. Alone in the black I reach out, finding nothing but air and metal.

I don't know where I am. I don't know if I'm asleep or awake. I can't even remember her name.

Something is terribly wrong.

II

For the record, I was against it.

It was called Revivranol. A compound that sent a huge blast of oxygen directly into the brain and shifted the body's repair mechanisms into warp speed. It extended viability for cardiopulmonary resuscitation from thirty minutes to twenty-four hours, and allowed the body to function in spite of massive physical trauma. The effects, however, were not permanent, typically only lasting around seventy-two hours.

To me, it appeared that the pain of losing so many to the great global pandemic known as the White Death was too much for our collective consciousness to bear. We couldn't cure it, we could barely treat it, but now we could beat it at its own game.

It was hailed as a miracle – the final frontier conquered by science. But soon the promise gave way to the reality. Those we revived came back broken, cold and distant. Far from the fairytale meeting of love across distant realms, it was usually a confused and perverse confrontation as people tried in vain to locate a tiny fragment of the person they once knew within the talking pile of human remains that wore their lover's skin.

And so, as has become the defining experience of my generation, hope turned to regret, and Revivranol was soon banned for use in all circumstances.

All but one.

III

"Tabitha?"

It's phrased as a question, but I don't know the answer. Am I Tabitha? I think that was my name, but I don't know if I'm still her.

I ache in the dark, and with every slight move of my body I become aware of a new pain somewhere within me. My wrists grind around, screeching like metal on metal. My throat burns like I've swallowed molten glass. My eyes...

I try to look around, but my body returns a null response. I twitch the other muscles in my face and feel the pull of fabric below my brow. I reach a hand up and brush the edge of a bandage.

"No, don't touch it." A gentle voice takes my hand and leads it back to my side.

"What happened to my eyes?" My words come out as a gurgle; it hurts to talk.

"You don't have them anymore. They've been stolen." Trying to offer a consolation, the voice adds, "we're getting a replacement camera on-line for you now."

I decide not to do anything until I get my sight back. Instead, I sit and listen to tiny sounds as echo around the cold, hard room, like water dripping in a cave. My hand touches metal – the frame of my bed – and it makes me wonder, *am I in hospital?*

Slowly my visual uplink connects to a tiny wireless camera in the latex-gloved hands of a medical technician. My new remote vision shakes randomly across the room before coming to rest on the bandages around my head, facing up at the fluorescent ceiling. Most remote-eye cameras include projective geometry and gyroscopic data to avoid generating these stomach-churning, dissociative experiences. This cheap, generic camera does not have such measures.

"We'd love to give you some proper replacement eyes, but with biotech as it is these days, we just can't afford it."

I painfully twist my head to the left and take in as much of the room as I can.

Bland white and sterile steel. Drains in the middle of the floor. Dim, cold lighting. Tiled walls. A woman in a suit stands beside me. A police officer behind her. The woman's ID badge hangs from her jacket pocket. Her name, rank and number zip around to the nauseating shiver of my body. At the bottom I read one critical word: Homicide.

This is not a hospital. It's a morgue.

IIII

Danielle, or Detective Chief Inspector Morris as the laminated card identifies her, is head of the CID Homicide department's Postmortem Division. She explains the procedure to me. If the body is determined to have died within eighteen hours of arrival, Revivranol will be administered and resuscitation commenced.

That's me. I am the body.

If resuscitation is successful, the case will be transferred to the Post-mortem Division, who will conduct interviews with the victim and monitor their state. The autopsy will be delayed until the victim is no longer responsive and can be re-declared deceased.

I ask Danielle how long have I got until the autopsy.

Two or Three days. Four at most. It depends.

I ask if she can explain what happened to me. She shakes her head. The only information she can give me is what's publicly available. I was last seen when I left the university around seven pm last night, but someone matching my description was seen near Rowen street around eleven. I was found early this morning stuffed in a suitcase along the edge of the canal in Camden. Any more than that could taint my recollection of the event and render it inadmissible.

I ask her what are the chances of me remembering it at all?

"That's up to you," she says.

Danielle explains that the revived often experience a disorder known as 'fracturing', where large sections of their memory, abilities and even identity completely vanish. A person may remember being a painter, but be unable to paint. They might only remember two of their three children. A migrant may lose all connection to their homeland, their native language or sense of culture.

Most commonly, people will have damaged emotional responses. They may find themselves apathetic to things they used to love. Feelings of grief, anger or happiness will not flow, but turn sharply on and off in response to stimuli.

The best way to deal with it, Danielle says, is to concentrate on what you do know. Focus on the memories that remain, the parts of you that have survived, and play them over in your head, like a mantra. It's likely that other parts will rise to the surface.

I sift through the broken shards of Tabitha that rattle around inside me, searching in vain for the name of the woman who lay by my side as I drifted in the twilight of consciousness, before I found myself awake in this room. I know the curves of her face, the sound of her voice, the smell of her hair, all to infinite detail, yet I can find no other memories of her. All I can deduce is that she was my everything, my soul-mate, and now she is gone. Despite the hurt, I cling to it as the only glimpse of true emotion I have felt since I was revived.

V

I take the secret back exit to avoid the gauntlet of protestors telling me that I have no soul and that my existence is an affront to the divine resurrection. The man who will drive me home calls them the PDM. The Pro-Death Movement.

The frozen night air feels oddly comfortable against my skin. It's my low body temperature, my driver tells me. Be glad I'm not out here in the middle of summer.

Sitting in the back of the unmarked police car, the driver tells me about a guy who walked into the sea down in Brighton. For the first six hours the Revivranol supplies all the oxygen to your system, which means you don't need to breathe. So this guy, he just spent the day on the bottom of the ocean. The driver tells me that you can survive almost anything within the first 6 hours. He met a guy who did a triple speedball and his heart kept ticking like a metronome. One guy ran into the path of a tornado, just, y'know, for fun.

The driver says that if you can get hold of another Revivranol shot you can extend your life for another day or two. He's heard stories of Revivranol junkies – undead addicts living in the sewers doing shot after shot to keep themselves alive. But it's probably bullshit. Eventually, he says, you'd just rot away.

And besides, black market zombie juice is fifty grand a hit. If you know where to get it.

The driver tells me how some people get this 'death vision', like they can see death. They know when someone's going to die or when something bad is going to happen. Some claim they can even control death – put it off a few hours, or speed it up.

I guess it's supposed to cheer me up; make me feel special, like I have a superpower or something. But as I take another diamorphine tablet to push back the agony rising through my broken body, I don't feel special. I feel like an abomination – a testament to the ultimate human need to ruin and destroy everything we see.

Ever since leaving the clinic (their polite euphemism for the morgue) I've had Danielle's voice running through my head. I had asked if I could contact my family, and Danielle produced a note – a message my mother had left when they first called to see if she wanted to be present when they revived me. I didn't have the courage to read it myself, and asked Danielle if she'd read it to me. Even in its brevity, only a few words from the short note remain in my mind.

"... very sorry ... can't go through ... again ... understand ..."

It's a surprisingly common reaction, (so she said).

I try to focus on all the things that are clear to me, but one curious thing rises to the surface. It occurs to me that I know everything there is to know about butterflies. I soon recall that I am (or was) a professor of entomology, specialising in Lepidoptery – the study of butterflies. The memory returns to me as fact, with no warmth of emotion, but it feels somehow satisfying to have a fragment of my identity back.

The driver tells me he knows people who will pay good money to have sex with me, as long as I'm willing to lay really still. Really, really good money.

VI

Back in my lonely two room flat, I sit on my bed, feeling my drugged body crumble a bit inside. I take off the camera and in a queasy, spinning movement place it on the bookshelf pointing directly at myself.

I look ridiculous – a frumpy grey blob with a head wrapped in bloody gauze. Carefully, I remove the layers of generic, oversized clothes given to me by the Postmortem Division. I undress as if unwrapping a mummy, like the slightest over-application of force would turn my entire body to sand. As the cloth gives way to skin, I can't help but catch glimpses of damage; deep red stains against my blue-grey complexion, rope marks like tyre-tracks around my wrists.

Slowly, I unwind the bandages from around my neck and eyes. I stand in front of the camera and stare at my own dead body.

The dead body looks back at me. A line of crude Frankenstein stitching runs across her throat like a necklace, reconnecting the carotid artery and sealing the split in the trachea. A cascading pattern of narrow slashes runs down her rib cage, over her left breast and down her body to her hip.

Dark maroon puddles wrap around her dislocated shoulder, from her broken collar bone to her hyperextended elbow. A black line remains where the fractured humerus tore its way through the surface.

I bring the camera closer, and focus on the empty eyes. The slashed, sunken holes, sockets filled with blood unceasingly leaking down her face... my face.

The wave of abject horror I steel myself against never comes. I stare myself down, daring my mutilated body to reduce me to tears. I concentrate on the splashes of blood red against my white skin, trying to fill my mind with raw, shocking truths about my visual aspect. The only thing that jumps into my head is "Jackson Pollock's Strawberry Shortcake."

And for some perverse reason, I burst out laughing.

Butterflies have extraordinary vision. They are tetrachromats, able to see well into the ultra-violet spectrum, and their compound eyes give them a 360° view of their surroundings. Many butterflies also have polarised vision, allowing them to see the direction of light, which they use to locate the sun on cloudy days.

VII

In the cold twilight of morning, I look out the window across the snow-bound city and a vague recollection – a memory of a memory, dusty and cobwebbed – wafts into my mind. I was a child growing up in East-London. It was hot and bright all the time. The sun hurt my eyes, my real eyes, even in winter. London seemed to be permanently covered in ash, like a city left in the oven too long. Following a tangent, the word *snow* brings up a whole album of painful schoolyard memories. Every where I went I was 'snow white' or 'snowy' or 'frosty'.

Snow White. White Death.

I remember the plague. Every week someone else got sick. Then every week became every day. Knowing nothing except the most vestigial, observable facts: you got sick, you turned white, you became agitated, then paranoid, then psychotic, and then you died. I remember how the panic was just as virulent as the disease. For the longest time the conspicuous dearth of scientific information was filled with superstition and fear. So I became the plague monkey. Patient Zero. Don't touch the albino kid, you'll get the White Death.

There was a point when the pathogen was finally identified. The death rate began to level out and the stigma started to abate. By then I had been forced to change schools twice, had my life threatened and one time some people broke into my house and covered everything in pig's blood. And like the disease itself it seems the superstition never really left us.

And in another drifting fragment, years later, I am holding her hand, skin mottled in shades of grey. She looks up at me from her bed, her deep blue eyes a foggy white. My love, wasting away, her pale lips part and she whispers, "It's not your fault."

In the cold twilight of morning, her hand slips away between my fingers and takes the memory with it.

VIII

Standing under the shower, I touch my skin, tracing the new lines and ridges of my body. The wounds are divided into antemortem and postmortem, meaning wounds inflicted before and after I died. I can tell the difference because the edges of the postmortem lacerations have not retracted and the blood clots are jelly-like, whilst in antemortem lacerations the blood clots contain platelets and form hard scabs, and the edges pucker and stretch open. This is why the antemortem wounds have stopped bleeding, but the post mortem ones never will. The cuts on my chest are antemortem lacerations. The cuts around my eyes are postmortem. No scabs, no bruises, no swelling, the wounds are as fresh as the moment they were made.

Later on I experience something like hunger, but without a functioning digestive system I can't eat anything. The advice from the 'clinic' was hot tea with sugar. Fluids are essential, and the warm tea will keep my temperature up. Sugars and electrolytes will help to prevent my muscles from going into rigor mortis. Sweets and lozenges supply sugar and keep saliva flowing.

I get a message from a friend. They're sorry that they haven't called yet, but they're still in shock. They don't know if they're going to be able to see me like this. They're really, really sorry.

Everyone's so fucking sorry.

IX

The camera runs out of battery and I can't be bothered charging it.
It's so disorientating and nauseating, I'd rather be blind. My old eyes – the
ones that were stolen – had LIDAR and 3D telemetry, which would build
and remember the exact layout of any space and track any moving objects,
essentially allowing you to 'see' what was behind you. They had an on-board
memory so you could record and store events perfectly. They had gyroscopic data, which increased your sense of balance, and full AR uplink so you
always knew where you were and what direction you were facing. They even
had projective geometry, where, based on shadows and the direction of the
light, your eyes could guess what was around a corner or behind an object.
They were great eyes.

My new camera has a zoom. But without any 3D data it just feels like
the room is flying towards me.

People were always surprised to learn that being blind was not like
having your eyes closed. Blind people don't just see black. I used to explain
it by asking them what they could see beyond the edge of their vision. The
answer was usually puzzlement and an objective "but I can't see *anything*
outside my vision." Saying it out loud was typically enough to get the point.

Of course, ever since the implants I'm never really blind either. Even
with my eyes stolen and the camera off I still see a small black square with
soft blue text saying "searching for ocular data stream..."

I know all this because three hours ago I decided to properly deactivate my vision systems, but needed to get some hardware from my study
to do it. Now I'm sitting on the sofa watching myself, and my house, and
the street outside, and a black and white cat on my neighbour's roof all simultaneously via eight remote, drone-mounted, three-sixty degree cameras
whilst steadily burning a hole in my brain.

X

Prior to being dead, I had been planning to release eight autonomous
microdrones – tiny robot butterflies – to follow the migrating swarms of
Vanessa cardui and collect data on everything from their numbers, flight
path, the weather, terrain and any other information I could grab. I had
built every little robo-butterfly to include cameras, gyros, GPS, geometry

scanners, ultraviolet, infra-red, ultrasonic and complex AI for navigation and investigation. And because I'm lazy, rather than design a bespoke protocol to communicate with them, I used the same one that my eyes ran on. Which is why went I walked into my office, the visual processor in my brain instantly connected to the eight butterfly drones that had been sitting on my workbench.

From total blindness, the room suddenly lit up in strange patches. I felt the quiet breeze of thirty-six tiny carbon fibre wings flapping frantically around the room. My view suddenly widened and I saw the whole office. Bookshelves full of academic writings and discarded coffee cups. Reams of weather predictions and diverted animal migration paths. And me, standing in the middle like a fish that had suddenly learned how to climb a tree.

And the light. The incredible spectrum of light, seeing the vibrant indigo lustre of the ultra-violet, and the curious patterns of polarisation. As the drones spread out, the room became alive with visual information that was almost too much to process. The tiny robots flapped about my head, looking in every direction at once. Ultrasonic, gyroscopic and LIDAR data streamed into my temporal and occipital lobes. It was a rush of information unlike anything I'd experienced before.

Then, as quickly as it had started, the data stream was cut off and the butterflies fell to the ground.

See, it turns out you can't just feed terabits of data per second into a person's brain without any consequences. The human visual cortex was never meant to process that amount of information and the overload quite literally blows your mind. So neuro-implants have safety switches on them to keep the data load below brain-exploding levels. At the intensity I was experiencing, it wouldn't take more than a week before I died from a tiny electrical fire inside my skull.

If I was going to live that long.

Which I am not.

As luck would have it, I happened to know how to access my own firmware and deactivate the safety routine. Thankfully, our brains have no pain receptors, so a small, blinking red circle in the bottom right of my sight was the only warning I had of the impending catastrophic overload.

XI

Sitting down, back on the sofa, the real challenge is just getting used to this absurd new way of seeing. Most unnatural of all is the shift in perspective; understanding and connecting to my own body in the space, when often I can see myself. Having full three-sixty degree vision is one thing, but it's the overwhelming wealth of visual information that knocks me down. Being able to see around corners, under tables, behind the fridge, down the road, it's impossible to describe. The active 3D scan means all the data is placed perfectly into a visual map inside my mind, so I'm never in danger of losing myself in the maze.

During one of its search and identify routines, a lone butterfly locates a framed photograph. It's of me and her, my lost lover, arm in arm, out on the streets of London. A rush of emotion floods my veins with such sudden intensity that I can scarcely identify it. Is it love? Loss? Heartbreak? Nostalgia? I don't know, and I soon am up in the room, searching through it, desperate to find out more.

Despite practically pulling the place apart, I find very little. An ageing flyer for a new café. A small gold crucifix on a chain, which I recognise from her photo. A vaccination card with a string of dates marked off. A silver ring with a peridot stone. A black ribbon and a business card with the name of a doctor based at the Enfield Hospice. The only other thing of mild curiosity I find is a small medical pamphlet entitled "Post-Surgical Care for Transgender Women."

I flick through the pages but can find nothing to indicate how I came to own it. Was it hers, or mine, or someone else's entirely? My first thought is to assume it clearly couldn't be mine, but I'm immediately confronted with a rather awkward question: How would I know? Could it not be one of those many things that had been lost, fractured, from my mind?

At that moment, I become oddly present in my body. I don't feel transgender, but then again, what does 'feeling transgender' even mean? If I had already transitioned, if my body aligned with my gender, what signs other than memories would I have that things were once any different? Reading through the pamphlet, I learn that biotech for trans women is practically indistinguishable from purely organic tissue in both appearance and function. Nanosurgical procedures leave no visible scars. A trans woman's body is for all intents and purposes unidentifiable as such.

The truth, as I'm forced to accept it, is that I can't be sure either way.

XII

A few hours later, I've reduced the number of active butterflies to two, just for a brief dose of normality (such as it is).

I look at my shaking hands and wonder if I've still got any cigarettes in the house. I was supposed to be quitting but, you know.

As I go to send the butterflies out on a search, I notice something: a file tucked away in my visual processor. A *memory*. Working backwards, I figure I must have been recording it when I was attacked, but my eyes were removed before it could be stored and so it remained – corrupted but intact – in the temporary file buffer of my visual cortex. My curiosity to watch it is slightly faster than my fear of what it may contain, and I instantly regret choosing to play it.

The memory is not like a movie, but like a full hallucination. It sends ripples out through my mind, restoring lost fragments of sound, of taste, of emotion. Darkness creeps in around me and I stumble back into it. I can hear my heart pounding itself against my ribs, trying to tear itself free from the straight jacket within my breast.

I feel pressure across my chest, like an arm, thick and heavy, wrapped around me.

I scream.

And a dirty voice stutters in my mind. "Shhh. Stop fighting."

And the memory envelops me and carries me away.

XIII

red: 0.9922311   – c%9

gr

een: 0.0000000000000000/err

:: there is a door. to my left approx 2.7m ::

my arm hurts my arm hurts my arm

my arm hurts my ar

.

the room is red so very red.

i can not move lying on my side my hands my hands

is   that

blooooooooooooo

where am i? small room where is he oh fuck fuck fuck christ what
happ

pened my arm is brrrrrrrrrro-
ken there is a lot of blood is it mine HELLLLLLLLLLLLLLLLLLLLLLLLLLLL
LLLLLLLL>>>>>ppp

{blu_____r.04_____}_____:

...

[red witch said//

what is that noise?

:: he his him himself male man ::

(bpm 182.9)

[Oh, you're awake. Ghost Girl is awake.

I was worried yo////////////knifeknifeknifeknifeknifeknifeknifeknife
knifeknifeknifek

_____ lost

[y attention Ghost Girl! Don't worry, it'll all be alright. I'm going to
put you back in the grave soon. I just need something from you first.] Kk-
kkkkknife.

Please, please... don't hurt me.../[Quiet, Ghost Girl. Ghosts don't speak.]
myarmh[Are you a real ghost, Ghost Girl? I want to see.]

No, no, no, no, no, ***red/red/red/red/red/
red/red/red

*pleas/*red/*e stop,* /red/red/*please, plea*/red/*se, n*/red/*o, no, no* [you bleed
like a cat, Ghost Girl. Do ghosts bleed? I guess they must.

Do you think I might/////////////_____
lost

null

[[[[[[UT UP! SHUT UP! BAD GHOST SH//////// lost ///red/

oh my god no why why *why, no, no, no, no, no*_____no_____
[Ghost Girl is quiet it now. Go to sleep Ghost Girl]

:: there is a window. To my _____ victorian era frame.

no

glass is   old.   distorted.no   wall has

crack   .

like

no

lightning   .

XIV

There's blood on my carpet and I'm all over the floor and there's blood on my carpet.

I feel like someone pulled a bag of greasy chicken bones out of the rubbish and called it a person. Have I been in formaldehyde all this time? Was I pushed off the shelf?

Stillborn. Flowing, liquid like glass.

I've fallen to the floor so many times, most of my joints bend backwards now. I'm like a glass jar pushed off the shelf. Blood and formaldehyde.

My thoughts are copying themselves.

Slowly, I get to my my knees. The flutter of butterflies around me is too much to handle right now, so one by one I deactivate them until I'm returned to the safety of darkness.

I try to remember what I was doing before I was dragged down into the sea of past trauma. I sift through the pieces, attempting to let muscle memory guide me but my head is still filled with fear.

Ghost girl is awake.

I fall back on the floor and cry.

And cry.

And cry and cry, crying blood. Crying for hours.

The Painted Lady Butterfly (Vanessa cardui) *has one of the largest migratory patterns of any insect, covering a nine thousand mile journey from Sub-Saharan Africa to the edge of the Arctic Circle. Using a complex system of bio-magnetic and solar navigation, millions of butterflies will journey across the earth and back again each year. However, because of the short duration of their life cycle, no single butterfly will survive to make the entire voyage, and in all, it will take six successive generations to complete the migration.*

XV

I've reached DCI Danielle Morris. She's unable to answer me right now, but if I'd like to leave my name and a contact number, she, or a member of her department, will return my call as soon as they can.

If it's an emergency, I should hang up and dial nine-nine-nine.

It's two in the morning, so Danielle is probably sleeping like a normal, non-dead person.

For the first time since I was revived, I try to remember what it was like to be dead. My memory of dying doesn't fade out, but breaks down into smaller and smaller pieces until it's impossible to tell if it's still there or not. Beyond it, there is nothing. No bright light, no angels or astral projections. Thinking back to my life is like remembering a dream. I wonder if I really am Tabitha, or if I'm just someone that's woken up in her reanimated body. Maybe Tabitha is up in heaven now, kicking back with Maya Angelou and the guy who invented Lego. Maybe I'm just the autopilot.

Staring at the twisted burns around my wrists, I start to wonder about the person who killed me. Who are they? Why did they hate me so much? Did they feel compelled to kill me, like it was out of their control? Was it simply a spontaneous hate crime, or was there a more deliberate, calculated motive? Were they horrified by their own actions? Did they enjoy it?

Bizarrely, whilst I dislike them on principle, I can't say I feel any real anger or hate towards them. I wonder if that's a symptom of fracturing, or if it's simply something our brains were never built to do – have an opinion of the person who murdered us.

Even taking the fracturing into account, I can't shake the feeling that I should feel something more than mild disappointment at the thought of being dead. I think about all the things I never got to do, all the people and places that I'll never see again, but it doesn't stir anything. Perhaps it's a blessing, perhaps I'm protecting myself from the immeasurable cognitive weight of truly comprehending my own death.

My mind naturally floats back to the one source of emotion I have left – my nameless lover. I stare at her image, her abyssal eyes and bold, crooked smile. It has the quality of the last surviving work of some lost, forgotten master. The one thing I managed to save from my gallery of memories as it went up in flames. I cling to it, yet can't shake the feeling that I've betrayed her by reducing her to a pretty picture. She was once a complete person and this superficial glance, this objet d'arte is all that remains.

Drinking my tea and stretching my cold, constricting muscles, I think about death in the way I understand it now, realising that we, as a species, have got it all wrong. For millennia, humans have deified death. We've exotified it, fetishised it, worshipped it and feared it, but what we've never been able to do is come to terms with the prosaic banality of it.

It's not a faint cough and soft bowing of the head.

It's not a whispered last word into the ear of your loved one.

It's meat and bone and skin and hair. It's tears and blood and bile and stomach acid. It's tendons and cartilage. It's a brain and a heart.

It's all the things a person isn't, left to rot and decay.

XVI

Snow crunches under my bare feet, but does not melt. Every step I take I can feel myself becoming more a part of the fog. My muscles feel like old elastic. The skin around my nails is receding and my gums are drying out. Drawing air into my lungs is like smoking metal.

Even in the freezing night, my breath doesn't cloud anymore.

Somewhere along the way to Rowen Street I dropped the bandage from around my face. I can feel the blood running along my body, down to my knees, dripping from the hem of my dress and making little red stars beside my footprints.

It reminds me of that joke with a dozen punchlines: What's black and white and red all over? Me. Dead. In the snow. At night.

When I was a child, people would dream of living on this street. Now, the few buildings that are safe to live in are home to those who can barely afford food. I allow a butterfly to venture off. It comes to rest on the windowsill of a collapsing house. Inside, I see a man in threadbare clothes ripping the wood from the walls to keep the fire going. It's a perfect metaphor for London – the city that ate itself from the inside.

In my brief moment of voyeurism, I in turn feel myself being watched. It stirs within a nervous recollection that tugs at me like a frightened child.

I think to myself, "I've been watched on this street before."

"Are you her?" A youthful voice whispers behind me. I instinctively turn toward the sound, then stop, trying to hide my grotesque visage. In front of me, a young girl – ten if she's a day – stands in the biting cold, watching me. She seems undisturbed by me, which in a way troubles me more.

"There's a witch who lives on this street. Are you her?"

"No, I don't think so." I look at this girl and wonder who takes care of her. "Shouldn't you be in bed?"

"My mum's got one of her boyfriends over. I don't like him."

"I'm sorry about that." Without thinking, I take my coat off and wrap it around her. "Here. This should keep you warm. Try not to stay out too late."

"Aren't you cold?"

"No," I assure her.

"Let me give you something." She runs across the road and picks a tall flower emerging from the snow in the mud of a once grand yard. She hands it to me, a luscious white blossom with a black star in the centre, and somewhere inside I crack a painful smile.

"Thanks."

The girl wanders off down the street for a moment. She stops immediately and runs back, throwing her tiny arms around me. For the first time that night, I feel the cold. I pat her head, only to have her jump away again and disappear into the night.

I hold the flower up as a butterfly encircles it. It droops down, wilted and desiccated, then slowly shrivels and falls apart in my grasp, as if days were mere seconds. I let it go and it falls to the snow as mulch.

I release my eyes on the wind and turn their gaze to my frozen form. A once-intact dress hangs from my skeletal frame, blood-drenched and in tatters. My white hair like shreds of straw, stained red at the tips. At my feet, a moth lies on its back, kicking its legs in futility.

XVII

Sitting in what was my favourite chair in the dark of the winter morning, I have a dream.

I see myself as an old woman, the last person alive on the face of the earth. I walk through rows and rows of pale stone blocks standing silent and ominous. There are no more roads, no more cities, just millions of cold marble stelae, stretching to the horizon in all directions. Alone I wander for years until finally I fall to the ground, exhausted and empty. As I lie amongst the monuments and cenotaphs, I see that every stone is covered with small bronze plates, each one bearing a name. I try to read the name before my eyes, but in my dream state, the letters are meaningless. With no one to bury me, I lay there as the world continues around the sun, and my body turns to dust.

From the outer reaches of the real world I hear a curious sound, like metal striking wood. Without the soft buffer of sleep between them, the dream world disintegrates and shoves me directly into waking life.

I hear the knock again. Somewhere in my brain, the right synapses connect and I realise there's someone at the door. I try to engage a few butterflies scattered randomly around the house, but in my addled state I can't put much of it together.

Still, I manage to make it to the door, remarking to myself the persistence of whomever has continued to rap for attention. I follow the motions of looking through the peep hole and my head makes a wet slap against the wood.

"Hello?" calls the persistent man.

I open the door, but have to wait a few moments until a butterfly catches up and peeks over my shoulder.

It's my driver from the other night. He's been sent to collect me. They've been calling me all morning, apparently.

XVIII

Number four looks straight at me.

Straight at me.

I've been told to look at all of them, but I can't take my eyes off number four.

They each step forward, one by one, and speak to me.

"Ghost girl is awake."

"Ghost girl is awake."

"Ghost girl is awake."

"Ghost girl is awake."

Stop. I scream at them. Stop.

"Are you sure?" I know she knows, but this is how it needs to be done.

"Positive. Number four."

XIX

Trembling, holding a paper cup sodden with the overflow of hot tea, I try to drink some before it all falls apart in my hands. I wonder if it's meant to be a metaphor for my life.

Danielle steps out of the office. Before I even look at her, I can tell she has a smile on her face.

"We've got him."

"For sure?"

"In the bag. Forensics is happy, CPS is happy. It's done."

"How did you find him?"

"A print of his we lifted from your cheek was in the database. He's got a record – mostly drug offences with some theft and animal cruelty."

"So, that's it? Case closed?"

"More or less, yeah."

It feels like an anti-climax, but I guess to a detective, a straight-for-ward case is a good case. I wonder if I'd feel better if my death was the crime of the century. The final cryptic clue to a tangled web of deceit and intrigue that shook the nation. Would I be happier right now if my biggest worry was who would play me in the movie?

"Who is he?"

"Henry James Wilson. Fifty-one years old. Suffers from substance-in-duced psychosis. He'd been living with his mother in Camden, but she said he was rarely at home. We haven't been able to get much of a statement out of him. He'll probably be found unfit to stand trial and spend the rest of his life at Broadmoor."

"Did he say why?"

"Something about snow and ghosts."

Snow and ghosts. Everything in my life is snow and ghosts.

"You feel sorry for him," she remarks, pretending like it's a question.

I sit and examine my feelings properly for this person, exploring my-self in way I haven't really done since I was revived. The truth is I don't really feel anything for this man. The vague sense of pity I feel seems to stem from a deeper kernel of anger, of disappointment and betrayal. I can't really tell what I'm angry at. Maybe it's society, or the system that failed him, failed both of us. Or maybe I'm just disillusioned at the notion of jus-tice – the idea that there's anything he or Danielle or the entire police force could ever do to make this even remotely fair, let alone right. As if finding him would bring me any kind of satisfaction.

"You look like death warmed up," she says with a smirk. If I had eyes, the look I'd be giving her right now...

"Anyway, you should go home. Leave the rest to us. I'll get you a ride home."

Before she can get up, I interject.

"No. I want to speak to him."

XX

"What are you doing here?"

"I wanted to talk."

"I don't want to see you."

"Well, I don't want to be dead, but..."

"Nah, I've got representation, real. I've got nothing to say."

"Nothing at all?"

"No, no, no, wha- what's your position, huh? What do you want from me?"

"Like I said, to talk."

"Look, I didn't know what I was doing, alright. I was dosed as fuck. I don't remember zero."

"You remember me, though, don't you?"

"You want me to say I'm sorry? Fine! I'm sorry! There, you blissed?"

"Do I look it?"

"Why're you keening me? What're all these fucking bugs?"

"They're my eyes."

"Your eyes?"

"All the better to see you with."

"You're fucking section, Ghostie. You should be locked up."

"Don't worry about them, just sit down."

"Nah, nah, something warped is going on."

"That's it. Just sit the fuck down and shut the fuck up."

"Get away from me. Get the fuck away."

"You think I'm fucking scared of you? You can't hurt me anymore, Henry James. I am fucking dead! I am a ghost. And I can flatline you quick as I can say your name!"

"Oh fuck."

"Now sit the fuck down!"

"Okay... okay. I'm down."

"Good."

"Now what?"

"I want to know why."

"I told you, I was fucking high."

"Why me, then?"

"Ahh I don't know... Young lady, late at night, walking alone. Whatever."

"No. I've seen you before."

"What?"

"Around Rowen street. I've seen you. I only just remembered when I came in here. You were watching me."

"I don't know what the fuck you're talking about."

"I wasn't just some random person walking alone. You chose me. You were waiting for me. Why?"

"You're crazy, you're fucking section. I've never checked you before."

"It's because you've got the Plague, isn't it?"

"What? Fuck you! I'm not iced! My blood is red as hell, bitch!"

"It's in your eyes. I can see it. It's an early sign, most people don't know to look for it."

"Fuck you. This conversation is disconnected."

"Was it just hate? Is that all it was? Or was it something else?"

"..."

"And the Red Witch?"

"What did you say?"

"Who's the Red Witch, Henry James?"

"There's no such thing as the Red Witch."

"Does she talk to you?"

"N... no."

"Is it in your sleep? Or while you're awake?"

"You can't hear the Red Witch, Ghostie. Only those with the gift can."

"What did she promise you?"

"You wouldn't understand. You don't have the knowledge."

"School me."

"..."

"I'm tired, Henry James. I'm tired of haunting people. I just want to rest. You owe me that."

"... a cure. She has the power to cure the plague."

"What's that to do with me?"

"She told me to bring her your eyes. The albino with rainbow eyes. That's what she needed. Said they had powerful magicks."

"So you stole them from me and gave them to her?"

"Yes. She did her magick, but I don't feel any different."

"That's cause it's bullshit, Henry James! There is no cure."

"But... she promised! She has the power!"

"If but that were true."

I get up and bang on the door. I hear the gears turn in the lock and Danielle lets me out. Behind me, Henry James howls into the void.

Danielle is telling me how brave she thinks I am, but the truth is I'm shaking. My cells are vibrating at frequencies so high I might turn to vapour. I'm quaking so hard I want to rip myself apart, but not with fear. It's something else, something I'd almost forgotten.

Rage.

I look at my hands and pry open my own clenched fists. Little rivulets of blood run from the tiny crescents in my palms down to my pointed elbows and all I want to see is more blood. But that isn't why I'm not listening.

Walking down the corridor, Danielle tells me about various superstitions regarding albinism and the white death. I've heard them all before, but that isn't why I'm not listening.

I'm not listening because I can't feel my heart beat. I cover my mouth and realise I'm not breathing either. A bit light-headed, I turn to Danielle and try to say "I don't feel well," but whatever sounds I make aren't words, and I fall back into the dark once again.

Many lepidoptera will not migrate and will instead enter a dormant phase during the colder months. Whilst most will overwinter as larvae or pupae, the Mourning Cloak (Nymphalis antiopa) is one of the only species that has been observed to hibernate as an adult through the winter. It is often one of the first butterflies to emerge as the cold abates, and is often referred to as 'the harbinger of spring'.

XXI

My fingers twitch and I wonder how many times I can wake up dead.

One by one, the butterflies come online again illuminating tiny patches of the morgue. This time, there's no one here to greet me. I'm guessing they didn't expect me to come back again.

I put my hand to my heart. After a long wait, I feel a faint throb. My breathing is so shallow it would evaporate in the sun. But I appear to still be alive. More or less.

I wrap a sheet around my naked corpse and stumble through the corridors.

The butterflies explore ahead for me. They locate a white slip in one of the rooms ahead. It's not mine, but I put it on anyway, watching the fabric go grey and musty as it touches my skin. Soon, I give up trying to find anyone who might know me and I step outside.

Across the parking lot, I see my driver sitting in his car lighting up a joint. I stammer towards him and fall against his window, my head swimming. In a blur I feel myself being lifted into the car and placed on the back seat.

I hear "I gotta call security," and I reach out.

"No... no. Need another shot." I gasp.

"Yeah, no shit. But unless you've got fifty grand, I can't help you."

"Please..."

"Don't do this to me. I'm just a driver."

"You said you know a guy..."

"What guy?"

"If I'm willing to lie still... really, really good money..." I hear a pause, then a sigh. The car engine starts.

XXII

If I'm completely, one hundred percent honest with myself – it's not the worst sex I've ever had.

XXIII

The driver jams the auto-injector into my chest and it's like being brought to life with a bolt of lightning. I kick and convulse all over the back of his cream leather seats, spewing blood everywhere. Gasping and coughing, my heart beats like a machine gun.

And all of reality is turned to stone.

The butterflies come back on line. Only five have made it this far with me. I grab hold of anything around me to try and sit up. My muscles are now steel pistons, but my joints can't quite bear the load. I bend around grotesquely like a puppet with severed strings.

"Jesus, girl. I thought you were dust for sure."

Gagging on blood I manage to say the word "drive."

"Drive? Where?"

I spit out a wad of red jelly and scream, "Rowen street!"

XXIV

Stumbling down the middle of the street on broken legs, in a now-vintage satin slip, dragging a veil of blood through the snow, I must look like a herald of the apocalypse.

Inside me, a thousand anguished souls are screaming from the depths. Every muscle is shaking with fury and bloodlust. Every fluid has turned to brimstone. Every cell in my body hungers for the same thing – to kill the Red Witch. I want to squeeze her soft throat with my bare hands and burn her whole world to a molten pit. I want drag her down to the centre of the sun and crush her to a point before ripping her into subatomic particles and scattering them into deep space.

The rage is so clear and consuming, I never think to ask why. After feeling so empty for so long, its presence feels like a gift.

Pretty soon, I find it. The only house in the street lived in by someone with money. The butterflies surround it, scanning the space, and then find various cracks and gaps, and make their way inside.

My eyes within the house, I see a tall man in a leather jacket by the door, another two in the kitchen. Upstairs a woman with bright crimson hair sits at a computer, surrounded by biotech.

In the pitch of anger, I clench my jaw so hard I hear one of my teeth crack.

I walk straight up to the house and bang on the door. It opens a crack and Leather Jacket peers through the gap, below a taut gold chain.

"Who the fuck are you?"

"My name is Tabitha Dyson. I've come to kill the Red Witch."

"Fuck off before you get into trouble." Leather Jacket tries to close the door but my hand shoots out like an arrow and jams it open. He gives it a kick but I barely notice the pain. Instead, my broken fingers worm their way backwards like tentacles and undo the latch. I push the door open and step forward.

In the corridor stands Leather Jacket. As I walk into the warm light of the house I drag with me a curtain of death. The man seems to age years for every second he stands frozen, watching me.

And he has a gun.

I think about the girl who hugged me in the street. I wonder how many years that brief moment of empathy has stolen from her life.

Leather Jacket points the gun straight at my chest. I step towards it until the barrel touches the skin. Rust creeps up the dark blue metal.

He pulls the trigger and a bullet explodes through my ribcage and out into the street.

The noise is deafening. I put my hands up to my ears and the world is filled with a high pitched scream. I shake my head, trying to rattle loose the ringing in my skull.

He tries again, but the gun misfires, the cartridge fizzing away in the cylinder.

He doesn't even bother with a third shot.

"You can leave now," I order, "and take your friends in the kitchen with you." He lowers his gun and two men appear around the corner. They stare for a moment, then swiftly leave past me, muttering blessings to themselves.

The gunshot has alerted the woman to a disturbance and she stands against her door, holding a crowbar.

I stand at the base of the stairs, screaming out to her, spitting blood from my lips.

"The crowbar will not save you, Witch!"

She panics and looks around behind her. She goes to her window and peers out, searching for prying eyes. Up in the corner of her room, she spots a butterfly. A few seconds later I see a crowbar hurtling towards me, then nothing. I let out an audible gasp.

Feeling back in control, she steps out of her room, searching for more butterflies. I panic and set them all to return to me, but one flies too close to her and she takes it out, causing me to stumble. Two manage to return, whilst one gets caught trying to go via the chimney.

I slowly creep up the stairs with a gnawing sense of fear. This woman is clearly intelligent and in her element. I worry I've let this sudden rush of bloodlust take me somewhere I am not prepared for. But the fear drains away in the face of a simple truth: This – this suicide mission, this march of death – this is all I have left. This will be my last action on this earth, even if it ends up meaning nothing.

I allow the addictive fire of rage to flood my body and drive it on. I reach the top and walk up to her door. With a raised fist I pound on the wood and my dead voice screeches out, "I have come to drag you to hell!"

A shotgun blast destroys the door, embedding dozens of small pellets into my chest and face. I stumble back through the splintered air and down a corridor. My last two butterflies get lost on the way, one disappearing under a flurry of wood, the other losing a wing to a stray pellet. I watch through the tiny camera as the fractured door opens, illuminating the Red Witch, double barrelled shotgun in hand. She steps forward and crushes the butterfly under her boot, leaving me in darkness.

"You picked the wrong house to come trick-or-treating to, little ghost!"

I get to my feet, spitting out a few pellets that passed through my cheeks. A long shard of wood has embedded itself into my chest, but I leave it in place. In the darkness I listen for any sound that might help me locate her, but my hearing now has the quality of a toy plastic microphone that's been shot twice in rapid succession. All I know is she must be back in her room around the corner, as it's the only explanation for why I haven't taken a shotgun blast to the head.

Suddenly and inexplicably my vision goes back online. It takes a second but I connect. The image is distant and blurry, but I can see, from the back of her room, the Witch creeping up around the corner, shotgun at the ready. I have just enough time to process this and duck when a violent explosion ruptures the air above me. I dive at the figure in front of me and I take her down onto the floor.

The moment I gain control without, I lose it within.

Kneeling on top of her, I scream at her with my whole body. I bludgeon her with my own bones. I rip and smash and crush her with the fury of a hundred stolen lifetimes. I tear off her fingers as she tries to protect herself. I put out her eye and snap her ribs. I tear the skin from her face. I rip out her collar bone. I am a maelstrom of hatred. I am hell.

Her body lies limp and in pieces. Through the mysterious distant camera I see myself stand up over her. Her face rolls to the side, teeth missing, nose caved in. Twisted, mangled, like an air crash.

I step towards the source of my vision. It becomes apparent to me well before I reach it.

My eyes. She has my eyes. I'm looking through them right now.

I lean forwards and take them off the shelf. They float around in their jar sending ripples through my sight. I scan the room with them taking in the stockpile of biotech around me, and for the first moment since I came through the door, I allow my brain to do its job.

This woman wasn't a witch. She couldn't cure the white death, or any of the other outlandish claims she probably made. She clearly didn't believe in any of that either. She was a Fleshminer – someone who stole people's biotech implants and sold them on the black market. She used people to do her dirty work. Frightened, disturbed and vulnerable people, desperate enough to believe anything.

I stepped back over to her and all I want is for her to die. I think I hear police sirens but can't tell if they're coming or going. I sit down amongst the debris and the Red Witch coughs up some blood.

No luck there, then.

Lost in my thoughts, I don't notice my optical system running the standard uplink procedure. Without any prompting, my visual processor links my brain to the eyes' on-board data storage and a million visions flood my mind. My gallery of memories. Hundreds of hours, all at once.

All of her.

XXV

I'd seen her around the campus before. She had been trying to get people to sign up for various social groups, but had the look of someone who wasn't having much luck. It seemed to her that no one wanted to do anything anymore, as if everyone was lost too deep in their own existential crises to engage with the world around them. I had felt sorry for her, that her rare sense of enthusiasm was going to waste in this temple of cynicism, but I'd never had the courage to actually talk to her.

Now here she was, talking to me, telling me to come by the opening of her friend's cafe. She had done all the artwork that adorned the walls, she says, and she'd love for me to see it. She hands me a small flyer with the name and address on it, and says she hopes to see me there. And, fighting every instinct to hand it back and run away, I smile back at her and tell her it sounds great.

She drinks her vegan spiced nut smoothie and doesn't judge me as I ask what the difference is between Assam and Darjeeling. She tells me about her art, her sculpture and her painting. She talks about the importance of preserving human culture in art – in objects that will outlive us – as the population continues to decline. She says every day another culture, another language, another mythology, is lost.

I watch her hands. How her long fingers push the air around as she talks. The drab light of the cafe turned magical through the facets of a pale green stone set in silver. I feel like a cobra being entranced by the movement of a flute.

She tells me about how, when she was a child, standing on the balcony of a ski resort atop a mountain once considered unsurmountable, she watched the International Space Station burn up in the atmosphere. She remembered how it looked as if someone had slashed through the blanket of night, allowing a searing sliver of daylight to shine through the gap. At that moment, it seemed to her that humanity's best days were behind us. We no longer had the ability, or the desire, to be explorers. We were now merely caretakers.

She tells me about her family. How she moved down to London from Birmingham to escape her religious zealot mother. How she grew up going to Sunday School, loving Jesus and looking forward to the rapture. It was only when the rapture actually came that she started to doubt its holy origins. As she talks about her evaporating faith, she fidgets with a small gold crucifix around her neck – the one she's worn every day for as long as I've known her. I ask her about it. She smiles and shrugs, and says, "You never know."

In another time, she stands beside me in silence. Instructed to wear only bright colours, save for a single black ribbon around the wrist, we look like giant clowns in a tiny model city that is the Trent Park Necropolis. It has been months since I'd been to a funeral, but no one can deny the painful familiarity in the moment, returning to a place we'd all dared to hope we may have escaped. As Bella's ashes are placed in the tiny vault within the great concrete monolith, I can almost hear the sound of her memory being absorbed into the inconceivable cosmic grief that hangs unspoken above the world.

At the wake, the conversation turns to the vaccine. It had been announced last year, to much rejoicing and fanfare, only for us to find out a few weeks ago that, according to several follow-up studies, it was largely ineffective. We all discuss our test results and how none of us, it seemed, had the lucky combination of genetics that allowed the vaccination to work.

Later in the cab, she asks me why I lied. I say I don't know, but the truth seemed inappropriate. I tell her about my dream – the one I've had every night ever since getting my results. I describe myself walking through the Necropolis. The last person alive, alone at the end of the world. I wander amongst the endless stones that cover the face of the earth, searching for the bronze plate with her name on it. That's how it is every night – wandering alone, looking for her amongst the dead, forever. She takes my hand and says that she can't promise never to die. All she can promise is that she won't allow me to spend every day until then just waiting for it to happen.

She unpacks a box of mine, placing books upon the shelf in her oh-so-particular order. From between the pages of a paperback falls a small pamphlet. She picks it up before I can snatch it from her, and after reading the title she looks up at me. My face tells her more than anything she might find within the pages of the old booklet.

She asks me why I never told her. I'm too ashamed to answer that I was afraid of her reaction, so I make up a water-strength excuse about how it's not really that important, and I'd rather be defined by other things. Things I've worked hard to achieve. Things I'm proud of.

She tells me I should be proud to be trans. That it is an achievement. That just to know it, let alone commit to it, is to confront a core truth of ourselves that most are too inflexible or too terrified to explore. I tell her that it's not about courage or determination, it's about survival and necessity. She looks at me quizzically and asks why those things should be mutually exclusive. Why should necessity make something easier or less frightening? Why an achievement born of survival has less worth than one born on a whim?

I had always thought of my trans self as an embarrassment – a birth defect, swiftly corrected, now nothing more than a note in my medical records. But perhaps she was right. Maybe I've been too quick to dismiss what it took become who I am. I would never dismiss how my albinism has shaped me, regardless of how it came about or what it lead life to throw at me. Maybe I should afford my gender the same courtesy.

In the light of the rising sun, I slowly awaken, before her, as I always do. She sleeps with the look of someone happy to be there, wherever she is. She holds me tightly, as if trying to draw me into her dream. For a moment, I allow her to pull me back to the edge of sleep and let the world around us fade away. I float on the edge of consciousness in a place were nothing, not hurt or sadness, not hunger, disease, or death, not even time itself, exists beyond us. It is a moment of subtle perfection, but even timelessness can't last forever.

My alarm goes off, signalling the end of our blissful morn. I reach over and terminate the dreadful noise, whilst she stirs and parts her eyes to the disappointment of reality. In the light of the rising sun, her eyes flick past me, and for a fraction of a second I glimpse a small red flare – like an old camera flash illuminating the blood orange retina.

And time stops.

She says it's nothing. Probably just the flu. She can barely lift the glass of water to her lips. She can't manage to stay warm, no matter how many blankets are piled onto her. She takes some codeine and tries to sleep, but can't. My heart is racing. I'm sick with fear. I tell myself everything will be alright.

The CDIR are here. My second test, like the first, has come back negative. They tell me how lucky I am and I want to punch them. Upstairs, they're zipping her up into one of those awful white tents before loading her into the ambulance and taking her to the Enfield centre. They don't even bother with hospitals these days. I ask if I can ride with them, but they can't take me because of some safety protocol. They tell me to come by in a few hours.

The white tent wheels past me on a gurney and I fall apart. I weep like a burst dam, crumbling, falling apart as the torrent washes away everything but an empty chasm. By the time I've pulled myself together, they have left. A small card with a name to contact is the only evidence they were ever here.

She looks at me with eyes that you can see through. Her hand rests on mine in a purely implied grasp. Her once athletic body wastes away at a rate you can almost see. Even the vibrant colour in her tattoos is fading. Between loving looks, her eyes dart around in random, frantic manoeuvres, tracking hypnagogic creatures crawling over the walls.

I promise I'll stay with her. Right to the end. No matter what happens.

She's sitting up in bed asking me about my day and wanting to know when she can go home. My finger rests on a panic button attached to a key-chain. I tell her again she can't go home, that she's still not well. She says she doesn't understand. She says she feels great. She takes a tissue from the box and asks me why her eyes keep oozing white blood. I explain that her organs have ruptured and are decaying inside of her. She laughs, and leans forward, putting her ivory hand on my cheek. It's ice cold, but her touch burns me. She smiles, then screams in my face. She grabs me by the hair and slaps me hard, over and over again, until my blood is spraying across the room. She tells me I did this to her. That it's my fault. That I'm a white plague monkey cunt and that she hopes I kill myself.

She lets go of me and I fall back onto the floor, shaking and bleeding everywhere. She looks at me in confusion and asks me why I'm crying. My finger floats above the panic button and I say I'm just sad about something.

In a brief moment of lucidity, she tells me I'm beautiful which causes me to recoil. I tell her I don't think much of superficial beauty, and that I'm surprised that adhering to some cultural notion of attractiveness is a quality she would value. She looks at me with faint disappointment. She tells me beauty is far from superficial. Beauty, she says, is what makes us human. The defining characteristic of our species is our obsession with beauty. We have an inability to do anything without turning it into an art form. Every great human endeavour, from fire to Mars has been lead by people who became entranced with its beauty. So when she says you're beautiful, what she really means is 'I see in you the essence of human passion'. I find it hard not to smile.

"We are all our own self-portraits." She says. "We are all works of art."

She said she didn't want a funeral. Didn't want that to be people's last memory of her. Standing alone, I slide the small box into the stone tower. In that instant, she becomes one of millions, all in identical boxes, in identical stone towers, stretching off to the horizon. I brush my fingers over the bronze plaque, feeling the ridges of the letters that spell her name.

Floating in the chamber of my memories, I examine the metadata of all my recordings of her. From first meeting to last goodbye barely four months had passed. That's all we had together. Four months.

The final memory was dated nine years ago.

XXVI

My time must be almost up. The pain is creeping back, soaking into my body through the myriad holes in my skin. My heart beat is erratic, bordering on fibrillation. My lungs are flooded bags of blood, leaking out the grapefruit-sized exit wound in my back.

Stumbling through the snow, I'm not even sure I know where I'm going. Every clear patch of grass or park bench looks as good a place as any to curl up and die.

Bleeding in the cold, I find myself thinking about the Red Witch, back at the house. As cryptically as it had arrived, the consuming hate I felt for her has vanished into thin air, leaving a bitter taste of mild guilt. I wonder if the ambulance arrived in time, if she was conscious, if she was afraid of dying. I wonder if, as a victim of a violent assault, she'd qualify for some decent biotech.

Then I see them: the stone towers. Rows and rows of them like poised dominos disappearing into the edge of the grey sky. Slowly I wander the endless paths, between the thousands of cold obelisks that hold the earthly remains of the millions laid to rest in the Trent Park Necropolis – from the Greek nekrós + pólis. Literally *City of the Dead*.

Even in this moment, I let a smirk grace my face hoping at least one news outlet runs with the headline "Corpse Found In Cemetery."

With every step, I feel myself hemorrhaging memories. The only thing I truly needed to save – my lover's afterlife – leaks out of me and disappears between the gaps in the graves.

A solitary butterfly, rescued from the cavernous chimney of the house on Rowen Street, is my only guide. I left my eyes behind on the off chance that, as evidence in an attempted murder, they (and the gallery of memories within) might be preserved long after my return to the earth. I read the names as I search for her in the library of ash and marble, hoping that some brittle filament of muscle memory can lead me to her.

And just like that, I find her. Amongst the crowds and the noise, I find her. The bronze is slowly rusting, and stone beginning to crack, but it's her. I reach down towards the plaque, but my body only just had enough left to get me this far, and I collapse into a pile of broken bones. I reach up and run my fingers over the letters that spell her name, reading it like braille.

Deanne Solarin.

Alone in the cemetery, I tell her I'm sorry.

She brushes a tear from my cheek and says, "It's not your fault."

Beneath me, the ground feels softer, and I sink into it, feeling myself slip into that timeless edge of consciousness. I roll over, sliding under the sheets, placing my arm around Deanne's waist. Her wild, vibrant hair in tight curls flowing down her back like a river, crashing over her spine and bleeding into her illustrated skin. Lips aflame with blood and passion. Irises that change colour like the ocean, from stormy green to clearest blue. And me, pale as a ghost, bone white hair in strands of silk.

She takes my hand and pulls me closer, and together we sleep.

The Spring Azure Butterfly, (Celastrina Ladon) *has one of the shortest lifespans of any Lepidoptera. Once it emerges from its Chrysalis, the Imago (or Adult) butterfly has only a few days to complete one single flight before it dies.*

Kid Ghost

NAT BUCHBINDER

Eia knew it was their fifteenth birthday; they were confused why everybody assumed they'd forget. They stood on a scale while Sila took measurements, did their best to keep from shivering. The wall in front of Eia was pale pink. Most of the research facility was pink or red like the ferric dirt outside its walls.

"You've gotten taller since you first came here." Sila tugged up Eia's eyelids with her thumbs. "You're taller than I am now. It's amazing."

"It really is." Eia had not eaten in two days. That is, Eia had not been given anything to eat in two days. "I'm supposed to have picked a new name by now."

"What's that?" Sila shone a light into their eye.

"In my culture. We have child names and adult names. I was supposed to pick an adult name by now." Eia kept their muscles tense, tried not to squirm when Sila took out the syringe. "Fifteen is usually the latest."

"But, isn't that supposed to coincide with your maturity?" She inserted the needle into Eia's arm and drew back the plunger slowly.

"Traditionally."

"Then why worry about it." Sila took out the needle and capped the blood-filled tube. "Brigg will be in soon."

Sila didn't shut the door as she left, and Eia looked down at their body. At fifteen, it was supposed to be "his body," or "her body." But it was still "their body." Smooth, hairless, none of the bulging or budding, scents or secretions that had come to their peers on Eyblil.

Brigg stuck his head in, voice cheery. "You can get dressed now, Eia. Today is going to be a round of mental tests."

Eia pulled up their too-short pants, the shirt that hung loose on their shoulders. They walked wobbly, the hallway shaking under bright, narrow lights as Brigg led them into a room with a table and two metal chairs.

Eia sat down, holding their back straight. They did not want to seem tired at all. Fear was not possible, yet their mouth dried at the sight of Brigg.

"How are you doing today, Eia?" Brigg opened a port-pad and started setting a timer for the first test.

"Fine, thanks. And you?"

"Not bad. I think you know that I want to take a look at how your abilities are progressing this morning."

"Alright."

"That blood sample Sila took will be used later in the week. Do you remember it?"

"Yes."

"Can you bring the test-tube in here?"

Eia took in a deep breath and thought of the test-tube, their own thick red blood, picturing it laying on the table between them and Brigg. And there it was, but Eia was on the floor, panting, covered in sweat.

Brigg picked up the tube and held it to the light. "Three minutes and four seconds. I think that's a new record for you, Eia. Do you think you can do it in three minutes flat?"

Eia got up from the floor and returned to their chair. "I don't know."

"I'll tell you what. If you get it to three minutes, I'll see what I can do about getting you some bread or soup. Doesn't that sound nice?"

It sounded wonderful. They always hoped that, at some point, hunger would stop being about food. It would become about something else. "I'll try."

"Great. I know you can do it." Brigg clicked the timer. "Can you bring me the port-pad Sila had in her pocket earlier?"

An object Eia had not actually seen. That made it harder. Not impossible, but harder. They would never be able to bring it in three minutes. But Eia knew what would happen if they accused Brigg of being unfair, of offering a deal and then taking that deal away.

Trying to picture the port-pad wouldn't help, so Eia pictured food. Not the measly rations Brigg was offering. Eia pictured thick slices of roasted meat, dripping in sweet red fruit sauce. They imagined crisp, crunchy, fresh greens from their mother's garden and hot cups of boiled root juice. Eia thought they could actually taste that juice, but it was salty instead of bitter, and they realized it was just blood. They had managed to not fall out of the chair, but bit their own tongue deep instead. The port-pad sat next to the tube on the table.

Brigg stopped the timer. "Just under three minutes. Excellent! Eia, you deserve some nice hot soup when we're finished."

"Thank you." Eia closed their eyes, and Brigg snapped in their face.

"Hey, hey, no dozing now. We've still got a bit to do today." Brigg glanced through his records. "By the way, it's your birthday. Birthdays are celebrated on Eyblil, aren't they?"

"Some of them. But not most."

"Interesting."

That morning Eia brought several more things into the little exam room. Rocks from outside the compound walls, pillows from their bedroom, a portrait of the Chairman from an office wall.

"Alright. Just one more test, and then we'll be finished and you can go back to bed. I bet you're tired, huh?"

Eia squared their shoulders. "I'm alright."

"Great. Can you bring the medium-sized cooler from the lab?"

A big object. Small enough to fit into the room, but Eia would have to concentrate on exactly where it was placed. But it was there, soon enough, sitting squat in the corner of the room. Eia was on their back, looking at the lights on the ceiling. They lifted themselves up onto their elbows. "Won't the stuff inside of that be damaged?"

"Don't worry about it." Brigg helped Eia up. "You can go back to your room now. I'll see you tomorrow."

"See you tomorrow."

There was a nurse waiting outside to escort Eia back to their room. When Eia made it, they curled up on their mattress and thought of hot broth. Their pillow was still in the exam room, and Eia wished they had remembered it. But it wasn't important enough to go back. They rested their head on their arms and closed their eyes for a few minutes, until there was a knock on the door. Eia wanted to get up, but their body felt too heavy, like their limbs were full of mercury.

"Come in, please."

A nurse Eia didn't recognize came in slowly, holding a tray with a steaming bowl on it. He set the tray down on the small table on the other side of the room.

Eia lifted their head. "Thank you so much."

"Do you need some help? Brigg said you might not be able to–"

"I'm fine." Eia sat up, then waited until the room stopped shaking. "I don't need any help."

"Let me know if you do." The nurse left, and Eia crossed the room and sat down at the table. There was no spoon, only the bowl. And inside no solid food, not even broth. Just boiled water with dissolved vitamins. Eia picked it up with both hands and took a sip. It burned their tongue and tasted like chemicals, but they were hungry enough to keep drinking in sips until it was gone.

Eia wanted to get back to bed, but it was too much effort, so they stayed in the chair. They crossed their arms on the table and put their head down. Their stomach still felt like it was sucking in on itself, looking for any scrap of nutrition left from their last real meal, weeks ago. Everything since had been supplements, tiny capsules of vitamins and calories.

Eia dreamed a memory. That was all Eia dreamed by then. Their brain had lost the ability to be inventive. It was about their brother's ceremony of age. By the time the family had gotten the relatives together he was nearly complete in his transition. Still, he stepped over the "river" – several long strands of wires that caught the afternoon sunlight and put it in Eia's eyes – and sang the songs, and declared his new name. He had picked Hatok, which, in Eyblil's old language, used before the annexation, meant *sophisticated*. Hatok was two years younger than Eia. The uncles and aunts all said he was an early bloomer, while Eia was...

But Eia would come into their own soon enough.

Eia awoke on the bed. Someone had picked them up and moved them in their sleep. The bowl and tray were gone. Eia rolled onto their back, allowing thoughts to flow unfiltered. It was a rare treat, like a special dessert after dinner. They had come to Mars not long after Hatok's ceremony. The research team who had taken them said it would only be a couple weeks.

Dispersal genetics, the head researcher explained to Eia's elders, was the phenomenon of a species stretched across space: distant pockets developed interesting abnormalities, traits that shouldn't be possible within humanity's genome. On the planet of Daks, all people are merges of two separate zygotes; on Muller's Planet, all people can produce their own vitamin C; on Eyblil, all primary sex characteristics appear at the onset of puberty. Mother, father, aunts and uncles, none of them understood what he was trying to convey, so he said it more simply: Eyblil is a special planet, and Eia is a special child, and we – the whole Republic – want to know what makes Eyblil so different from the rest of the galaxy.

Eia tried to fall back asleep, but the sucking pain in their stomach kept them up. The broth had probably contained a stimulant as well. Eia knew sometimes Brigg had certain drugs added. So Eia reached under their bed and picked up their chess box, which fit into the palm of their hand. The director had given it to them after Eia had been told they'd be staying on Mars for an extra three weeks.

Turning the box on, Eia tried to pick an opponent. Whenever Eia played, they chose someone to pretend to be playing against. Eia acted as themselves for the blue pieces, then how they imagined that opponent for the green moves. The director seemed like an alright candidate. Eia had only met him a few times, but once they held a stylus of his and saw an argument with his daughter. Eia couldn't tell what the fight was about, but they saw the shouting and the tears, red faces and hoarse voices.

The director seemed the type who'd play fair but distracted. Eia opened with a blue pawn, spun the board around and did the same with the green, what the director might do. Eia moved the blue knight, and then another green pawn.

Whenever Eia played as Brigg, they always cheated. In small ways, on occasional moves. A square too far with a knight, a diagonal shift for a rook. It was an extra challenge, to try to keep up.

The chess game didn't even take ten minutes, so Eia played another with Sila in mind. Then with their brother. The real Hatok never learned how to play chess. He would have done it cautiously, slowly, thinking as much as possible. That one took twenty minutes.

Then Eia put the game away. It had limited distraction potential. They wanted to go to the small reference room and read, but they were afraid of fainting on the way. That had happened, once, and for a week everyone was asking them if they were *alright*, how they were *feeling*, and it made Eia want to cry.

After sleeping a few hours, Eia was awakened by someone shaking their shoulder. Sila.

"Get up. Brigg thought of another test he wants to run."

Eia sat up slowly, nausea bubbling. "I thought we'd finished for the day."

"You did, but he's got something else for you now. Come on." She tugged Eia's shoulder.

They followed her back to the exam room. "He'll be in in a minute."

The objects from before were still scattered around. There was a port-pad on the table. Eia knew it was their own case file and opened it. Eia had read it before, but it was interesting to see the updates as they came in. Brigg thought of it as an opportunity to educate. The most recent thing was the day's earlier tests. The blood work hadn't even been added yet.

The top of the page read Spritius Neotenus. Spirit child. Mozlet Eia, too different from anything else in the galaxy, was a species of one. Brigg had come up with the name, following the old system. Neotenus for the immaturity, the lack of development, the original promises underneath their genetic code. Spritius for the powers. The first one, invisibility, had been discovered when the scheduler made a mistake and had forgotten to give Eia food for three days. At least, that's what they were told. A janitor went into Eia's room thinking it was empty, only to have them appear on the bed, moaning, curled around their empty stomach. Eia was thirteen. The janitor described it as seeing a ghost.

Since then, it had been found Eia could do all sorts of things, under the right circumstances. Move objects without touching them, make an object disappear and reappear elsewhere. Brigg's hypothesis was that the objects were being sped through time while simultaneously moved through space. By the same principle, Eia could levitate themselves slightly off the ground. Sometimes, Eia could touch a personal object and experience a hallucination that usually depicted a scene from the life of the owner of that object. When they held onto Sila's shirt, they saw her signing her marriage authorization form. It was always an event in the past, and silent but colorful.

In states of extreme sleep-deprivation Eia spoke in garbled, unintelligible babble, but they never remembered doing this. A linguist was brought in who concluded Eia's speech followed the patterns of language, but not any language known to the Republic. He had taken several hours of recordings and was supposedly working on a paper about it.

One of Brigg's assistants had become convinced, based on the spontaneous combustion of a lighting fixture, that Eia could light things on fire using only their mind, and set out to prove it. After a week with no food except a few sips of broth and sleep only in twenty minute increments every eight hours, the side-project stopped because the chamber Eia was kept in needed to be used for something else.

After that, Brigg had Eia brought to his office and shut the door behind them. "Eia." Brigg sat down. "Eia, I have good news."

"Yes?"

"The Party has expressed an interest in using your abilities in the military."

"Really?"

"You should be excited."

"You told the Party about me?"

"They asked me, 'How does your research help further our mission?' And I told them, 'I have a kid here who's a monster.'" Brigg must have noticed Eia's face change with disgust, because he laughed. "I mean, if you weren't so thin, you'd be completely horrifying."

Eia only nodded.

"They want me to study you extremely closely, and find out everything that I can about you. But, if they get the impression that I can't do that to the fullest extent possible – either because you're too uncooperative for me to handle, or because we're not well equipped enough, or any number of reasons – well, the only option the military will have will be to bring you to their own facilities. That was the deal we just made."

"When?"

Brigg paused. "Just now. They wanted to take you to their own testing center, but I said that you'd feel better here, where you know us and you know we don't mean you any harm. Do you understand what I'm saying?"

"Yes." Eia sat up straighter.

"What I'm saying is, you must be cooperative, if you want to stay here. Any fooling around, and the Party will know about it. Do we have an agreement on that?"

"Yes." Eia raised their hand, a moment, to shake on it, but Brigg was already standing, walking past the portrait of the Chairman to open the door. He called for a nurse to escort Eia back to their room.

Eia heard footsteps approaching the exam room and turned off the port-pad.

Brigg was carrying a small metal wrist band. "Sorry to drag you out of bed, Eia, but I had an idea and I really didn't want to put it off until tomorrow. You know, the military is waiting for my report."

Eia touched their right wrist. "It's fine." The military was always waiting for the report. The military, speaking through the trumpet of Brigg, had innumerable demands. If Brigg didn't meet them, they'd take Eia to their own facility, where there were never any pillows or hot bowls of soup, never any messages back to Eyblil, and they would not be nearly as hesitant in administering punishments.

"I'm wondering how a sudden change in your pulse might impact things mid-transport of an object." He placed the band between them. "This device will administer a short but powerful shock that should do it. I can control it with the port-pad."

Eia stared at the dull metal. "Should I put it on now?"

"Please."

Eia slipped the band over their thin wrist. They remembered a book they read, once, about a ghost who could materialize or vanish at will. Eia could only appear to vanish.

"Please bring me your other suit."

Like always, Eia pictured the suit, imagined its touch and smell. But instead of blacking out and finding the suit there in a few minutes, there was a jolt, a thorny vine that wrapped around their arm and reached out to their chest, up their neck and down their back, pricking them all over with razors. They stayed in the chair but kept their eyes closed, feeling their lungs and heart panic and convulse. The pain became finer and finer, spreading and deepening, and even when the shock had ended Eia could still feel it.

They opened their eyes slowly, and the suit was hanging off the side of the table.

"Interesting." Brigg touched Eia's other wrist, the one without the bracelet. "What differences did you notice?"

Eia's mouth was dry. "I was aware of the entire thing. Usually I'm not. As you know. It kept me right here."

"Huh." Brigg made a note on his pad. "Let's try it again."

So Brigg and Eia tried the experiment again, and again, and again. The same result each time, pain and presence. Eia wondered if anyone could hear their screaming outside of the room, and then wondered whether they screamed out loud at all.

In the morning Sila brought them a thick slice of warm bread topped with butter, and left it on the foot of the bed. There was sunshine coming through the window as Eia ate. There were marks up their arm.

"I think you're going to get a break for a few days." Sila touched Eia's hair. Eia felt warmth in their scalp as Sila spoke. "Brigg was very pleased with yesterday's results. He's eager to restart the tests, but he said you deserved a reward for being so tough and strong."

Eia didn't look up until all the bread crumbs had been licked away. "When does he want to start again?"

"I'm not sure, he didn't say." Sila picked up the tray. "He's going to report his findings directly to the office of the Chairman."

"He is?"

Sila put her hand on Eia's shoulder. "Exciting, isn't it? That's what he told me, at least. He thinks the Chairman will be very interested."

"Why?"

"Your skills could be extremely useful, you know. You could rescue people who were trapped, or move really big things for people. Oh! You could predict crimes before they happen."

"I can't see into the future."

"You can't? I thought you saw people's future when you touched them." She rested the tray on her hip, holding it with one arm.

"No. Nothing happens when I touch people, I don't think. Only when I hold their things."

Sila shook her head. "Eia, you're the strangest little girl I've ever heard of."

Eia scowled for a second. "I'm not a girl."

"You're right." Sila's eyes widened. "I'm so sorry." She reached to touch Eia but they shifted away.

"It's alright. I think I'd like to be alone for a few minutes, if that's alright."

"That's fine. I think Brigg wants you to have a chance to get outside for a little while today. It's supposed to be warm."

Sila left, and Eia looked out the window. There was a row of trees off the official premises of the research station. They took on the red of the soil, drawing it into their branches and leaves. All they had to do was look to the sunlight, keep their roots in the soil, and they could live.

Later, the nurse from the day before brought Eia out onto the grounds. There were no wheelchairs, and Eia fell after a few steps. The nurse carried them again, and sat with them in the dully orange grass.

"You're new here, aren't you?"

The nurse plucked a blade from the ground. "Just came in a few days ago."

"How are you liking it?" Eia lay down, sun on their face, arm over their eyes.

"It's strange. I didn't expect it to be like this, when I was assigned. How long have you been here?"

"Years. Almost exactly three years."

"How do you like it?" The nurse tied a long blade into a knot.

Eia moved their arm away from their face. "Do you know how to play chess?"

The nurse shook his head. "No, sorry."

"It's okay." They covered their eyes again. The sun was bright, and large and bulbous yellow. "None of the nurses or assistants here do. Brigg showed me how, but we never play."

"Brigg is a smart man. He would be tough to beat, I would imagine."

"I wouldn't know. Where are you from?"

"Venus. I'd never left the planet at all before I came here."

"Me, neither, until I came here. I'm from Eyblil."

"I know. I'd never heard of that planet before but Sila told me everyone there is like you."

They imagined the sun on Eyblil. It was smaller than the one brightening the facility. A young star, in cosmic years, with only one planet surrounding it. Young, and alone, a longing sun. "That's right. Everyone on Eyblil is exactly like me."

"You know, when I first got this assignment, I was reading down the list of projects at this facility. It was written in Venusian, you know, translated. And, for this project – for you, but I didn't realize it – they didn't translate it that well, because it said 'Kid Ghost.' I spent hours wondering what that was supposed to mean. Right there between projects about cell growth and longevity and things like that, all it says is 'Kid Ghost.' I was baffled."

Eia smiled. "I'm baffling to a lot of people anyway."

"Have you had a nice break from things?"

Eia kept their eyes on the table, hardly hearing what Brigg said. They had gotten food that morning, but no sleep had been allowed the night before. Sila had given them a green pill in the afternoon that had made their blood feel cold and fast.

"Have you had a nice break?"

"Fine."

"Excellent." Brigg took his seat. "I might have an audience with the Chairman himself regarding you."

Eia rested their feet flat on the floor. "When?"

"Very soon, perhaps. He's very interested in what you might be able to offer the Republic. I'm told he thinks you could be placed on a ship. You'd get to travel the entire galaxy. Would you like that?"

Eia nodded slowly.

"I thought so." He slid the bracelet towards Eia. "But you need a lot more training. Two minutes won't cut it. It needs to be as close to instant as possible."

That morning, Brigg and Eia brought the transport time down to a minute and forty-five seconds. The room was filled with small objects, and larger ones. The biggest was a two-foot metal cube that sped up the mitochondrial action of cells, causing organisms to rapidly age. Eia recognized it because Brigg once ran a sample of their cells through the machine, ostensibly to see if Eia would ever be able to develop normally.

Apparently, no matter how fast Eia's mitochondria acted, they never died.

In the afternoon, after a quick break for Brigg's lunch, the two of them tested an elevated heart rate on Eia's psychometry. Eia already knew a lot about everyone who worked on the facility, so Brigg arranged for other items to be brought in.

First, a suit jacket, the same kind worn by every citizen. Eia held it in their hand, and on top of Brigg's face they could see the inside of a transport ship. Then the shock was delivered. The picture in their mind became bleached, elongated, muted. The back of a seat, the white metal ceiling. A list on a port-pad, in a language Eia didn't know, letters all melting.

"This belongs to the new nurse."

Next, a blue chess piece. The queen, with her rounded crown. Eia closed their eyes, and they saw gray. Waves blurred, crashing solid shaded walls.

"This belongs to no one."

It turned out, a prolonged electrical shock only dampened and distorted the image Eia received. It took several tries before Brigg gave up on the idea.

"See you tomorrow, Eia." Brigg turned to step out.

They were shaking. "Don't call me Eia." Eia felt a great dark wave underneath their skin.

"What?" He looked back.

"Don't call me Eia anymore. I'm fifteen. Eyblilans change their names at this age. My new name is Kid Ghost."

"Is this really the time to play games?"

"I'm very serious. Kid Ghost. To call me Eia after today would be the gravest insult."

"Kid Ghost. That's the stupidest thing I've ever heard."

"You dishonor me and my traditions to say that."

"Do you think the military is going to acquiesce to your demands like we do here? Don't you realize how good you've got it?"

"It's from the name you gave me. Spritius Neotenus. Spirit Child."

"I'll call you by your name."

Eia looked at the cell-aging device from before, thought about it, pictured it moving through the air. Then the heavy metal cube was hurtling towards Brigg's head. He tried to dodge it, but the edge grazed his crown, and he screamed, clutching his wound as the device clattered behind him. "How dare you! How dare you, you little shit!"

"That's what monsters do."

Brigg radioed for security guards to bring Kid Ghost back to their room.

The three men carried the thin sleeping ghost down the hall.

Back in their room, Kid Ghost looked for a wire. A silver wire. But the room was bare, clean and tight, nothing fraying at the edges. So they had to imagine one instead, a wire catching sunlight like a river. Inside they held a gentle warmth, the tiny spark that ignites a sun. Kid Ghost hummed the song softly while taking the ceremonial step across the imaginary wire towards their parents and siblings, new nephews and nieces, uncles and aunts, all waiting in the shade.

The Gift

RYKA AOKI

"Freddie? You home?"

The air was bright with the sounds of a spring Saturday. Mrs. Fernandez was clipping back her chrysanthemums; the cute UPS guy rumbled past in his big brown truck; the neighborhood cycling club buzzed by like cicadas; next door, little Heifetz Wong was sawing away at the Bach bourée from Suzuki Violin Book Three.

Yet Martha McRae was unaware of any of it. Instead, she was focused on her child's footsteps. She frowned. A child should never walk like that.

"Freddie. Come over to the kitchen. Are you feeling okay?"

"Yes, Mom."

"Freddie." Martha looked at her son. It wasn't just his feet. His entire body trembled like it was holding up the sky.

Freddie paused, then bit his lip.

"Uh, is Dad home?"

"Are you in any trouble?"

"No Mom! I mean—not *trouble* trouble. It's just that I have something I need to tell both of you"

"Okay," Martha said gently, "then why don't you wash up for lunch? Dad'll be home soon."

Sure enough, when Freddie McRae returned to the kitchen, both of his parents were waiting.

Martha ladled some of her trademark minestrone for Hank, Freddie, then herself.

They said grace, then began to eat. Martha's minestrone was amazing as usual, but unlike most lunches in the McRae household, no one said a word. His parents tried to make eye contact with their son, but it seemed as if Freddie could not look up from his bowl.

Martha glanced to her husband, who nodded back and leaned toward their son.

"What's up, Kiddo?"

Freddie stopped. Then slowly, he looked up.

"Whatever it is, it's going to be fine," Martha said.

"We're a family, right?" Hank winked. "What's going on?"

"Well, you know I've been kind of distracted lately."

Hank and Martha looked at each other, then back at Freddie.

"How couldn't we, Freddie?"

"It's not about school, is it?"

"No..."

"You do know if you're gay, that's fine. I mean, I'm bisexual."

Freddie shook his head.

"Then maybe girl problems?"

"Well, maybe sort of. You see... I've felt something was wrong with my life. Not bad or anything. Just...wrong."

His parents nodded.

"So, I've been talking to the school counselor—she's been real helpful. And doing some reading, and well, last night, it all came together. I realize that I'm transgender. I'm a girl. "

"HA!"

Minestrone splattered everywhere.

"Oh no! Sorry honey!"

"It's okay. Does anyone else need a napkin?" Hank asked.

"Mom!?"

"Sorry! I'm just relieved that it wasn't something bad! Wait—singular? 'she' and 'her'?"

"Yes Mom. That feels right." And it did. It really felt right. OMG, it felt sooo right.

"Oh honey! How I missed that smile! Fre... Uh... Fredericka?"

Freddie crinkled her nose

Martha laughed. "Okay, no Fredericka, then. Do you have any names in mind? I'm sure you've thought of some."

Um... I was wondering if you might call me Samantha?"

"Samantha... My, that *is* nice. Your great aunt was a Samantha. But I'll bet you knew that, didn't you?"

Samantha blushed.

"Hank? *Hank?*"

Samantha's father, who had been wiping the table, nodded and swallowed. "Well, I think you should rest on it for a few days and see if you're sure."

Samantha's smile disappeared.

"Hank! Martha scolded, "Why would you ask if she were sure? Of course she's sure. If she says she's your daughter, *then she's your daughter.*"

"No!"

"NO?"

"NO! I mean—no, not about being a girl. I mean about the name."

"Dad?"

"I mean, I want to make sure that it's 'Samantha' before we change all the paperwork, the insurance forms, and the birth certificate, and everything, so I just want him to be sure—I mean *her* to be—"

He paused.

"I really said "him," didn't I?"

Hank put down the washcloth and sighed.

"Damn. I swore if my child were transgender I'd always respect their pronoun choice." He sighed. "And here I am, messing up your pronouns right at the beginning. I'm so sorry."

"Dad... It's OK. I've been 'he' and 'him' to you for 15 years."

Martha got up and rubbed Hank's neck. "Honey, I think we can change the paperwork just fine. It's not so hard to do, even if she changes her name later."

"Well, you know this sort of stuff best," Hank said. He cleared his throat, winked then grabbed the ladle.

"Now who wants more minestrone soup?"

That night, Martha peered into her daughter's room. Samantha was on the bed, motionless, with pillows over her head.

"Pumpkin?"

"I don't think Dad's too happy," said a voice from under the pillows. "He didn't say anything to me after dinner. I mean, we usually talk, work in the garage, or do some Mad Libs... "

"Oh Samantha, it's not that. He's just worried about getting everything right. You know your dad. Now he's pestering me about how to raise a daughter."

"What?" Samantha sat up. "*Really?*"

Martha stroked Samantha's hair.

"Yes, *really*. He'll be fine. Now, since you've got your computer here, let's take care of some school stuff."

Martha helped her daughter complete the school's online Gender Affirmation Form to change her gender ID to "female." The form was its usual simple self, so everything was finished and effective immediately.

The next morning, as Samantha slept, Martha and Hank went to church. Pastor Truong was always an inspiring presence, and this was a particularly spirited sermon, full of commitment to God and not compromising one's morals.

After Pastor Truong concluded, and one of the deacons reminded everyone about the bake sale next weekend, the pastor asked if anyone had prayer requests.

Hank stood up. "My wife and I would like to request a prayer. Of thanks. You know our Freddie."

Many in the congregation nodded.

"Well, Freddie has been troubled lately. And his mom and I have been praying for our child's happiness. This weekend, well, God answered our prayers.

"Last night, our child sat with the both of us, and told us that she is transgender. Her name is Samantha now. We'd like a thank you prayer for our child's happiness, and to celebrate the gift of our new daughter."

The congregation broke out into applause.

But then, Pastor Truong cleared her throat.

The applause abruptly stopped.

"Hank," Pastor Truong said firmly. "Our community is a God-fearing respectful one, is it not?"

Hank looked at his wife, then out at these people, who had been friends of the McRaes for years.

Pastor Truong continued.

"Since God created us all as we are, it is our duty as Christians to celebrate this. God made gender a spectrum. Just because one is trans, we can't assume a binary reaction to gender. Hank and Martha, have you asked your child which gender and pronouns are preferred?"

Martha stood. "Thank you, Pastor, for your concern. That was the first thing I asked. And it's 'singular, she, her.' She's a *girl!*"

Pastor Truong smiled.

"Such is a mother's love!" she shouted. "Well then, let's send a prayer of thanks for the McRaes, and their daughter Samantha, starting her new life in our House of God!"

The congregation broke out in applause.

"Can I get an Amen?"

"*Amen!*"

On Monday, Samantha left for school looking much the same as before, save for a little powder, lip gloss, and pencil eyeliner. Her Mom suggested that she start easy on the makeup, to take her time.

"Makeup takes practice. And selection. Some cosmetics want to cover you up, and there's no reason for a girl like you to do that. Why hide the face you were given? It's beautiful."

Martha smiled.

"After all, you *do* take after me."

As she approached campus, Samantha became nervous. How would she address her name and gender change? But then she realized that many of their parents attended the same church as the McRaes, and of course, all parents all spend too much time on Facebook. So even before her first-period teacher could say, "I'd like everyone to welcome your classmate Samantha McRae's new identity," many of her classmates were already waiting to congratulate her.

The attention was different from anything she'd faced as the school's quarterback. Of course, she'd been popular, but that was for what she had done on the football field. This was all about *her*. Everyone wanted to tell her how much they supported *her*, and how they were so happy for *her*.

Then, just as things were getting overwhelming, someone grabbed her arm.

"T-Tammy?" It was Tammy Weinstock, her ex from sophomore year.

"You. Bathroom. Now."

"Hurry *up!*" Tammy pushed Samantha through the door.

"Uh…" Samantha hesitated.

"What's wrong?"

"Nothing—I mean it's just that I've never been in here before."

"It's a *bathroom*. What's the big deal? You've identified female; this is the one to use."

"But I don't have to pee or anything."

"*Duh!* I brought you in here to talk."

"Tammy, you know I'm sorry about how things ended between us—"

"Shut UP!" Tammy snapped.

"Huh?"

"Just because we're not dating doesn't mean I don't care about you. Whether you're Freddie or Samantha, we can still be friends, right?"

"Sure?"

"Now, I've read in all the magazines that starting as a trans girl can be complicated. And it's not the same for everyone. But seriously, we'll need to go shopping."

"My mom said she'd take me shopping whenever I was ready."

"Your *mother*? You've *got* to be kidding. Seriously, Samantha, we need to find your look. I mean, you're smart and charming and—"

"But I've not even started electrolysis or hormones yet. What about this?" she pointed to her facial hair.

"Like that would matter." It was Tammy's friend Jeanette Chung, in front of the mirror, brushing even more shine into her silky black hair. "Besides, trans women just starting out are hot. Right, Tammykins?"

Tammy turned red. "*Jeannie!* That's not the point. Samantha is finding herself."

Jeanette laughed.

"Well, I'm sure the rest of the school will find her…mmm…" She blotted her lipstick, then looked Samantha up and down. "You were sorta cute with the quarterback thing, but this trans stuff just gives you so much more…mmm. Yesss."

"Uh—" Samantha blushed.

"JEANNIE!!" Tammy shrieked.

"But, Tammy's right. Ugh. Lose the shopping date with Mom."

"But I *like* shopping with Mom."

Jeanette flipped her hair and walked away.

"I am *so* not arguing with you. Tammy, *fix her.*"

As first period passed, then second, Samantha felt less nervous, and more like herself. She was about to sit down to third period history, when her teacher gave her a note from the school nurse.

Mr. El-Sayed smiled. "I think we know why the nurse wants to see you. Good luck."

It was customary, whenever students affirmed as transgender, to visit the school nurse. Of course, most all students had doctors, but since school nurses played such an important role in maintaining the health of each student, they were naturally seen as the ones best able to guide them in this important time.

The nurse met with Samantha for almost an hour, listening to Samantha's goals and concerns while explaining all of her options. Sie gave Samantha a pamphlet on hormones, androgen inhibitors, nutrition and health, as well as a month's supply of estrogen and spironolactone.

"I can provide these whenever you need them. But I advise you to follow up with your doctor, since you'll need blood work and there's no endocrinologist on staff at this school.

"Plus, you'll most likely be wanting other procedures done as well."

"Well, Mom's found a surgeon for breast augmentation. Seriously, I just told her this weekend, and she's already boob hunting on Google."

"You let your mother know already?"

The nurse chuckled and rolled hir eyes.

"What is it with parents and transitions? Let them know you're affirming your gender and BOOM! It's like they're planning your wedding! But remember that it's *your* life, okay?"

Samantha nodded sheepishly.

"You kids these days! Always telling your folks right away. Where's the fun in that? Back in my day, when we affirmed ourselves as trans, we at least had the sense to wait a couple of weeks to keep the good news to ourselves."

After school, Tammy and Jeanette were ready for shopping, but when they came for Samantha, she shook her head.

"I'm sorry, but I have football."

Tammy tilted her head. "You're going to keep playing football?"

"No, but I haven't told Coach or the team yet, and they are my buddies. Maybe go ahead, and I'll meet up with you later?"

"Okay!"

Jeanette winked. "Just don't get trapped in the locker room."

"JEANNIE!" shrieked Tammy.

"Just kidding, just kidding..."

"MCRAE!"

Before Samantha even reached the athletic building, Coach Calavicci bellowed out her name.

"Yes, Coach?"

"I heard about this transgender stuff this morning. So, you're a girl."

"Yes, Coach."

"Well," Coach Calavicci cleared his throat. "You're still going to play ball with us?"

Samantha had been quarterback, and All-league, at that. And these were her teammates, and they were going to win it all this season. But still...

"McRae."

"Yes, Coach?"

"Now, I do care about our team. And with you coming back as QB, we'll take the league title for sure."

He exhaled and took off his sunglasses. His eyes were green.

"But I'm not just a coach. I'm a teacher. And it's my job to guide and encourage you to hold to your convictions and goals, whatever they are. So, again, McRae, will you be playing with us next season?"

Samantha trembled. But she did not cry. Instead, she raised her head and looked straight at her coach.

"No sir. I really love this team. But I want to find more about this girl I want to be."

"Well," Coach Calavicci exhaled, "I can't say this won't affect our team." Then he chuckled. "But as a teacher, I'm proud of you." He patted her on the back.

"Come on—Samantha—let's go tell the crew."

The chatter stopped as soon as Coach Calavicci and Samantha entered the meeting room.

"Okay, ladies and germs. I have an announcement. McRae is leaving the team."

"WHAT!?"

"NO WAY!"

"Just because she's a girl doesn't mean she can't play football!"

"Quiet. QUIET! Samantha just affirmed her identity this past weekend. She told me she wants to find out more about herself. I'm sure she's needing to make a lot of adjustments."

"But we were going to win it all next year!"

"And we will *still* win!" Coach snarled. "But not at the cost of a student's well-being. McRae's on a different journey now. I expect you to treat her with the respect and support any of you would ask for. Do I make myself clear?"

"Yes, Sir."

"Did someone say something?" Coach sneered.

"Yes, Sir!"

"Huh?"

"YES, SIR!!"

Samantha tried not to cry as she told her teammates what it had meant to be part of their team. The Sweeney twins, all 550 pounds of them, hugged her and wished her well.

"McRae, you'll always be our quarterback. Let us know if anyone gives you trouble, and we'll be there to protect you."

"You guys…" Tears began rolling down Samantha's face.

"Monoi," said the cornerback, Derek "Deacon" Young.

"Huh?"

"Monoi. Repairing conditioner and hair mask. Carol's Daughter makes it. My sister still swears by it. It's all natural."

"Deac?"

"Well, I may not talk much, but I'm a trans man. I used to have a *lot* of hair before I chopped it all off. I mean, I don't want to jump to conclusions, but you'll probably be trying out different looks. If you don't have a good repair regimen, all that heating and teasing and relaxing will murder your cuticle."

Coach Calavicci blew his whistle.

"Okay, that's it for the touchy feely stuff! Samantha, good luck and congratulations. The rest of you lowlifes, get ready for pain!"

"YES, SIR!!"

There was one last person to talk to.

Bobby Hernandez.

She had been All-league quarterback. He was the star receiver.

"Bobby—"

"Shit, Freddie... I mean, Samantha. Wow. I mean..." Bobby made a weird face, like he was about to either burp or pass gas. Samantha could understand why he was angry.

"I wish it could be different."

"Sure you do," Bobby mumbled.

"Hernandez!" Coach Calavicci shouted.

Bobby shrugged. "Gotta go."

"I'm sorry, Bobby," Samantha said. She turned to walk away.

"Well, now you're a girl, enjoy all the cock."

Samantha froze. When she finally gained enough composure to turn around, Bobby had a disappeared into the locker room.

"He said *what!?*" Tammy was furious. "That little shit!"

"Maybe it wasn't supposed to be mean." Samantha had caught up to Tammy and Jeannie at the mall.

"Uh, hello? In what way could that not be mean? You sure you don't want some pizza? It's vegan."

"No, the salad is fine. Guess I just don't want think of Bobby like that."

"Well, it's your life. But that was still a jerky thing to say. Forget him. He can find someone else on the team to play catch with."

Samantha cringed. It felt like someone had jabbed her heart with an electric needle. What was that? Why?

But before she had the chance to ponder this any further, Jeanette skipped over to their table.

"Victoria's Secret's having a sale! Check this out!" She reached into her bag and retrieved a band of shiny black fabric.

"So... Is that a belt?" Tammy ventured.

"They're shorts, silly."

"Seriously? They're gonna pull halfway up your butt."

"And? Why do you think I do so many squats at the gym? Right, Samantha? Samantha?"

"Bobby Hernandez just said something really stupid to her."

"Of course he did. He *so* likes her."

"I knew you'd say that."

"And am I wrong? He's a boy and boys say stupid things when they like someone. Right?"

"Yeah, I guess," Tammy conceded. She turned back to Samantha.

"It'll be okay, Samantha. *Samantha?*"

"She's spaced out again," said Jeanette. "Hello? Earth to Samantha!"

But Samantha's mind was racing. *Bobby likes her?* But then why was he mean? Or was he trying to be mean? Did it mean something else? What did he mean? And boys. Boys! Boys? *Boys!?*

"This is so complicated! How do you handle boys?"

"Well..." Jeanette smiled.

"Jeannie! Samantha didn't mean it *that* way," said Tammy.

Jeanette looked into Samantha's eyes. Samantha tried not to swoon.

"So you want to do it?"

"Huh?"

"Go out with boys."

Samantha bit her lip. This was all happening so fast.

"I guess so? I think?"

Tammy held Samantha's hand.

"It's okay. You don't have to rush. You don't even have to choose. So you're a girl. It doesn't mean you have to like or not like any gender." She winked.

"Yeah. Take your time and have fun, Sammie," Jeannie said. "That said, you'll probably be fine, but you're cute, and boys can be pigs. So keep our numbers on your phone, just in case. Don't do anything you don't want to, carry protection because most boys won't, and be careful."

"Now you sound like my Mom."

"No way your Mom can rock these shorts like me."

"JEANNIE!"

Samantha laughed, the first good laugh she had had all day.

"Can we do this again tomorrow?"

"Oh gosh, Sammie, we can't. Tomorrow's Tuesday and we have practice."

The cheerleading team. Of course! They had practice too. Tammy was the captain, wasn't she?

Suddenly, Samantha had an idea.

"Hey! Do you think I can try out for the team?"

Tammy and Jeanette looked at each other and frowned.

"Samantha," Tammy said gently. "You have been a great quarterback. But cheerleading is totally different."

"I learn fast, and I'm good on my feet. I mean, I had to be when Coach Calavicci switched us last year to a run and shoot offense."

"Tell you what. Why don't you come to the field tomorrow at 3, and just watch what we do? Then we can talk."

Samantha nodded excitedly. "I can be on the cheerleading team," she thought to herself. "Why not? A new life, a new team... it was perfect!"

It was Tuesday, 4 pm. Tammy and Jeanette were still at practice.

Samantha, however, was walking home alone.

She had met them as promised at 3. In less than fifteen minutes, she had felt silly. Sure, she had played football, but the things she saw that cheerleading squad do... Being All-league quarterback was nothing compared to that.

At least Tammy and Jeanette were kind. They recommended that she try out for the drill team. But the drill team was mostly freshman and she was going to be a junior.

Which meant, in her new life, Samantha McRae would not be on any team at all. She felt so lost. What was wrong with her? And why couldn't she stop crying?

Suddenly, Samantha stopped at a familiar sound. Footsteps. The same ones she had heard so often on the football field.

"Bobby?"

"HEY! Wait up! I'm—" he gasped, "so glad I caught you!"

Samantha waited as Bobby coughed and bent over to catch his breath.

"Hey—" he said between breaths," I'm really sorry about—what I said at practice. Of course—gender and orientation are—two different things— and yes I was being a total douche and—uh—hey, you okay?"

Crap. She was still crying! Oh, why did he have to see her like this?

"I'm fine." She tried to wipe her eyes, which made them red and smeared her liner.

"You don't seem fine. What's wrong?"

Bobby listened quietly until Samantha had finished. He felt badly for her, but one thing didn't make sense.

"Samantha, I don't want to seem mean, but whatever made you think you'd make the cheerleading team? You've never been to a cheerleading camp. You've never taken dance. You don't even like dancing. Why be a cheerleader?"

Samantha sighed.

"I thought, well, since I'm a girl—"

"Aw, Samantha. Geez. What the hell?" Bobby started laughing.

"Don't laugh at me, Bobby!"

"No, no, Samantha, I'm not trying to make fun of you. But geez, you don't have to be a cheerleader because you're a girl! You can be anything you want!"

He was right. Of course he was right. But so what if he was right? That didn't mean she wasn't feeling alone. That didn't mean she wasn't scared. That didn't mean—

"You're going to be *fine*. You're being you."

Yes, those were nice words. But Samantha couldn't help it; tears were just coming and so what if they were?

Suddenly, Bobby Hernandez realized he wasn't just chatting with his quarterback anymore.

"Yeah, well, I guess, now that you're a girl, um—"

Part of him wanted to hold her. "I mean, you've always been a girl—"

But they weren't even going out! "I mean—"

And why was he even thinking that? "Maybe I could take you out—Wait! I don't mean it like that. No! I mean I do, I mean. SHIT! Wait I—um—

"So you still like hamburgers?"

Samantha watched Bobby stammer and stumble like a big dumb puppy. She had never seen anything so stupidly cute in her life. Yes, she was sad. Yes, she was heartbroken.

But Samantha started giggling, even as she wiped her face on her sleeve and sniffled.

"Doofus. Of course I still like hamburgers."

Visions

MORGAN M PAGE

He's been waiting for her to jump his whole life.

The truth is, he doesn't know who she is, he's never met her, doesn't know a thing about her. But ever since Avery could remember, he's been seeing her.

The first time Avery ever saw her, it wasn't in a dream – those would come later – it was in a reflection on the side of a bus. White girl in a long green dress, dark hair, all distorted in the shiny metal. His first memory in fact. Even earlier than his memories of throwing fits over dresses he never wanted to wear, earlier still than his first stirrings of arousal catching a glimpse of Glenn Close in Dangerous Liaisons on the TV as his parents tried to shoo him off to bed. She's been with him a long time.

Avery gets off the metro at La Salle in Verdun and slowly makes his way up the escalator. Even before he gets outside, he can feel the cold. He puts his hands into the pockets of his second-third-fourth-hand leather jacket, the one with the Beyoncé back-patch his last girlfriend skillfully sewed into place in June, two seasons and a whole lifetime ago.

Inside his pockets, he clenches and unclenches his hands. Been doing that ever since the dentist told him that his jaw pain wasn't some infection or abscess, that it was all the stress, that if he didn't stop clenching his teeth so hard, he'd break them. Now he's moved all that tension into his hands, but it looks so aggressive if other people see it, like he's the kind of man looking for somebody to punch. Keeping it in his pockets and out of sight is one of the many adjustments he's had to make to balance how differently the world treats him now.

Outside it's another shitty, wet night. Usually this time of year, Montréal is two feet deep in snow and slush, the Saint Lawrence River frozen solid so that dozens of Québécois fathers can take their sons fishing on the quietly creaking ice. But winter just won't come this year. Avery thinks maybe – not in the way that things are but the way that things feel – it's because the mayor dumped 14 billion tons of raw sewage into the Saint Lawrence a month before. Mother Nature's too sick to do her duty. Or maybe She just doesn't want to freeze in all that shit and garbage.

He shouldn't complain. Avery hates the cold. And worse, he can never get his shit together to buy gloves, or a scarf, or anything to protect him from the cold. Only has this pair of long-johns under his jeans because they were a gift from the back-patch sewing girlfriend.

Avery looks around for a cab. Takes a few minutes of walking to find one. Not so many cabs out here in Verdun, and he wishes he didn't have to be out here at all, that he could just be back at home in Parc-Ex, primping and pre-drinking for New Year's Eve like any regular guy his age.

He could turn around now, go home, be that kind of guy, couldn't he? He looks back in the direction of the metro station as he climbs into the cab. He could go home, and maybe then whatever might happen, whatever could happen between him and this girl wouldn't. It could all just be some lifelong delusion, early onset schizophrenia – that bitter possibility somehow an even worse option than being guided by visions.

But he knows where he needs to be and when he needs to be there. As he explains, in his awful broken French, where he wants the driver to drop him off, as he assures the driver it'll be ok to drop him right there and this is all on the level, his eyes go to the clock on the dash. Still got time before she comes.

They became dreams when he was young, became erotic fantasies with the flood of hormones from his first puberty. And when that happened he could feel it – whatever it was that drove these messages – get annoyed. Like he was going off script. He wasn't supposed to grab her, to slip his hands around her waist, to feel the warmth of her chest against him. He definitely wasn't supposed to run a hand up the long green skirt of her dress, shove aside her black lace panties that just happened to look like what he saw at age 9 when he caught all the cis boys in the neighbourhood gawking at lingerie in the Sears catalogue. He wasn't supposed to think

about that. It would interrupt him. And the fantasies would snap back, return to the unflinching, unchanging, cold truth of what was to happen.

He was only allowed to wander so far. His whole life he was only allowed to wander so far, before God or whatever threw him back on course.
As Avery got older he began to feel claustrophobic all the time. He realized
his choices were not his own. He's not even sure becoming a man was his
own choice. Whether that was genetics, or the cold hand of whatever hateful
spirit drove him on to this girl and this moment, it all felt predetermined.

Messages came from all around him, to remind him of his duty or his
curse.

Once, in college, he was driving around listening to an oldies station.
Jukebox music. Had taken to driving around back roads in Vermont because his roommates were always fighting or fucking. Suddenly the DJ cut
the song half way through. "Sorry folks, but we've got a special announcement, a real important message. This one goes out to a listener by the name
of Avery. You know where you're supposed to be, to watch her fall," he said,
pure radio voice. "Thanks for your patience folks! Now, back to another
classic from the late, great Buddy Holly himself!"

The music in the cab is nothing special. Inoffensively Top 40. Avery
wishes he could smoke, have something to occupy his hands besides making and unmaking fists on his knees. They're getting close now. He can see
it in his head, where he's supposed to be, but more importantly, he can feel
it. Like this place has got hooks in him, right through his heart and his guts,
reeling him in. It gets stronger every second.

Halfway across the bridge, he tells the driver to stop. It comes out
Stop!Stop!Stop! all together. His French isn't good enough to really understand what the driver says as Avery hands him a couple of bills, but he gets
it. *This is the middle of a bridge. Where are you going to go?*

Avery gets out of the cab, shuts the door, and gives the driver a little
wave. Like, get lost. You're not part of this. And, eventually, the guy drives
away.

Once the driver leaves, Avery gets off the road. He hops over the railing and onto the pedestrian sidewalk. He could've just walked across the
bridge, but it's so damn bitter out. He already knows he's got a while before
it all goes down. Before this girl he's been seeing and dreaming about and
jerking off over and afraid of and afraid for all these years comes up – if she

comes up, if there even is a she to come up. No use being out in the cold even longer than he needs to be.

Opening his jacket to grab a cigarette lets in the air, stealing away some of his body heat. Avery takes one from the pack he keeps in the inside pocket. He lights it and takes a deep drag, walks right up to the railing at the edge of the bridge. Down below, the water is fierce. The Saint Lawrence moves so fast, even now that it's full of the unprocessed human waste of Montréal. He wants to imagine that the water is a little yellow or a little brown, but the truth is it's too dark to see any colour in it.

Something is telling him she'll be here soon. When he was younger, Avery tried thinking up facts about her. He's given her half a dozen names over the years. He daydreamed about what she did for a living.

He wondered most of all whether she was seeing him everywhere, too.

Now that he's here, actually here, his feet planted more or less right where they are supposed to be, where they've always been meant to be, he doesn't really care.

She's stolen his whole life. If not her, someone or something else that tied the two of them together and, worse, let him know about it. Each decision, from which girlfriends would propel him to leaving rural Vermont, to which schools to go to so he could get a job in Montréal, they've all been for her. And what's she ever given him in return? He's played the vision in his head over and over, and it's never ended with her giving anything back. All those years, all that heartache back. The vision is just the two of them right here on this cold bridge, on this cold night, for this one fixed moment in time.

A car speeds past him on the bridge, the sound of drunk Quebeckers on the New Year nearly louder than the sound of the engine moving wet tires across slushy pavement. He turns to watch them pass, just in time to see something whiz by his head. The empty beer can hits the rail and the drunks erupt in laughter. Would this be his life if he didn't have to be right here, right now, waiting on some girl he's only seen in dreams and visions? Some girl he's never met? For a brief moment, he's thankful that, whatever else it may have done to his life, the pull to bring him here shielded him from becoming that exact type of asshole.

When she finally walks up, she looks different. It's subtle. She's definitely the same person from every dream, every fevered vision, every

half-whispered message from a stranger over the years. The same girl that
Bobby, the six year old Avery used to babysit, once drew for him and said,
"you gotta be there, when it happens. You gotta be there."

As she gets closer, he can see her face is a little more cut than he had
pictured it all these years. Angular bones, only just covered over in soft fat.
She's skinnier than he remembers. And taller, too. He hadn't figured on her
being trans at all, had half-hoped his own transition could've been an act
of rebellion against this predetermined life. But when he sees her up close,
she's familiar in that way that trans people are familiar to him. And he can
see it spread across her face too, that recognition, that deep knowing of the
fact between them.

"Oh," she says, like she was expecting him. Or maybe that's just what
he wants to believe. The girl sidles up beside him and they both lean over
the railing to look down at the poisoned Saint Lawrence. "You stole my
place."

"Didn't mean to," he mumbles, not sure what to say. Talking was never part of it. Is this going off script? He shifts weight back and forth between
his feet. Avery takes a long, final drag off this cigarette to calm his nerves,
goes to toss it into the river then drops it by his feet instead. Crushes it out.
The river's taken enough as it is, and still might take more tonight.

"You know, it's really rude," she says. "I had a plan, I had it all figured
out. I wanted to be alone."

The sound of the river and passing cars fill up the space between
them. Avery's not sure what to do, and that not knowing begins to fill up
with all those old sex fantasies he used to have about her, about this girl he's
never met before but knew he'd have to. His eyes trace the sharp cut of her
jaw, her high cheekbones, the fat curl of her lower lip. All his years of wanting condensed into a single flash of eyes over bare skin. He could touch her
now, if he wanted to, if she wanted him to. Slide his hand around her waist,
press her chest – broader now than he'd imagined – against him. And maybe that would change things. For him, or for her – it doesn't matter. Instead,
he turns around, puts his back up against the railing.

"I get it, you're my angel," she says, staring down at the rushing water.
"You're here to *It's a Wonderful Life* me into not jumping, right?"

"I'd make a pretty terrible angel," he says. Avery fishes another cigarette out of the pack with shaky hands, shoves it in his mouth, and lights it
up. He wants to go home, he doesn't want to be here, doesn't want to have

this responsibility. "Maybe I'm here to tell you to do it. Maybe I'm here to make sure you don't chicken out this time, like you probably have every other time. Maybe I'm not here to save you at all. You ever think about that?"

The girl looks at him, maybe disappointed or maybe just tired. It's hard to tell in the cold and the dark. For a while they just stand there, the two of them alone on the Champlain Bridge in the cold, wet, snowless December night.

"I'm guided by voices," Avery says sheepishly, his eyes studying the wet pavement at their feet. "Until you showed up, it all could've just been twenty-eight years of crazy."

"These voices—" she starts, then seems to lose the thought. He moves in a little closer, imagines how his hand might feel on her waist, how warm her breath might be against his neck. "I've seen you before," she says. "Not seen-seen. I don't think. But in a different way."

"I've been seeing you for as long as I can remember," Avery says. He searches for the right way to describe it. A whole life of living with the unspeakable – forget trans shit, this is unutterable. "You've been here, with me, for many years."

"So tell me how it ends," she says quietly, so quiet the words almost slip past him in the cool wind. "I've never seen how this ends. You've seen this before, you've got all the cards. Tell me. What happens? Do I jump? Or do I go home and come back next week? And the week after that. And the week after that."

The girl looks into Avery's eyes. She takes in the whole of him – the small, vertical line a life of constant consternation has cut above his untended right brow, his lips chapped and broken from anxiously biting them. And he returns her gaze, imprinting what might be the last of her – the way her scarf is too loose to protect her from the cold, how she stands almost imperceptibly slumped forward as if equally ashamed both of her height and her shame for it. For a moment, they really seem to see each other. The urgent pull of visions fades away, and this girl is just a girl to him. He wishes he could know her.

Avery wants to comfort her, to give her an answer that makes sense, to lay out a sequence of events that go from here to wherever they're supposed to end up. But there's nothing. He's never known anything. He opens his mouth, looks at her square in the eyes, but nothing comes out. Avery shrugs and looks away, guilt and shame weighing down his shoulders so he can hardly move them.

"Don't you care?!" she says, real emotion in her voice for the first time. "Don't you want me to live? You haven't even asked my name. You haven't even asked me why, why I'm out here, why it's not worth it anymore."

"All I know is I was supposed to meet you here," he says. He should care, he should know what to do to save her, he should be the man that can save this girl. But he shrinks at the task, curling himself around the same helplessness that ran through him as a child, unable to come between his father's anger and his mother's face. He squeezes his hands into a tight fist, so hard his short fingernails dig into his palm.

If he saves her, what then? Can you ever really save someone from themselves? He runs it through his head, a whole life returning here again and again, talking her back from the edge. Every week. What kind of life is that for him? What kind of life is that for her? Who is he to decide that she should keep living a life he knows nothing about?

And if he lets her go?

The visions always stop here. Will there be a new vision to drive him, or does his life become his own? Will Avery be a free man – no more voices and signs pushing him through every decision big or small? The thought sends a chill through him – freedom, absolute freedom, seems impossible and terrifying. A life without meaning or purpose. A life with no one to blame but himself for his failures.

"You don't care," she interrupts, her voice cold like the night.

"You think I haven't done this?" he says then. The words come out angry, tripping over each other. "You think we haven't all done this? What makes you so special? You're trans and you're sad – big fucking deal. Me too. But we keep going."

He's not sure if he's angry at her, or at the futility of trying to save her. Or if he's just angry that this is it – nearly thirty years leading up to this moment and she's just another depressed transsexual, like all of his friends, like everyone he knows. She could've been more. He could've been more, more than this half-frozen punk clenching his fists on a bridge, unable to make a decision, in the damp early hours of New Years.

A car passes by on the bridge. And then it's quiet for a while. Quiet between them.

"Well, I guess I oughta get this over with then," she says. The girl climbs up on the rail, shaky and awkward. The sharp wind blowing through her hair nearly knocks her back.

Avery turn around to watch. He takes one last look over the edge and whistles the sound of a falling bomb. He makes a big splash sound at the end. Then he looks up at her face. She's framed by pitch black night all around, not even a star. Only the motion of her dark hair whipping around to distinguish it from the sky.

She looks down at him. There's a pleading in her eyes. A call he doesn't know how to answer.

"Okay then," she says.

"Alright." He wants to reach out, to touch her, maybe even to pull her back. That invisible thread that's been dragging him along all these years, it ends. It ends in her.

"Okay."

And then,

Angels Are Here To Help You

JEANNE THORNTON

PART ONE.

1(A)

With the money she'd embezzled from her cat, Viola bought a mid-market warp drive kit and started to construct her spaceship.

The foldout instructions called for her to assemble a collider out of twelve arcs of plasteel, each piece labeled with hypersharpie: Part G, Section 04, etc. She didn't mind assembly—hands shaking, told herself she didn't mind—but the final collider hoop was going to add up to what, eight feet in diameter? She studied her shitty freelancer's apartment, looking for any hunk of floor space that might accommodate an eight-foot particle accelerator rig among the milk crates full of primers for foreign languages she hadn't gotten around to learning, hypercardboard boxes from three moves back, the gated area full of toys, litter boxes, and holoimagers owned by her cat Duncan's production company, Big Goof LLC (Duncan himself yowled at her for treats within), the big synthesizer she swore she needed to learn to play, the sewing machine with its needle still plunged into a halfway-completed muslin mockup of a summer skirt (it was winter), the shelves of preserves she'd laid up months back but suspected she'd fucked up on sealing and was now terrified would open in a spray of botulism death.

She tried canting the collider on its side against the synthesizer, which sort of worked, space-wise, but maybe put the part on the bottom under too much pressure during assembly, which could lead to a coolant leak and her asphyxiation in the cold vacuum of space. She tried to do yoga breathing, worried she was doing it incorrectly, and sat on the carpet beneath the canted ring, sloppy plaid skirt clashing with the clawmarked Persian rug, looking up at all the unbonded joints hanging loose and totally antiproton-permeable above her.

Give up, suggested her Helpful Angel, fluttering around her head.

1(B)

The Helpful Angel install had been a three-month anniversary gift from Viola's now ex-girlfriend, Thoth-Lorraine.

Thoth-Lorraine worked on a rolling contractual basis for a bunch of holography firms that fixed texturing errors in force-feedback UI systems, though her side hustle was designing apps at a couple hundred hyperdollars a pop. Someone else had designed the Helpful Angel app, but Thoth-Lorraine and some of her online followers had been the ones to jailbreak it. Normally, the Helpful Angel was the kind of install you'd buy for a Christian bookkeeper aunt—a sand-haired, porcelain-white cherub that read your emotions, mood-rock style, through your pulse and skin temperature, and that then offered you cheerful encouragement when you were in a good mood and even more cheerful encouragement when you weren't. The cool tech kids all had them too, got trashed on hyperwhiskey at parties and tried to make the bewildered little cupids dogfight while chirping out New Testament verses. Within a month, the inevitable mod community had sprung up, and Thoth-Lorraine and her buds hacked the SQL table and replaced it with Nietzsche quotes and Burzum lyrics in iffy translation.

Viola's jailbroken Helpful Angel was still a prototype, released before the complicated mood-detection algorithm stuff had been worked out, and mostly its depressive text data was placeholder. But the texture modding was first rate: Hummel-proportioned legs tricked out in fishnets and scarlet domme boots with red leather demon wings that erupted from just above the hemline of its plump corset, sick violet flames that flickered in the pupils of its wide, trusting eyes.

Viola had no idea how to uninstall the Helpful Angel from her visual cortex mod slot. She could invisible-mode it when she had to go to the bank or whatever, but it was only invisible externally: she could still see and hear it, circling her like a wasp. She thought every day about asking Thoth-Lorraine to please uninstall it, but she didn't like admitting to a tech person that she couldn't do it herself.

Secretly Viola thought Thoth-Lorraine and her whole Cool Tech Geek set were kind of shallow and tiresome and hateful. Maybe those words were unfair, she always told herself. But she'd been through enough bad hang-outs at tapas bars with good Yelp reviews, double enough bad game nights in some FPS server or Team Puzzler. They all had good apartments and health insurance, their estrogen nanobot implants never ran out, and their produce was all exotic asteroid hydroponic whatever.

They had money, so they had confidence. Viola found any show of confidence uncomfortable, like she was watching a pathological liar at work. How did these people feel that way? How had they formed a whole industry built around feeling that way?

There were exactly two activities Viola enjoyed with her girlfriend. One was going to the holo-puppetry performances Thoth-Lorraine put on monthly at the open mic place downtown. The stories were *zany* in a terrible way, insipid and pop-referential, sure, Viola thought. But Thoth-Lorraine really was excellent at holography design, and Viola loved to watch her disappear on stage into each character, however shallow Viola privately thought those characters might have been. Thoth-Lorraine took her puppetry seriously; she was vulnerable about it, always asked Viola after every show if the performance had gone okay without really asking her. (—That asshole who cut across the stage to pee halfway through!, she'd say, —It really took everyone out of it. —No, everyone was with you, Viola would say quietly, wondering why Thoth-Lorraine couldn't just be like, *I'm sad about this*, and Viola could tell her that everything and everyone was always sad.)

The other activity they both enjoyed was sex. This mostly happened online. Viola wasn't totally cool with this—like she did kind of enjoy in-person sex and didn't totally Hate Her Genitals as you were maybe supposed to, thought of them more as a corny uncle or something, the one you never look forward to seeing but who can still make you laugh in spite of yourself —but Thoth-Lorraine was always really anxious and out of it when naked IRL, talking a lot and not meeting eyes and just kind of unglued in a way

Viola was never sure how to assist her in re-gluing. Suppose she made it worse if she tried.

Viola never totally got Thoth-Lorraine's weirdness about her body because she and her tech pals were much more advanced trans women than Viola. Viola, shamefully, was still registered with SoftPackr, the terrible app for fresh-from-egg trans people who wanted to meet other trans people. The app was not what Thoth-Lorraine called a Good Hack: it worked by registering your avatar in a government database of trans people, so you were basically *trans forever* once you used it, doomed to have the app bleat at you whenever another SoftPackr user approached. It was mostly now used by masc guys and women into them. Thoth-Lorraine had told Viola many, many times how to get her SoftPackr registration out of the government database, but the command line stuff involved intimidated Viola. And being on SoftPackr was the very lowest level of trans you could be: experimental genehack firms were dumping beta phys-modding products on the market through every backchannel their executives could devise. Thoth-Lorraine's labmate, with whom she DJed and did a really funny Twitch livestream show, had a guiding laser installed in her clit plus dual-boot uterine transplants stocked with buccal mood cells and a FitBit. Thoth-Lorraine was more vanilla, but still fabulous.

How did tech people even know that mods like this were available? Viola tried reading the same holoblogs and mailing lists as them, but always found them tedious and gave up. Any thought she had of installing dysphoria-easing devices into herself reminded her of a day she'd spent weeping while she tried to get a wireless 3D printer to talk to an old haptic laptop before giving up and calling tech support, resulting in a bunch of annoying corporate app installs at the borders of her vision and bills it had taken her six months to pay. The more intentional decisions she made about her own body, the more specialists, doctors, device support systems, and maintenance/upgrade cycles she'd had to synchronize her life with. Tight underwear and estrogen-delivery nanobots were about all she could bear responsibility for. Basically, she could tend to her body by spending a bunch of money on tech, or she could tend to her anxiety for free. One choice seemed healthier.

But vis-à-vis sex: Thoth-Lorraine, though modded, still tended to check out IRL more often than not. So they mostly just did it via witch-adventures roleplay stuff on a private server. Which Viola guessed was fine

—she liked seeing Thoth-Lorraine's avatar clad in busty plate mail bikini and wide-hipped in Perfect Cis Simulacrum, all fending off the lightning bolts and acid arrows Viola's Sex Necromancer avatar flung at her as she rushed closer with the Manacles of Soul-Bondage +4. Plus she could mute the volume whenever Thoth-Lorraine tried out dialogue. But in a way it was everything that bugged Viola about tech: too confident, too easy a solution. Whenever they had witch cybersex, she spent at least an hour after they signed off lying on the floor, wondering whether Thoth-Lorraine was at her apartment, doing the same thing, unable to speak about it later. Or maybe she had an app she could speak about her sad feelings about her body to. That would be a more efficient solution, Viola guessed.

At first, in their relationship, she'd talked to Thoth-Lorraine about what Viola felt stupid about calling *her depression*. But it seemed to make Thoth-Lorraine sad, so she didn't talk about it as much now, which she guessed was progress.

Thoth-Lorraine had originally pursued Viola to get closer to her cat. Viola knew that.

Viola's cat, Duncan, was mid-level famous. He wasn't a superstar as cats went—like he was no Calico Starbuck or Black Dimitri or _cat5_, cats you recognized from hit multiplex holomovies. Viola knew, rationally, that she and Thoth-Lorraine had stayed together probably for reasons that had more to do with Viola personally. But her insecurities about her cat were deep, their roots carefully and complexly woven into the soil of her being to the point where it wasn't certain whether the insecurity was feeding on Viola or whether that insecurity was the only structure keeping her personality from wilting away (as she feared it might be, five tall glasses of tea into a freakout.)

Duncan was mostly famous as an advice columnist. It was an early experiment in animal holography that Viola's cis high school pal, Jana, had convinced her to undertake while they were undergrad suitemates. Conventional wisdom held that the only propositional ideas cats could communicate through body language were *back off* or *give me food* or *I am content and stretching*. But Jana proved conventional wisdom totally wrong via her technique: (1) convert natural language strings into emotional primaries, (2) cause them to manifest on an extremely well-rigged holographic avatar of a cat, (3) allow a Legit Cat to react to the Hologram Cat and record its physical responses (stance, head orientation, blink rate) via fractal motion capture, and (4) convert the resulting shades of emotion back into text chains. For example, a certain kind of yawn might convert to *content/sated/follow your bliss*, a warning paw extended into your space might be *foreboding/alarm/ time of great change for you.*

Granted, the technique was only as good as the translation algorithm, so any advice you happened to elicit from a cat in this way was about as accurate as you'd get from an aspirant yarrowstalk caster: really you were talking to yourself. But who cared? It was *so awesome* to use holograms to talk to a cat, especially one as affable and holophotogenic as Duncan: twenty pounds, pink ears and green eyes (watermelon combo) on cream white tabby backdrop with legit spitcurls and a winning meow. After a week of playing with the technology, Jana set up an app that let visitors submit questions to Duncan about situations that were going wrong in their lives, to which he'd give encouraging answers. The website was set up using student hosting, and by the second week, their bandwidth invoices from the university were so high that Jana had to contract Duncan out to a VC company.

Initially, Viola had been the one to do the heavy lifting of glossing Duncan's gnomic emotional primaries into human grammar, *nudge/mark/ yowl* into *Right now, your moon is in Pisces, which means it's time to shore up new business connections!* She was an equal partner in the whole thing, she liked to think. And she enjoyed the work—it was so stupid, frankly, that she never worried about it—added little flourishes and quotations when she felt them appropriate, urge people to take actions that she'd never feel comfortable taking herself. She liked to think about it when walking to class or changing hyperbuses, their neon ad panels lapse dissolving in alpha rhythms. Anyone she saw could maybe be someone in trouble, someone with an abusive partner or crippling debt anxiety or a dire sexual secret, someone who shook alone in the three a.m. LED glow of their alarms, someone who gratefully sought out her cat for relief. Her cat connected her to people. She could do things and nothing bad would happen.

It was nice right up to the moment when Duncan's management team at Big Goof Entertainment LLC fired her from the writing job. Big Goof controlled everything, had used careful VC investments to slowly acquire title to the website, promotional accounts, personal appearance rights, etc. in the year or so since the Advice From a Huge Cat website had first gone viral. As severance, they contracted to pay dividends on Duncan's new personal wealth as a stipend to Viola in exchange for providing the talent with shelter, fish treats, and love. Alternatively, they suggested, she could sell all rights and title to him, as well as all derived intellectual properties, in exchange for a lump sum and modest stock options.

She kept Duncan, less out of affection—by this point he had gotten kind of Hollywood—than spite. The management team wanted title to her cat? No, she would *keep* her cat.

She had never told Thoth-Lorraine, or anyone, that her cat's business partners had fired her. She never outright lied about this, just implied that the cat stuff had been distracting her from her other projects. The stipend was mostly enough to pay her rent, and she was able to hustle up the difference in good months—months when she could get out of bed at least 40 percent of freelance-hustle days—or borrow it from Thoth-Lorraine otherwise.

You know, you're smart, Thoth-Lorraine told her once. —If you need money, you could *totally* work in tech. I mean you and your friend made that website, right? I could train you, and there's always entry-level stuff available.

The idea of starting on the lowest rung of the ladder that Thoth-Lorraine had climbed didn't bother Viola so much as the idea that in the end, all roads had to lead to tech, that any other path she might choose to pursue was unachievable, or at least unachievable by her. Only tech would give you what you needed to survive—the monoculture, the Done Thing. It made her sick.

Yeah I'll put together a portfolio, she said.

She thought about that now, as she sat on the floor of her apartment, busted warp drive ring propped against the door, blowing furiously into the air nozzle of the inflatable gangway connector of her spaceship kit's habitat module, cheeks red and hair sweat-welded to her forehead: she should be photographing this. The photos could be her portfolio.

In the next room, Duncan was on his back, biting a kick toy and changing the life of a delighted petitioner. Viola breathed into the nozzle; she fucked up the rhythm; the nozzle breathed her own dead air back into her mouth.

1(c)

Thoth-Lorraine was the one who'd turned Viola onto Spoor. Spoor—which was chemically very close to wheat bread in a way that was unexpected for a Cool Alien Drug—came folded up in little pouches of hyper-aluminum foil, a magenta resin still sticky despite the dessication process necessary for interstellar transit. Thoth-Lorraine, who'd already babysat a pair of friends through a Spoor trip, measured out the resin and primed the SCUBA equipment while Viola filled the bathtub to the line Thoth had marked in lipstick on the porcelain. They took turns applying the packets of rhino slime to one another's shoulders, which would help the resin absorb into their skin, according to Erowid forums.

Are we doing this naked, she asked hopefully. —We can, said Thoth-Lorraine. —I mean, we did, my first trip. But in a way it was kind of distracting. It's harder to get into vegspace. That's what the high is called. Vegspace.

Viola hated subculture facts. —Oh rad, she said.

I mean if you want, go wild, Thoth-Lorraine shrugged.

And she sort of got why going naked was a bad idea once she and Thoth-Lorraine had strapped their respirator hoses into their mouths, fat oxygen tanks each with a three-hour supply propped up against the toilet tank, and plunged their heads and shoulders into the iced-down water, her back arching painfully over the tub rim, ass bone crushing into diamond, Viola's genitals crabwalking out.

Yet beneath the water—her hair and her girlfriend's hair meeting like twining snakes in the fuschia cool of dissolved resin, trying to stay calm with her head and lungs inverted, to breathe as normally as she could through the hyperalloy tube invading her lips and the resin invading her ear canals, her brain steeping in it—she realized how badly sex missed the point of intimacy.

How would she describe the experience of taking Spoor to someone who'd never done it? *Imagine you're sitting in the back patio of a crowded hypercafe, thinking about bills or tax reforms or girl drama. You look up and catch sight of a friend across the way, also caught up in bummer things. She doesn't see you the first time you look up, and then you look up again. You smile, some. She smiles, some. And then a recursive reciprocal action begins: she smiles wider, so you smile wider and activate her smile, and soon you're laughing and sad at once, laugh where she cries, cry where she laughs, all other café patrons vanished, all space between you vanished, all barriers down like brains floating in the same jar, every thought you think rippling the fuschia waters and transmitting the ripples to her.*

Both of you translucent; there is no both of you.

When enough Spoor has absorbed into the blood-brain barrier, diluting the water to a pale rose, first you, Viola, then you, Thoth-Lorraine, wake up. Viola, you see her eyes blinking across the bathtub; Viola sees Thoth-Lorraine's eyes, the respirator in her girlfriend's mouth, the black rubber taste of it in her own. She saw them as separate. Together, on three, they rose out of the tub, spitting the tubes out in rising, or in Viola's case, in trying to rise and then slipping, falling back in, rattling her sacrum and splashing pink across the tiles.

She guessed it was residual empathy from the Spoor that made Thoth-Lorraine wince for a moment before she broke down and started to cry.

It was fascinating to watch, she thought, in the portion of her mind that wasn't itself crying in frustration in the tub, or with the portion still mired in comedown empathy and identification. It was abstractly fascinating to watch Thoth-Lorraine cry; she never did, even in the most intense fights. Her voice just got soft, withdrawn and aggrieved around the edges, like a middle school teacher at seventh period. To see her out of control for a moment was like seeing an eclipse. It made Viola feel at ease, in awe.

You hate me, Thoth-Lorraine was saying. —You've always hated me. Why would you even date me if you're afraid of me like that?

I dunno, Viola said, numbly. Their submerged psychic connection was fading, and she still couldn't process all of the reasons she'd learned that Thoth-Lorraine had been dating her: the image Thoth-Lorraine had of her, someone serious and shining, covered in thick, wide cracks. Of someone sick, of someone who this tech maven wanted very much to see become better. *To help unlock human potential,* Viola thought. —Why does anyone date anyone?

Her girlfriend cried, and Viola looked into the surface of the water, its rosy volume swirling with flakes of dead skin she and her girlfriend had shared. And she realized: *I could sell this alien empathy drug so hard.*

1(D)

In the void left by the breakup, Viola read a bunch of anthropology and pop science papers on the initial contact with the planet Undine, mostly written in the heady period after the cosmonauts and imagineers involved in early planet exploration realized the masses of floating broadleafed root plants covering every ocean on Undine were not only plants but sentient animals, or something in between.

She studied the same crisp hyperPhone video clips that had passed around social networks, eventually gathering crude satiric captions in Impact like barnacles:

In the shallows, warmed by Undine's twin baby suns, a laughing scientist in a wet suit treads water before something like a cross between a paper lantern and a floating bonsai tree. The scientists have allowed the rest of the colony of Undini to drift further away, taking their thick fuschia clouds of Spoor with them; only this single creature remains. Just below the surface, the shadow of its single fat taproot is just visible; the pink miso clouds around it slowly dissipate.

And then the plant begins to move—its leaves droop, slough off; its root uncurls into a broad otter's tail, the flippers it keeps hugged tightly about its body during its sleep unfurl. Its planarian eyespots open, wink. And with a sudden twist and chirp, it dives into the water, chasing the dispersing patches of Spoor around it like a dreamer mid snooze button cycle. Finally it wakes fully, blinks at the camera, squirms away beneath the surface to chase its departing city.

Surprise: the only other intelligent life in the universe besides humanity looks like adorable space otters. Everyone squeals, likes, shares.

After many such experiments, the scientists figured they had a reasonable description of the Undini life cycle, thus:

1) To swim the endless oceans of Undine, burning lipid energy, until they found clouds of Spoor excreted by other Undini,
2) On finding them, to fall asleep,
3) Sleeping, to sprout,
4) To draw energy from the sun through the leaves they sprouted,
5) To transform that energy into bulging, sugary storehouses of protein, and
6) To produce two wastes: Spoor, and dreams.

7) Through the exposed axon bulbs concealed like cloacae at the base of their taproots/tails, to pass those dreams via electrical impulse to other nearby Undini.

In other words: the planet was a gigantic, oceanic brain. Only instead of neurons, it had adorable space otters who shared spooky psychic visions with one another.

Humans, lacking huge, exposed access nervous system ports in their butts, could never really understand the Undini Dream. This was the opinion of the human scientists who'd studied the nuts and bolts of it in terms of electrical potential, myelin, neurotransmission. It was miraculous that the first scientist who freaked out from an overdose of Spoor (brought on by a seemed-rad-at-the-time amphibious/romantic interlude with another member of the landing party in the middle of a highly populous vernal reef) was able to realize that there might be a good, smoking-gun reason she'd hallucinated furious aquatic beasts mid-climax.

As humans actually experienced it—for example, Viola and Thoth-Lorraine, heads upside down in the bathtub with their hair interlocking—the Undini dream manifested as a kind of empathy-on-crack. The Undini experience—insofar as lexographers and registered literary critics could make sense of the allegorical imagery the Undini poet-shamans patiently tried to beam into the thoughts of the invading scientists and space tourists—was a lot more like a shared lucid dream. Undini society, lacking scarcity (the only things necessary for life were sunlight and the shit of other Undini), was pretty much anarchy, and the most psychically sensitive of the Undini, the poet-shamans, occupied the positions of greatest social power and influence by their capacity to direct people through their occult visions. The Undini cities—less stable municipalities, more functions of axial tilt, current, and NPK ratio per inch of water—were hotbeds of shared dreaming, metaphysical speculation, counterfactual history, and elaborate puns involving water pressure and smell.

In other words: conversation with any given Undini was not only one-sided but boring. It was like listening to an Aleister Crowley audiobook about sacred geometry. This, plus the goody-goody regulations that governed contact between cultures and the fact that there was nothing of (initially) obvious value on Undine, explained why the thrill of First Contact had quickly modulated into excitement about how the next alien contact would totally be better than this one, now that there was proof of concept.

Earth slapped a "wildlife refuge" designation on Undine to protect it from immediate capitalist exploitation, and people crowdsourced expeditions in search of better species, ones with maybe awesomer, deadlier technology for us to buy. Only a few hundred thousand or so people still cared much about Undine—i.e., nothing, percentagewise, and most of them academics or isolated teenagers or sensitive twentysomethings who were already planning their holo-zines of Undini *symbol-poetry* in dubious translation.

This was before everyone realized that Spoor could get you fucked up.

Not many people outside of Thoth-Lorraine's early adopter circle knew that yet. Viola was sure of it.

When you see an opportunity, Viola knew, you go for it. Even if it seems like a bad idea; especially if it seems like a bad idea. That was the secret behind tech, she knew: indifference to result. Failure was inevitable, but it was just like that ancient Tracy Chapman song said: if you drove fast enough, you could outrun failure. If you failed enough, soon you would succeed.

That was how winners thought. That was how Thoth-Lorraine thought. If their breakup was to have any meaning, it was time for Viola to win.

I'm going to *win*, she said aloud to the fucked up spaceship she had built in her apartment.

Only her Helpful Angel replied: —No one wins.

PART ZERO.

Viola had always wanted to join Starfleet. She had even tried once, in her late teens, shortly after warp drive had been made affordable for middle-class kids.

She found out about Real Starfleet from comments on an old SF review site she haunted at the time. Some kids had written to Paramount for the content license, and they were building the whole thing from scratch, all primary color uniforms and red stripes down the corridors. The kids' web holoportal had lots of text, plus reasonable spreadsheets and slideshows that detailed just how the fleet would organize itself, establish an academy to train recruits, promote worthy captains and lieutenants, and finally commission, construct, and launch vessels on a series of five-year missions to distant stellar clusters. They had a donation bar shaped like a thermometer and a promotional quote taken from a feature on Local Nonprofits.

The night she discovered the site, Viola stayed up until sunrise, chatting key lines to Jana (who responded HOLY SHIT CAN'T DEAL to like sixty percent of it.) That weekend, she and Jana got trashed on cough medicine to build up their courage and took the hyperbus, giggling and speculating and making the other passengers turn up the noise-cancelling static on their avatars' ear slot apps. Every building they saw was the Last Time They'd Ever See That Building, every shitty chain restaurant's sign the Last Time They'd Ever Order Those Fries. Finally the wriggling dread that each of them felt (that Viola speculated each of them felt) would relax, fill in with the warm cement of purpose in the Poetic Void Beyond.

H-hi, Jana giggled when they arrived at the recruiting station, Viola standing just beyond her shoulder, to which she would have clung if she wasn't terrified of all human touch. —We're here to enlist in Starfleet!

The recruiting officer looked up; above the trim two-pip uniform collar bordered in crisp red he was a kid, junk food fleshy with a buzz cut and teenage pubic mustache. He was no older than they were. He straightened, stood in a confident Rikerish kind of pose.

You've come to the right place, he said.

He began to explain the overall mission, the obligations of service, the eventual career advantages a spell in Starfleet would bring someone, etc., and how coincidentally a group of them were getting together just that very evening to talk about purchasing warp coil components and assigning research groups to go over the engine assembly procedure in order to report it out the following week, all while Viola and Jana watched, smiles dimming and frequency of giggles decreasing, beginning to sway on their feet as reality made a perpetual Hell Zoom in and out around them. The recruiter maybe didn't notice, preoccupied with them being women with an interest in joining Starfleet—or anyway preoccupied with Jana being that, since she was the fancy cis one with good bone structure or whatever, as opposed to Viola, the weird clunky trans one with bad skin and weird boots and stringy hair, whom the recruiter probably figured should be welcome in Starfleet anyway (IDIC and all), but who'd inevitably be assigned to some cruddy junior astrophysics position while Jana and the recruiter became cool captains and got possessed by anaphasic lifeforms and fucked sometimes. Totally this asshole was thinking all that, Viola knew. The floor was becoming abstract expressionist.

Let's, Viola began. —Bail, she concluded.

Jana nodded, looking sick. —Can we—take these applications home to fill out later, she said. —We, we really would like to join your Starfleet club.

The recruiter's face flickered in expected pain. —Sure, he said. —Not exactly *boldly going*. But sure, take your time.

The worst part of the hyperbus ride home—aside from the horrible feeling of sinuses filling with smoke and menthol and lava that you could never ever ever cough out again—was the certainty, upon seeing the bus take what seemed like ten years to turn off of the main channel and into the tiny tributary that serviced the shuttles to Jana and Viola's houses, the same old posters and textbooks and bedspreads and albums and clothes waiting in their bedrooms to receive them—that Viola had never seriously expected any other outcome. The possibility that she'd have to leave any of her life behind had never once seemed real. The mission had been something to fantasize about in order to fill up a teenage evening. Hadn't it been that?

She and Jana didn't speak on the whole final approach to the station, the bus's gravitators flattening the dandelions that sprouted around the edges of the plasteel landing pad, scattering their spores.

Starfleet broke up not long after. No ships were ever constructed, and Paramount reclaimed the license to use on some kind of new holo-series that never got funded. Some of the organizers vowed to continue the five-year mission under a new Creative Commons name, but without recognizable IP, who even cared?

Jana had dropped out of college after creating Duncan's website and giving Viola her only income. These days she was heading some alternative school movement in Fiji probably, raising her two natural-born kids and cultivating nanomachine cheeses. Or Viola guessed; they hadn't actually spoken in years.

LAST PART.

3(A)

Viola perched high in orbit above the planet Undine, the metal plates of her ship's habitat rings and cells of her solar sails pitted, cracked, peeling from the Incident just days before, her busted nose just able again to taste the methane tang of her spaceship's recycled air. In the cockpit module at the ship's core, her eyes locked on the haptic screen twelve inches front of her eyes like a monocular Viewmaster, she pulled up archival images, holoprojections, fan art of Undine from hyperTumblr. Even the most inept MS Paint kids drew cartoon concentrations of fuschia within the planet's watery blue, pink spirals in rough correspondence with the tides. Yet as she entered the landing codes and brought her craft closer and closer to Undine, the approaching world presented itself as an eerily monochrome blue beneath its swirl of clouds. Two wide red spots floated somewhere in what she guessed to be the Southern Hemisphere like vampire's punctures.

Keying in, for reference, the coordinates of the rudimentary gravity elevator the early researchers had set up, she set Duncan's cage on her lap —he growled, sticking first nose and then butt fur through its bars at her— decoupled from her cargo sphere and propulsion system, and dropped into the atmosphere, aiming for the rosy wounds, humming ancient Lana del Rey tracks as she dropped—life imitates art—cirronimbus streaks of dark vapor slapping the heatshield tiles and vanishing.

The rosy spaces, seen from a mere thousand feet up, turned out to be rectangular pens like tilapia pools, a thin polarized line of virtual fence that divided pink from blue. It took her a moment to realize that the floating green bushels that filled each pen, steeped in rich fuschia Spoor, were living—alien!—creatures, the ones she'd come to make a deal with. The Undini were taller than any she'd seen, deep in dreams, swaying in the extraterrestrial wind.

So why were they in steel pens? Why was the Spoor-water surrounding them thick, glutinous, yeasty? These are the questions it occurred to Viola to ask just before the swarm of violet-eyed interceptor drones threw a graviton net around her and dragged her craft into the water.

3(B)

The corporate compound itself was modest, halfway between a lighthouse and a water tower, floating on wide helium cushions like a hovercraft. The shuttle garage that floated nearby had its own rough gravity elevator, two shuttles parked in it, each with a gloriously stenciled logo: Big Goof Entertainment LLC. Numbly, Viola sat in the outer reception room and watched the garage bob, mug of stale rehydrated jasmine tea in her hand. Duncan, freshly brushed and perfumed after his passage through decontamination, yowled in contentment. Her Helpful Angel, in her ear, told her she should hurt herself. The tea, as inhaled through the shattered cartilage and blood of her slowly healing broken nose, was nearly tasteless, but at least it was warm.

The person who she guessed was the sole occupant of the lighthouse—anyway the only one who'd met her when the drones had dragged her and her cat in from the ocean—was dressed casually for someone whom she guessed was technically engaged in space piracy: hyperdenim shorts and ball cap with the Big Goof logo on it, expression at once nervous and eager. When the drones escorted her in from the decon chamber to meet him, both of their phones started bleating.

Ha ha ha ha ha, he'd laughed, very evenly. —App jinx!

He'd introduced himself as Sebastian and explained that he had to confiscate her cat.

I mean technically I'm granting him refugee status, he explained. —Since he's a wealthy holovid star under contract to Big Goof whom you abducted after cleaning out his bank account to come to a restricted world.

I am a serious businesswoman, Viola said, suddenly imagining the entire lighthouse disassembling itself rivet by rivet under her feet, herself plunging after it, perhaps to the planet's molten core, perhaps to somewhere even lower. —I'm creating a wagon train to the stars.

Sebastian let this pass. —What exactly were you doing on this planet? he asked. —You're not one of those lefty alien poetry people, right? No offense! You just kinda look like one! Calling it like I see it here!

Viola inhaled. —I was coming here—with a lot of bread, I mean like, wheat—to try to—

Cutting her off, Sebastian swung his fist through the air in front of her; she stepped back.

That was the punch, he explained. —We beat you to it. Ha ha ha ha ha! —He threw up his hand as if to ward off a slap.

3(c)

She let him take her on a shuttle tour of the production facilities, showed her the different grain mixes they'd found to produce an optimal state of Undini narcosis, the bubbly storage tanks of Spoor ready to be winched to the gravity elevator for export to Earth's moon, where the empty bottling and packaging facilities sat waiting to receive. He showed her the vast forests of Undini, their evenly distributed stalks bound with zipties, a carpet of gray wilted leaves floating like cigarette cinder lilies over the pink.

Sometimes they overfeed, Sebastian said, shrugging. —It's sad. We're trying to optimize it out.

Isn't this all really illegal, Viola said, with respect and envy.

Sebastian turned to her; his lips still smiled; his brow scrunched in weary irritation.

Facts on the ground, he said. —I mean ha ha, no offense, but you can't be that naïve. Someone's going to break the law to make money until the law recognizes how much more money it could be making and changes itself. Think of it as civil disobedience.

Or colonialism, Viola suggested.

Uh huh, said Sebastian, wince ridge deepening. —Sure. Uh huh. Except don't give me that bullshit. I mean, ha ha, no offense, but you were coming to do the exact same thing as me. Maybe you thought you were better because you've read some Tumblr kids whining about the poor otters, or you know, some debatable historical parallel or something. It's not like they're *unhappy*. Their whole life is spent swimming around, looking to connect with one another, and look, now they don't have to do that anymore.

He stopped talking. Again he laughed, very evenly, and then he got quiet. —I mean, you understand that this isn't colonialism, he said. — That's important to me. It's important not to focus on the negative when you're trying to build something.

Her rib cage flooded out at the bottom, a kind of despair overcoming her: and despair, unlike anxiety, sometimes has a bottom to it. It is soporific, grounding. It's the lamp that the moth, given its druthers, moves to instead of the darkness. She was familiar with that.

It was important, she knew, that she have the moral high ground here over Sebastian. But she pictured an Undini in her mind: a hoary one, trunk whorled and eyespots wizened, or no, maybe a young one: taproot slim, meat leaves seductively curled at their tips. What she pictured, when she pictured other lives, was fan art. Did she actually, at bottom, care about the fate of these individual beings who she guessed were now technically enslaved? Every time she felt like she found something that seemed like caring, she looked at it closely, and it fell apart. (Every time she thought of Thoth-Lorraine's picture of her, that fell apart too, the baby breaking up along its fault lines.) She was silent, turning these questions around for so long that Sebastian finally took out his phone and started texting through subspace, and she guessed that the moment had been lost. The questions must have been settled.

You're a horrible piece of shit, she finally said.

Don't apologize, he said brightly and immediately, not looking up from his phone. —You didn't do anything wrong. I mean, nothing you can't recover from, probably.

She checked into his avatar; he had a lot of apps, many of them glowing with an early-adopter halo. An alien sun, she realized, will warm you just as little as your own.

You're confiscating my cat, Viola finally said. —Do I get to just like —go back to Earth, then? I don't want to be in space anymore. She cleared her throat. —My girlfriend is on Earth, she explained. —She does puppetry.

Sebastian looked up. —I'm not sure, he said. —Gee, I'm probably legally obligated to hold you here until the authorities can extradite you. You're welcome to stay, you know! It'd be nice to have someone here to talk to.

He snapped his fingers and drew a hypertablet from the glove box of the flyer. —Just fill this out and we'll let you know our decision within a week, he said supportively.

3(D)

Back at the lighthouse, she took Duncan—a tracking collar secured around his neck, his name spelled out on it in rhinestones—and checked out a rowboat from the vehicle register. With great effort, she rowed herself and her cat out to one of the Undini pens, its bowling ball gluten tanks feeding their silent excretory dream cycle, Duncan lowing and the boat swaying against the roots of dreaming, ziptied alien beings that bumped her hull and drifted along. She leaned back—felt leaflights of shade and sun move over her neck and chest and forehead, let her Doc Martens steep in the pools of collected water—and worked on filling out the job application.

What do you consider your greatest strength as an employee? What do you consider your greatest weakness?

Know when to quit, whispered her Helpful Angel, flitting about her shoulders beneath the sound of the wind.

3(E)

After a long time, she set the job application down. She looked into the water, tried to remember everything she knew about its chemical contents.

Her Docs weighed her down; she untied them, shucked her socks, and let them drop into the darkness far below sight. *The first litter on an alien world;* hers. They'd remain down there for generations; poison dyes siphoning off the vegan leather, taking up great polluted clouds of space whether she decided to stay or not.

She lay down on the water outside the boat, let it bear her up.

I'm a winner, she said to the sky. —I've won.

Part Two.

The night before she launched, Viola didn't sleep. She knew it was going to be important to attend to details once she was up—when traveling astronomical distances, fractions of decimals in a 3D radian could send you hurtling into some zero galaxy beyond—but she couldn't lose consciousness. She thought, inexplicably, of Jana, how old her hypothetical babies might be now.

She packed Duncan's camera setup and put him in his cage, all the while looking through the Venetian hyperblinds to make sure no one had stolen the pilot module and warp intermix ring she'd left bike locked in a corner of her apartment parking lot. She packed a bikini, three skirts and blouses, underwear, and toiletries in a backpack with some trail mix and a bar of astronaut ice cream she'd saved since childhood, and she hitched the module to a rusty boat trailer she'd bought on Craigslist while Duncan screamed.

At every exit vector on the highway, her spaceship rattling and jouncing unpromisingly on the trailer hitch behind her, she told herself: *you can stop this any time you want. Think this over. You are doing something unsafe and wrong.*

Give up, whispered her Helpful Angel, and Viola gripped the wheel and tried to disassociate, to make it through.

Successfully checked out, heart beating somewhere beneath dirty ice, she presented her launch passport (still with the wrong gender marker on it) to the bored spaceport security dude, gave appropriate and bogus answers about her destination and cargo, went through the body scanner and the patdown, watched as the kids working on the hangar floor hitched on her rented solar sails, centripetal habitat rings, and hyperrubber storage balloon full of stale bread bought in bulk from the registered advocacy group who brokered trade at the Costco dumpster. At T-minus-120, cat carrier in her hand, she crossed the tarmac to her spaceship, waiting for her in the gravity elevator. Slowly the hydraulics drew her up—the first jolt, even cushioned as she was in the capsule with her feet on the pedals, eyes and fingers on the haptic viewscreen, cat on her pelvis and shivering. *Now I have to fall ten feet to reach the surface. Now I have to fall twenty, fifty, a hundred, a thousand*—and the atmosphere got thinner, thinner, darker, gone; her spaceship perched like a gargoyle atop the tower.

You're going to die up here, said her Helpful Angel. —You will have killed yourself.

And then the mass accelerators hummed—her cat cried—and with a lurch and a momentary jolt, she was floating free, lifting against her straps, only her thrusters between her and infinite dark.

She touched the haptic screen; somewhere behind her, an impulse driver went off, and she spun just as she had desired to spin, Earth's circumference circling the viewscreen slowly like the greatest revolving restaurant; she touched the screen and she rotated back in the other direction. In the sky all around her were other spaceships with other people just like her, everyone bound somewhere.

Alone, she started to cry for a long time, stars moving, cat whimpering, Helpful Angel saying things to her she tried not to hear.

The solar sail took some time to charge up the ship systems for warp, so she set it to autoengage her on a course for Undine, started the artificial gravity in the habitat rings, and went to settle in. The rings came standard with built-in camp shower, revolving closets, and daybed; she set up Duncan's litter box and plugged in her old SNES emulator to run through some *Super Mystic Knights III* while eating her astronaut ice cream. After a while, she found it hard to keep her eyes open through the repetitive battles, and she lay down on the daybed and wondered whether masturbating in centripetal gravity would feel any different.

Thoth-Lorraine would have been more careful about this, she thought. Thoth-Lorraine wouldn't have had the courage to come out here. Everything's going to fail, anyway—if you don't accept that and try to do things anyway, what in life do you end up accomplishing? Thoth-Lorraine didn't understand that. She expected things to go well for her. Like a *coward*, Viola thought.

She fell asleep with her underwear still on.

She woke up to red alarm lights and the digitized sounds of a gentle Australian-accented cis woman's voice telling her that she and her cat were about to die.

Out the window, the stars streaked past in warp rainbows. Everything looked distorted around the edges—the haptic screen displaying her emulated RPG a storm of static—molecules of her astronaut ice cream wrapper crushed into liquid that slid over the concave linoleum of the habitat ring. And she felt weird when she stood up, like one instant she was in a moon bounce, the next instant she and her bones, straining against themselves, might crack and join the trade goods melting all over the floor. From the direction of Duncan's holographic enclosure, there was only silence.

The first action she took was to do nothing. She sat on the daybed, skull squeezing and flexing. *The warp drive I built failed. The warp bubble is going to become more and more unstable until everything tears into pieces.* She thought about how she was going to die in space. Should she really have expected anything different?

When had she begun to feel this way?

After a moment—the thought crashing through her like a runaway train, its last car uncoupled, too terrible for any connection—she swung her fist at her face, and the rapidly changing pressure and mass relationships within her shoddy warp bubble made her screw that up too, and she felt her nose break.

She sat on the linoleum, trying to breathe through the nets of blood and mucus, thinking about how far away the airlock might be.

When she was a kid, Viola loved Transformers. One of her favorites could turn into a lion, a boat, an eagle, a standard affable masc robot, etc. She would sit for hours on the hypercarpet of her bedroom, mutating the toy into different forms, turning it in her hands to look at it from all angles, frozen between two states, imagining what it might say to her, what people said to one another. She never brought out her toys on the infrequent occasions when friends were over, feeling private about them. She never spoke out loud when she played.

How did one cheap hyperplastic toy take six forms? Thoth-Lorraine and her friends could probably explain it down to the last detail. But Viola knew it depended, somehow, on one screw. She knew this because one day she managed to dislodge this screw, lost it within the body of the toy itself midway between mutations. She could hear it rattle when she tried to shift from lion to boat, the parts clicking and failing to join.

She'd set it on the carpet, panic rising, alone. Just as it never occurred to her to speak while she was playing, it never occurred to her to ask anyone for help. Who could she trust to ask? All she could think was: she'd fucked it up. Her favorite toy; she'd fucked it up and broken it. It was gone. In panic, she turned it in her hands—upside down, rightside up, the screw rattling within.

There was no one she could trust but herself, and she couldn't trust herself.

This is what she thought with her conscious mind—useless, unreliable, hopeless, and she wished she could cry about it without something in her brain throttling her tears. While with some other part of her mind, some eerie still place, she turned the toy, listened to the screw inside click, the changes in its pitch corresponding to some imagined inner architecture of plastic, guiding the screw steadily through, letting it fall back to where it had started—failure, breathe—starting again. And suddenly here it was, silver and bright stud on the carpet.

The sphere of distortion around the hammer thinned Viola's muscle to the diameter of a straw when she reached in, and the effort of lifting the wooden handle nearly pitched her forward. *Concentrate*, she told herself; she focused; pitched forward, waited, teeth biting her lip, until the unstable bubble fluxed and the hammer swung wildly behind her, pitched her back. Duncan cried, his meow misshapen across the lips of folded space. Holding the hammer tight in one fist, Viola gripped the ladder that radiated up to the spoke of the habitat ring. As the walls buckled, rungs twisted, meows warped around her, she let her feet lift her one Doc Marten at a time toward the airlock.

By some miracle, the hyperglass of the pressuresuit stashed at the join between the cockpit and the spoke was intact. She strapped it onto herself in zero-g, felt the crush on her tucked crotch as the suit depressurized, forced herself to forget it.

Outside the airlock, there was only cold and dark, beyond the gravity of any sun: just the inflatable walls of the ship, reflected dimly in her suit's headlight and by faint bug-zapper smears of galaxies too far away to swim to. The glass might crack. Or space might warp and snap her neck. Or the bubble might flux again, slip her out of her comfortable envelope of relative motion; suddenly her top half might be cruising away from her bottom half at many times lightspeed, globules of cerebrospinal fluid merging and floating in her wake.

Why do you think you can do this, asked her Helpful Angel.

Relax, she told herself. *Be kind. Wait for the screw to drop.*

She opened the airlock, silencing the Helpful Angel with space.

Hands on the handholds, teeth gritted, she worked her way around the tiny module to the outsize hula hoop on its stern. One of the panels had peeled back like the edge of a crepe filled with buzzing blue plasma. She kept her eyes on her craft—told herself not to let go—raised the hammer to strike the panel back into place.

And the first swing of the hammer missed, and she hadn't been as careful to hold on as she *could* have been as she *should* have been, and she felt herself begin to float away from the ship.

Earth was gone. Undine was gone. She would fall away from the ship, away and away without sound or increasing speed, until she was no longer conscious of her fall as a fall: just a suspension, hanging in featureless void that she knew her malfunctioning brain would find an eternity of ways to fill—

—she thought of this with a white flash as the force of her swing with the hammer, unimpeded by friction, brought her around full circle, so that the head of the hammer locked improbably into place on a handhold.

She clung to it, tethered at ninety degrees to the ship.

She hyperventilated in the fishbowl space of her helmet for what was maybe two minutes, maybe nothing, before she pulled herself up the hammer, grabbed the ship's handhold again. Then she righted herself, and she bit her tongue, and she hammered the hula hoop into shape.

And the warp bubble corrected itself, and the stars grew clear, and she and her cat and her cargo of illegal bread and commercial hopes streaked forward again toward an alien world. And for a moment she existed in silence, and for a moment she felt good about what she was doing, and for a moment her Helpful Angel was circling just outside of her helmet, whispering curses to her that the empty seas she'd taught herself to sail swallowed up.

And before she returned to the airlock, to see if her famous cat was okay, she told herself to lie. *Pretend that the rest of your life was the aberration. Pretend you have the confidence you need. Try, try so hard.*

MEANWHILE,

Afterword

When we conceived this book three years ago, we had two goals. First, we wanted to make a book by trans writers that centred a trans reader as much as possible, that dispensed with the worry of explaining ourselves to cis people, and that would allow us to talk to each other. We believe this gives the stories in this book an intimacy that makes them more enjoyable and meaningful for everyone. Of course, trans people are a varied lot and there is no universal trans reader—on this, we tried our best.

Second, we wanted to offer a vision of what transgender sci-fi and fantasy might look like as a genre. We guessed, or hoped, that instead of simply ending up with a book of traditional SF/F stories that happened to have trans people in them, we would receive stories with new and exciting themes and ideas, stories that would make a distinct contribution to the conversation about what genre fiction can be. We were right—but not in the way we expected.

Historically, science fiction and fantasy have tended to the spectacular. Even when SF/F writers have commented most incisively on our own world, they have often done it through characters who have incredible adventures, heroes and archvillains locked in battles on which the fate of nations or universes hinge. When we put out the call for submissions, we assumed these would be the stories we would receive—space opera, epic fantasy. We didn't. The stories we got, by and large including those we did not select, seemed to be telling us something eerily consistent: It was something about not saving the world—

—Or, perhaps more accurately, about redefining what saving the world looks like.

Throughout this book we follow transgender people in fantastical, strange, often brutally difficult and unpredictable circumstances *not* redeeming a universe, *not* heroically and single-handedly rescuing the masses (how possible is that, even in galaxies unknown?) but carving out small pockets of knowledge, strength, and survival,—even though, as you know by now, the characters in our stories do not necessarily survive, do not always succeed in being strong, they sometimes attempt greater knowledge and fail.

For a long time, trans people have been treated in science fiction and fantasy as part of the spectacle: either as an amazing future technology (people can *change sex*!) or as awful unlikely monsters. We hoped to challenge this by making a book of stories that allow room for the heroic everydayness of real trans people's lives, even among outer space or apocalypse, and we hope that it might, in a Janus-like fashion, act as both an escape from the current world and manual for your own possibilities.

Cat Fitzpatrick and Casey Plett
July 2017

Acknowledgements

Our first thanks goes to Tom Léger, without whom the two of us would never have found each other and without whom neither this book nor Topside Press would ever have existed. Thanks to Riley MacLeod, Red Durkin, Katie Liederman and Julie Blair, who ignited the initial Topside engine and gave it a spectacular lift-off. Thanks to Courtney Andujar, our cover designer, for her talent, her taste, and her patience. Thanks to the fabulous Jeanne Thornton, who gave us the benefit of her own experience as an SFF editor. Thanks to all the authors in this collection, both for their inspiration and their perspiration—it has been a pleasure working with you. And thanks, above all and with deepest gratitude, to everyone who submitted stories, including those we regretfully turned down—five years ago, neither of us could have imagined a world in which we would get to pore over hundreds of manuscripts from trans writers, but we are very excited to actually live in it.

We would also like to respectively thank Ali Howell and Sybil Lamb, who supported, inspired and, most importantly, put up with us during all the work it took to bring this book to fruition. We love you!

Extra special thanks to Daniel Cruz, Associate Post-Reality Engineer.

Author Biographies

Emma Addams is a trans woman, writer, former educator, and current homemaker. She is fascinated by the intrusion of fiction into reality, the moments when characters bleed into our lives, the ways that stories shape our world.

Colette Arrand is a transsexual poet from Detroit, Michigan. She is the author of *Hold Me Gorilla Monsoon* and *To Denounce the Evils of Truth*. She is currently a student at the University of Georgia and is the founding editor of The Wanderer.

Ryka Aoki is the author of *Seasonal Velocities, He Mele a Hilo (A Hilo Song)*, and *Why Dust Shall Never Settle Upon This Soul*. She has been honored by the California State Senate for her "extraordinary commitment to free speech and artistic expression, as well as the visibility and well-being of Transgender people". She has MFA in Creative Writing from Cornell University and is the recipient of a University Award from the Academy of American Poets. Ryka is a former national judo champion and the founder of the International Transgender Martial Arts Alliance. For her work with youth, Ryka was named an Outstanding Volunteer by the LGBT Center's Children, Youth and Family Services. (It's her favorite award ever.) She is also a professor of English at Santa Monica College, a half-decent pianist, and is starting to learn to play the violin.

Sadie Avery is a writer, actress, and performer in Tiohtià:ke, unceded Kanien'kéha territories (Montreal). She bikes fast, talks fast, and is consistently late. Anna Paquin once asked for her email. She's a young white tran trying to cut off every driver in the city and finish her chapbook about how it blows to have PTSD. Follow her on Twitter @lake_scum to see how that's going.

According to Google Drive, some topics **Beckett K. Bauer** writes about are "Finger, Skull, Gold (Color), Dust, Human back, Face, Friendship, Hearing." They make other creative stuff too like songs, little movies, doodles, etc., but not really professionally. They are interested in all kinds of liberation, especially kids' liberation. Beckett grew up in DC and lives in Philadelphia right now. You can find them on twitter @callmecapnbecks.

Imogen Binnie is a columnist at *Maximumrocknroll*, wrote the novel *Nevada*, and makes the podcast *Imogen Watches Classic Films*. #blacklivesmatter

Cooper Lee Bombardier is a writer and visual artist based in Portland, Oregon. His work appears in many publications and anthologies, most recently in *The Kenyon Review, CutBank, Nailed Magazine, Original Plumbing*, as well as the anthology *The Remedy–Quer and Trans Voices on Health amd Health Care* (ed. Zena Sharman). Cooper's visual art was recently curated in an exhibition called "Intersectionality" at the Museum of Contemporary Art in North Miami. He teaches writing at the University of Portland, Clark College, Portland State University, and at various Portland-area high schools as a writer-in-residence through Literary Art's program Writers in The Schools. Visit him over at www.cooperleebombardier.com

Paige Bryony taught collegiate rhetoric and argument for several years before transitioning and becoming an escort. She leaves it up to the reader to decide which is the more honest profession.

Nat Buchbinder is keeping an eye on the stars.

Ayşe Devrim is a world diplomat, champion of the burly, well-oiled working man, and radical Marxist revolutionary who currently resides in an undisclosed bunker with her organized cadre of militant tabby cats.

Dubbed "The Ancient Jazz Priestess of Mother Africa" **Lady Dane Figueroa Edidi** is an African, Cuban, Indigenous, American performance artist, author teacher, choreographer, oracular consultant, healer, advocate, and a founding member of Force Collision. Also an actor, singer, and dancer, Lady Dane made her cabaret debut at the age of 17 and in 2011 made her New York debut. After beginning to study the dances of her ancestors, Lady Dane began combining African and Native American rhythms into her shows. Although primarily known for her explosive cabaret, in December 2013, Lady Dane Figueroa Edidi became the first trans woman of color author in DC to publish a novel (*Yemaya's Daughters*) In 2015 she received the Pioneer Award for work with the DC trans community and was honored as one of the Trans 100. She is a 2016 Helen Hayes Award nominee for her choreography in *Dontrell Who Kissed The Sea*. She has had work featured in *Queer of Gender*, *Black Femme Witches Brew*, and *Trans Faith*.

RJ Edwards is a writer, podcast host, and librarian. Their work has been featured in *The Collection: Short Fiction from the Transgender Vanguard*, *Capricious Magazine*, and the "Queers Destroy Science Fiction!" special issue of *Lightspeed Magazine*. RJ currently resides in Vancouver, but considers Providence home.

Aisling Fae is a transexual woman of colour, writer, scientist, and activist. Dominican born, she now resides in Berlin, Germany, where she organizes spaces for trans women, hangs out with anarcho-communists, and tries to foment and create a trans literary scene in the city. More of her work can be found on her website Transfaerie.com, and she's on twitter @ transfaerie.

Cat Fitzpatrick has been an editor of prose and poetry at Topside Press since 2014, and is also a professor of English at Rutgers University-Newark. She is the author of the 2016 poetry collection *Glamourpuss*.

Calvin Gimpelevich is a fiction writer whose work appears in *Electric Literature*, *Plenitude*, *Glitterwolf*, *cream city*, *THEM*, and other publications. He is the recipient of awards from Artist Trust, Jack Straw Cultural Center, and the Kimmel Harding Nelson Center for the Arts. calvingimpelevich. com

Sybil Lamb has worked for over a decade as a self-styled underground documentarian of the rare and beautiful characters of underground and edge culture, the recording angel of a particular milieu. Her detail obsessed scenes and hyper articulated portraits collect stories and characters from all around North America to document the lives and cultures of Nomadic Squatter Punks, the many facets of historied yet evolving extremes Trans-culture and the modern Artists and Inventors Underground. A keen Sense of Modern Graphic Design drawing with Bold Lines and Colors create ultra-detailed alternate worlds, upon examination every limb and object has seemingly been drawn from overly enthusiastic memory. Like a dream about what happened just before you fell asleep Lamb is at once familiar yet somehow more, invoking the viewer on multiple levels with a recognizable yet "otherly" visual semantix. Her detail obsessed narrative genre scenestold in a high resolution vision of high contrast over saturated color contrast her chaotic, elusive and gritty subject matter. Thusly Lamb uses her studio method to turn unlikely people and settings into something in between cartoons, diagrams, and graphic design. Lamb perfects the formula for magical realism; upon perusing any number of Lamb's deeply imaginistic images it becomes evident that there is a highly personalised coded richly woven tapestry of mythos of girls demons punks robots spare parts and clues hidden in trash. And then in 2014 she got all famous from publishing a 350 page illustrated punk rock road trip novel *I've Got A Time Bomb* with Topside Press. The End. Also she lives in the House of Lamb SANDWICH in Windsor, Ontario ATTN: Attic.

Bridget Liang is a mixed race, queer, trans feminine, autistic, disabled, fat fangirl. They came into their queerness in Hamilton, Ontario and now live in Toronto. They're a budding academic, community researcher, workshop and group facilitator, performance artist, and writer. They can be found lurking on Ao3 reading excessive amounts of fan fiction. They are especially interested in monsters and desirability politics, autistic and queer/trans things, and arts-based research. Blog: https://bridgetliang.wordpress.com/

Janey Lovebomb, a self-described witchy artist sweetheart, is actually poorly-behaved and, we have reason to believe, a threat to law and order. From the sultry cracks and edges of New Orleans, lately she's trouble in cutoffs in Portland, Oregon, where she is accepting gifts and looking for a band to be in. This is her first (probs problematic) published work.

Tristan Alice Nieto is a time-traveler from the late nineteenth century who appreciates phonographs, flying machines, and antibiotics. She is currently involved in the production of moving images for the cinematograph, but wishes to further explore the medium of the written word. Tristan currently resides in a decaying mansion in London, England with her partner, their nineteen cats and the ghost of a local pirate.

Morgan M Page is a trans writer and artist in Canada. She's a 2014 Lambda Literary Fellow, and her work has been published in *QED, Montreal Review of Books, Feministing, Plenitude, GUTS*, and other magazines and anthologies including Cleis Press' *Best Sex Writing Vol. 1* (2015). She currently runs the trans history podcast *One From the Vaults*. She can be found @ morganmpage on Twitter.

Casey Plett wrote the short story collection *A Safe Girl To Love*, winner of a Lambda Literary Award. She has written for *McSweeney's Internet Ten-*

dency, *The New York Times ArtsBeat*, *Maclean's*, *The Walrus*, and *The Winnipeg Free Press*, among others. Her first novel, *Little Fish*, is forthcoming Spring 2018 from Arsenal Pulp Press.

Trish Salah writes poetry, fiction, criticism and other less categorizable stuff. Of mixed Arab and Irish-Canadian heritage, she was born in Halifax, and has lived most of her life between Montreal and Toronto. Her books are *Lyric Sexology, Vol. 1* and *Wanting in Arabic*, for which she won a Lambda Literary Award. She co-organized the *Writing Trans Genres* conferences at the University of Winnipeg and is assistant professor of Gender Studies at Queen's University.

M Téllez is a heavily cyborg sci-fi writer from the 215/occupied Lenni Lenape land. They are a founding member of the corner store sci-fi & action collective, METROPOLARITY. In 2015 they received the Leeway Foundation's Transformation Award. Eighteen is exhausted/pissed with institutional legitimacy, global anti-Blackness & white forgetting, and fixed treatments of language and identity. They consider the common a word handy and inexpensive tool for deconstructing oppressive world-ordering narratives. Find them across cyberspace @cyborgmemoirs.

Jeanne Thornton is the author of the books *The Black Emerald* and *The Dream of Doctor Bantam*, a Lambda Literary Award finalist. She is also the copublisher of Instar Books and created the webcomics *The Man Who Hates Fun* and *Bad Mother*. She lives in Brooklyn.

Brendan Williams-Childs' work has appeared on NPR, in Midwestern Gothic Literary Magazine and has won the Larry Neal Writers' Award. Originally from Wyoming, he now lives on the East Coast. Though where he will be when you are reading this is uncertain, like most of the future.

Kaj Worth lives in Berlin and Devon.

Rachel K. Zall is an erotica author, performing artist, poet, and hat enthusiast who lives with her partner in The Bronx. Her fiction has appeared in *Nerve Endings* and the Lambda Literary Award winning anthology *Take Me There* as well as *Exiles*, a comic book she co-created with artist Christianne Benedict. She can be found on the web at www.radiosilent.net. "Control" was originally written for Metropolarity's *Laser Life* reading and the author would like to thank Metropolarity for their light and inspiration.

CPSIA information can be obtained
at www.ICGtesting.com
Printed in the USA
LVHW101445020419
612401LV00036B/190/P